THE UNIQUE CREATION

HEATH A. HAGUE

authorHOUSE®

AuthorHouse™ UK Ltd.
500 Avebury Boulevard
Central Milton Keynes, MK9 2BE
www.authorhouse.co.uk
Phone: 08001974150

First published by AuthorHouse 12/11/2008

ISBN: 978-1-4389-2842-5 (sc)

Printed in the United States of America
Bloomington, Indiana

This book is printed on acid-free paper.

DEDICATION

Throughout my life I have come into contact with so many different people in so many different places, and yet, across the years I have only ever met one that gave me the encouragement and the inspiration to complete this book.

This work is dedicated to the one.

CHAPTER 1

The waking dream returned; the squeal of tyres, the tormented rent of metal, the shattering of glass and the screams of agony. Steve Westerman squeezed his streaming eyes tight shut, but the images still flooded his consciousness, burned into the insides of his eyelids as if he had been staring at a hundred watt bulb filament for days. Head bowed, a tremor of sobs rippled up and down his body, broad shoulders shuddering as another wave of remorse and grief crashed upon the shore of his composure.

Slowly he lifted his heavy head, opened his eyes and looked through the mist of tears around the chapel into which the two-dozen or so people had been seated. It was a typically sombre building with rows of customarily uncomfortable wooden pews facing a raised pulpit and the three coffins, neatly lined up in front of the 'final' curtain of the crematorium. The three simple wooden boxes looked ludicrously small to contain the hopes and aspirations of his wife and children. Their lives and, what felt also like his, neatly packaged finite. To his left a priest stood and mouthed words of solace and feeling, never a pious man, Westerman looked at the priest and although he could see his mouth moving, he heard no words and like the light from a nearby fluorescent tube, he felt no warmth. His attendance for the religious side of the ceremony was only to placate the wishes of his Mother and Father-in-law. Glancing sideways slightly he could see that the aged couple were clinging to each other as if to keep themselves afloat in this sea of grief. Once again he bowed his head and closed his stinging eyes. Once again the drama began to replay itself within his tortured mind.

A clear warm summers evening, the sun had not yet fallen low in the azure sky and clouds of aphids swarmed and danced hypnotically above the passing fields. It was a beautiful night for a drive in the country and the Westerman family were taking full advantage of the conditions, their family hatchback moved rapidly along the country lanes collecting specimens of the local insect life in the form of smears across the leading edges of the vehicle.

They would often, when the weather permitted, go for these runs. The kids enjoyed them because it would invariably mean a stop at a public house, which was usually equipped with a children's play area. The in-car entertainment system throbbed out a bass beat that magically seemed to be maintaining perfect time with the deep throb of the engine as the road snaked ahead. A left, and then a right, the wide low profile tyres gripping the warm dry roads with consummate ease and no audible protest; the cat's eyes and white lines smeared into a continuous blur as the light grey of the dry stonewalls flashed by.

Westerman loved his driving, he was good at it, always within his limits and the conditions of the road, and tonight the conditions were very good. A steady right hand curve doubled back into a tightening left-hander; brake in a straight line, move out towards the crown of the road, down two gears – the needle on the rev counter leapt to 5,500. With a smooth precision the car turned into the apex of the bend and accelerated effortlessly out of the corner, short-shifting to stop the front wheels spinning and scrambling for grip Westerman looked over at his wife.

"You enjoyed that didn't you?" She said smiling her own peculiar little knowing smile at her husband; she enjoyed the speed as much as he did. Looking in the rear view mirror he checked on his son and daughter, Mark and Lucy, both looked totally non-plused about the whole experience, although it was fair to say the they had probably covered enough miles in a car to go to the moon and back in their short lives of eleven and nine years.

"You know I enjoy having a little play now and then." He replied, peering over the top of his sunglasses and giving a cheeky grin to his wife, Rachel.

The way ahead was clear and the visibility was excellent, the sun had not yet descended low enough into the evening sky to create a hazard. They passed through tunnels produced by the roadside trees being in full foliage, the inside of these natural passages being lit by a strange, greenish shifting light that was made by the leaves waving in the evening breeze. The vehicle growled along at around seventy miles an hour, suspension effortlessly soaking up the undulations in the tarmac. Life did not get much better than this, the entire family taking pleasure in the beautiful conditions.

After rounding another bend the road resolved itself into a straight that sloped gently downward, heading toward a valley in which nestled a picture postcard perfect little Dales village. This straight section covered almost two miles and had been proclaimed an accident black spot by the local police authority many years earlier, the gentle gradient coupled with the generous width of the road had led to vehicles attaining unsafe speeds for entry into the village and several fatalities had been recorded.

Aware of the environment in which he was operating at about half a mile along this piece of asphalt, Westerman backed completely off the throttle, the fuel injected engine burbling and popping on the overrun through the unburned fuel igniting inside the exhaust system. Around a small curve at the start of the village an inconspicuous lorry appeared, beginning its slow, steady climb up the incline, Westerman had seen the vehicle; it was still over a mile away. The simple white cargo carrier produced a thick haze of blue-grey smoke as it laboured up the hill. "We'll see if there's a nice pub in the next village boys and girls." Westerman said and shot a smile at his family. He then returned his full attention to the road ahead. In addition to being straight and wide, the road was lined with dry stonewalls which had been painstakingly constructed from the locally quarried limestone. On one side beyond the wall was a small ravine along which a small stream picturesquely babbled, the uphill side had the wall acting as a retainer for a two metre high embankment which was topped with vivid green grass upon which one could see the odd sheep precariously placed, grazing away the evening. The car was now a third of the distance down the hill, the truck was still accelerating upward.

Westerman suspected that he would relive the horror of the approaching event for the remainder of his life, and he would never be able to explain what happened.

The two vehicles closed upon each other, the car had lost speed due to the engine braking effect, it was now moving at around fifty miles per hour. The truck was still accelerating and was moving at a speed in the region of forty miles per hour, they closed upon each other at a combined closing velocity of ninety miles per hour.

In retrospect, Westerman thought that he had had a premonition, that something was not right. As the two vehicles drew nearer to each other he looked up at the driver of the approaching truck, the man stared back at him; time appeared to slow down.

With a violent swing of the steering wheel of his vehicle the oncoming driver turned his truck towards the car. In slow motion the lorry appeared to jump across the road onto his side, the ferocity of the manoeuvre causing the vehicle to lean wildly in both directions on its soft suspension; Westerman's reactions were good but there was nothing he could do. Within a split second the cars brakes were fully applied, the vehicles anti-lock system kicked in producing the characteristic lock release action causing the brake pedal to judder wildly. The tyres squealed and released, squealed and released, the rubber compound bit into the surface of the road rapidly retarding the velocity. The braking systems were operating at their maximum efficiency, but the truck was still accelerating, the closing distance was too small, a collision was unavoidable.

His wife realised the oncoming impact and screamed, at the last moment Westerman swerved to his right so that rather than head-on, the combined impact of fifty miles per hour would be on the front left quarter of the car. The two vehicles came together, metal, plastic and glass tore and smashed, screaming in protest, time slowed even further. The collision spun the car around, slamming the rear into the stonewall on the uphill side of the road. The back of the vehicle crumpled along the predicted stress lines of its safety cell absorbing the energy of the smash, unfortunately the forces involved were too great and the rear continued to fold, the hapless children being forced mercilessly forward into the rear of their parent's seats. Compression could not be infinite, limits were reached and the tattered wreck of the car was propelled at what seemed like a ballistic velocity forward across the road into the opposite stonewall.

This man made barrier was approximately one and a half metres high and half a metre thick, even after losing a large fraction of its velocity this obstacle still offered no resistance. Large blocks of local quarried stone burst asunder as if they were made of Plaster of Paris; the twisted mass of metal reared up as the sturdier base of the wall refused to move, it was now airborne, plummeting into the awaiting ravine. The car designers had never catered for such titanic forces being applied. Anti-burst locks burst. Crumple cells could crumple no more. The last impact with the second wall blasted the driver's door completely from its hinges, pent up pressures released in a cataclysmic moment of force. Along with the driver's seat belt mountings, Steve Westerman was flung, catapulted from the vehicle onto the grass and heather slope of the ravine.

The laws of ballistics and gravity are well established and a body set in motion will continue along its path providing nothing intercepts it, the opposite slope of the ravine intercepted the flying wreckage. Any remaining integrity of the machine failed in a spectacular fashion, any remaining glass shattered, the engine block moved through the front of the cabin with terrifying ease. The concussed body of Steve Westerman had, in a final gut wrenching twist of fate, been deposited so that he could witness this personal carnage.

"Noooo!" Was the scream issued from his tortured lips as he watched the remains of the car tumble down the remaining three metres into the babbling brook below. Fate is a fickle mistress and whist the combination of impacts had stolen the lives of his family, he was remarkably intact. Despite feeling pain coursing through every part of his battered body, he propelled himself onto his feet and down the uneven banking to the steaming carnage that once was his family. If you had asked Westerman to describe the scene he found there, he could not. The human body has a safety mechanism that cuts in when scenes of mental and physical trauma become too great, he blacked out.

When he came to a flotilla of police and ambulance vehicles had arrived upon the scene. Spectators stood by and watched with morbid curiosity. The stretcher he was being strapped to was being gingerly hoisted up the ravine towards the gap in the wall his car had created, he could see people pointing and shaking their heads. At the very end of this line of onlookers a man stood apart from the rest, he was a long way away, the daylight had begun to fade, but still Westerman was sure that he recognised this man. Against the aches and heartaches that were racking his body he raised his head to gain a better look. The man appeared to notice this action, turned and vanished into a twinkling ball of light, which faded away to nothing. Westerman passed out again.

Slowly he opened his eyes and raised his head, tears streaming down his face, to look at the priest stood at the raised lectern. He felt a hand gentle press his shoulder from behind, turning around he looked into the red-rimmed eyes of one of his oldest friends. He mouthed a silent word of thanks, his friend smiled and nodded. The service was drawing to a close and descending from his dais the priest crossed to the three coffins, made a sign, stepped back and a set of curtains closed. Westerman reeled and had to grasp the back of the pew to stop himself collapsing into a puddle of spineless jelly. This one simple act of closing a simple set of curtains had produced a feeling of finality and futility within him. If he had not known it was over, he knew now.

"Goodbye! I'll love you always." He whispered to his departed wife and children.

An usher gently took his right arm and gestured that it was time to leave; he turned and began walking up the centre aisle towards the exit. Rows of people nodded and scrubbed at red eyes and noses, sobbing could be heard all around, the doors opened as if on cue to allow his exit.

The outside light was brighter than in causing the emerging mourners to shield and squint their eyes. The surrounding memorial gardens glistened in the summer sun, which was peeping ashamedly through the storm clouds, the door of the traditional black hearse swung silently open and Westerman entered. Within minutes the solemn procession was on its way to the funeral reception venue, the rain had begun again, forming rivulets down the side windows of the vehicle, the grieving man looked outward with unseeing, glazed eyes. Inwardly his thoughts were confusing, he still felt the intolerable grief of his loss but the closing of the curtains in the crematorium had provided him with a point of closure, and although at this present time he did not particularly care whether life went on, he knew it would. He perceived that a simple analogy of this was the few shafts of sunlight poking through the dull drab coverage of grey cloud. He had always been a 'get on with it' kind of person and he knew he would have to. It was at this very point in time that a resolution formed within his tortured mind.

For years he and his late wife had paid good money into various pensions and insurance schemes and, by and large, they were always the right ones and had survived the ups and downs of stock market fluctuations and financial fashions. The house would be paid for; he had savings, he would do something that he and Rachel had always dreamed of. He would travel; he would see the world. What was wrong with him? He had just seen the bodies of his wife and children disappear behind a velvet curtain forever, how could he contemplate such a thing? At that moment, only seconds after reaching such a momentous decision he nearly backed out, but one person convinced him that he should go ahead with his plan, Rachel. She had wanted to do this and like any sensibly minded adults they had discussed the eventualities of death and they had concluded together that life should go on.

A murmur of tears and the sniff of a nose brought him back out of his own personal little world, in the car with him sat his Mother and Father in law. How would he explain this to them? There would be no easy way, he would have to take the bull by the horns and do it. Not now obviously, but soon. His reverie was then broken as the car pulled to a halt outside the doors of the local community hall that had been hired to host the reception, the door swung open and he stepped out into the pouring rain. His companions climbed from the vehicle and went to stand by his side in the doorway, ready to do their collective duty and greet the guests. Westerman had done this particular chore at his parent's funeral, this he was sure would be a great deal harder.

Within four weeks all the loose ends had been just about tied up. He had quit his job, a process that had, to his surprise, given him a feeling of great satisfaction and accomplishment; it was not that he particularly hated his employment but he had deep down always felt that the time devoted to the daily grind had never sat well with his character. He had processed all the legal paraphernalia and begun selling off the unwanted bits of his life. There were bystanders and friends who thought that, and even said to his face, that he was out of his mind, but it was his life, his grief, and he would deal with it how he wanted.

The much-dreaded ordeal of informing the parents was not as bad as he had expected. His father in law, had looked dumbfounded when he had been told of his son in laws plans but he too knew of his daughter's love for travelling and had agreed that there was nothing to keep Steve there, his mother in law still immersed in a sea of grief and anguish said very little. So, as they say, that was that.

The pain was still great. The dreams of the accident were still as vivid as ever, but life had to and was going on and, for what seemed like the first time in a thousand years, he was doing what he felt was right for him. His plans were pretty straightforward; he would travel to London and from there onto the Eurostar link to Paris, then Italy and Greece. Rachel had always loved London, even though he had not, he would spend a night or two there as a sort of lop sided memorial, or tribute to his late wife.

It was mid-August when the taxi pulled away from the front of his home. The summer sun was beating down on to the front of the brick built detached house, he took a long hard look at the structure, the place where he had lived for a good few years. Memories of various occasions popped into his mind, happy times, sad times. He was feeling the full gamut of emotions, mentally once again he said goodbye to his departed family. Westerman felt the grief swell up inside of him like a massive wave building to crash onto the beach of his feelings, but he was learning to handle it and sheer willpower forced him not to be smashed mentally open by the wave and descend into a blubbering wreck. The car turned out of the small housing estate and made its way towards the local railway station.

CHAPTER TWO

The plain white Ford Transit van moved effortlessly in the mid day sun along the French motorway. Inside sat two everyday ordinary looking men, both in their mid-thirties, both had no criminal record, both held clean driving licences and impeccable financial credentials. They looked and behaved like nobodies.

The driver, Joseph Rodgers, had grown up in middle England, gone to Birmingham University and gained a degree in theological studies. The passenger, Michael O' Grady, had been born in Londonderry, gone to the University of Manchester and gained a degree in nuclear physics. To the casual observer and acquaintances of these people what these two had in common was very little; however they did share an allegiance to an obscure religious sect that appeared to have been started in the back streets of east Sheffield of all places. The leader of this order was enigmatically called 'The Warden', his teachings were simple and his followers were growing.

Rodgers had been one of The Warden's first recruits or converts. Around two years previously he had been made redundant from a position of some influence within a manufacturing company. The job had been his life, he was not married and without an emotionally stable background to offer support in this stressful time he had drifted into the all too familiar cycle of despair and drink. It was whilst sat in a bar drowning his sorrows that a man had appeared at his side and had started talking to him. To Rodgers the man appeared to understand his situation perfectly, seemed to empathise with his emotional state with a perfect synchronicity. The man used various theological standpoints in his discussions, which gelled perfectly with Rodgers' own ideals. After a few hours of talking, during which the consumption of alcohol was noticeably reduced because Rodgers was so rapt by this mans eloquent conversation and expansive knowledge; he was invited to visit the meetinghouse of his newfound friend. Soon after this first meeting Rodgers became a member of The Warden's sect.

O' Grady's induction followed a similar path. Whilst growing up in Londonderry he had witnessed the troubles that had racked Northern Ireland. He had seen friends murdered and the injustices endemic in the flawed system. The Warden had met Michael in a bar and after a number of hours talking the affinity O' Grady felt with this man was unbelievable, he seemed to understand everything; he even thought that he could hear a faint Irish lilt in his voice. Once again he too became a member of The Warden's sect very soon after.

The two men's route was both long and meticulously planned. They had left southern Spain ten days previously, driving up the east coast via the Costa Blanca, Costa del Sol and through Andorra and finally over the Pyrenees into the South of France. The journey had taken in many stops to legitimately pick-up and drop off items. The items that had been collected looked innocuous in themselves but when combined at a point in the not too distant future their deadly purpose would become all too apparent.

The trek continued through southern France to Monaco and then northwards towards Paris. Throughout the entire trip the two men had been 'sustained' by listening to CDs of The Wardens teachings. These lengthy diatribes of hate against the state and other related agencies showing the listeners the injustices they were destined to strike against, the evils and the atrocities they would avenge. They were completely brainwashed into The Wardens doctrine and the subliminal messages using ultra-high frequency carrier waves embedded within each soundtrack that would ensure that they would lay down their lives in the name of the cause.

After stopping in Paris and performing a final collection they continued on the Autoroute toward Calais and then England. Their final destination was London and here they would deliver a blow that would signal the beginning of the end of the perceived tyrannical oppression and cost the lives of nearly 10 million people.

CHAPTER THREE

Westerman sat bolt upright in his bed; sweat streaming down his face and back, his tears mingling freely down his cheeks with the rivulets of perspiration. Yet again he had relived the accident; he had watched the mass of tangled metal crash to a sickening halt.

Since the accident the mornings had been pretty tortuous. Despite not being seriously injured the impact had detached and torn a large amount of muscle tissue at various locations in his body and this was taking some time to heal. The process of getting out of bed was not what one could describe as being a rapid movement; eventually he hobbled over to the sink in the bathroom of his hotel room and began the ritual of morning ablutions. This particular room was in a Holiday Inn in the East End of London near the terminus of the Docklands Light Railway. He had chosen the hotel because it was reasonably priced, clean and was ideally placed to get to the centre of the metropolis. The previous night he had taken in a show in the West End, Les Miserables. Truth be known he had hated every minute of it but his wife had once been to see it and had always wanted to see it again with him, therefore he had felt honour bound to carry out this act.

Today he would do the sight seeing, tourist route and see all the landmarks. Dressed and ready to go he looked at himself in the full-length mirror.

Steve Westerman was a man in his mid forties; his height of around two metres had enabled him to carry his weight better than some of his fellow Englishmen, because waistlines had followed the model of the Americans and Westerman was no exception.

"El touristo!" he proclaimed aloud to himself looking at the camera slung over one shoulder and a rucksack over the other. He allowed a smirk to play over his features, then checking that everything was neat, tidy and all his possessions were stored safely, he turned and exited the room.

After only a short walk he stood on the platform of the Beckton railway station, very soon afterwards he was aboard one of the carriages of a London Docklands Light Railway train. The scenery slipped past, the London City Airport, the famous or, as some say, infamous Millennium Dome. He was doing the sights but in all honesty his heart was not really in it, this was for Rachel, not himself, he had always held an aversion to the capital. Truth be known it was probably a North / South divide thing but nevertheless his wife had really loved the place so he would stand it for a couple of days. Silently the train slipped into the labyrinth of skyscrapers that dominated the central London skyline, winding along on its raised track and eventually pulling into its terminus. From this point easy access was available to the underground and with it any of the well-known landmarks. Westerman exited his carriage and moved to stand in front of a large wall map of the Tube system, mentally planning his route, looking for the locations of all the places that Rachel and the kids would want to see.

At the Dover ferry port the unobtrusive Ford Transit lurched off the cross channel ferry's uneven loading ramp, both Rodgers and O' Grady spun around and glared rearward at their cargo. After a few seconds they both let out the breath that they had been holding, turned to each other and giggled like a pair of naughty school children. O' Grady was the first one to regain his composure.

"Keep to the left Joe. Booth number six is the one we need." said the Irishman in his thick brogue.

"I see it! Keep calm!" His companion replied realising he was shouting. He turned to the other man and smiled sheepishly.

"Sorry Michael."

"It's okay. Just stay focused." he answered also with a smile.

The White van bore all the hallmarks of a long journey. Insects spattered across the front and brown-grey streaks along its flanks, evidence of the various climates through which it had travelled. Booth number six appeared in view guarding the gate that would allow access to the country and their path to their ultimate goal.

A small family saloon pulled away allowing the two men to pull up to the barrier. The uniformed officer leaned out of his window; Rodgers slowly lowered the driver's side window.

"Good morning gentlemen. Could I see your documents please?" asked the chubby, moustached official. Rodgers passed over the two passports; the customs officer stared at them carefully. He would have found nothing wrong, the documents were genuine and valid, and raising his eyes he asked the million-dollar question. "Have you got anything to declare?" Rodgers glanced across at O' Grady, he could feel the tension rising in his body, his hands were wet and clammy upon the steering wheel he was gripping as if his life depended upon it. Rodgers replied.

"My total belief in The Warden." The official's face adopted a blank and distant expression, after a couple of seconds he blinked three times in quick succession, put the two passports neatly together and handed them back to Rodgers.

"Belief is total!" said the man, sweat prominent on his forehead. "You may go."

The vehicle engaged first gear and pulled away through the open gate in a cloud of blue-grey exhaust fumes. The customs officer watched them leave, gave another set of blinks and returned to his paperwork, blissfully unaware of the compliment of nano-probes that were now dissolving inside his brain.

Weeks before he had been in his local bar, having a quiet drink, when an unfeasibly attractive woman had approached him and made polite conversation. They had spent a good four hours discussing work and everything in general, however at one point in the night she had leaned closer and whispered something into his ear and, seemingly by accident, caught the back of his hand with her ornate bracelet. He pulled sharply back as if he had been stung.

"Oh! I am sorry," she said, "this silly bracelet is always catching on things." The man rubbed his hand and politely laughed the incident off.

"It's only a scratch." He had replied and continued their conversation. Inside the pin prick of a wound a molecule sized machine activated its programming and began its journey through the blood system of its unsuspecting host until, some hours later, it reached its destination; the brain; once there it multiplied and embedded itself together with its brothers awaiting the activation sequence to promote the response that Rodgers and O'Grady had received.

The unwitting host left the bar with the woman. He made the predictable pass, let's be honest he was no Adonis and chances like this did not come along everyday, but she gently declined saying it was late; and then walked away into the summer's night. Turning away the dejected man headed for home. What was that? Out of the corner of his eye he could have sworn he had seen a brilliant flash of light, but no. He continued along the Dover street wondering why such a beautiful woman had wanted to talk to him for so long. Little did the man realise that such an unfortunately innocent meeting, which had left him all dressed up with no where to go, would contribute ultimately to costing so many lives,

Westerman walked alongside the Houses of Parliament. This ancient citadel, the model for so many governments around the world, looked shiny and slick in the rain that had begun to fall out of the darkening sky, the grey clouds marching relentlessly in ever increasing numbers across the summer sky. In the days since the terror attacks of 2001 it was no longer possible to get close to the building, large concrete blocks had been deposited in strategic places to stop any potential car or truck bombs, security fences surrounded the grounds. But a small number of determined tourists still stood and took pictures of the landmark. Westerman decided that he would do the same, and taking out his digital camera he carefully recorded two images, which he could splice together at a later date, that would allow the full grandeur of the scene to be displayed in a panoramic view. It was strange but he noticed that this act of banality had brought to his attention that he had actually gone a precious few moments without dwelling on his loss. He felt instantly ashamed and putting away his camera he headed off to find a café for some much needed liquid refreshment.

The white van was now moving purposely along the M20 towards London, keeping within the speed limits so as not to attract any unwanted attention. Rodgers was still in the driving seat but O' Grady was now in the rear of the vehicle, opening the boxes of machinery and connecting wires and switches.

"Michael, it's starting to rain."

"It won't affect this baby." O' Grady continued his work. Despite his nuclear physics background the speed with which he was constructing the device was breathtaking. His own I.Q. was in the region of one hundred and fifty, however the nano-probes coursing through his body were significantly augmenting his abilities. Neither of the men realised that these micro-machines were occupying their bodies, cousins to the now deceased versions inside the Customs Officer, but still programming in the blind allegiance to The Warden. The instructions for the men and machines coming from the CDs supplied by The Warden that were constantly playing on the vehicles sound system.

The M20 was now awash and slick with the rain that was now constantly falling.

"I'll knock the speed back a bit. I don't want to have an accident," Rodgers shouted to O' Grady in the back of the vehicle, raising his voice to be heard above the drone of the diesel engine and the splashing of the spray from the road.

"Not a problem, we have a window of around two hours to get to the target area. It's only the final moments that need to be perfectly timed," replied the Irishman as he opened a final box and extracted a long, sword-like, piece of equipment, which he then inserted into a correspondingly shaped hole in the side of the now completed machinery. Lights winked on and a low throbbing powerful hum could be heard from the device. "We have a heartbeat!" exclaimed O' Grady. Rodgers risked a glance over his shoulder away from the rain-drenched road.

"Belief is total!" beamed the man from alongside his handiwork.

"Belief is total!" smiled the driver who turned back to his duties, tears brimming in his eyes with happiness.

The rain was beating steadily down on the pavement outside Buckingham Palace and a constant rivulet of water had formed in the kerbside. Along with the American and Japanese tourists, Westerman focused the lens of his camera and took the obligatory picture. After spending another few moments to safely store the photographic equipment he pulled the hood of the kagool he was wearing further forward over his head. The rain had now turned into an all soaking steady drizzle, his mother would have described this form of precipitation as the type of rain that would go through plastic mackintosh jackets. Out of one pocket of his wet weather attire he produced a map of the city and began to carefully fold this item so as to not have too much exposed to the downpour.

He had 'done' the Houses of Parliament, Bond Street, Buckingham Palace; what was next? Glancing up The Mall he decided that he would walk along the tree lined avenue to Admiralty Arch and into Trafalgar Square. After all, he thought, he could surely not get any wetter. As if on cue thunder rolled through the atmosphere overhead.

"Oh, perfect!" Westerman muttered to himself as he began his steady walk.

In a multi-storey car park in the West End of London, well inside the congestion zone, the white van had arrived. Both Rodgers and O' Grady sat in the back of the vehicle either side of the throbbing device. Rodgers glanced at his wristwatch.

"Time to call The Warden," he said.

O' Grady nodded and pulled out a mobile phone from his jeans pocket. At that very moment a tap on the vans rear door snapped the two men to attention. They sat in silence; presently another more insistent tap was heard.

"Is there anybody in there?" A confident, commanding voice boomed out. Rodgers snapped a glance into the vehicles side mirrors. A policeman.

"I don't like the look of this Jim." A second voice confirmed the presence of at least two police officers. Since the Twin Towers incident in America, in most major cities across the world, any suspicious looking vehicle required at least a cursory inspection. The policemen were about to leave when from inside the van came a metallic sound.

O' Grady had shifted his balance slightly and, even though nano-technologically enhanced, had clumsily knocked over a box of tools. Outside the two officers backed a step or two away from the vehicle, the older more experienced of the pair had begun to reach for his radio. The back doors of the van burst open and with almost unbelievable speed Rodgers and O' Grady exploded forth.

The two unfortunate policemen never stood a chance. With precise speed and force Rodgers had struck one man in the throat, the blow so severe that he was already dying with a crushed windpipe, leaving him gasping frantically for breath. O' Grady had landed around the second officers neck and with a backwards heave, a loud crunch could be heard and the lifeless body crumpled to the ground into a misshapen heap.

The two luckless constables were then bungled unceremoniously into the back of the van. O'Grady and Rodgers resumed their places next to the device, once again the mobile phone was produced and a pre-stored number was activated. The phone was then placed atop the device and, seconds later, a thin high-pitched modulating tone could be heard, and both men stared blankly ahead, blinking intermittently. After two minutes the tone stopped and Rodgers picked up the phone and placed it into a specially designed connecting port on the front of the machinery. The hum of the device rose to a higher pitch. The two men climbed into the front seats of the van. Rodgers started the engine and looked at O' Grady.

"Trafalgar Square?"

"Trafalgar Square," answered the smiling O' Grady.

The walk along The Mall was not one of the most pleasant experiences that Steve Westerman had endured. The constant downpour had made his feet and the bottom of his denims wet, the kagool he was wearing was making him sweat and so his shirt was also wet. The storm had taken a turn for the worse and now lightning flashed and thunder boomed as he went under Admiralty Arch.

Even with the rain the tourists were still out in force, as were the pigeons. Over the years a few half-hearted efforts had been made to clear the birds, their excrement blamed for many things from ruining clothes to defacing famous landmarks. Westerman looked up at Nelsons Column and the bedraggled creatures nestling amongst the ornate stonework. Again lightning flashed and thunder rolled.

Busily looking around for a vantage point to take the best shot of this historic vista, he was blissfully unaware of the plain, dirty white van which had pulled to a halt about twenty metres away from him. Inside the vehicle Rodgers and O' Grady sat motionlessly staring through the rain soaked windscreen. A passing policeman noticed the stationary vehicle and approached, O' Grady noticed him and began winding down his side window. "Is there a problem gentlemen?" asked the young constable politely. O' Grady smiled and said.

"No officer there is no problem; belief is total!"

At that split second conditions of cosmic chance came together. In a window overlooking the square The Warden held a device that was counting down to zero. At zero a signal was sent to the mobile phone connected to the machine in the back of the van. The smiling Warden vanished in a flash of light; a bolt of lightning flashed, and a millionth of a second later the van, Trafalgar Square and the surrounding area of ten square miles disappeared into a brilliant white hot nuclear fireball.

The world had seen its first act of nuclear terrorism, five million people would die in the immediate blast and millions more would perish from the secondary effects. The world would decline into a global financial meltdown as bank records were destroyed. Criminal gangs would begin a reign of terror as their records had been erased from police and security services databases in the massive electro-magnetic pulse.

It would take decades for the United Kingdom to recover from the hammer blow of the nuclear blast. Parliament had been in session; nobody had survived. The Queen had been in residence at Buckingham Palace together with most of the immediate royal family, nobody had survived.

The world would suffer the political, economic and ecological after-effects from the outrage for nearly a century. It is with some passing irony that it would also take that long for the conscience of the world to come to terms with the fact that nobody would ever claim responsibility for this abominable act or any related convictions occur. It would eventually be consigned to history as a mad, random attack.

CHAPTER FOUR

Pain! Searing pain! That was slowly receding together with a strange blindness. Steve Westerman found himself laid on the floor, his vision full of what seemed like exploding stars of brilliant white, this effect was also starting to recede. He staggered to his feet and promptly fell back down; there was no life in his legs only a tingling sensation, he tried again to get up, this time with more success. What had happened? He could remember standing in Trafalgar Square; the rain; the thunder and lightning; a burst of pure white light and then nothing until he had tried to stand up.

His vision was clearing and through the transient flashes of red blurs that were dancing across his view he looked at his surroundings. This was definitely not Trafalgar Square.

He appeared to be standing on a plain of what looked like dark grey marble that reached away into the distance for as far as his improving eyes could see. Over to his left Westerman discerned what looked like a low building that was made out of the same dark grey material, in fact it looked as if the structure had organically grown out of the ground. Allowing his gaze to pan upwards he beheld an early evening sky full of stars and amongst those stars hung the glorious sight of two full moons.

"Two Moons!" he yelled aloud, his voice echoing and rolling across the empty plain.

"Two Moons?" he repeated, this time in a quieter voice. "Where the hell am I?" With steadying legs he resolved to walk over to the nearby building. The very action of walking assisted his trembling legs to recover even quicker; this allowed his mind to concentrate on his situation.

The first thoughts that tumbled into his consciousness was that he had been struck by lightning and he was dead, he would discover later that this synopsis was not all that far removed from the truth. He was not a religious man and if this was the afterlife it certainly was no paradise; neither, did it appear, was there any number of demons and fire like in the other commonly perceived alternative.

The scale of the building was beginning to reveal itself, it was not the small squat dwelling he had assumed it was, his perspective had been all wrong, he had been at first stumbling but now walking for about half an hour and the distance to the structure did not seem to have diminished. He casually glanced at his wristwatch; the second hand was not moving. Taking the timepiece from his arm he shook it repeatedly, this was strange, he had only had a new battery fitted less than two months ago. Putting the watch back on his wrist he noticed that he was still wearing the kagool, he immediately felt foolish, it was quite mild here and definitely not raining, he began to extricate himself from the garment. It was then that another strange observation was made; the kagool, his jeans and footwear were all still wet. He turned around and on the marble like floor he could see spots of water and damp marks made by his feet receding into the distance, this fascinated Westerman, as he turned and began to follow the trail back to where he had set off from. The journey back to the site of his appearance in this strange landscape did not take long, he had now fully regained the use of his legs and at a steady jog he arrived at his destination. Looking intently at the ground he could see puddles of water on the ground, the dampness tracing the outline of what had been his prone body. This was not as strange as the fact that all around this area up to a distance of around half a metre away from where he had laid the floor was covered with raindrops, undisturbed as it they had fallen on the roof of a stationary motor car. He looked down at this strange sight for a few minutes and then realising he would get no more answers at this place he turned and once again set off towards the structure, this time however he moved across the barren plain at a steady jog.

After what he estimated to be about an hour, he finally arrived at the structure. Its appearance was that of a dark grey marble block standing at around twenty metres high by approximately two hundred metres in length with no apparent openings. Westerman walked to the nearest corner and peered around it; this face also appeared to be about two hundred metres long with no openings. For the first time since he had arrived in this place he felt helpless and without purpose; if this was heaven or hell somebody had better come and tell him what to do next.

He turned his attention away from the structure and allowed his eyes to scan along the horizon; it is perhaps a testament to how his brain worked in an analytical fashion that he perceived that he had no idea of knowing how far away the horizon actually was. However he was sure that he could see no further structures, a feeling of loneliness began to spread a chill across his soul.

As if on cue, out of the corner of his eye he caught a flash of brilliant light; he spun around, before him stood a statuesque woman of about thirty years of age.

"What the?" blustered Westerman as he backed away a pace or two. The woman just smiled and advanced slowly, her left hand outstretched.

"Jal Ja var va!" she muttered. Westerman shook his head.

"I'm sorry. I don't understand," he stammered. The woman smiled and carried on advancing. Suddenly in a movement as quick and agile as any wild cat, she sprang and knocked him on to his back. He had no time to react as she deftly rolled him over and pinned down his head.

"Ow! What the fuck are you doing?" he yelled as he felt a sharp stinging sensation behind his ear; he then noticed that she had released him. Scrambling to his feet he backed away until his back was flush against the dark grey marble wall of the building.

"What the fuck are you doing?" he spluttered, his hand rubbing the area of his head that had been 'stung'. The woman looked surprised and replied.

"I don't think that there is any need for such profanity, do you?"

This was definitely weird city. Westerman could hear the words plainly but his attackers lips were moving out of synchronisation with them, just like a badly dubbed foreign movie. It was at this point whilst touching behind his ear that he found what felt like a small stud. The woman stretched out her hand and showed Westerman a device in her palm.

"Translator," she explained. "This is an injector; it puts the device in direct contact with the hearing centre of your brain. It can translate any language after a few words have been spoken." Westerman had adopted the look of a frightened rabbit caught in the headlights of an approaching motorcar.

"It's totally harmless and after a short while you'll forget about it being there," she continued. "Look! I've got one." And with a flick of her long dark hair she showed him behind her own ear; the stud was plainly visible.

"Harmless you say?"

"Yes completely," she beamed, "I'll bet my lips even look to be moving in sync now." Westerman hadn't noticed but she was right, they no longer appeared to be the delay that had been apparent. He nodded.

"Good, good. That means that they've integrated successfully," she smiled, "you should only experience the delay when you encounter a new dialect or language from now on."

This was starting to prove too much for the confused man. His legs buckled and he slid down the wall until he sat on the dark grey marble floor. The woman gave a pitying smile and placed the device in her hand into a pocket in the one-piece coverall she was wearing.

"This is going to take some time to get your head around." She leaned forward and offered her slim hand. Westerman shook his head and took a deep breath.

"If this is a dream, it's a beauty!" He took the offered hand and with a push from his free hand he picked himself up and stood facing the woman.

"My name is Zalar," she stated and nodded encouragement to the baffled man.

"Mine's Steve Westerman," he replied.

"Of course it is. We've been expecting you."

Westerman took this opportunity to look at the woman. She stood at around two metres tall, slim and obviously attractive; her head was tilted skyward showing off her unblemished skin in the double moonlight.

"We had better get inside. We are pretty near the galactic centre here and the background radiation is quite high, this moon's atmosphere is only thin and there is hardly any magnetic field to protect us," she said in a matter of fact fashion.

Westerman looked up; the light level had dropped a bit now and even with the background radiance of the two moons being fairly bright he could see that the celestial panorama above him was plainly not that as seen from anywhere on earth. There were just too many stars and they seemed much too bright.

"Come on. This way," said Zalar, she was still holding his hand and gently led him off along the side of the building. Approximately one-third of the way along the wall they stopped and the woman pointed to a small round marking which she then touched. A section of marble two metres square detached itself and swung upwards and inwards revealing a dark portal through which she was urging him to step. They entered the pitch black and as quickly as it had opened the door closed behind them.

They stood in the complete blackness; the air felt cool and still but something about the situation gave Westerman the impression of being stood inside a massive chamber.

"Lights!" said Zalar. A silent explosion of white light flooded the room, his impression had been correct; the area appeared to be a long wide corridor with archways leading off at regularly spaced intervals.

"Wow!" breathed the shell-shocked Englishman. The woman turned toward him so that her face was very near his.

"Impressive? Trust me you haven't seen anything yet." She tossed her hair to one side. "Come on you must be hungry." They walked towards one of the open doorways, above which there was a strange symbol.

"What does that mean?" he asked casually.

"Can't you read it? That's strange the translator stud should be interpreting visual signs for you." She reached into her pocket and produced the device that she had used to perform the implant earlier and advanced purposely towards him.

"Oh no you don't!" he exclaimed and moved a pace backward. "Just tell me what it says." She shrugged and put the machine away.

"Refectory, of course." With a smile she entered the darkened room, which immediately illuminated. The décor of the room was spartan, the same dull drab grey colour but there was what appeared to be tables uniformly spaced throughout, with cubic blocks situated for seats. In one wall was an alcove positioned about a metre above the floor, this gave Westerman the impression of an old style oven but missing the doors. Zalar approached this opening.

"Yag-zablich!" she enunciated clearly. A dull glow issued from the alcove, which then faded to reveal a plate of what was obviously food of some description resting on a shelf inside.

"I'm sorry, I didn't catch that. What did you order?" Westerman queried, inspecting the food. It had the appearance of a fruit salad.

"It's Yag-zablich," she answered matter of factly. "It's a native fruit dish from Taboran." The confused look on his face encouraged her to continue. "You just ask for anything you want. The alcove uses a low powered brain scanner to find out what you really want. Try it." Westerman took a deep breath and stepped forward. "Cheese sandwich and a glass of beer!" he said clearly aloud. Nothing happened.

"Give it a minute or two. It's the first time anybody or anything has asked for that particular selection." Twenty seconds later the alcove glowed and inside had appeared a plate containing a sandwich and a half litre glass of beer. Zalar had already gone over to one of the tables, sat down and begun eating; Westerman picked up his meal and moved to join her.

She watched with interest as he first sniffed at the sandwich and drink and then tasted both. She was amused by the way he nodded and then proceeded to devour both items. They ate in silence, he was watching the way that she delicately consumed the fruit, eventually, after demolishing what tasted like the Red Leicester cheese sandwich he took a long swig of the beer, a deep breath and said.

"Okay! I've played nice. I've allowed you to inject machines into me, I've eaten the food and drink you've magically produced, oh and by the way the beer needs some work, so I've played nice so will you now tell me what the fucking hell is going on! Please!" The change of the demeanour of his voice from pleasant to hostile made the woman flinch backward.

"I said earlier there is no need for foul language."

"Oh cut the bullshit! I awoke on a seemingly endless marble plain underneath two moons, when the last thing I remember was getting piss wet through in Trafalgar Square." His voice had taken on a menacing edge. He stood up and leaned over toward Zalar with his fists planted firmly into the table. Gone was the carefree smile from the face of the woman, she was troubled; this was not going as she had expected or wanted.

"This is going to be difficult to explain," she replied

"No shit Sherlock!" retorted the agitated man. Something in the troubled face of the woman made him realise that perhaps this was not the time for a confrontation; he decided to try a different approach.

"Please tell me where I am." He had softened his voice, which in turn allowed Zalar to relax; she looked down at the empty plate and then back up at Westerman's confused face, he in turn slumped back down on to his seat holding her gaze.

"You were in Trafalgar Square; you were also at ground zero for your planet's first nuclear terrorist attack." He stared at her, his brain trying to grasp what he had just heard; his mouth moved soundlessly searching for a response. Nuclear attack, this was absurd but yet his senses told him that he was being told the truth.

"So I am dead," he eventually said and slumped forward on the table. Zalar gently reached across and placed her hand upon his; he looked at the hand and then at her face.

"No. You are not dead. You are Unique. A set of circumstances have turned you into a Natural."

"A what, a Natural?" He appeared to have calmed down which gave the woman encouragement to press on.

"Yes a Natural. As far as I have been told at the exact same moment as the EMP…"

"Electro-magnetic pulse?" Westerman queried.

"Yes that's right. The same moment as the EMP hit you were also struck by lightning. I don't know all the technical stuff but you must have some quantum DNA; you opened a wormhole and you transported yourself here." Westerman stared at her for a long period and then he began to laugh. This laugh started as a giggle and developed into a full-blown cascade of laughter. Eventually he brought himself under some control.

"Well if it was something as simple as that, why didn't you tell me this first off?" he said sarcastically. This had a totally unexpected effect on the woman; she sprang to her feet, infuriated.

"Simple! Simple! Have you any idea of how many people and how much computing power went into the calculation of your final destination? How many millions of terra-watts of energy were expended to stop you materializing in space or in the centre of a star? How many Wardens are deployed in this sector to greet you?" She paused and took a deep breath. "And it's me who gets the 'honour' of greeting the first Natural in years only to discover that he is a giggling idiot!"

Westerman was brought bolt upright by the sudden force of her verbal assault, he felt himself bristle and stop laughing.

"Look, this is all a bit difficult to take in. It's not everyday that you wake up on an alien planet and a beautiful woman tells you that you've stepped into a sci-fi novel!"

"It's not a planet, it's a moon and … and… do you really think that I'm beautiful?" she asked bashfully. Westerman turned a bright red with embarrassment. "Yes. Yes you are beautiful." An awkward silence descended in the refectory. The two people regarded each other across the table; eventually it was Westerman that broke the reverie.

"Look, I'm sorry but this is a hell of a lot for me to take in. My race of people only learned to fly just over one hundred years ago, we've only been to our own moon a handful of times in the last forty years." Zalar looked down at her feet and replied.

"Yes I know all this and I should apologise for expecting you to accept this strange situation on face value. Let's start over again. Please?" She looked back up at Westerman, her bright eyes twinkling in the room's overhead illumination, to Westerman they appeared to shine with an inner fire or passion.

"Okay let's start again, but I've got to warn you I'm going to need some more proof and a long time before I can really start believing in this fairy tale." He smiled as disarmingly as he could at the woman and in this particular instant a new understanding had been reached between them. Zalar stood up and nodded her head in the direction of the door.

"They say that a picture is worth a thousand words," she said and started walking, Westerman stood up and followed.

"Isn't that a Human saying?" he offered. She glanced around and retorted.

"Are you kidding?"

Westerman and Zalar exited the building and once again stood on the featureless dark grey plain. Night had fully fallen and the alien sky was ablaze with billions of stars. He was gazing upward at this awe-inspiring vista when the woman moved closer to him and pointed up into the heavens.

"It's over there," she whispered.

"What is?"

"The Earth, the Moon, your home." She smiled. He blushed again.

"Thanks. How far are we away?" She frowned and produced a small credit card sized device from a pocket of her coverall, which she studied, for a short time before replying.

"I think that it's about three hundred light years."

"Wow! That far?"

"Yes that is why you caused such a problem. Nobody was expecting you to do such a big jump for your first time." He turned towards her. She was intently looking at the stars, her face bathed in the glow of the twin moons, her perfect jaw line emphasised by the shadow beneath. She was a naturally beautiful woman, the type that would not age badly. Conscious that he was staring and ashamed that in this 'alien' situation he was actually beginning to feel turned on; he looked away to the stars. "How far was your first time?" She glazed across at him, puzzled and then with realisation of the meaning of his question replied.

"Oh no; I'm not a natural. I can't jump without the correct equipment."

"Neither can I!" he stated forcefully.

"Oh but you will." She answered in an all-knowing, matter of fact manner. With that she looked down at the calculator like machine and expertly, with one hand, pressed a series of small keys, whilst she was doing this she moved toward Westerman so that her face was about two centimetres away from his.

"What happens next?" he said looking into her slate grey eyes, she looked back into his; Jesus she smelt good, he could feel his loins starting to stir into action. She appeared to be thinking and then replied.

"I came across this saying in my research into your culture."

"Which is?" He adopted a puzzled frown.

"I'm taking you to see the wizard, the wonderful wizard of Oz!" With that she wrapped her slender arm around his neck. Westerman looked down at the device in her hand; her perfectly manicured thumb pressed the single red button that was in the centre. They disappeared in a brilliant flash of white light.

CHAPTER FIVE

To Westerman, when Zalar pressed the red button a milky-white sphere appeared to form around them, this sphere had then begun to glow, brighten, become hotter looking. She was now hung tightly around his neck.

"St…ay cl..o..se!" she yelled in a peculiarly distorted voice, appearing to be talking in slow motion. The brightness continued to intensify to an almost intolerable level, and then a silent explosion blew the sphere away just like the popping of a soap bubble.

They were hanging in space above a slowly rotating galaxy. For some reason he felt no fear but Zalar was hung tightly on to him, like a drowning child. They were slowly turning, orientating themselves towards some point or other, the motion stopped and the woman's grip tightened even more. They began to fall towards the spiral galaxy below at an ever-increasing speed. The stars moved from being pinpricks to short bars of light hurtling toward them. Their speed increased again, the short bars became solid shafts of light that disappeared into the distance to a single point. He risked a glance over his left hand shoulder; although the sphere was no longer visible the boundary of it could be clearly seen as it was marked with a ultra-violet luminescence, titanic energies flaring in mutual destruction.

He looked forwards again and the point at which the shafts of light met had grown to a blazing white disk that was increasing as they raced towards it. Within moments the light appeared to engulf them and then with a noiseless explosion of brilliance, it was gone.

As his eyes adjusted to the lower light level, Westerman could see that he was stood upon a raised platform in the middle of a medium sized room. Zalar still hung around his neck and she was trembling like a leaf.

"It's okay. It's okay," he breathed whilst gently rubbing her back; slowly the woman regained her composure. This time however gave the perfect opportunity to fully take in the surroundings. The first impression was the sound of a large fan or blower that appeared to be working over time to cool some form of apparatus. Although dimly lit his eyes had now adjusted and he looked about the room and his immediate feeling was one of disappointment. Apart from the raised round platform they stood upon it was completely bare, the surrounding walls were decorated with various shapes, squares, rectangles, circles and the like, but no evidence of any highly technologically advanced machinery. What light was in the room was cast from a number of small panels, which had been sunk into the walls at about ten centimetres above the floor. He turned his attention back to the trembling woman.

"Are you alright?" he asked. The still slightly shaky woman looked him in the eye. She looked ashamed.

"Every time I do that it scares me to death!" she gulped down a lungful of air and continued, "but riding with you? I've never known it to be so fast and violent!" She smiled helplessly and began to extricate herself from around his neck.

At that very moment a large door set into one of the walls swung open with a loud hiss.

"Are you both alright?" asked a robed man who rushed in through the opening. "We've never seen so much energy in a non-cargo jump. Seven back-up kinetic dampers have been fused." This approaching man had the appearance of being in a euphoric state of concern and excitement.

"You must be Steve Westerman? I'm Tang-Zal-Far; I'm so very pleased to finally meet you." He offered his hand to Westerman who took it and then quickly recoiled.

"Ow! What the?" Looking down he could see a small spot of blood on his forefinger.

"I'm sorry. This ceremonial jewellery is so sharp," said the man holding up his hand upon which sat a large ornate ring on his middle finger.

"It's only a scratch. It's hardly bleeding," he answered looking at the small wound.

"Come, you have had a very long journey, we have reception rooms awaiting," the robed man then turned to Zalar, "You must come too, I think that Mr. Westerman would welcome a friendly, familiar face around for a while." He moved of through the door, the two new arrivals followed, Westerman quietly flexed his hand. It had stopped hurting but he was blissfully unaware of the new microscopic nano-probes, which were now multiplying and beginning to flow through his veins.

In a small room, a few hundred metres away, two sinister looking robed figures sat, huddled over a small visual display monitor.

"Do you think the nano-probes will take?"

"Some will. Some won't," replied the second man who turned to face the other. "If the control ones don't he'll either jump one day and appear in the middle of a sun or we'll just have to put him with the rest of the Unique's."

"I hope you're right. I have got a bad feeling about this one. Did you see the power that leeched off him into that last jump?" His colleague frowned and studied the monitor for a while and then said.

"You could be right but I think that we should be able to handle this one okay. Just in case, we will maintain an extra scan-watch on him." His gaze then fixed on the screen, watching Westerman, Zalar and Tang-Zal-Far as they walked along the nearby corridor.

Westerman had the uneasy feeling that he was being watched, not in a menacing way, but in the same way as in any modern town centre with the advent of CCTV. He returned his attention to the corridor he was walking along. It appeared to be constructed from the same dark grey marble material as the building on the moon they had just left.

"You people don't go much on bright colour schemes do you?" he whispered to Zalar. She looked at him in puzzlement and then realisation.

"Oh, the dark grey colour?" Westerman nodded. "Well it is not our selection. The buildings have been here for over a million years. They were built by a race we refer to as the Ancients."

"The Ancients, they just let you use them rent free?" Tang-Zal-Far turned to face the inquisitive man.

"The Ancient are no longer around. For some reason they simply disappeared about two hundred and fifty thousand years ago, nobody knows why, but they left a galaxy wide network of outposts all very much of the same in construction. Some of our scientists have theorized that the Ancients are responsible for so many humanoid races populating the Galaxy.

"Just how many humanoid races?" Westerman asked.

"At the present time, just about one million but we are finding new ones every cycle," Westerman shook his head and gave a low whistle. The universe was indeed a stranger place than he had ever imagined.

Presently they arrived at an opening, the hooded man gestured to him to enter.

"This is where you can rest and gather your thoughts, give yourself time to acclimatise."

"Thank you. I'd better put in an alarm call for a thousand years time." Tang-Zal-Far looked puzzled.

"I'm sorry. I mean it will take me that long to get my thoughts together." The robed man nodded.

"Ah, Earth humour. You will have to excuse my ignorance."

"It's okay. It wasn't a very good joke and you two are my first aliens." he quipped with a thin smile.

"If you require, I'll stay with you," prompted Zalar.

"No it's okay," he replied but he couldn't help thinking that the woman looked slightly offended, he continued, "just show me how to close the door and I'll be fine." This appeared to darken her mood even further.

"Just say 'private' aloud when you're inside!" She snapped and with a toss of her hair she walked away. His other companion gave Westerman a quizzical look and gentle nodded and walked away in the same direction.

Shaking his head he said the 'magic word' and an opaque film appeared across the entrance. The room itself was about three metres square, with a two and a half by one and half metre slab along one wall, which he assumed was the bed. In the centre of the other wall was situated the now familiar feature of the food alcove. "Coffee, white, hot," he said loudly and was rewarded by the appearance of a steaming beaker of liquid; he took the beverage and moved over to the slab.

"Well you don't look particularly comfortable do you?" he observed and sat down. The construction of the 'bed' responded immediately, altering its shape and texture; underneath his behind it suddenly became very comfortable.

He finished his drink and placed the mug back into the alcove, which promptly vanished. He was beginning to feel tired so he gingerly laid his weary body on to the slab; once again the surface moulded itself to the shape of his body and became extremely comfortable. Within seconds he was beginning to fall asleep only to be struck by the thought that he should not really be this at easy in such an unusual environment, perhaps something or someone was exerting a mysterious force making him relax? He didn't mind either way and very quickly sleep consumed him.

His slumber proved to be a busy affair. In total Westerman slept eight hours. However, this time had been interspersed with many dreams that all seemed to have a repeating theme.

He was stood on the dark grey marble plain of the moon he had first arrived upon; he would extend his arms and disappear in the flash of light he was beginning to recognise as being the norm. Next he was floating in space high above the Galaxy, he would select a point in the spiralling swirl of stars and then, as gracefully as an Olympic diver, swoop towards that point; seconds later he would be stood on an alien world with vastly varying features. Then as if in reply to the question forming in his mind, "Where am I?" a voice would utter an alien sounding word, instinctively he knew that this was the name of the moon or planet upon which he was standing.

In the nearby observation room the two robed men sat, Praying Mantis like, over their instruments.

"His brain appears to be absorbing the navigation information."

"Yes, but look at the speed! Forty thousand jump termini coordinates and still going!" A worried look passed over the man's face; he turned to the other and whispered. "Do you think that he is the one, the Prime Navigator?" With a startled look of fear his colleague quickly responded.

"Don't say that! You know the myth and the chief Warden's don't exactly reward talk like that." The other man nodded slowly and cautiously returned to his observations of the sleeping human.

His sleep was almost at an end when once again his dreams summoned him to the point high above the Galaxy. This time however he did not select a point and dive, instead he turned away from the beautiful spectacle of the mass of stars and looked into the surrounding blackness.

"Steve Westerman," called an eerily disembodied voice from an unknown point far away.

"Steve Westerman, help us! Please help us!" Westerman gentled pin-wheeled in space looking for the source of the voice. Suddenly directly in front of him a hazy cloud seeped into view and gently formed into the shape of somebody's face. It was the face of his dead wife Rachel. Her lips began to move.

"You've got to help them Steve. Please help them."

"Rachel! How? What? Help who?" Westerman's senses were reeling. The image of Rachel's face simply smiled and said.

"The other Uniques, they need your help my love." With another smile that was this time visibly tinged with sadness the image began to dissolve. He held out his hand trying to grasp the dissipating particles, trying to capture pieces of his lost love.

"No! Please No!" he yelled and started to fall back towards the Galactic spiral. He awoke with a start on the slab, sweat flooding from every pore of his body; he sat up shaking his head. It had all been a dream, a cruel dream; but it had been so real, so vivid. This was an experience he had never had before even in the darkest moments of his grief.

Standing up he stretched his aching body, he needed a shower, a shave and a change of clothes. It was then that he realised he desperately needed to use the bathroom, necessity would prove the spur to Westerman finding out about his surroundings for himself. Approaching the doorway the opaque film vanished and revealed the empty corridor.

"Boy do I need the bathroom!" he said aloud to himself and on cue a red spot materialised on the wall ahead of him, announcing its presence with an audible soft chime. The light then faded only to be replaced by another a metre along the wall of the corridor. This pattern of events continued until a door some forty metres away had its complete outline illuminated by the same red colour.

"Now that's impressive!" Westerman said under his breath to himself as the cycle began again. He walked along the indicated route and entered the room.

Yet another room of dark grey décor greeted him; once again three metres square with the customary alcove sited in the middle of one wall. The only difference from his own 'Bedroom' was that instead of the low slab upon which he had rested, this room had a low trough and in the ceiling above it was a row of what appeared to be a set of nozzles. After activating the privacy function, Westerman stripped off and stood in the low trough and almost instantly was rewarded with a powerful blast of water, which was just the right temperature to refresh and cleanse his aching body. Looking down he noticed that there was no plughole in the trough but the water simply seeped away through the material of the trough's base. He remembered, or was reminded that he needed to relieve himself desperately so, feeling as guilty as a schoolboy, he just let go there and then in the shower. No dramatics no alarm bells, the liquids simply combined around his feet and leeched away.

When he had finished showering he stepped out on to the cool grey floor, behind him the shower stopped. He needed something to get dry on; a thought entered his mind that maybe the alcoves were not only for food.

"Towel," he said and sure enough a dark grey towel materialised. Westerman promptly used this to thoroughly dry himself.

"Underpants," was the next command he issued and as he was putting on the dark grey items he was suddenly struck by the comical absurdity of his situation. Here he was millions of light years from home shouting "underpants" at a machine, he began chuckling to himself as he set about ordering further items of clothing. After about twenty minutes of experimentation he was dressed, the length of this period could have been reduced dramatically if he had realised at an earlier point that he needed to specify the colour of the garments he required, later he would also learn that the actual voice activation of the machinery was not needed, psychic pattern recognition circuits required that you only had to concentrate on the finished item you wanted. He looked at the pile of old clothes on the floor and bent down, picked up one of his socks and threw it into the alcove. The sock vanished, waste disposal! He tossed the remaining items in after the vanished sock and everything was soon gone, with the exception of his old jeans. He carefully went through the pockets, emptying the contents into the pockets of what he was wearing. He did pause however as he opened his tatty leather wallet to look at the small photographs of his late wife and children, seeing Rachel's face again reminded him of the dream he had had, he felt a shiver of dread pass over him, he couldn't put his finger on it but something didn't feel right. He finished stowing his possessions, threw the last garment into the machine and, feeling more refreshed he headed for the door.

The privacy field deactivated to reveal Zalar leaning against the opposite wall, apparently waiting for him.

"Hello. Did you sleep well?" she enquired formally.

"A little restless, but I suspect that is to be expected." He had already decided that he would keep the details of his dreams to himself for the moment, especially the final ghostly warning.

"The Elders want to meet you, please follow me." Again the tone was so formal as to be on the point of being hostile.

They began to walk along the corridor in silence, after a few paces Westerman reached out and gently grabbed Zalar's arm, turning her around to face him.

"Look! I don't know what I said or did to upset you but I'm sorry." The woman flinched in his gaze and then hung her head and looked uncomfortably at the floor.

"It is I who should apologise. I was not told until after we parted last night that you have recently lost your life partner and offspring," she continued to look at the floor, "I should not have made advances towards you." The truth hit him like a thunderbolt, the woman was ashamed, embarrassed. Compounding this was also Westerman's inability to spot a 'come on', gently he leaned over, and placing his hand under her chin, lifted her lowered head up so that he could see her face.

"You haven't offended me or upset me," he said softly, "it's not every day that I get an offer from an attractive lady." He beamed a smile, seconds later she responded with one of her own. The moment had been broken, the tension eased.

"Come on Dorothy, let's go and see the Wizard!" he quipped and taking her hand they set off along the corridor, Westerman whistling a very poor version of "Follow the Yellow brick road".

CHAPTER SIX

The Council of Elders sat in the main meeting chamber, the full council was twelve members, and only four sat in session at this time.

Tang-Zal-Far was looking seriously at the read outs on his display unit, the other three looked on, impatiently awaiting his prognosis.

"Well? What do you think it means?" asked Zan-Pek. He had been an elder for the past decade and was not well known for his patience.

"Give Tang-Zal time to completely study the data. You must learn the value of patience Zan-Pek," said Tol-Zan, an elder of nearly thirty years standing, in a condescending voice. His comment was greeted with a scowl and a slight grin from the final person in the room, Far-Zel. This final member of the depleted council was a relative newcomer with only five years service. Presently Tang-Zal-Far broke his reverie and looked up from the displays, their light illuminating his face from below giving it a ghostly, eerie appearance.

"This is very interesting. Never has a humanoid brain absorbed so many termini coordinates in one session.

His processing capacity must be phenomenal!" Zan-Pek could contain himself no longer.

"Yes! Yes! But what about the final four minutes of the sleep teach session?" The man's stubby finger pointed avidly to a data array displayed on the screen. Tang-Zal-Far studied the symbols again.

"I'm not sure exactly. But this could be a random data stream or free formed thoughts?"

"I knew it!" snapped the excitable Elder, "he should not have any free formed thoughts during sleep teach. The nano-probes are not in control! He should be processed."

Tang-Zal-Far flinched involuntarily at the vehemence of his colleague's verbal onslaught. Quickly he regained his composure and replied.

"My dear Zan-Pek we don't know this. Steve Westerman is the first Earthman to achieve uniqueness, we all know that although all humans seeded throughout the Galaxy came from the same basic genetic stock, but environmental conditions on different worlds give rise to variations in DNA etc. This could just be a natural Earth Unique response." His tone had been measured and conciliatory, it had soothed the fiery beast within his verbal combatant.

"You could be right Tang-Zal, but just in case you are not, what steps are you taking for this eventuality?"

asked Tol-Zan leaning forward to fold his arms on the tabletop.

"One of our most trusted operatives is spending all her time with him. The nano-probe control integration should have reached maturity within forty-eight hours. If we don't have complete compliance, we process, Tang-Zal-Far replied in a matter of fact, businesslike fashion.

"Will that keep you happy Zan-Pek?" asked Far-Zel suddenly making his presence known. "If everybody agrees then we will give the man 48 hours, but I think that we should maintain maximum surveillance level." Zan-Pek looked over at Far-Zel and nodded his agreement and gratitude. Tang-Zal-Far looked back to his display.

"We shall meet this Earthman soon enough. Zalar is bringing him to meet us as we speak." The four robed figures looked at each other and then returned to their respective displays and began analysing the scrolling lines of data.

CHAPTER SEVEN

Westerman and Zalar continued their steady progress along the corridor. During this walk he noticed a pair of doors opposite each other bearing the words 'Emergency Exit'.

"Are these the escape routes in case of fire or something?" he asked his companion. She started to answer and then brightened visible.

"Why do you ask that?" she playfully queried.

"Well they say Emergency exit on them and so I...." his voice trailed off. Zalar was smiling and nodding encouragement. "...Holy shit! I can read what is on the sign, and I'll bet that it is not in English."

"Yes you're right on both counts. That is what it says and it is written in Ancient," she beamed at him as if he was a puppy that had finally learned a new trick it had been practicing for a long time. She continued," the translation nanos must now be totally integrated which is good."

He absently touched the stud behind his ear. He wasn't convinced it was a good thing; he still remembered how much it hurt. Along the corridor the news that this integration had now been achieved had been relayed to the council members via the scanning equipment and through exchanged glances, they also greeted this as a positive sign.

Back in the corridor the pair continued their walk. It suddenly occurred to Westerman that he appeared to be constantly moving uphill on a very slight incline. He glanced over his shoulder and the floor behind him also climbed upward at the same inclination.

"What gives? Are we walking uphill or downhill?" he asked Zalar. She replied with a puzzled look.

"What do you mean?" she questioned. He stopped walking and nodded up the corridor in either direction.

"The floor rises in both directions," he said

"Oh, the curve!" she exclaimed with comprehension of the question. A wicked and playful smile played across her full lips and turning to the corridor wall she said.

"Observation dome." The wall replied with a soft chime and a line of light spots along the wall reaching into the distance until an entrance had been illuminated about thirty metres away.

"Come on," said Zalar and with that grabbed his hand to drag him along. "You're going to love this!"

They entered the indicated room and once again the three metre square dimensions were evident. However, this room was completely empty, no alcove, no sleeping slab, but laid into the floor was a circle of approximately one and a half metres diameter; the woman led him to stand beside her in the middle of it.

"Activate!" she shouted out loud with obvious excitement. The edges of the circle began to glow and from the floor, upwards, grew an opaque wall of light that reached up to the ceiling. When this circular wall of light touched the roof it dissolved and Westerman became aware that he was steadily rising. This lasted for about two minutes and then abruptly stopped; he looked at Zalar's face bathed in the glow from the light walls.

"Are you ready for this?" She looked and sounded like a teenager, her face shone like the sun from the excitement within.

"Reveal," she purred, confidently holding Westerman's gaze. The walls of the tube snapped from opaque to crystal clear.

"Oh! Fuck me!" he gasped. His senses reeled; he squeezed and hung on to Zalar's hand to stop himself falling over in a demeaning attack of vertigo. His senses were flooded with stimuli from the most breathtaking panorama imaginable.

They appeared to be standing on the top of a large, taut ribbon of dark grey that was about one hundred metres wide, which just hung in space. The 'ribbon' receded into the distance, narrowing with perspective, and at the same time rising into the star encrusted blanket of night; it continued climbing and narrowing until it disappeared from view overhead.

Following the line of the improbable road upon which he was stood; Westerman's eyes were drawn to a blue-white ball of fire that hung directly overhead. He shifted his footing so that he could look behind himself and found that the 'ribbon' trailed away into space in the same way as the opposite direction.

"A complete ring, how big is it?" he breathed.

"Five hundred kilometres in diameter, by one hundred metres wide and one hundred metres thick." Her beautiful eyes were twinkling with a brilliance that rivalled the stars surrounding them.

Once the initial shock and awe of the celestial spectacle had passed, he started to notice that the ring's inner surface was not completely flat, at irregular intervals strangely shaped structures sprouted upward. The nearest of these 'growths' was about two hundred metres away from them, a large bulbous object that mushroomed into the sky. Atop this structure sat a slender needle, which pointed resolutely at the overhead ball of fire.

"What's that?" asked Westerman, pointing at the structure.

"It's our power source; watch." As if on cue a tongue of blue-white flame erupted from the ball and leapt at an astonishing speed across space to the needle. Sparks and excess energy flicked in different directions.

"The Ancients created the mini-sun to supply fusion power to sustain the ring," explained Zalar, "I was once told that the ring maintains and contains the sun, and the sun powers the ring. They are bound together in a form of Symbiotic relationship. The sun is fuelled from interstellar dust and gases." Westerman shook his head slowly.

"Incredible! Where are we?" he continued to clarify the question, "where in the Galaxy are we?" Zalar thought for a while and then turned and pointed to a red, angry looking, hung nearby in the sky.

"You see that Red Star over there?"

"A star, it looks like a moon!"

"That is a star, a red giant. It's about ten light years away." She pulled the small calculator-like device from her pocket, tapped a sequence of keys and read the display.

"Your people have named this star Betelgeuse." Westerman gave a low whistle.

"That's thousands of light years from home." He fell silent. Home! He was on the other side of the Galaxy, seeing things with his naked eyes that nobody on Earth would ever see even with their strongest telescopes. And yet the thought of home and all that it entailed, despite the enormous distance, still brought a wave of melancholia crashing over him. Zalar sensed the tide of sadness rising within him, she moved closer.

"Come on. Let's get back inside, the council will be waiting." She gently grasped his arm and squeezed it with a tenderness that invoked a warm feeling in the pit of Westerman's stomach, a simple touch of companionship and compassion.

"Deactivate," she said aloud and the walls turned opaque again, shortly afterward they were descending back inside the ring.

Upon exiting the Observation Room they continued along the corridor in silence. The awesome spectacle of the ring had profoundly moved Westerman; it had also created a good few questions in his mind. What had happened to the Ancients? How could a so technologically advanced race just simply move away? Was there evidence somewhere on Earth of these galactic demigods? He was about to ask Zalar about these matters when something caught his eye.

"What's that?" he enquired pointing to a door a few metres away along the corridor. What had caught his attention was that the door was surrounded by an angry red glow that was accompanied by a repeatedly oscillating siren like noise. She looked at where he was pointing.

"Oh, that's the entrance to the power generation facility. You can't go in there! I was told that there were a sizeable quantity of nuclear particles floating around freely in there, I think that they are a side effect of the generation procedure." Westerman nodded but he couldn't believe this excuse; he could not accept that a race as advanced as the ones who had constructed this ring artefact would be so careless with their radiation shielding. He also had a very weird feeling about this area, it felt as if something was calling to him from beyond the door in front of him, but now was not the time; he would file this particular conundrum away for a later date.

"We're here," Zalar said and turned into one of the open doors, Westerman followed. They entered the council chamber.

"Mr. Westerman. It is good to see you," said Tang-Zal-Far, rising to his feet. "Please join us. Please sit at the table." He made an expansive gesture with his arm towards the free seats on the other side of the dark grey table. Crossing to the centre of the room, Westerman and Zalar seated themselves facing the four robed figures.

"We hope that you are refreshed after your long journey. The council of The Wardens bids you welcome to Ring Station Fourteen," said Tol-Zan, an elderly looking gentleman who seemed genuinely pleased to make the Earthman's acquaintance. The remaining two members were then introduced, firstly a younger man, Far-Zal, who had a quizzical smile playing across his lips; secondly a short man who moved restlessly in his seat with the appearance of a smouldering volcano waiting to erupt called Zan-Pek. The latter of these two wore a constant sneer of disgust, which seemed to be directed towards Westerman. Tang-Zal-Far had sat down and began talking, forcing Westerman to prise his gaze away from the ambivalent individual.

"You must have many, many questions. Please feel free to ask some of them now, we will try to answer as many as possible if we can." After shooting a glance across at Zalar, who in return nodded encouragement back to him, he asked.

"The first one is easy! Why am I here?"

"An excellent question!" boomed Far-Zal, "and one that deserves an answer," he continued turning toward Tang-Zal-Far, who paused for a moment before replying.

"As we have told you already, you are unique. Your genetic and chemical make-up is subtly different from that of your fellow Earth-Humans, you have a feature that we call Quantum Energy.

You would have been totally unaware of this quality and your primitive medical instruments would never have been able to detect it. This energy would have remained dormant within your body all of your life if not for a random sequence of events leading to it being activated."

"You mean being at ground zero of a nuclear blast and simultaneous lightning strike?" replied Westerman.

"Yes precisely! We have instruments and a very limited potential for temporal viewing that enables us to predict the emergence of uniqueness and we use our resources to 'shepherd' a fledgling Unique through their first jump." Tang-Zal-Far spread his hands wide on the tabletop as he finished.

"Well I appreciate the concern shown over my safety on the journey but the thousand, million, dollar question is, why? Unfortunately my Human nature makes it hard for me to believe that anybody could be so altruistic." Zan-Pek exploded with all the fury of a supernova.

"Only your primitive mind would be so suspect of advanced beings assisting them!" he spat at the earthman, which then started rallying his composure to retort when Far-Zal stepped into the breech.

"Zan-Pek, please! Our guest has endured so much in so short a space of time," the young man continued in a conciliatory tone," we must endeavour to answer the question." Zan-Pek returned to his pre-detonation state but maintained a look of high instability.

"Thank you Far-Zal. Mr Westerman the Galaxy is a vast area and is not the peaceful place that one would want it to be. Many factions fight openly for control of territory and resources. Most terrifying and dangerous of these factions is the Calaxians." Zalar twitched uncomfortably and glanced across at the council and back to the man beside her, she had been clearly upset just by the mention of these people.

"The Calaxians are a biped race evolved from reptilian ancestors rather than mammalian, they are roughly the same size as a human but they are immensely strong and warlike." Pausing for a deep breath, Tang-Zal-Far operated a control beside the viewing screen in front of him. A three dimensional, holographic image of the Galaxy sprang into existence, hovering above the table in front of him.

"This is our Galaxy about two hundred years ago. The Calaxians first appeared here." A star on the outer edge of one of the spiral arms of the galactic representation turned into a vivid bright red speck of light.

"It is believed that they have travelled here in massive multi-generational ships capable of faster than light travel…"

"I thought that faster than light speeds were impossible," Westerman interrupted. Zan-Pek snarled in a derisory fashion, Tang-Zal-Far continued.

"In normal space you are correct, but using massive gravity compression fields the Calaxians are able to move their craft beyond normal space and achieve phenomenal velocities." He turned his attention back to the 3-D representation. "That was two hundred years ago. This is now!" The image of the Galaxy showed all the stars around the original place of 'infestation' turn the same colour one by one, spreading just like a virus, until a vast area of one of the spiral arms was coloured blood red.

"They are like a certain Earth insect, the Locust, they descend upon a solar system and one by one they strip the resources completely from every world or moon and move on."

"What about any life forms in these systems?" asked Westerman.

"During the first assault they use weapons of unimaginable power to destroy centres of civilisation, after that they appear not to bother with the inhabitants of a world unless they offer resistance, but it must be remembered that once the Calaxians have gone there are no resources left to continue existence, they leave a dying husk, and if the population do not have any interstellar capability they are doomed."

Even though man had and was capable of some horrific crimes, he was having a great deal of trouble accepting that an advanced, space-faring race could be so brutal, without compassion. He needed more information.

"Do we know why they behave as they do?"

"They are communal animals and prodigious breeders; they need to expand to survive. Some worlds they settle upon they do not strip bare immediately, they set up communities but these very quickly become over populated so once again the resources are depleted and supplies have to be brought in from elsewhere. Eventually when there is no more space or the supply chain is too long they migrate to another virgin world. We have been to the original colonisation point, this is nothing but an empty rotting rock in space with a poisonously polluted atmosphere, this same world was once home to three billion Oxygen-Nitrogen breathing humanoid life forms." Westerman looked at the growing red stain on the holograph.

"The Wardens are fighting them?" he asked. Zalar who had been quiet through the meeting finally spoke.

"Steve. We do not have great enough numbers to fight the Calaxians directly so we infiltrate the threatened races and help organise their people into resistance groups. Uniques like you are important in this process."

Westerman looked at the woman and then directed his attention back to the council.

"Why are the Uniques important? Surely you have the technology to take the fight to the Calaxians. Why do you need the likes of me?" The council chamber suddenly adopted a very uneasy atmosphere and in silence the members exchanged furtive glances with each other, At length the elderly looking Tol-Zan broke the reverie.

"The technology we use to travel about the Galaxy is not ours! It was left behind by the Ancients, the devices you have seen used by Zalar for transportation are relatively few in number, our best scientists have spent decades trying to replicate them, but we cannot.

Therefore when we spot a 'Unique' event we do our utmost to recruit that individual." The four robed men looked across the table toward Westerman.

"Are you expecting an answer now?" quipped Westerman. Tang-Zal-Far smiled.

"Of course not," he stood, pressed a button and the floating holographic galaxy vanished, "please take your time. You have a great deal of new information to assimilate."

"Thanks for that," breathed the relieved Earthman.

"Zalar will show you around the Ring and look after you. We'll meet again tomorrow." With that the four council members stood up and, followed by Zalar and

Westerman, headed for the door to the corridor. Suddenly Westerman had a thought.

"Tang-Zal-Far!" he called, and when the Warden had turned around he continued, "how long before they reach Earth?" The council regarded each other and then he answered.

"Two hundred of your Earth years." Westerman nodded, obviously deep in thought, and then turned to join Zalar as they walked away down the corridor.

"Do you think he will go for it?" quietly asked Tol-Zan amongst the group.

"Either way we will have what we want!" growled Zan-Pek.

The rest of the day proved to be a bit of a blur of amazing technology and awe-inspiring sights for the hapless human. Zalar steered him around the Ring pointing out the places of interest, they stopped and had meals and drinks in various identical looking refectories at intervals throughout the day. Eventually he became aware of a growing need for sleep.

"Zalar, you've finally worn me out, I need to crash." The woman looked puzzled.

"Sleep," he clarified.

"Oh! Of course! Come on, there is a dormitory along here," she said and led him along the now familiar corridor. Presently they arrived at the door of the room, Westerman entered, Zalar did not. He turned to face her as she stood in the doorway; her face was troubled map of uncertainty. He smiled at the woman and then gently reached over and took her hand.

"I would appreciate some company tonight." She smiled back and walked into the room being gently led by the hand.

They made love during the night, gently, reassuringly and slowly. The thought of having unprotected sex with a stranger on 'the first date' as it were, would have been unthinkable back on Earth, but he reasoned that he had survived a nuclear attack, a lightning strike and also he was well past caring about what may be. Their movements became more frantic as they both climaxed at the same time; they stayed entwined in the afterglow of their orgasms and fell asleep in each other's arms. The dreams began again for Steve Westerman.

"Help them Steve. Help the Uniques," said the amorphous soap bubble image of his dead wife that was hanging in space before him.

"Please help them. Only you can help them!" pleaded the vision.

"How, what do you want me to do?" entreated Westerman.

"You'll know when the time comes," was the haunting reply and with that the image blew itself apart into tiny specs and vanished.

He awoke from his sleep gasping for air just like a drowning man.

"Are you okay Steve?" asked Zalar as she gently laid her hand on his perspiring shoulder.

"Yes, yes, I'm okay; just a bad dream." He turned to look at the beautiful woman laid naked beside him; he felt immediately ashamed. How could he have made love to Zalar so soon after his wife's death? He had always been faithful to his late spouse, what he had done felt like a betrayal.

"Your dream was it about your wife?" she asked with obvious concern. He took a deep breath, hung his head and nodded. Zalar got off the sleeping slab and moved to her clothes.

"I'm sorry," she said, consciously keeping her back to him. Westerman got up and crossed the room to her. "Don't be sorry. I'll always love Rachel but life has to go on. Please don't be sorry." She turned to face him; tears running gently down her cheek. He wrapped his arms around her and gently kissed the damp cheek and said.

"Come on. Let's get washed and dressed; I want to find some food. I'm starving." Her demeanour brightened and they left together for the washroom and then the Refectory.

CHAPTER EIGHT

It was during breakfast that Westerman had an epiphany; a name suddenly sprang into his consciousness.

"Zalar, does the name Xal-Ha mean anything to you?" She thought for a while.

"I don't think so." Reaching inside her coverall she produced the calculator like device, tapped a few keys and studied the display.

"Xal-Ha is a planet in the…" her voice trailed away.

"What's wrong?" he asked

"It's in the Calaxian infested quarter. It was one of the first planets to fall," she explained. Westerman was deep in thought; there was something about this planet's name that was troubling him.

"Let's go there," he suddenly said. Zalar was clearly taken aback by this request.

"I don't know if it is allowed?" she thought and then continued, "I'll have to ask the Council."

"Could you do that please? And if they ask why tell them that I want to see what we are up against before I commit to anything," he continued, "also it will give them the opportunity to show me what I can do with this 'Uniqueness'."

"I'll try but I'm not promising anything." She smiled, stood up and left the room. Westerman returned to his silent reverie and the cup of coffee he was holding.

"He wants to go where?" blustered Zan-Pek with a ferocity that made Zalar step back slightly.

"Xal-Ha, it's a planet in the infected sector," she replied timidly.

"I know what it is and where it is. Why does he want to go there?" Tang-Zal-Far stepped, deftly, into the exchange.

"Zan-Pek, he has been given the termini coordinates for all known worlds, it is expected that one of these would seep into his consciousness." Zalar turned to the robed figure.

"He says that he wants to see what he is going to be up against before he'll commit." The man thought and then nodded.

"That is understandable."

"There's one more thing, I think that he wants to initiate the jump himself," Zalar said and then braced herself for the explosion she knew was coming from the direction of Zan-Pek.

"He what???" Tang-Zal-Far held up his hand to pacify his agitated colleague and then turned to the woman. "Zalar, would you wait outside the chamber please whilst we discuss this." She nodded and then walked out of the room.

"Privacy!" said Far-Zel aloud and was immediately rewarded with an opaque film forming across the doorway. Zan-Pek could control himself no longer.

He cannot be serious! Visit an infested planet? Be shown how to access his jump capabilities? What next?" "Be calm, please Zan-Pek!" said Tol-Zan and then continued to his fellow council members.

"This was only to be expected. We have loaded his brain with information that his subconscious is burning to use." The other men nodded, deep in thought.

"How long before the control nanos are effective?"

"Somewhere in the region of fifteen hours," answered Tang-Zal-Far, looking at a readout. Tol-Zan studied his clasped hands for a while and then closed his eyes saying.

"I think that we should grant his requests."

"What! You can't be serious?" barked Zan-Pek.

"Please explain your reasoning Tol-Zan," asked Far-Zel. "Firstly, I think that he will be stubborn about this and we would prefer him to join our group 'willingly'. We know from past experiences that resources can be damaged if the situation is not handled correctly. Secondly, if he has fully activated his uniqueness, he will be a formidable asset." The council members nodded. "Finally, in a few hours time the controls will be in place to enable us to use his Unique powers as and when we see fit."

"A logical argument Tol-Zan, also we will ensure that he is accompanied by Zalar, we know that her controls are fully in place and have been for many years," said Tang-Zal-Far looking back across at Zan-Pek for a sign of accord.

"Alright, we allow this but we send Zalar with the equipment to neutralize Westerman and return him here if there are any problems." The seething man grudgingly conceded.

"Agreed, now let's call Zalar back in and explain what we need her to do," said Tol-Zan spreading his fingers wide on the table.

One hour later Steve Westerman and Zalar stood on the raised dais they had arrived at the ring upon. Both were wearing black, close-fitting, body suits that were very similar in style to a scuba diving wet suit. Westerman had quipped that Zalar looked better in hers than he did in his. She was wearing a small backpack containing supplies that could be needed on the trip. Tang-Zal-Far had accompanied them to the embarkation room.

"Remember Zalar no more than ten hours. There is the possibility of existing background radiation from the conflict." Zalar nodded and returned to checking the fastenings on her equipment. He turned to Westerman. "Now you my friend, you need to access the quantum effects of your Unique genetic make up."

"We don't have to set off a nuclear warhead do we?" he replied laughing uneasily. Tang-Zal-Far smiled.

"No we don't. But you have to remember what it was like."

"How do I do that?"

"I'll show you. Zalar stand next to him please." The woman took up her place close to Westerman. The robed man began to speak.

"Now close your eyes and concentrate, concentrate very hard, try to remember what happened in Trafalgar Square."

Westerman was visualising the scene on that fateful day; the pigeons, the rain. Thunder rolled overhead and his skin began to tingle.

"That's right. Remember the sensations, the smells and the people," breathed Tang-Zal-Far who was studying a small device in the palm of his hand. Quantum flux levels were rising.

In his minds eye he could see a white Transit van in front of him, a bright light, and a flash.

"Zalar hold on to him, quickly he is about to go!" She threw herself around his neck. Westerman could imagine and feel the electromagnetic pulse wash over him;

he felt the lightning strike. The room filled with a blinding white light and then the two travellers were gone.

Just like in his dreams of the previous two nights he found himself floating in space, looking down on the Galaxy below, only this time it was different he could feel Zalar clinging to him with tangible desperation. He looked down on the stars below and instinctively thought about Xal-Ha, he began falling, accelerating towards a point on one the Galaxy's spiral arms, faster and faster until, flash!

They were standing in a darkened alley, not too dark because a large bright moon in the night sky overhead provided ample illumination. He turned his attention to the woman wrapped tightly around his neck.

"Are you okay??" he asked gently as he gently rubbed her shaking back.

"Yes. I'm fine, I think?" she replied in a quivering voice and disentangled herself enough to look at Westerman, he smiled and gently drew her back into a comforting embrace and gently kissed her cheek, with this reassurance he could feel her body beginning to relax. It was then that the two travellers noticed a strong burnt smell in the air and this seemed to be accompanied by a hissing noise. Looking around they could see that the building next to them had had a two metre diameter hemisphere burnt out of it and the material used for its construction, which was some fibrous organic material similar to wood, was still smouldering. It was the rock surface upon which they stood that was hissing as it cooled.

"Did I do that?" he whispered sheepishly, Zalar had by now entangled herself from around his neck, looked at him and slowly nodded her head.

"I've never seen so much energy go into a jump Steve; it's terrifying!" She was clearly shocked and shaken. Westerman reached over and gently took hold of her by the elbow.

"Come on. Let's have a look around." With that they moved off along the alleyway.

After covering fifty metres the alleyway opened into a wide street that ran between two rows of buildings, these structures all stood at about one storey in height. Westerman signalled and they moved of to their left, the street had the appearance of an old Wild West cowboy town complete with what looked remarkably like hitching posts sited at regular intervals. It was immediately apparent that the place had been deserted for many decades, evidence of natural erosion and decay could be seen in various places and manifested itself as rotting wood-like material and native vegetation taking root in cracks that had formed on the walls.

"How long ago did the Calaxians come here?" he asked.

"About seventy five years ago," breathed an obviously tense Zalar. It was then that he noticed she carried a device in her hand that looked like a flashlight, he pointed at it.

"Ray gun??" he asked.

"Thermal disruptor," she replied in a matter of fact way. "Oh good!" he said sarcastically and continued walking. Presently they came to a T-junction offering a choice of two more streets in either direction.

"Which way Steve?"

"I don't kn…. Wait a minute!" Something had caught his eye in the moonlight and he set off at a steady trot to his right, a puzzled Zalar rushed after him. The street they were on revealed itself to be only about two hundred metres long at which point it opened out into a dark grey marble plain. Westerman stopped at the start of the expanse.

"Ancient technology?" asked Westerman as he stood with his hands on his hips surveying the scenery.

"Yes it looks like it," she answered and pointed away to the left. "Look over there; the building." Looking toward where she was indicating he could see the same low dark grey construction as he had encountered on the moon where he had met Zalar.

"This is odd?" he gestured back to the buildings they had just walked amongst, "back there we have really primitive structures that are probably one hundred years behind in design and construction to what we had in my country back on Earth." He pointed at the building on the plain. "But there we have something that comes straight out of a Sci-Fi comic book." She moved to his side.

"If you were to date the two materials of construction you would find that the structure on the plain is many millions of years old and yet the settlement is probably only a hundred years old. You see the Ancient's came and went a long time before the inhabitants of this world evolved into communal building entities. We find that on many worlds that the natives seem to congregate near the Ancient sites, we presume that there is some religious attachment that has been created," she offered "I thought I had heard somebody say that the reason that there are so many humanoid species spread throughout the Galaxy is down to the Ancients?" he countered.

"That is one belief, but nobody has found any definitive proof of a link between the two things, but it does seem to follow that they go hand in hand." Westerman pondered this new information whilst looking at the two differing examples of alien architecture.

"So some people look upon the Ancients has Gods?" he finally asked.

"Some cultures have elevated the Ancients to deity status. Why do you ask?"

"Oh it's just my sense of humour. I have a picture in my mind of one of these Ancients dressed in a white robe together with a long white beard and halo," he quipped. Zalar looked confused and said.

"Nobody has ever seen what the Ancients look like. Nobody has found any images of them or found anything on their computers." Westerman shook his head smiling and started out across the plain towards the solitary building.

"Perhaps we should be getting back?" Zalar said.

"I need to see this," he shouted back over his shoulder, she decided to join him and trotted up to his side.

They had been walking for about half an hour and the building grew in size as they neared it, when Zalar point off to her right and said.

"Steve what's that?" He looked at the point she was indicating on the horizon and sure enough there appeared to be a pile of something, from this distance it looked like a tangle of twigs or strips of something or other. Zalar had taken the pack from her shoulders and produced out of it a pair of spectacles; she offered these to Westerman.

"Put them on," she said. He did as instructed and looked again at the object in the distance. With dizzying speed and clarity the pile of material jumped toward him and resolved itself into the twisted superstructure of some kind of massive craft of some description.

"What is that?" he asked, passing the glasses back to Zalar. She put them on and studied the wreckage.

"It looks like a Calaxian Multi-generational ship," she offered.

"Okay. But what is it?" he countered. She removed the glasses and looked at him her face bearing an attractively quizzical smile.

"When the Calaxians travelled to our Galaxy they did it in massive ships which held thousands. You see even with they're faster than light technology the distance between galaxies is still too great for creatures like us, or Calaxians who have the about the same lifespan, to cover the distance before they die of old age." Westerman nodded and continued the train of thought. "So you have a massive ship where a tightly controlled population number and closed environment, nature takes its course and renews the population, through the generations until they reach their goal."

"Yes that's right," she answered and began to look nervously around.

"We should go and have a look at that," he said. Zalar started laughing.

"Have you any idea how far away that is? One of those ships is over three kilometres long!"

"You're kidding! This bloody grey plain plays havoc with your perception," he said shaking his head and turning to Zalar. The woman was clearly very nervous.

"Are you okay?" he asked moving toward her.

"The Calaxians could be near; I think that we should be starting back." Gently he moved his arm around her waist and whispered.

"I really need to see the building. Besides I won't let anything happen to you." She looked into his eyes; there was something that told her that he somehow was telling the truth. They're faces were only a couple of centimetres apart, they looked deeply into each others eyes and then leaned naturally into a long and passionate kiss.

When they finally broke away from each other Westerman smiled.

"Come on," he said gently leading her by the hand across the featureless plain.

The building steadily grew as they approached; this was not the same construction as he had seen previously. In the middle of the wall they were nearing was a large jagged, gaping hole, its positioning seemed to coincide with where the door should have been situated.

"Wow, the Calaxians?" he asked, glancing at Zalar. She nodded nervously; together they entered the gaping blackness.

"Lights!" shouted Zalar and the interior was illuminated by a feeble, flickering glow. Westerman looked around the dimly light chamber.

Covering all the walls were holes of various shapes and sizes, some as big as two metres in diameter. Around the edge, and hanging out of these apertures hung filaments and twisted metal bars.

"Looting?" Westerman asked.

"Typical Calaxian technology pillaging," she said with loathing.

"Why do they do that?"

"It's their way, they don't actually develop or invent new technologies. They forage or steal the technology from the worlds they conquer and the Ancient equipment is a gold mine to them," she explained.

Westerman was examining one of the holes when out of the corner of his eye he thought that he saw a movement. The wall beside them exploded in a concussion of light and sound, the blast hurling them to the floor and showering them with marble material fragments. He opened his eyes to see a figure in a cloud of dust standing over the prone figure of Zalar.

"Warden!" hissed the creature. He looked at the bipedal entity, it appeared to be about two metres high and covered with a dark green leathery skin; the face was a curious cross between a human and a snake. Its narrow eyes fixed in a deadly gaze upon the helpless woman, in a clawed four-fingered hand it held a lethal looking, needle nosed pistol.

The creature hissed again and pointed the weapon at Zalar, in that very split second Westerman looked to his left; the woman's weapon was laid only a metre away. He sprung to his feet and shouted.

"No!" The Calaxian spun around to bring its weapon to bear on the other human target. It would be too late; Westerman was just coming out of a rolling dive clutching the thermal disruptor he had just collected from the ground. The creature tightened its grip around the firing stud of its weapon; Westerman depressed the button on the top of his own weapon with his thumb. A stream of tortured light and energy leapt from the device, a brutal scream filled the air; there was an explosion and the Calaxian lay in a mass of mangled smouldering flesh, thrown against the nearby wall by the force of the blast.

Zalar scrambled to her feet and threw her arms around her saviour's neck; in return he gentle rubbed her back with one hand, the other still holding his weapon that was still trained on the smoking corpse.

"Oh Steve, are you okay?" she breathed. He simply nodded, a strange feeling of triumph and disgust was passing over him. He felt proud because he had protected Zalar but disgust that he had killed a sentient being. A loud whooshing noise shattered his reverie.

"What the, come on we have got to get out of here, now!" He dragged the woman towards the large gaping hole and on to the plain outside. Overhead a formation of three small triangular craft banked sharply and swooped towards the couple fleeing towards the nearby township.

"We've got to jump out of here," shouted Westerman.

"I can't activate the jump engine whilst we are moving!" she shouted back. He looked over his shoulder the menacing looking machines were almost upon them.

"Down," he yelled and threw them both to the ground; the section of the dark grey marble plain ten metres in front of them exploded upwards showering them with more fragments. The craft climbed high into the night sky and banked round for another pass, they started their dive straight towards them. Looking around desperately, Westerman spotted a craft the same as the ones attacking them standing on the plain.

"That must be the dead Calaxians craft," he shouted, pointing, "What is it powered by?" The three attacking machines were now diving directly for them.

"Quick! What's it powered by?" he barked

"Liquid hydrogen, oxygen mix I think," she replied confused. He dragged her forwards and together they jumped into the crater created by the first salvo from the Calaxians. The three arrows of death drew closer, holding the thermal disruptor in front of Zalar he asked. "Can you turn the power up on this thing?"

"Yes. But you'll only get one discharge and then the power cells will be depleted."

"Do it!" he commanded the force of his voice compelling the woman into action. Snatching the weapon from Westerman she turned a ratchet on the base fully clockwise and then thrust it back into his open hand. In one smooth action he brought the device to bear on the craft sat one hundred metres away from them on the plain; he pressed the firing stud and a white hot bar of light leapt across to the target.

"Down," he called out and threw himself on top of Zalar. A massive explosion shook the ground and a ball of fire spread upward and outward, huddled in the crater they could feel the raw heat on their bare skin.

The attacking formation of Calaxian craft were almost directly above the exploding vehicle; white hot fragments of metal of varying sizes arced into the sky at nearly supersonic speeds. The lead machine was literally torn apart, shredded by the blast; one of its companions was now sliding along the dark grey plain in a stream of flame and debris. The third and rearmost of the formation had been luckier and was now banking away, hard, leaving a trail of smoke from its minor damage. Climbing out of the crater Westerman and Zalar watched the fleeing vessel climbing into the night sky.

"Come on let's get back to the town. I've got a feeling that they'll be back in force," he said. The woman nodded and followed him at a steady run across the plain towards the comparative sanctuary of the town.

High above, the surviving Calaxian attacker had been in immediate contact with its base craft and asked for reinforcements. Reptilian eyes flicked across the instruments, the craft was in no condition to engage an enemy but the pilot was confident that it would be able to make it back in one piece to the docking cradle.

Twenty dart-like ships roared past heading toward the Wardens, the creature gave a hiss of satisfaction to itself and then returned its full attention back to piloting the damaged machine.

Westerman and Zalar trotted along one of the streets of the deserted town, the woman stopped.

"Steve, Steve, stop a second please!" He came to a halt and turned to face her.

"Steve, have you had any combat training?"

"No. Is this important? I think that we could really be in the shit in a big way here," he answered impatiently looking upward at the sky.

"Yes I think that you could be right but the way that you have just handled yourself, you were like a trained solider." He continued looking anxiously overhead.

"I was just doing what came naturally, self-preservation," he said.

"So on your none inter-stellar, oil powered, low tech, world you all learn instinctively at an early age to fire particle weapons and fight reptilian aliens?" Her words sunk into him as deep as if she had fired them out of a canon. He stopped looking overhead and turned his puzzled gaze to Zalar.

"What?" he said. She smiled and moved closer and gently grasped his elbow.

"Steve," she said softly, "look at what you have just done. Look how rock steady and confident you are. This is a totally alien situation for you; nothing in your life on Earth could ever have possibly prepared you for this." He looked deeply into the woman's eyes. She was absolutely right, only months ago he had been an office worker and now he was some kind of inter-stellar troubleshooter.

"I don't know how I know what to do," he countered searching for the words to describe the emotions boiling inside his head. "This is strange but this all seems so natural and familiar."

The wall of a nearby building exploded asunder shocking the couple out of their reverie.

"No time for this now. We have to get out of here now!" Overhead the flight of Calaxian attack craft roared by. Westerman looked around and through the settling dust he could see a narrow alleyway.

"Quick! Over here!" He dragged the woman with him as he ran for the newfound cover.

"They shouldn't be able to spot us easily down this alley," he said as they entered their new refuge. They both pressed themselves tight against the wall.

"We can't stop here long. They'll start using infra-red to find us," she said. Westerman nodded and replied.

"Okay I think it's time for you to get us out of here." Zalar smiled and nodded pulling out the calculator-like device and frantically punching the buttons; something was definitely wrong, the machine was not working.

It was then that he noticed in the half-light a dark slick wet looking patch on her suit, it appeared to be coming from the pocket where she kept the jump engine.

"Are you wounded?" he asked concerned. She looked at him, puzzled, and then turned her attention to the area of her clothing he was pointing to.

"No. I didn't think that.... Oh shit!" she exclaimed and held to jump device out to Westerman.

The casing had a large split along one of its edges, a dark liquid dripped from the crack.

"It looks like blood," he exclaimed. She nodded.

"It's bio-mechanical. And this one's dead!" They both stared at the damage to the equipment, slowly he put his had out and allowed on of the drops of fluid to land upon his upturned palm. It was just as if he had received a massive electric shock, he pulled his hand back quickly, his brain filled with a tortuous scream. Wild with panic he looked at Zalar.

"I can hear it! It's screaming in agony!" The woman turned her gaze to the device in her hand. She could not hear anything, what did he mean?

A split second later and they were both blown off their feet by the concussion of the blast that the Calaxians had unleashed upon them. Coughing and covered in dust they staggered back to their feet.

"Over to you Steve. It's up to you to get us out of here, but I think we need to be quick about it." Once again the fleet of craft roared overhead, Zalar moved closer to him and locked her arms around his neck, aware of the intense look of concentration etched across Westerman's face; another explosion.

"We have to go now!" she gasped. He could feel the tingling beginning; he was remembering the jump sensation. The building upon the other side of the alley burst apart into flame and dust, above them a pilot locked his weapons on to the building against which they were stood and depressed the firing toggle.

The Calaxian was too late for as it fired it was sure that it had seen a brilliant flash of light from the alleyway. The building it had targeted disintegrated in a ball of flame.

CHAPTER NINE

A flash of brilliant white light and the man and woman stood once again in the ring's jump room, a cloud of fine dust gently settled to the ground, the particles that had been in the air on Xel-Ha captured by Westerman's jump field. Zalar stood clinging to his neck, her face buried deep in his chest.

"It's okay. We're safe, back on the ring," he said soothingly whilst gently stroking her hair.

"I thought that we were going to die," she breathed looking up at his face; he smiled back and whispered. "So did I." They clung together for a long while before she gained her composure and extricated her self from his comforting grip.

"I must find Tang-Zal-Far and report what has happened." He nodded and followed her through the door.

Walking in silence, Westerman was deep in thought, for some strange reason he was remembering the dreams of his dead wife asking him to help the Uniques. Something was compelling him to act, to do something; suddenly he turned to Zalar.

"Can I look at your broken jump engine?" Puzzled she nodded and passed the small box over to him. He turned the object over and looked at the split along the side, fluid still oozed from the damage; instinctively he placed his finger in the liquid.

Pain! In side his head he could once again feel and hear a convulsion of agony and despair, he recoiled and dropped the machine as if it had stung him.

"Steve?" asked the concerned looking Zalar as she stopped and picked up the equipment, "are you alright?" He looked at her hand, which was in contact with the same fluid but it was not causing her any distress.

"Yes. I'm okay. Delayed shock or something I suppose," he replied weakly. The scream was fading in his mind; she hadn't heard anything. Obviously, something was very wrong and he would have dismissed the experience altogether if it had not happened before on the planet and also he could now hear a faint voice.

"Help us? Please help us," said the ghostly voice.

"Zalar can you hear anything?" She shook her head and they continued along the corridor.

"Help us, please help us," repeated the voice, this time louder and clearer. Ahead was the chiming, red-fringed door of the power generation plant; Westerman somehow he knew that the voice was coming from behind that door; he walked over and stood in front of it. "I need to get in there!" he stated in a matter of fact fashion, staring at the closed metal portal.

"You can't. You're not allowed," she replied. He turned, stony faced toward Zalar.

"I need to get in there!" She backed away slightly.

"You can't, I don't have the access codes either." He continued to look at the door; the voice inside his head was persistent.

"Help us! Please help us!" repeated the phantom.

"I can't get in!" He shouted aloud holding his hands out in frustration. Zalar backed away even further with an ever more concerned look on her face. The voice inside his head stopped pleading and answered his last statement.

"Jump!" it simply said. Westerman turned to Zalar, smiled at the terrified looking woman and then vanished in a flash of light.

Behind the closed door there was a small corridor into which Westerman re-materialised.

"Impressive control Steve," whispered the voice.

"Where are you?" he shouted.

"Please go forward," came the disembodied reply. The short corridor opened into a large circular room that illuminated automatically as he entered, revealing two large, upright, cylindrical objects that stood three metres tall in the centre. Cautiously, he walked around the two metre wide milky white towers.

"Where are you?" he asked aloud

"I'm here," replied the voice. Westerman approached the nearest cylinder, reached out and touched the surface. Abruptly, the structure became transparent and to his horror suspended inside was the body of what looked like a thirty-year-old Negro male. The man appeared dead, wide-open eyes staring lifelessly ahead. At various points tubules had extended from the base of the cylinder and inserted themselves into his body, the whole structure was filled with a viscous, slightly cloudy fluid.

"I've looked better," said the voice. A stunned Westerman stood staring slack jawed at the horrific scene.

"My name is Xander. I was born on a planet somewhere in the Tau Ceti region of the Galaxy." The body did not move but within his mind Westerman could visualize the man talking to him.

"How did you get here?" he asked.

"The same way that you did, I jumped, I became Unique."

"I mean what happened to you? Why are you here inside a test tube?"

"The Wardens happened. They brought me here, filled my mind full of jump coordinates whilst I slept and pumped nano probes into my body."

"Nano probes?" Westerman did not like the way that this 'conversation' was going.

"Yes. Incredibly small machines designed to control you by altering the synaptic pathways of your brain; so that you will do their bidding." As if in a fit of understanding, Westerman looked at his hand, searching for the scratch that had already healed.

"Your instincts are correct, Tang-Zal-Far's ring. But don't worry about that because the nanos do not work on Uniques," explained the voice.

"The bastards!" he spat and looked back at the floating figure.

"Are you dead?"

"To all intents and purposes I am dead. My entire body is kept functioning in some form of stasis and the brain is dead."

"If that's the case, how come I'm talking to you?" said the confused Westerman.

"You are talking to me because the brain is not the nested seat of intelligence of a Unique. When we transform or evolve into the next stage of development by a process that is not understood, magic if you like, our essence or soul becomes part of the very structure of time and space."

"Do you mean that a Unique can never die?"

"No, in the natural order of things when your body dies so will your essence be lost." Westerman struggled to get his mind around these new concepts and facts. Shaking his head in the vain hope of some form of clarity he asked.

"Why have the Wardens done this to you?"

"I think that you already suspect the answer to that question." The voice of Xander paused for a while and then continued. "The Wardens are basically as parasitic as the Calaxians. They stumbled upon faster than light travel and one of their very early explorations discovered a nearby Ancient ring structure.

Naturally inquisitive they managed to gain access and eventually found the jump technology. Unfortunately the jump engines are bio-mechanical and require…"

"Quantum DNA!" interrupted Westerman with a flash of comprehension.

"You are correct. So when I would not join their happy little band and fight the Calaxians, who incidentally are after the same Ancient technology, they effectively killed me and I have been like this for the last forty years. They process my bodily fluids to provide the materials for their jump engines."

Revulsion welled up inside Westerman as he thought about the nightmare that Xander had endured. Slowly he forced his brain into considering his next course of action.

"How can I help?" he eventually breathed.

"Simple. Destroy the ring and release me. My consciousness is trapped by the static condition of my body." Westerman tangibly felt the warm feeling of relief that Xander was expecting; he wanted it very badly.

"What about Zalar and the other Wardens?"

"The Wardens are evil. They have no altruistic motives, they are no better than the Calaxians, however Zalar is different, she is not doing their bidding voluntarily; the control nanos are compelling her actions. Her control is complete you cannot trust her Steve Westerman."

He stood in front of the cylinder looking into Xanders dead eyes, pondering all the new information he had received.

"If you require further proof look at the records in the council chamber, particularly your own," insisted the voice.

"How many Uniques are imprisoned like you?" A great wave of sadness washed over him as the voice replied. "Around four thousand dotted around the Galaxy."

If Westerman was going to articulate a response he did not get the chance. A sharp crackle filled the air of the chamber and he could no longer feel any part of his body; he crumpled to the floor total paralysed. The way that he had fell did however afford him a view of the open doorway in which Tang-Zal-far stood holding a small tubular device in his hand. Behind him was, Zalar tears streaming down her face. Slowly he slipped into unconsciousness.

CHAPTER TEN

He eventually awoke and to his horror discovered he was naked and inside the second cylinder alongside that of Xander. He scrambled to his feet; in front of him stood Zan-Pek and Zalar.

"You are awake I see," gloated the robed man.

"Let me out of here you bastard!" shouted Westerman slamming the palm of his hand against the inside of the tube.

"Save your strength, you cannot smash your way out and don't think of trying to jump, an inhibitor field is operating within this room," sneered Zan-Pek. Zalar's face was awash with emotions, horror and helplessness. She looked as if she had an internal battle with her feelings going on. A chubby finger reached out and depressed a control stud on the cylinder.

"Soon you will be dead but helping the Wardens for centuries to come." Zan-pek said smugly.

"Let me out of here! If I get hold of you I'll tear your head off you fuck!" the cylinder had begun to fill with the thick liquid and out of the base extended the tubules. Westerman looked at Zalar.

"Zalar, please help me!" he pleaded.

"Don't waste your breath," turning to the woman the man continued, "belief is total!" She looked at Westerman and back at Zan-Pek.

"Belief is total," she replied in a faltering manner.

The fluid was now above Westerman's knees and the tubules snaked around his legs until one darted forward, burrowing into his right leg. He winced and bent down to pull it away and another stuck into his other leg.

"Yes. Belief is total!" exclaimed Zan-Pek obviously watching the man struggling against the increasing depth of fluid with great amusement and satisfaction.

A scream of tortured energy filled the air and the robed figure fell to his knees looking in amazement at the large smoking hole, which had appeared in the middle of his chest. Behind the mortal wounded Warden stood Zalar clutching a thermal disruptor in her hand, still aimed at Zan-Pek.

"Belief is not total!" she spat. Looking up from his wound Zan-Pek tried to say something but it was at this point that his brain realised that his body was dead and with a protracted gurgle he pitched forward into a lifeless heap on the floor.

Zalar, still horrified looked up at Westerman; the fluid was now over his head and more and more tubules had attached themselves, she could see the life seeping away from the man that she now knew she loved in front of her eyes. Without a second thought she carefully levelled her weapon at the cylinder and fired. Her target blew apart spraying its contents across the room and leaving Steve Westerman laid on the floor coughing and gasping for breath, the dead tubules falling from his body.

Ironically, it was the very act of love making, of which he had been so ashamed that had saved him from the same fate as his fellow Unique.

The reason why the nano probes that had been introduced into his body to control him had not worked upon him or any other Unique was because they had been reprogrammed at a sub-atomic level by the effects of his quantum DNA. The altered microscopic machines had then been passed on to Zalar by their intimacy, the resulting battle between the two versions of the probes within the woman's system had led to the extermination of the control function, allowing her to have total free thought for the first time in many years.

It had felt like she had been walking along a long tunnel of grey, which had become brighter and until, fuelled by the emotion of witnessing the impending death of the man she had come to love, daylight flooded in. Indeed the sight of the loathsome Zan-Pek falling forward, his face a picture of disbelief at the smoking hole in his chest, had caused only feelings of contentment, because although she was free of the control she could still remember the acts that she had been commanded to do.

Stowing the weapon in her coverall she knelt beside Westerman who was trying to regain his composure.

"Are you alright?" she asked tenderly placing her hand on his shoulder.

"I am now!" he coughed as he heaved and brought up another mouthful of sticky fluid. He looked up at the woman's concerned face, he continued, "what happened? Why did you help me?"

"I don't really understand myself. As I was watching you inside the tube I started feeling disgust at what was happening. The feeling just kept getting stronger and stronger until I had to do something about it," explained Zalar. Westerman was now back on his feet, wiping away the remaining traces of the fluid from his body.

"We've got to get out of here. All hell is about to break loose when the rest of the Wardens find out about this." He smiled and leaned over to give his rescuer a kiss on the cheek but she leaned into him and firmly planted her mouth upon his, a very passionate kiss and embrace quickly developed. Eventually the couple broke away from each other; Zalar stared deeply into his eyes and said,

"I love you Steve." Westerman could see from the look burning within her eyes that she was deadly serious.

Conflicting emotions welled up inside of him, his dead wife and his children. He felt like he should answer.

"I…." Zalar cut him short by placing a finger upon his lips, saying.

"I know that you have other things on your mind Steve. Please don't answer." He smiled and limply nodded agreement. Jesus! This woman was beautiful he could feel his body beginning to respond.

"First stop is for clothing I think," he said. Zalar stepped back and looked down his body at the stirrings in his loins, giggled and nodded, turning to lead the way out of the chamber. Westerman turned to the remaining cylinder.

"I'll try and help," he said aloud and then in a lower voice added, "I promise!" With that he followed the retreating Zalar into the corridor.

"Thank you, there is hope," said the disembodied voice of Xander in Westerman's head.

Within minutes, fully clothed, Westerman exited another room on to the main corridor. He had opted to put on one of the 'Jump' suits he had worn on his trip to Xel-Ha, the material comfortably cool against his skin.

"What now?" asked Zalar who had changed into the same style of outfit.

"We need some munitions. Is there a storage area, equipment room or even better an arsenal?"

"Yes it's pretty nearby."

"Good. Show me the way." He beamed encouragement to her; it was obvious she had got something on her mind.

"Steve, what was going to happen to you inside that tube?" It was obvious that she had never been inside that particular room before; this filled Westerman with a feeling of happiness that Zalar had never been directly involved with the crimes against the Uniques.

"I'll tell you a little story whilst we are walking." he said. "Does it have a happy ending?" she joked back.

"It could do," he replied and began to relate the whole sorry saga. He told her about the Uniques and how the Wardens were using them to supply the raw materials for their jump devices. Zalar listened to the tale in silence, her face portraying many emotions from disbelief to disgust.

They reached the equipment storage area just as Westerman finished his story.

"What are we going to do now?" she asked, wearing a dazed sickened expression.

"I've made somebody a promise and I've got to keep it," he stated in a matter of fact manner.

"Which is?"

"I'm going to destroy the ring and release Xander from his perpetual nightmare." He turned toward her, studying the emotions etched into her features. She nodded, looking towards the ground, her eyes staring at a nameless distant point.

"And then what?" she finally replied with an air of reservation about her voice. This question had stopped Westerman in his tracks; it was something that he had not considered, such was his desire and fury to mete out vengeance and destruction upon the Warden inhabitants of the ring.

"I'm not sure," he answered at length. Zalar looked at his resolute features, his eyes seemed to be burning with an inner fire she nodded and said.

"It's here." They had arrived at one of the anonymous doors that punctuated the main corridor only seconds before another Warden had discovered the body of Zan-Pek. They barely had walked through the door when shrill alarms began to sound and the security doors and defences closed throughout the ring.

"It looks like the balloons gone up!" said Westerman as the entrance behind him turned into solid wall of dark grey. Zalar smiled thinly in reply and they both turned toward the rows of shelves in front of them.

"What do we need?" she asked. Westerman studied for a while, he knew they would only get one opportunity for this so he would have to be sure.

"Firstly we need a jump device for you; I somehow think that we won't get the chance to repair yours." Nodding in agreement she crossed over to a shelf in the centre of the storeroom. Meanwhile the racks directly in front of him were occupying his attention; rows and rows of thermal disruptors lay neatly in custom made compartments, more worrying was that some of the compartments were empty. This would mean they would probably meet armed resistance.

"I've got one and a couple of spares," said Zalar as she returned to his side.

"How many Wardens are on the ring?" he asked.

"About forty, some are away on missions but usually about forty. Why?" Pointing to the empty spaces in the weapons rack he answered.

"There are about forty of the disruptors missing. This could get messy!" The woman nodded in agreement. "We have another problem. The alarm has activated a ring wide jump-inhibiting field. I just found out whilst I was checking this out." She held out one of the jump machines she had appropriated, he could clearly see a line of small red lights flashing along the upper edge of the device.

Returning his attention to the shelves he took three of the weapons from their storage compartments and handed one to Zalar and placed the other two into the pockets of his suit. He then noticed another shelf a couple of metres away upon which were placed a row of devices. What had caught his attention is that these instruments actually looked like stereotypical ray guns. "What are these?" he asked crossing over to the shelf and picking one of the items up.

"Be careful Steve! It's a new type of disruptor," she continued, "It fires a charged plasma bolt, very powerful!" Westerman grinned and felt the weight of the weapon on his hand, next to each example laid a belt and holster. He quickly picked one up and fastened the belt around his waist and slid the weapon into its holster. "Suits you," remarked Zalar. He smiled back in reply as they both picked up a rucksack from a nearby shelf and began to load their booty into them.

Zalar who was more acquainted with the applications of the various devices made their selection; scanners, medkits, portable food synthesisers and short-range communication equipment were all stowed into their bags.

Suddenly the wall of dark grey blocking the doorway vanished and a man ran through the now open entrance, his weapon drawn. Desperation had begun to hone the reflexes of Steve Westerman for, as the man appeared, his hand shot down and jerked his gun from its holster. A ball of silvery white light exploded from its muzzle and shot across the room. The Warden was propelled backward by the impact of the bolt, blood and scorch marks scarred the wall directly behind the point of impact. Looking down at the gun in his hand, Westerman nodded and said.

"Now that's what I'm talking about!" He was feeling exhilarated by his handiwork.

"The door's still open!" yelled Zalar and they both picked up their rucksacks and raced through the open portal.

The corridor outside was deserted in either direction, they both scanned along the dark grey walls.

"Where to now?" she asked.

"We need to shut off that jump inhibitor so we are not trapped here. Where are the controls?" The woman had the look of 'I don't think your going to like this' on her face as she answered,

"The Council Chamber."

"Oh perfect!" he sarcastically commented. With a nod she started walking to their left, "how far?"

"It's on the right, roughly three hundred metres this way." They continued their journey in silence for they had both realised in unison that the Wardens would be expecting them to come after this strategic location. In mutual understanding they both drew their weapons.

"Are you expecting an ambush?" said Westerman. Zalar nodded a reply.

"You take that side of the corridor, I'll take this." Following his instructions the pair moved to the outsides of the dark grey coloured passageway and began to inch forward, backs pressed flat against the walls.

Presently they came to the first open doorway that they had encountered; being on Zalar's side she pressed herself hard against the wall next to the aperture and with his gun pointing steadily towards the offending opening, Westerman inched along the opposing wall. The room was dark producing a multitude of shadows deep inside the chamber, shadows where anybody could have been hiding. Westerman held up his hand and gestured to Zalar to get ready. He then began counting down visually with his fingers, 5 – 4 – 3 – 2 – 1. "Now!" he yelled. The woman threw herself across the mouth of the door to the other side; a beam of light lanced out from the darkened room and impacted upon the corridor wall opposite. Westerman was already in motion, diving low and sliding on his stomach across the corridor he brought his gun to bear and fired twice. Two bolts of white-hot energy crashed inside the room, twin explosions blew fragments of dark grey material out of the offending doorway followed by a belch of acrid smoke.

"Lights!" yelled Zalar and leaned through the doorway. The illumination responded and revealed a scene of destruction. Their attacker had been sheltering behind a table that had been rent totally asunder; the Warden had been reduced to a smouldering heap of flesh and rags against the far wall. A quick check through the clearing smoke produced no further would-be assailants.

"One down?" she asked.

He smiled and replied, "One down."

They moved back into the corridor and continued their steady progress, weapons drawn in readiness.

Movement along the corridor was slow, but they encountered no further resistance, eventually they reached the door of the council chamber. The security device had done its job and this opening was now a solid dark grey wall, Westerman gestured Zalar to stand back as he levelled the muzzle of his weapon at the obstruction.

He was just about to fire when a sizzling beam of agitated particles shot past the side of his face.

"Down!" he called out as he threw himself to the ground, and was further rewarded by feeling the reassuring bump of Zalar landing beside him. The space they had been occupying became criss-crossed with the beams from two or three weapons. Westerman rolled over and fired in the general direction of his attackers, fifty metres along the corridor a Warden was thrown to the ground by the bolt exploding against the nearby wall.

A second robed figure was quickly regaining his composure and about to fire again; he was too late, Zalar had already pressed the firing stud on her disruptor, her shot struck the man squarely in the throat and with a sickening spluttering noise his head bounced along the floor behind him, after what seemed like an eternity, the headless body toppled over to join it.

The remaining Warden was scrambling to his feet and, giving up all thoughts of fighting, was starting to run away, his feet skidding on the fragments of ring material covering the floor. Westerman stood up and aimed carefully along the barrel of his gun; he pulled the trigger and the fleeing mans back erupted into smoke and flame, the force of the bolt sending his dead body tumbling along the corridor.

Turning to the sealed door of the council chamber, he fired again. The bolt of energy struck the dark grey barrier with devastating force, the explosion threw debris in every direction and, after the smoke and dust had cleared, a jagged hole large enough to allow entry had appeared.

Slowly, holding his gun two-handed in front of him, Westerman advanced into the room. The smoke was still quite thick causing him to use his left hand to cleave the air to help clear it. He was barely through the door when something struck his outstretched gun hand making his weapon fall from his grasp; he turned to the direction from which the blow came.

Tang-Zal-Far stood a metre away from him holding a thermal disruptor, which was firmly pointed at his head. "You have caused us a great deal of trouble Mister Westerman," he said slowly and deliberately. After a short pause he gestured with his weapon and continued, "you could have joined us! You could have been one of the team! You could have helped us rule the Galaxy! But no, you wanted to be the hero."

"I'm no hero! I just can't stand the injustice of what you are doing to the Uniques. You're no better than the Calaxians!" Slowly he backed away into the room, Tang-Zal-Far advanced, maintaining the same distance his weapon still trained, unwavering.

"You know nothing about anything! If it wasn't for us you wouldn't even be Unique," he spat.

"What?" replied Westerman, puzzled.

At that very moment Zalar, who had entered the room unseen, moved up behind the robed man and pressed the business end of her disruptor into the back of his head.

"Don't even breathe," she said and, as if struck by an electric shock, Tang-Zal-Far stiffened.

"Zalar what are you doing?" he stammered a sudden panic entering his voice. In desperation he continued, "Belief is total!" Moving around, she gently reached down and removed the disruptor from the Wardens hand and whispered.

"No it isn't"

"Thanks Zalar" smiled Westerman, a smile that she returned with a slight nod. Turning to the control panels on the desks of the council chamber, he began to think about what the Warden had just said. How were they responsible for his Uniqueness?

"What did you mean, if it wasn't for you?" he asked without looking up from his studying of the switches and dials.

"In your vernacular, go fuck yourself!" replied Tang-Zal-Far defiantly, looking smugly across the room, arms folded.

"I would really like to know what you meant by saying that I would not be Unique if it wasn't for you?" Westerman's voice had been steadily rising in volume until the last few words had been practically shouted, their tone full of venom and anger.

"Go to hell!" was the terse reply. Westerman picked up his gun from the floor and, in a smooth, dramatic arc, brought it to bear on the Warden.

"Zalar come over here please. I've got him covered." The woman backed away from their captive hardly daring to take her eyes off the man.

"I need you to look at these controls. I want to know how to turn off the jump inhibitor field." He noted the man flinched ever so slightly when he had mentioned this device. Zalar had begun to look over the instruments when another Warden burst through the jagged opening from the corridor.

"Steve!" she yelled. By the time this warning had been issued Westerman had swung his gun over, fired and was swinging it back to Tang-Zal-Far. The incoming Warden was now a heap of smoking flesh and bone; Tang-Zal-Far had tried to react to this diversion but had only moved half a pace before he brought himself to an abrupt halt, hands raised.

"Don't even think about it," said Westerman. Zalar returned from studying the panel and said.

"I've found it! As you thought the Jump override is controlled from this panel." The robed figure shifted slightly as Westerman glanced momentarily away, however his attention quickly returned and he slowly shook his head.

"Do you want me to kill the field?" she asked.

"Not yet. Could you check if there are any back-up activation sequences?" he replied. The woman began scrolling through the various menus and schematics being displayed on the panels monitor.

"Can't find any, no, I'm pretty sure its centrally control from this point."

The Wardens earlier comments had put a germ of an idea inside Westerman's head, he was curious as to the basis around Tang-Zal-Far's earlier claim.

"Zalar, Can you access their database?" he queried. The Warden shifted uneasily.

"Yes, what do you want to know?"

"See if you can cross reference and do a search on me." Her fingers danced over the keyboard, initiating the routines that had begun to interrogate the data files; the Warden was becoming increasingly agitated.

"What do you hope to find? You primitive fool what could you hope to achieve?" He was hiding something Westerman thought; he was becoming worried by what they might find. A small chime-like noise sounded bringing Zalar's attention back to the screen.

"I've got it Steve," she said. Nodding he crossed over to her.

"Keep him covered, if he as much as farts, burn a hole in the son of a bitch!" The woman nodded and raised her own weapon, aiming it at the Warden.

Westerman looked intently at the screen; against his name there was a list of sub-files labelled 'Record', 'Processing' and 'Conversion'. Using one of the keys, he scrolled down until 'Conversion' was highlighted. The screen changed and presented another short list; he was immediately drawn to the file titled 'Activation'. Hardly daring to breathe and occasionally darting a look at the nearby Warden, he operated the controls and opened the file.

The display showed lines of text interspersed with photographic inserts; the first picture was obviously a mug shot of him; the second was at his family's funeral and the third was of him getting off the train in London. His heart pounded as he began to read the text, the translator device changing the characters into pure English. It told of how he had been identified as a potential Unique five years ago, apparently the death of his mother with all the emotions and subsequent chemical imbalances within his body had first prompted the Quantum DNA into action. The death of his wife and children had provided a further catalyst; however, what was needed for the final metamorphosis was the application of a massive quantity of electro-magnetic energy.

The realisation hit him like a solid iron brick.

"You set the bomb off in London!" he said looking up from the console into the worried Wardens eyes.

"It was necessary to initiate the change in you," he answered in a smug, condescending way and began to shuffle uneasily.

"You killed millions of people just to get me?" Westerman barked incredulously.

"Yes. You were or had the potential to become Unique. We had to act, it was in our interests."

"Your interests, all you wanted was to be able to use me with your mind control nano-probes to fight your wars and if that didn't work, stick me in one of your test tubes and use pieces of me in your jump devices!"

"You seem to have grasped the basic concept. Yes!" said Tang-Zal-Far superiorly.

This was far too much for the irate human to bear, with a growl he picked up his gun and leapt over the console toward the Warden, and with a heavy swing of his arm, he pistol whipped the focus of his torment, sending him sprawling to the ground.

"Your interests!" spat Westerman, his shoulders trembling with burning rage. The prone Warden turned over and glared at his attacker.

"The strongest best position, to achieve that we need the advantage that jump capability gives us; the only way to make the jump devices work is with Unique tissue. We were forced into doing this."

"Don't give me that bullshit! You were using Unique material along time before the Calaxians came. You're just a bunch of interstellar parasites!" spat Westerman. This tirade had helped him cool down a small fraction, he turned and crossed back to the console and the record it was still displaying, he continued reading, a thought occurred to him.

"What about the lightning strike?" he asked. The Warden said nothing.

"What about the lightning strike? When I first arrived you said that it was the EMP and the lightning strike that had triggered my transformation. What about the lightning strike? Did you arrange that too?" He pressed the point home hard.

"Even we do not have weather control to the sort of degree that could generate a lightning bolt in a specific place," was the sneering reply. Raising his weapon, Westerman continued his line of questioning.

"What about the lightning strike?" With a smooth movement, Westerman levelled his gun and fired; a section of wall close to the Warden's head exploded outward prompting the robed figure to throw himself to the floor and cover his head with his hands.

"Alright, I'll tell you!" He said as he knelt up and held his hands high in the air in a submissive gesture.

"The lightning strike was a pure coincidence, we knew nothing about it."

"There's something that you're not telling me. What is it?" Westerman jerked the weapon up to align perfectly with the man's head. Clearly now very afraid, Tang-Zal-Far cowered away, but eventually spoke.

"The lightning strike was nothing to do with us, but it has further enhanced your Quantum DNA. We have never before seen anybody who can generate so much jump energy, your travel capabilities could well be not just be interstellar but, intergalactic!"

"Steve," said Zalar, "I think that he is telling the truth. When I travelled with you the power was awesome. I've certainly never experienced so much power in a jump." He looked over at her and smiled.

"The next time we fly I'll try to be a bit more careful." She smiled at his reply and Westerman turned back to the display; after a few moments of study he shifted his attention back to the Warden.

"What about my family?" he asked

"You're family? I know nothing about your family," Tang-Zal-Far replied giving a creditable impression of someone who was confused by the question.

"When we had the accident in which my family was killed, I was thrown clear of the final impact. I was stunned, barely conscious when the paramedics loaded me into the ambulance, but I distinctly remember seeing a robed man watching everything that had taken place, this same man vanished in a flash of light!"

"I know nothing about this. It wasn't the Wardens," he replied. Westerman tightened his grip on the weapons firing stud.

"It wasn't us! Check the data records if you don't believe me!" pleaded the now clearly terrified man. Nodding and slightly lowering the gun, Westerman returned to studying the displayed text.

"Zalar," said Tang-Zal-Far, "do you think that you can hope to escape with this primitive? You will be hunted down like dogs even if you make it off the ring."

"Don't make me laugh, I've come to realise that the Wardens are just parasites; you can't do anything for yourselves!" she snapped in reply, Westerman smiled to himself listening to the exchange, however his amusement was short lived for as he read the text he stumbled across an important fact causing him to level his gun on the Warden again.

"You set off the bomb! You bastard! It was actually you who set off the bomb!" he shouted, the object of his rage cowered away. Westerman glared at the man; the perpetrator of the largest single act of murder in man-kind's history was at the business end of his gun. There were no courts to mete out justice, no judge or jury, he would act as man's avenging angel, and this creature had to die!

Two Wardens had been slowly inching their way along the corridor; it had taken them a while but they were now at the council chamber door. As they got with-in a couple of metres of the entrance they could clearly hear the interrogation, they could also clearly hear the direction it was heading, they realised that they had to act now otherwise their colleague would soon be dead.

His finger tightened on the firing stud; Westerman could feel the bile of hatred building up in his throat, he had always tried to be a peaceful man but he knew that at certain times extreme measures were called for. This was one of the certain times.

A motion caught his eye and instinctively he ducked; a beam of energy sliced through the air in the precise location of where his head had been and went on to tor-ture the dark grey wall. A second blast narrowly missed Zalar who had followed Westerman's lead and dove for cover; they carried on moving and weaving until they had found shelter against the wall near the door, out of sight of their attackers.

Tang-Zal-Far had also been prompted into action and he took his chance; he knew that he was about to die, he had nothing to lose; he propelled himself across the chamber and launched his body over the desk. This action had taken the preoccupied Westerman by surprise; a hand appeared around the opening holding a disruptor, a single shot was fired and the beam glanced Zalar's shoulder sending her spinning to the ground, her weapon clattering into the middle of the floor.

"Zalar!" cried Westerman. He jerked up his own gun and fired, the wall next to the doorway exploded into smoke and flame.

"Are you alright?" he panted; in reply the woman looked up, nodded and smiled thinly.

"It hurts like hell!" she eventually said through gritted teeth. As gently as he could, under the circumstances, he reached down and dragged the wounded woman closer to the wall; his attention then returned to Tang-Zal-Far. The robed figure looked up and grinned manically back at him.

"You're too late!" he spat and held up a Jump device, his thumb already depressing the activation button; he disappeared in a flash of light.

"Bastard, he must have turned off the inhibitor field when he hid behind the desk!" raged Westerman, only to be interrupted a wild beam of energy lancing across the room.

"I have had enough of this!" he barked and jumped out into the middle of the room. In one smooth movement he began firing his weapon repeatedly at the doorway; explosion after explosion rang out, debris scattered in every direction. Zalar looked on as he continued to fire wildly wondering about the motive behind his strategy, it became obvious seconds later.

The sheer violence of the onslaught had forced the attacking Wardens to back away from the doorway and shield their faces from the flying fragments of ring material. Taking this opportunity Westerman closed his eyes and concentrated; he vanished in a flash of blinding light and reappeared in the corridor behind the two cowering Wardens. Alerted to his materialisation they began to turn, he fired twice and at such a close range all that remained was a few scraps of clothing and lumps of charred flesh.

Walking up to the chamber door he shouted.

"Zalar, don't shoot! It's me. I'm coming back in." He entered the dust and smoke filled room and crossed to the woman who was now stood up and leaning against the wall.

"How are you?" he asked, his voice full of concern.

"I'll live, I think." she replied through a wince of pain from her shoulder.

"Let me take a look at that." He began to inspect the wound. She had been lucky the beam had grazed her jump suit and the resulting injury was just a burn, it looked painful and sore but he suspected that it was not too serious. Crossing to the remains of the dead warden on the floor, Westerman retrieved a clean piece of the robe and made it into a makeshift bandage, which he applied to the wound.

"Ow!" she yelped, but managed a smile of gratitude.

"I need you to look at the console for me. I need to know what that piece of shit has done," he said gently rubbing her back for reassurance and also steering her behind the desk. She studied the readouts.

"Oh no," she groaned eyes widening.

"I take it that this is one of those good news, bad news moments," he said ironically.

"The good news is that the jump inhibitor field is off," she said nodding.

"I gathered as much. What's the bad news?" Zalar looked up from the screen.

"Before he departed our friend issued a system wide alert." The vacant, questioning look on her companions face prompted an explanation.

"Sorry. Using quantum devices the Wardens can communicate instantaneously across interstellar distances, but the signal gets badly degraded the further it travels so actual verbal communication is not practical. However, frequency modulation can be detected so they have a set of prearranged signals to use in case of certain eventualities."

"I suppose that they had a signal for attack from an angry human?" he said. This was obviously not the time to try and inject some humour, he continued, "I get the picture. How long do we have?"

"Standard procedure is for an armed response unit to be mobilised. I would say no more than an hour, tops," she replied tenderly cradling her damaged arm.

"I think that it could be sooner rather than later if Tang has anything to do with it," he commented. She nodded in agreement and crossed to stand by his side.

"Well, what now?" Zalar asked. Westerman knew that they had to get off the ring but he had made a promise he had to keep. He started to move to the door.

"Come on. We've got to get to one of the power generation rooms." Without question the woman followed him out of the room.

Once in the corridor, after carefully checking that the coast was clear in either direction, they asked the guidance system for directions to the power plant. In the familiar fashion their way became illuminated.

Progress was steady due to the need to check every open entrance in case the Wardens lay in wait for them; they encountered no resistance. Westerman suspected that the general alarm and the procedures in place had dictated that they had withdrawn to plan a re-offensive to coincide with the arrival of the rapid response team. Eventually they came to a door on their left that glowed red, indicating that they had reached their goal.

Being of strategic importance the entrance to the power plant had been sealed, Westerman frowned and looked at Zalar, she shrugged, and taking out his gun he said. "Better stand back." He aimed and fired, his target exploded in light and flame but, when the smoke had cleared, the aperture remained sealed.

"What the?" breathed Westerman. Zalar raised her thermal disruptor and fired, the beam of light appeared to strike the door, flame and sparks radiated around the impact area, but no effect.

"Damn!" she said and winced at a jolt of discomfort from her shoulder.

"What's wrong?" he queried approaching the blacked doorway. Zalar gasped, surged forward and forcefully dragged him back.

"Don't go near it!" she barked and continued, "There's an additional security field been erected over the door. It's deadly to the touch!"

"How do we get in?" he pondered, studying the offending obstruction. Zalar turned his head to face her; she was smiling in a strange way, a way that suggested to him that she knew something that he should know. Seconds later it hit him like a brick.

"Oh! What a bloody fool I am!" he proclaimed and closed his eyes.

"There should be an override panel next to the door," she shouted, barely in time before, with a flash, he disappeared. Seconds later the door opened and Westerman peered out.

"Come on!" he said cheerfully and, returning his smile, she moved through the door.

Inside was a circular chamber that was about twenty-five metres in diameter by fifteen metres high, at its centre stood a large, impressive looking, piece of machinery, which was also circular, standing about fifteen metres in diameter and all the way up to the roof. The entire equipment was covered with lights and circuitry, however directly facing them was a single desk, above which was situated a display screen.

"This must be the control console Steve," she said moving towards it, Westerman operated the door controls, re-sealing the aperture and then crossed to her side.

"What do you want to do?" she asked, he gave her a quizzical look.

"Do I really need to tell you?" She nodded and began to study the read outs scrolling across the screen, her fingers danced across the keyboard prompting ever more complicated sets of numbers and diagrammatical displays to race across the display. Presently she said. "I'm afraid you're out of luck. You can't just initiate a self destruct sequence from here, there are too many fail-safe devices incorporated into the system." He nodded and frowned, contemplating his next course of action; Zalar continued looking at the schematics, double-checking her conclusions.

"Are there any sub-systems that could be affected to start a chain reaction inside the mini-sun?" he asked. Nodding she punched the appropriate keys and the display changed, after several minutes of study during which Westerman kept very quiet so as not to interrupt her concentration, she said.

"We're out of luck there too. The fusion reaction is tightly controlled by powerful magnetic forces generated throughout the ring itself." A germ of an idea formed itself in Westerman's mind.

"What if we stopped some of the magnetic force? You know, there must be generators. What if we disabled them?" Would that allow a chain reaction to start?" he suggested, looking at the screen over her shoulder.

"No. If the fail-safes were not disabled taking out a few of the magnetic generators would not be enough. Anything lower than a fifty percent failure would just make the ring wobble...." Her voice trailed off and she began to furiously punch a new set of commands into the console, her eyes scanning wildly over the displayed data, various diagrams of the ring appeared and disappeared.

"I don't believe it!" she eventually exclaimed, "I can't believe that the ancients could be so stupid!"

"What?" said Westerman.

"If we were to take out just three of the magnetic generators and prevent the others compensating the ring will begin to run out of true and eventually crash into the sun.

If we take out more generators the 'wobble' is more pronounced and the collision occurs quicker!" Zalar stated triumphantly.

"How do we do it?" he eagerly asked.

His companion explained how to bypass the fail-safes and stop the reactivation process; a certain console had to be disabled. The process of cutting the power to the generators would then have to be done manually by severing the actual power feeds.

"How many generators are there on the ring?"

"Five hundred," she replied.

"So they are all around us and we only need to take three out?"

"Three would start the cycle but the more, the quicker the desired effect."

"Okay beautiful. How do we cut the power?" He smiled. She returned his smile, nodded towards his holster and replied.

"The tool you need is right at your fingertips." Westerman looked down at the weapon hung from his belt and laid a reassuring hand on its grip.

Their attention was sharply focused by a loud explosion; the doorway to their chamber blew inward.

"Zalar, Look out!" shouted Westerman as he drew his weapon. Beams of tortured light lanced into the room; luckily the dust and smoke from the destruction of the door precluded the attacking Wardens from using their disrupters with any degree of accuracy and the shafts of death impacted harmlessly against the wall and ceiling of the room. However, the same obscuring fog of smoke and dust also hindered any return fire accuracy, Westerman fired three times in the general direction of the destroyed doorway, the resulting detonations adding more airborne debris to the already laden atmosphere. "Keep down!" he whispered to Zalar who was also sending her own beams of destruction towards the shattered aperture, "they can't see us, they're firing wildly," he continued as he sent another couple of bolts of energy towards the target. He looked over at the tower of machinery in the middle of the room.

"Zalar, which console would activate the fail-safes to compensate the magnetic force imbalance?" She also looked over at the machine.

"The main console would allow manual input and the automatics are run from a smaller console around the back." She realised immediately what he had in mind and scrambled to her feet.

"I'll do the honours around the other side," she said and darted off to their left, keeping low to avoid any of the stray energy beams that were periodically lancing through the door.

Westerman sent another two bolts towards the billowing cloud of smoke and then spun round and took aim on the main console; he fired once and the screen and keyboard flashed into a ball of sparks and flame. Seconds later another explosion lit up the room around the rear of the machinery; Zalar had carried out her part in this act of vandalism.

She reappeared, throwing herself to the ground beside him as two more beams sizzled into the room from the corridor. He placed a comforting hand on her shoulder and asked.

"Where are the magnetic generators?"

"That's the tricky bit. They are in the roof of the main corridor, or at least the power conduits supplying them are." He nodded toward the latest high-energy rays flashing across the room.

"So getting out of here is the first problem then," he smirked. Zalar moved beside him and a wince of pain momentarily flashed across her face.

"Is the shoulder still hurting as much?"

"I'll be alright," she replied with a thin smile. Westerman rose to his feet and closed his eyes, seconds later he vanished in a flash of brilliance.

Listening carefully she noticed firstly that the beams coming into the chamber had stopped, this was followed very quickly by the unmistakable sound of her companions gun discharging.

"Don't shoot, it's me!" called Westerman as he eased through the battle damaged doorway cleaving at the thick smoke with his free hand.

"Come on. The ways clear now!" Zalar stood up and moved to his side in the corridor, two smouldering piles of cloth and flesh lay before them.

"The first conduit access point is about two hundred metres that way," she said pointing. He nodded and together they moved off in that direction. Westerman looked troubled, and as they walked in silence Zalar became worried.

"What's wrong Steve?" she enquired, laying a concerned hand on his arm.

"Oh! It's nothing," he said, sapping out of his reverie.

"Something's wrong. What is it?" she persisted. It had become obvious that she was not going to take no for an answer. He stopped and turned to her.

"When I made that last jump it didn't feel right."

"How do you mean?" she asked, puzzled.

"The jump didn't feel as powerful as the previous ones I've done. It felt as if I faded into the corridor, not popped like before. In fact I thought that the Wardens nearly had time to turn and shoot, it was a close thing," he said rubbing his chin with the back of his gun. Zalar thought for a while and then offered

"Perhaps you're getting tired?"

"How do you mean?"

"Well, when we use the jump boxes I have heard that there have been occasions, when they are used frequently, they stop functioning," she continued, "however if you leave them for an extended period of time they do start working again. Perhaps your batteries are run down."

Westerman couldn't deny that he was feeling tired. He nodded and they moved off towards the power conduit access point. Shortly after a few metres Zalar stopped and looked up at the ceiling.

"Up there I reckon," she said. Westerman looked up at the continuous section of dark grey material.

"How do we get in?" he said. Simply smiling she aimed her thermal disruptor and depressed the firing stud. A thin ray of ruby light struck the roof, producing a shower of sparks; holding her finger on the stud, Zalar dragged the beam steadily across the surface of the roof until she had completed a rough circular shape, as she shut off her weapon and a twenty millimetre thick piece ceiling crashed heavily down to the floor.

"How's that?" she said, smiling.

"Great, now what?" he asked as he peered up into the hole that she had just created. A complicated crisscross of wires and tubes had been revealed; some of the tubes appeared to throb with raw energy, pulsating with coloured light.

"We have to cut the conduit, the deep red one to the left." She pointed upward and deep inside the maze a tube of about ten centimetres in diameter flashed with a reddish, evil looking glow.

"How do we cut it?" he asked, standing with his hands folded across his chest.

"Easy!" she stated and raised her weapon again. The thin beam of tortured high energy particles struck the conduit, sparks and flame erupted as Zalar played the beam across the tube, and then the red glow simply faded leaving the conduit looking like an empty opaque plastic pipe.

"That easy, you should have let me do the honours."

"You must be joking!" she spluttered in reply, "that little baby of your would have gone straight through the conduit and the roof of the ring! A woman's touch was needed." She turned away and moved off down the corridor, he looked at the gun in his hand, shrugged and set off after her.

They encountered no resistance at the following two magnetic generators and the 'deactivation process' went smoothly. They continued along the main corridor to their next target.

"How long will it be before the ring starts to get out of shape?" Westerman asked. Zalar was just about to respond to his enquiry when a piercing alarm sound echoed down the corridor and around the entire ring.

"I guess that has answered my question." he joked as they carried on.

"The next generator is about fifty metres ahead…" She stopped dead in her tracks. "Steve! Look out!"

The warning had barely left her lips when their way became blocked by a wall of brilliance, which quickly faded to reveal four Wardens standing, weapons ready, directly in front of them.

Westerman's gun was already out of its holster and spitting bolts of energy at their attackers; Zalar lurched against the nearest wall, wincing from the pain of her injured shoulder, and fired. Two Wardens fell, one with a neat hole drilled through his forehead and the second was sent tumbling from the force of Westerman's pistol. The two remaining fired in retaliation, beams lancing towards their prey. Fortunately for their potential victims the aggressors had both decided on targets at the opposite sides of the corridor, this presented a less than perfect angle of attack and led to the beams of thermal energy splashing harmlessly against the walls near their targets; diving forward into a roll, Westerman came up to his feet and fired, blowing the nearest assailant into smoking fragments. The remaining Warden had had his attention distracted by these actions giving Zalar enough time to cut the man in half with an almost casual wave of her disruptor.

Standing in the middle of the carnage, Westerman said. "Do you get the impression that they don't like us?" He smiled across at Zalar, who responded,

"We'd better get on with it; they'll be back in force." Nodding, he started once more along the corridor, the piercing alarm still ringing out its message of impending destruction loudly in their ears.

After another thirty minutes had passed a further three magnetic generators had been deactivated, the effects their actions were having was definitely becoming noticeable. A series of tremors began to take place, which seemed to race along the corridor, increasing in strength with every passing minute.

"I think that we've managed to do it," said Zalar. Westerman nodded and turned to the corridor wall.

"Observation dome," he said loudly so as to be heard above the alarm. The wall responded and indicated the way to a door approximately fifty metres to their left.

"Come on! I want to see this," he said and set off at a steady trot towards the highlighted door. With a shrug, Zalar followed.

The observation dome turned transparent to reveal the evidence of their handiwork. It was immediately obvious that the Mini-Sun was off centre by a massive margin. The dome they stood in was at this moment on the inside of the ring that was furthest away from the ball of atomic fire. However, because the entire ring was spinning to impart gravity for the inhabitants, they could see the proximity of the brilliant object reducing by the second.

"Wow!" breathed Zalar, taking in the spectacle unfolding before her.

"Wow, doesn't somehow seem enough," he replied, "This is awesome. Look down there, ahead of us; you can see the skin of the ring surface burning off!" He pointed at the area concerned.

The ring material had begun to turn from its usual dark grey colour to a powdery white in places; these sections then peeled backward from the direction of spin and flew off into space. From a distance they appeared to be like snow flakes, but as one of them sailed past the observation dome it resolved itself into an object of roughly a metre square and a couple of centimetres thick.

"We'd better get ready to jump. I don't think that it will be long before it tears itself apart," said a concerned Zalar. The point at which they would be closest to the

Mini-Sun was fast approaching and the ring seemed to be shedding 'skin' at an alarmingly increasing rate.

"Where are we going to go?" she asked. This simple question stopped Westerman dead in his tracks.

He hadn't considered where he would go. Earth was out of the question, he did not want to take this particular galactic struggle back home as they had got enough problems at the moment, he only two other places that he had visited were both inhospitable, one naturally and one unnaturally.

"I have not got a clue," he said with honesty and resignation.

"We could go back to my home world, Bailon," she offered.

"Can they track where we've jumped to?" he queried. "Only from the base point and that will be soon gone," she answered, nodding over her shoulder towards the ring.

"Bailon it is then," he said, extending his arms towards her, she nestled into his embrace. He was all set to initiate the jump when he looked into the eyes of the beautiful woman in his arms, the increasingly bright light from the Mini-Sun bathed the side of here face, making her seem to glow with beauty, she looked back into his eyes and they drew each other into a long, passionate kiss. Westerman could feel the heat of the sun on the side of his face; it matched the heat of the passion of their kiss, for that split second nothing else in the universe seemed to matter.

An extra strong tremor nearly shook them off their feet; they broke their kiss and looked out along the ring to where a piece of material about twenty metres square tore itself free and cartwheeled gracefully into the sky. "We'd better go now I think," said Westerman, turning back to Zalar. She simply continued looking deeply into his eyes and nodded.

He closed his eyes and concentrated on the jump, the familiar tingling began but then abruptly faded away; he slumped forward on to Zalar who struggled to support him.

"Steve! Steve! Are you alright?" she yelled into his ear. He felt as though all the life energy had been drained from him, he was struggling to just barely stand up and breathe.

"D-Don't know... So tired..." he panted. Gently cradling his head Zalar comforted him.

"It's okay. I've got you. You just need to rest," she said soothingly. "You need to recharge your batteries."

"You must be right," replied the drained man.

"It's okay; I'll make the jump... Look at that!" she shouted, looking over his shoulder.

She had been facing toward spin ward and half of a kilometre ahead of the observation tower stood a power generation tower, this same tower was about to brush against the artificial sun.

Westerman had mustered enough strength, with Zalar's help, to turn around to watch the spectacle. The tip of the tower approached the ball of atomic fusion and promptly exploded into a million pieces, sending shrapnel in every direction. The cycle of destruction had now firmly begun; the force of the blast, in addition to peeling the sunward surface backward, had pulled out the roots of the tower. The integrity of the ring itself had started to fail; the massive structure was now violently shuddering and bucking, throwing the two spectators to the floor of the observation dome. Westerman looked across at Zalar and with a thin smile said,

"It's time to go."

Smiling back she produced the jump device from her coverall and entered the co-ordinates into the key pad, with her thumb hovering over the red activation button she crawled over to her kneeling companion, they wrapped themselves in each others arms.

"Time to go, I love you." she whispered into his ear and gave him a small kiss on the cheek. The button was pressed and a split second later the couple disappeared in a flash of light.

Ahead of where they had been watching from the titanic forces exacting themselves on the ring finally exceeded the failing tolerances of the construction and with a series of complicated twists and undulations the structure flew apart. With the last remnants of the magnetic containment field gone the Mini-Sun blossomed into an expanding bubble of nuclear energy. The ring was gone and ages later a lone astronomer would witness the event on Earth and catalogue the explosion as some miscellaneous stellar event.

CHAPTER ELEVEN

Zalar materialised on Bailon at the jump exit coordinates accompanied by the customary flash of light, promptly falling forward against a nearby wall. Her centre of balance had been fooled into thinking that she was still supporting the eighty-nine kilos of Steve Westerman, but he was gone. She collected herself and stood looking helplessly at her empty hands, and then throwing back her head she looked up at the sky and let out a wail of anguish.

Steve Westerman materialized in a blaze of light; the brute force of the energies involved sent him sprawling, face down on to the ground. Tentatively he opened his eyes and focused on the rough-hewn cobblestones upon which he was laying, slowly he raised his aching head and then got to his feet, taking in his new surroundings. He appeared to have landed in the middle of a village square, he was about to make a more detailed study when an awful truth hit him; he spun around, the execution of this action making his head swim, he staggered slightly. Where was Zalar?

He quickly did a full circle sweep of the square, she was nowhere to be seen; he was alone. A wave of anguish swept over him adding to his disorientation causing him to stagger again. Despite the tumult of emotions flooding through his mind he noticed that he was not alone, he was surrounded by a number of people who all seemed to be going about their daily business whilst giving him protracted looks of amusement. Fighting against the massive urge to start shouting Zalar's name out loud he began to take a careful note of his surroundings.

The area he was standing, or reeling in, was approximately fifty metres square and as he had noticed upon first opening his eyes, covered by slate grey cobbles of differing sizes. In the centre of this plaza stood a single, strangely carved, golden coloured obelisk; this object glowed in the rays from the yellow sun that was directly overhead in a clear deep blue sky. The entire area was enclosed by single storey buildings made from irregular sized red bricks, these structures varied in size but all were topped off by a sloping grey slate roof. Along the front of the, what appeared to be houses, was a half metre border of earth from which sprung plants of various shapes and sizes from small flowers to medium sized trees. These trees looked very similar to the olive trees that could be seen anywhere in the southern Mediterranean, if point of fact Westerman thought the actual buildings looked almost Greek. The square was not totally enclosed because over to his left he noticed a two metre wide gap between two of the structures, it was through this opening that three men strode purposefully towards him.

"Hello Mister Westerman. We are so very pleased to meet you," said one of the men, all of which were dressed in very formal two-piece grey suits. Westerman noted that these gentlemen did not appear to be armed. "Who are you? Where am I?" he asked, his hand hovering over the grip of the pistol hung by his side. The furthest right of his welcoming party noticed this defensive posture, smiled and said.

"Please, there is no need to be apprehensive or frightened. You are amongst friends here." The other two smiled and nodded their encouragement. Some sixth sense made Westerman look closely at these men, there was something strangely familiar about them; they seemed to give off an aura that he was able to perceive. "You're Uniques!" he blustered with sudden realisation. "Your instincts serve you well Mister Westerman," said the man who stood one the left-hand side of the trio as he offered his hand to shake. Westerman had become aware that the people in the square had moved over to where the 'reception' was taking place; he looked at their smiling faces, one or two of the onlooker's nodded encouragement.

"We are indeed Uniques. Welcome to what we call home," continued the man still holding out his right hand whilst making an expansive gesture with his left. Westerman stepped forward and took the offered hand and shook it formally; suddenly he remembered something very important to him. Snatching back his hand to rest on his weapon and taking a step back he barked,

"Where's Zalar? What have you done with her?" The ferocity of his inquiry immediately took the three men by surprise, however after regaining their composure one of the party replied.

"Please do not worry. She has completed her journey and is now safely on Bailon."

"How did you do that? We were travelling together, in each others arms." A wave of sadness washed over Westerman.

"We are Uniques! We have far reaching understanding of 'jump' mechanics. We can track another Unique in transit if we need to and affect the termini of the jump if we want to."

Westerman began to guess at the awesome power required to intercept a jump; he also started to relax now that he knew that Zalar was safe because somehow he could instinctively tell that he was being told the truth.

His thoughts drifted back to the woman he had travelled across a galaxy to find. It had torn through his very soul when he had discovered that she was no longer with him, he found himself mortally shocked by the depth of his feelings for the woman who had declared her love for him only a short while ago.

"Please, I can sense your distress and you must have many questions; let us move to somewhere more comfortable to discuss things," said one of the group, gesturing towards the opening between the houses. Presently Westerman nodded and the four of them walked into the alleyway leading out of the square.

The passage led to a narrow street, which was lined with single storey buildings echoing the same style Westerman had seen in the square. People passed by, all of which seemed to nod and smile a greeting whenever they crossed the party's path. The population of this unobtrusive looking town all seemed to be wearing the two piece grey suit, men and women; they continued along the street past numerous doorways and even the occasional shop window displaying various items for sale.

"Not much further now," smiled the man nearest to Westerman.

Five minutes later they stopped outside a large red double door, which was firmly closed, one of the men stepped forward and extended his hand, palm facing forward, silently the door swung open.

The Bailon sun had passed its zenith a good number of hours before, its yellow-orange hue beginning to cast shadows of steadily increasing length. Crouched, huddled in one of these shaded areas was Zalar, her back pressed firmly against the reassuring bulk of an ancient stone wall.

The torrent of raw emotion that had flooded out of the young woman had been staunched a great deal, but only by supreme efforts on her part, only occasional sobs raced uncontrollably through her body. She desperately tried to recall what, if anything, had gone wrong during the jump, nothing unusual sprang to mind, except that she had had a strange uneasy feeling, a feeling that they had not been alone whilst travelling. Deciding to mentally put this current line of thought to the back of her mind for the time being, her attention returned to her surroundings. She had materialised in a large thoroughfare, although deserted at the moment, the earthen surface of the road showed no sign of growth of the native grass species indicating that this was not an unfrequented route. Behind the opposite wall, the shadow of which she was crouched in, trees grew majestically skyward; recognising them as Poylock trees, Zalar noticed that their leaves had begun to take on the deep brown hue, a sign that the Autumn of the Bailon seasonal cycle had started on this particular continent. She raised herself to her feet to get a better look around the area; a jolt of pain from the injured shoulder reminded her of the current less than perfect condition she was in.

With the loss of Steve Westerman the wound she had received had been almost totally forgotten, however this was no longer the case as the movement had re-opened the rupture in her flesh, Grimacing against the pain and using the wall as support she unfastened her coverall from neck to waist and then, with her good arm, began to tease the top of the one-piece garment away from her body.

The sun was now sinking near the horizon and the temperature of the air in the shadows had also began to fall, the cold breeze forcing an involuntary shiver to pass through her body and making her now exposed nipples harden. Finally, with a great deal of discomfort, she extricated the injured arm from its covering. A massive stab of agony shot through her as the material that had been fused into her broken skin by the thermal disruptors beam came away with a tearing sensation. Tentatively, with eyes streaming with tears of pain and anguish, she examined the now exposed injury.

Immediately she realised that she had been very fortunate. The beam that had struck her had gouged a cut six centimetres long by two centimetres wide across the top of her arm, if it had been any deeper it would have gone straight through the actual shoulder joint. Delicately she probed the skin around the wound, even the gentlest touch sent spasms of red-hot pain flashing to her brain. Blood had begun to seep out of the cut sending lazy rivulets of red trickling down her arm.

Reaching inside the backpack she had brought from the ring, she produced a palm-sized, white box that she turned over in her hand until it was orientated with one side, which was covered with a metal grill, facing the wound. There would be no easy way to do the next part of the procedure, with a deep breath she depressed a button on the side of the machine and pressed the grill hard against the cut. Pain! A sharp stinging pain caused her knees to buckle; she sagged back on to the wall. This unpleasant sensation was thankfully short lived as the filaments that had now extruded from the device started to deliver pain-killing compounds, effectively isolating the inflamed area.

As the pain receded, Zalar stood back up and gazed up and down the road; there was still nobody to be seen, which was fortunate because she knew that she would have to stand, semi-naked, with the first aid device pressed against her shoulder for at least another ten minutes. Leaning back against the wall, the coldness of the stone on her naked back making her flinch, she closed her eyes, with the pain from her wound now gone she devoted her mind back to the ill-fated jump. With the new clarity that the release from the agony had brought, Zalar retraced every second of the journey from the ring to Bailon.

She began to perceive the point at which she had lost her love in transit; it was at the very top of the jump, the point at which the universe in all its glory is laid before the traveller. Zalar started to recollect sensations, feelings that were not part of a normal journey, she could now definitely remember the feeling of not being on their own, but now the sensation of invisible hands and fingers working upon her own digits to release them from the grip that she had upon Steve Westerman was also remembered.

Who could do such a thing? Who would have the awesome power to intercept somebody in mid journey? The sheer magnitude of these questions and their implications triggered a huge wave of futility within the weakened woman; tears began to flood from her eyes, she started to sob uncontrollably and violently, so much so that the medical device emitted a loud warning beep announcing that it was in danger of losing contact with the affected area. Noting this Zalar produced a massive effort of self-control and brought herself back into a more stable state, in spite of being half-naked, injured and alone in the twilight of a world that she thought she would probably not visit again in her life.

Westerman and the group of Uniques entered the open doorway and walked along the dimly lit passageway within; the door closed behind them and low-level illumination flickered into life. The corridor they walked along in silence had begun to slope downward and after a distance of about one hundred metres, opened into a large chamber.

As they entered the lighting of the room activated revealing a circular area with a large round table at its centre, around which was arranged a dozen or so high backed chairs.

"Please Mister Westerman, be seated," indicated one of the entourage. Westerman did as he was bid and slid himself on to the nearest seat; the other men positioned themselves around the table and also sat down.

"Okay! I think it's about time I had some answers don't you?" pressed Westerman as he sat forward allowing his hands to rest on the table. The three Uniques looked at each other, there was nothing sinister about the way that they did this, it merely seemed to be a question of manners. Presently a member of the trio gestured to himself and nodded to the others, turning to Westerman he said,

"I or we feel that some introductions are in order. Do you agree?" With a silent nod of his head, Westerman consented.

"We are the current representatives of the Council of Uniques. My name is Wendle and these are my colleagues, Landon and Bolas." He gestured toward each individual as he spoke, "we are very pleased to make your acquaintance." The others smiled and nodded agreement enthusiastically. Landon picked up the conversation obviously with some sense of personal interest.

"You are Steve Westerman from the planet Earth and you are truly unique as you are the first of your race ever to achieve full Uniqueness," with gestures of encouragement he continued, "You must be very proud!" Still feeling weary and lonely from his exertions on the ring and the loss of Zalar, Westerman smiled thinly.

"Oh! Very proud! It's only cost the lives of many millions of my people to produce me!" he said with heavy sarcasm. Landon was all set to continue; oblivious to the tone of the reply he had received. Bolas interjected.

"Mister Westerman, Steve. My colleague is very much a scientific person and has a great deal of passion for the study of Uniquism," he gestured towards the now tongue-tied Landon, "I on the other hand have detected that a current of animosity is present in your voice. Why is that?"

"Don't you know?" said Westerman glancing at each of the Uniques across the table in turn.

"Don't you know how the Wardens detonated a thermo-nuclear warhead in one of the major capital cities and population centres of my world just so that the electro-magnetic pulse from the explosion could activate my quantum DNA?" The three men looked on in genuine horror.

"You cannot be serious?" gasped Wendle.

"Surely no race of intelligent creatures would commit such an atrocity?" blustered a horrified Landon.

"Well I am! And they did!" snapped Westerman.

The Uniques all tried to speak at once and then stopped and looked at each other; Westerman sat back in his chair and firmly folded his arms across his chest. Wendle held up his hands to silence the others and took charge of the situation.

"Please, Mister Westerman! We had no knowledge of this. We knew that the Wardens were desperate to acquire quantum bio-mass for their jump devices but we never thought that they would actually 'farm' worlds to create their own Uniques." Bolas stared down at his hands and said.

"My God, will these people stop at nothing to further their ends?"

"I think that you now have the answer to that particular question," said Westerman

"How did they know that you were ripe for activation?" said Landon, deep in thought, he was answered with a shrug of the shoulders from the irate earthman.

"Please Steve. Tell us your story so that we can better understand what you have been through," said a concerned looking Wendle, who was leaning forward to listen intently.

Westerman laid out the entire saga of his recent past; the death of his wife and children, the nuclear blast in London, his meeting with Zalar. When he mentioned her name he again felt a great sadness well up inside of him, he must have drifted off into his own private reverie because one of the Uniques, Bolas, who was sat nearest to him gently reached over and grasped his arm, shocking Westerman back into the real world.

He told of his journey to the ring, his trip to Xel-Ha and the Calaxian encounter, the trio of men nodded understanding at the mention of the reptilian race, these gestures changed in nature to those of disgust and revulsion when he related the episode of his return to the ring and the discovery of Xander, the perpetually imprisoned Unique.

As he finished his story with the destruction of the ring he thought that he had detected the glint of satisfaction in Wendle's eye. The tale completed the four men sat in silence; eventually Bolas roused himself from his thoughts.

"You have done our people a great service with the release of our deceased brother, a great service." The other two nodded in agreement. Westerman had had another train of thought pop into his mind.

"I have a question or two if you don't mind?" he offered. The Uniques looked at each other and then Wendle made a sweeping gesture of approval with his hand.

"I was wondering why you have waited until the last jump from the ring to bring me here?" He asked. Wendle nodded to Landon to reply.

"We can track a Unique in flight, but only when the jump is initiated by him or herself. Your first few jumps were under the Wardens control; true we could detect your residual energy but it was not focused enough to give us an accurate track." Landon said in a matter of fact manner.

"Okay so how come you were able to intercept me on my jump from the ring to Bailon? Zalar had to initiate that one; I was practically dead on my feet," he pressed.

"When you had done your own jumps we were able to get a positive identification of your quantum signature, once we had that even in a flight not of your own making we could still discern that you were involved," he continued, "we could also detect the signature of an unidentified Unique like entity travelling with you, this of course was the bio-mass within the jump device used by the Warden that you were with." Westerman bristled.

"That Warden was Zalar, the woman who saved my life!" he spat venomously.

"Please we did not mean any offence," offered a conciliatory Wendle, "we know from past experience that the Wardens or their associates have controlling nano-probes inside their bodies and minds. We have always found them untrustworthy."

"Not this one! Something broke her programming. I was about to die and suffer the same fate as Xander, she saved me and killed more than one of her own kind," retorted an agitated Westerman.

"This is most interesting. How could she have broken the conditioning? What could have facilitated such a thing?" pondered Landon.

"I've no idea," answered Westerman, "but I do know that she did and I genuinely believe that she is on our side." "You could be right, but it is just that we have never witnessed this in our experience," offered Bolas in an attempt to defuse the potentially volatile situation.

"All I know is that she will now be alone and she's been wounded. She needs my help!" he said rising to his feet, pressing his knuckles firmly into the table. A wave of nausea and light-headedness swept over him, he staggered and flopped back down into his seat.

"Are you alright?" asked Bolas

"I don't feel too good. Weak, wiped out," he answered

"You have expended too much energy, too quickly." said Landon with a knowing frown.

"Yes you are like a new-born child, you have all the muscles but they are not yet fully developed. It is the same with your Unique powers," added Wendle.

"So what do I do?" asked Westerman

"Simple; rest and with use your strength will grow and your endurance will build," replied Bolas,

"I'll bet that you have not eaten for a while, have you?" Westerman smiled thinly.

"Not for a while and I do feel very tired."

"Come then, let us take you to somewhere that you can get some nourishment and find a place to rest your body," said Wendle standing up and walking around the table to where Westerman was seated. The other two joined him and assisted Westerman out of his seat and then supported him as they walked out of the chamber and back along the corridor, back out into the afternoon sunlight.

After what had seemed like an eternity of being stood in the cold air of the evening the medical unit finally issued a long beep and Zalar tentatively removed it from her injured shoulder. She had no need to be concerned because upon inspection all that remained of the disruptor blast she had received was a six centimetre long, thin, red scar, which she knew from her training in use of the device would fade in a matter of days.

She had forgotten how fast the sun set on this world, this being due to the size and rotation being at odds with many other of the Warden frequented planets. After stowing the first aid machine safely in her backpack, re-dressed her upper half, the shoulder proved to be fine and giving no pain what so ever, only a little stiffness remained to remind her of the trauma it had received. With the coverall back in place she vigorously rubbed her chest and arms to put some heat back into herself. The one-piece suit was constructed of a composite material, specially designed to maintain optimum body temperature for the wearer regardless of external climatic conditions, within a certain tolerance. Even though the integrity of the garment had been compromised with the tear across the shoulder, Zalar soon felt warmer as her shivering subsided.

Despite the warmth of her body the coldness that had grasped her very soul at the loss of Steve Westerman still remained. She felt totally helpless, she did not believe that he was dead, but she knew that he could be potentially anywhere in the galaxy and there was no means at her disposal to find him. The total futility of her situation started to overtake her again, tears began to fill her already red-rimmed eyes, and once again she fought back control of her emotions.

Survival is a powerful driver for any sentient creature and it had started to assert its influence on Zalar. In spite of the grief gnawing at her very essence she realised that she needed to find food and shelter. Something else had started to grow out of the darkness within the woman, hope! Deep down she knew Steve was alive and, although he had not said the magic words, she suspected that he loved her; he would find a way to get back to her and the best chance for this eventuality would be for her to stay on Bailon.

She reasoned that he knew their destination and he had been given the coordinates to this world. Yes, the best chance for the future of them would be to remain on this planet. With this renewed hope to cling to she resolved to find the nearest settlement and a place to stay.

Twilight was now giving way to full blown nightfall, looking up and down the road she thought that the horizon looked brighter in one direction than the other indicating that there could be a settlement of some description. Swinging the backpack up on to her shoulder she set off in the direction of the light source at a brisk march.

Westerman had been led to small taverna, off one of the side streets near the council chamber, where he had been given a rustic meal of bread, some form of cheese that tasted very similar to Feta, and local salad leaves, this was accompanied by a large glass of a red local beverage, not dissimilar in taste to a passable Merlot. During the repast he had been joined by Wendle and Bolas, Landon had been called away to attend to some business or other. They talked about various topics, mostly related to the spread of the Calaxians across the galaxy and the Wardens efforts to stem their expansion, Westerman finished his meal, drained his glass and turning to Wendle asked,

"So, how many Uniques are there here?" Wendle seemed deep in thought for a few seconds and then replied.

"At the moment there are ten thousand, three hundred and fifty one of us on the planet."

"Exactly?" said Westerman with a hint of incredulity.

"Not exactly, twelve individuals have just jumped off world."

"How do you know that so accurately?"

"You obviously cannot feel it yet. We Uniques all share a telepathic link between each other, at short distances, worldwide for example, we can sense every single individual present."

"No shit!" blurted Westerman

"It is one of the many powers that we have at our disposal," added Bolas.

"What do you mean many powers? I thought that the ability to teleport ourselves across vast distances was our talent?"

"We have teleportation, telepathy and telekinesis. Some of our number has developed greater gifts," said Wendle in a matter of fact way as he turned and reached out his hand into which a spoon promptly flew from a nearby table. A totally amazed Westerman sat, open mouthed, for several seconds looking at the spoon, which was now rotating slowly in mid-air above the Uniques hand. "Why don't I have any of these powers if I'm Unique?" pressed a suddenly wide-awake Westerman, sitting forward in his seat.

"We have to use the young child analogy again I'm afraid. Children are born with many abilities, which they have to learn to use; walking and running are good examples. You have been recently 'born' with these abilities latent within you; the next stage is to learn how to master them."

"I feel that our guest must master sleep at this time," said Bolas observing Westerman producing a massive jaw-snapping yawn.

"Of course you are right Bolas," agreed Wendle who turned to a young man who was sat in the corner of the room watching the exchange with interest.

"Willan, please take this gentleman to the guest rooms." Eagerly complying, the young man stepped forward and gestured for Westerman to follow.

"You will have to use speech Willan. Mister Westerman is not adept at telepathy yet," said Bolas. Willan stopped, gave a shrug and said,

"I'm sorry! Could you come with me please?" Westerman gave a similar shrug, stood up and followed his guide.

He was led to a nearby building, inside of which he now laid on a comfortable single bed. The room itself was very spartan in décor consisting of a small set of drawers, a chair and a bedside table that held a bottle of clear liquid, he assumed was water, together with a glass. The single source of lighting originated from a metre square window set into the wall opposite the bed head. Before his departure, Willan had drawn a simple blind across the pane of glass making the room comfortably dim in the afternoon sun.

Westerman laid looking up at the imperfections in the plaster of the ceiling; he was taking the oasis of calm as an opportunity to reflect on the events of the last few days. He mused how quick the human body could adapt to new and different conditions; one minute a widowed office worker, the next he was an interstellar freedom fighter.

He considered what the Uniques had told him, he believed that they had been truthful but something in the back of his mind made him feel that he was not getting the whole truth. He had had this peculiar sensation of mistrust since his appearance on their world and for some reason or other it had refused to go away. This had been the main driver behind his decision not to tell them about the coincidental lightning strike in Trafalgar Square, he had purposefully also omitted certain facts about the accident that had claimed his family; namely the certainty that he had seen somebody disappear in a flash of light very similar in nature to somebody initiating a jump.

His thoughts turned to Zalar. She must be going through absolute torment at this moment on Bailon. The one hope that he was clinging to was that she would remain where she was and when he got his strength back he would travel to her planet and be reunited with her. Whilst thinking about his missing companion he found that his eyes were beginning to brim with tears. It hit him like a bolt from the blue; he was in love with her and nothing else mattered to him at that moment.

A strange feeling swept over him, a mixture of joy and pain. He had thought that with the death of his wife he would probably never love again, how wrong he had been. This new love however had been cruelly plucked away from him by the Uniques intervention; could this be the root of why he mistrusted them?

The thoughts tumbled in ever-complicated precessions across his consciousness until eventually the necessity for sleep outweighed his need for answers, Westerman slid seamlessly into welcomed slumber.

In an underground chamber, not very far away from the sleeping human, Landon and Wendle sat at a control desk, observing a number of screens.

"*He's finally asleep! I thought that we would have to consider using chemical methods to facilitate it,*" said Wendle telepathically.

"*Yes! I was coming around to thinking on the same lines. He's away now so we can begin our scans,*" replied Landon without breaking his gaze at the readouts or opening his mouth.

"*We have to discover why he created such a massive signature when he became Unique, the power registered was incredible, I've never seen anything like it before,*" observed Wendle as he turned and gently touched Landon on the arm. Landon turned to face him and then he said out loud.

"You're thinking of the Prime Navigator aren't you?"

"I'm trying not to think about it! Can you imagine what would happen if this got out amongst the Unique community? Mass panic! You know the legend as well as I do; a Prime Navigator will herald the Ancients return." The other man nodded sombrely and turned back to the displays.

"*Start scan,*" said Wendle telepathically.

Zalar could clearly see the approaching horizon becoming brighter and brighter with every single step she took. The sky itself was now fully black with a sprinkling of stars, only the very brightest managing to compete with the steadily growing source of light pollution. Luckily the road that she was travelling along had a reasonably flat surface so that even in the darkness her progress was not hindered by embarrassing trips or stumbles, she had already thought to herself that in all the equipment she carried heavily on her shoulder there was nothing that could be used as a simple flashlight.

The landscape abruptly resolved itself as she crested a small rise; laid out below her was a small town, ablaze with street lighting, clearly marking out the streets and avenues. Seeing this centre of population had a profound effect upon the young woman, after walking for several hours and not seeing a single person she was beginning to fear that some strange catastrophe had befallen her home world,

Home world, for some unexplained reason the thought of being on the planet of her birth filled her with strange emotions that she had never felt before. Perhaps, she thought, that the control program that no longer had a hold upon her will had blocked all feelings relating to home? She reached up to her eyes and caught a tear that was rolling lazily down her cheek.

"Bloody Steve Westerman!" she said to herself aloud and started down the gentle slope towards the hamlet.

As she entered the town she still had not encountered anybody, this was starting to become a cause for concern, but then she was sure that she had heard a distant noise, the roar of a crowd. She followed the sound as best she could, it became louder and louder until after a few minutes she was standing outside a huge rectangular structure. The cacophony of raw noise being generated from inside the building was deafening, there was a large sign on the end wall of the edifice.

"Pizoka Stadium," she read aloud, the translator nano-probes obviously still working within her body. Something stopped her in her tracks, Pizoka? Of course this was actually her hometown, long since forgotten memories started to flood back.

One of these ancient, suppressed trains of thought brought a realisation explaining why she had seen nobody since arriving. It was the Bailon equivalent of Saturday and this was the night that the Ji-pak match took place; she could barely recollect from her childhood that this was something that absolutely everybody attended. Smiling to herself she walked over and entered the stadium.

Inside the population of Pizoka sat or stood shoulder to shoulder on sharply inclined terraces, all of them focused on the central area of the stadium upon which two teams clad in garish strips competed in a form of ball game. Cheers erupted from one faction of the crowd as the ball was taken through a complex series of passing manoeuvres across the pitch.

Zalar smiled to herself, the memory of such an event returned to her. She had attended with her father and mother, the smile evaporated from her features, her father and mother. She had always thought that she had been an orphan, heroically rescued from the streets by the all-benevolent Wardens. Was that true? She was very quickly coming to terms with the fact that nothing that the Wardens had told her was based in fact. She wondered how many false memories had been hardwired into her by the control nanos.

The game ended abruptly with the sounding of a claxon, the crowd cheered and applauded loudly as play ceased, the players began to leave the pitch waving at the adoring masses. Presently the great throng of people started to filter out of the stadium, Zalar allowed herself to be swept along in this organic tide.

Eventually the crowd began to disperse leaving her deposited upon a pavement of one of the main streets of Pizoka; she looked about at the surrounding scenery. It could have been any street on any of the numerous worlds she had visited, lined with stores, all having large window areas displaying their respective wares. A sign in the middle distance caught her eye, in bold illuminated letters it read, 'Hotel'.

She made her way through eddies of Ji-pak supporters involved in animated discussions about the action they had just witnessed. Upon arriving at the hotel door she noticed a smaller sign, this time labelled 'Tariff'. Damn! She thought; this world was still using money. Her backpack contained items that could potentially have a value of thousands of Failics, the local currency of Bailon, but her pockets were completely devoid of even the smallest coin.

It is said on many humanoid worlds throughout the galaxy that necessity is the mother of invention; Zalar noticed a small alleyway on the opposite side of the street beside a store that sold agricultural implements. Crossing over she looked around, with the thoroughfare still being so busy nobody noticed her slip into the opening where she promptly disappeared into the shadows, aided by the black coverall she was wearing. Twenty metres down the alleyway she found a door that, she presumed, led to the rear of the store, it was locked. Producing her disruptor she adjusted the settings and a pencil thin ruby red beam neatly cut the lock out of the door with a seamless wave of her hand; fortunately no other securing device had been employed so, with a gentle push, it opened and allowed her access to a small yard at the rear of the shop. Another door barred her entry to the interior of the store; this was summarily dealt with in the same way as its counterpart in the alleyway. The outside street lighting produced ample illumination for the woman to see around the inside of the store, the serving counter was immediately visible; keeping to the shadows, she edged around the back of the desk where she began to look for anything of value. A dull thud made her duck for cover; stealthily she looked up from behind the counter towards the front of the store where she located the source of the noise. Her eyes filled with tears as she watched a young couple kissing each other eagerly in the shop doorway, in their passion they had tumbled against the door causing it to rattle.

Zalar's thoughts drifted back to a night, which seemed like a thousand years ago when she and Steve had shared an equally passionate embrace. Presently the couple broke their kiss and set off down the street, happily holding each other's hand, Zalar watched them leave and then, wiping the moisture from her eyes, returned to looking behind the counter.

The very first drawer that she opened was divided into many smaller compartments, in which laid a large quantity of small, round and flat metal objects, she recognised these as Failics of assorted denominations. Grabbing a handful she started to head for the rear door; a thought occurred to her. The lack of security devices probably meant that this was a pretty honest society; the news of a robbery would quickly travel across the globe, a robbery would be unusual but a robbery where only a small part of the total money available had been taken would be very unusual. She knew deep inside her that the Wardens would be coming; such an inconsistency could potentially alert them to her whereabouts. She emptied all the coins from the drawer into her pockets and backpack; she then made her exit through the rear door.

Exiting the alleyway, she strode purposefully across the street, slipping in and out of the knots of people, as far as she was aware nobody had paid her any attention. Smiling inwardly she pushed the front door of the hotel open and entered, Zalar, renegade Warden and now a master criminal, should she really be deriving so much pleasure from being so bad?

The sun was visibly dimmer against the outside of the blind that covered the bedroom window; Westerman awoke and wondered how long he had been asleep. He noticed the drop in the ambient light level and reasoned, based on Earth standards, that it must have been only a couple of hours.

Moving to his feet he was immediately aware of the stiffness that had set into his bones, he stretched and bent to re-introduce some suppleness into his body, only to be greeted with numerous sounds of a creaking and cracking nature.

"Definitely not as young as I used to be!" he said to himself, as he discovered that he had the urge to use the bathroom. Swiftly exiting the room he found a door to his left that, when opened, revealed an object that could only have been interpreted as a toilet or a bidet, he reasoned that he did not have the luxury of the time to look any further; firmly closing the door, he used the facilities.

With nature taken care of he had then found a room next door to the 'toilet' contained a washbasin, which he used to wash his hands and face, making a mental note that he should try and lay his hands on a toothbrush, he followed the outside corridor, through a door and into the street.

The sky still carried the same azure blue colouring, but Westerman realised that the sunlight was coming from the opposite side of the sky from when he had retired to bed; a figure moving purposefully towards him caught his eye, it was Wendle.

"Good morning Mister Westerman," he said warmly

"Good morning? Please it's Steve."

"Yes, of course. Steve."

"Morning did you say? How long have I been asleep?"

"About thirteen hours. I trust that you are well rested?"

"Thirteen hours! I've never slept that long before in my life. Boy was I tired!" stated Westerman.

"You were indeed. Now perhaps you would like to freshen up a little before a spot of breakfast?" said Wendle who had produced a medium sized bag, which he offered to Westerman.

"I think you'll find everything that you need in there. The white tube is a cleansing balm, just rub it on and then rinse off. The blue tube is tooth gel."

"Where's the toothbrush?" he replied, rummaging through the contents of the bag.

"A toothbrush? Oh I see. There's no need for another appliance just put a small amount of the gel into your mouth for a couple of minutes and then rinse it out," smiled Wendle, "I'll be back in about half an hour." He finished, bowed and walked away down the street.

Westerman looked again inside the bag, shrugged his shoulders and returned to the bathroom he had found earlier.

Feeling very much more refreshed, he re-emerged into the morning sunlight. Together with the toiletries, Wendle had supplied a fresh pair of baggy, linen trousers and a loose fitting long sleeved shirt, both in a neutral grey colour. He definitely felt so much better than the previous afternoon, he sensed that a vital spark had been re-ignited inside of him; inevitably his thoughts returned to the missing Zalar.

He was now beginning to feel a trifle concerned for her safety; he suspected that it would not be long before the Wardens would come looking for the pair of them and the home world of his love would be the most likely place to start looking. The current planet he was on, he reasoned, would not be on the list of the most frequented by the Wardens, he felt that he would not be receiving any unwelcome visitors soon. A brilliant flash of light broke his chain of thought and announced the appearance of Wendle beside him.

"Good morning again," said the grey suited man.

"Good morning to you. People popping in and out of existence beside you could take some getting used to," he observed. Wendle smiled and nodded his head slightly and gestured the taverna that they had eaten in the night before.

"Breakfast?" he asked. Westerman became aware that he was actually very hungry and nodded his agreement.

A simple meal of a muesli style cereal and a cup of a liquid that tasted very similar to coffee were soon consumed and their attentions turned to other matters.

"I need to get to Bailon as soon as possible! Zalar needs me," asserted Westerman.

"All in good time, you have to learn to control your powers first; in any case you are still not strong enough to make the jump," replied Wendle.

"I'm sorry but I feel that time could be an issue here. The Wardens are bound to come looking for me and Zalar, Bailon will be the most likely place for them to start," he pressed.

"What makes you so sure of this?"

"Bailon is Zalar's home world; surely they will be reasoning that any threatened creature always makes a run for the safety of home?"

"This is very strange. Normally the control system used by the Wardens selectively removes all memories of the individual's birthplace and related emotional ties. This is very strange indeed."

"I told you! She has broken that programming. I don't know how, but she has!" insisted Westerman. Wendle thought a moment or two and then gave him a look as if he was about to ask something but he was finding it difficult to frame the question.

"What? What do you want to ask me?" pried Westerman, having picked up on his obvious discomfort. "Did you have relations with this woman?" asked Wendle, sheepishly.

"What do you mean relations? Oh! I understand! Do you mean sexual relations?" he replied. Reddening slightly and shifting uncomfortably in his seat, Wendle nodded. "Yes I did." said Westerman in a partially hushed voice. "That could well explain it then." offered Wendle thoughtfully.

"Well could somebody explain it to me?"

"Oh! I'm sorry. Although I don't quite share Landon's passion for the sciences, I too sometimes get caught up in the trying to make sense of it all," smiling the Unique continued. "The Warden's continue to try and use their control nano-probes on us, what they have never discovered is that the quantum DNA we possess actually reprograms their microscopic machines at a sub-atomic level rendering them useless.

"You say that the Wardens don't know about this. How can that be? Surely they know that their control nanos don't work; they must have tried to get to the bottom of the problem," interjected Westerman.

"You forget or don't yet know the true nature of the Wardens. In a great deal of respects they are as big a galactic, technological parasite as the Calaxians, they actually invent very little. Agreed, they have the intelligence to adopt and utilise any advancements that they stumble upon, but any actual homegrown innovations are very few and far between. Ironically the over use of the control devices only served to foster this endemic condition, as the control only works successfully when the centres of the brain devoted to questioning the way that things are done are totally suppressed."

Westerman nodded to himself quietly. He could see the logic of Wendle's assertions, but in the back of his mind other questions began to form; surely the entire

Warden culture could not be injected with the control nanos, there had to be an overall guiding intelligence somewhere in the galaxy. He turned his attention back to Wendle.

"Okay. So how does this explain how the control was broken in Zalar?" he pressed. Wendle smiled and said. "When the nanos have been neutralised they pass harmlessly out of the body through natural methods of waste disposal, this process does take a number of days however. What has probably happened is that during your sexual relations with Zalar, the exchange of bodily fluids has transferred a quantity of the altered nanos into her body." Westerman began to grasp the concepts of Wendle's explanation.

"So the altered nanos I gave her actually reprogrammed her own versions?" He asked

"Yes. That is correct. The nanos are basically self replicating devices; they build newer versions of themselves until the population in the hosts system is sufficient to implement the control."

Westerman realised that these micro-machines were actually Von Neumann devices. Many years ago a scientist called John Von Neumann had postulated that if you have a massive task to undertake, strip mining the Moon for example, there were two possible courses of action. You could create massive construction plants to endlessly turn out gigantic machines to carry out the operation; however this would be costly and, in energy terms alone, inefficient. The other way would be to build a single machine that not only did the task, but also had another purpose; this was to build an exact copy of itself, programmed with the same dual goals. The result would be a greatly reduced cost and the job would actually take less time.

"So the altered nanos took the place of the originals and broke the control?" Westerman offered.

"Exactly, this could open up many possibilities, Zalar has been a pretty high profile operative for the Wardens, she could have knowledge of their operations and infrastructure that may well be invaluable to us." Wendle was visibly excited by the options that could now be available to the Uniques; however his mood darkened. "What's the problem?" said Westerman.

"I'm afraid that I have to broach a very delicate subject with you," said the obviously uncomfortable man.

"What is it?"

"A great deal of our number are unhappy with you carrying that weapon in public." Wendle gestured to the pistol hung in its holster around Westerman's waist; totally as a reflex action his hand moved to feel the reassurance of the guns metallic gip, Wendle recoiled slightly from this action.

"Sorry, reflex action." offered Westerman, consciously removing his hand and placing it on the tabletop, the Uniques mien eased visibly.

"You can see our point of view, we are totally unarmed." "No weapons at all? I'm sorry. I can't believe that!"

"Oh, we do have some heavy, planetary defences, but we do not carry any personal armoury." Wendle said in a matter of fact way.

"I'm sorry. I have a problem accepting that you are living in what seems like a hostile universe with no form of personal protection."

"Your views and perceptions are based upon your own world and the limited experience you undergone since your 'Unique' rebirth." Wendle stopped and thought. "Come. I think that you could find this very interesting." And with that the Unique abruptly stood up and gestured Westerman to follow him.

After a short walk along the street they turned and walked down a narrow alleyway, which in turn, opened into a small square, not too dissimilar to the one that Westerman had arrived in only the day before.

Looking around at his new surrounding, he was immediately struck by the fact that the particular plaza was totally enclosed by solid bare walls; no doors or windows broke the bland beige expanses. Wendle made a grand sweeping gesture.

"This is one of our training areas, it is in such squares that our new recruits learn how to utilise their talents." The walls were completely blank with the exception of the alleyway through which they had entered; the surface of the fifty metres square was not rough and cobbled but covered with a dark grey bitumen-like material. Tentatively, Westerman shuffled his foot and noted the exceptional level of grip the coating seemed to offer. Along the opposite wall to the entrance stood a line of pedestals, which tapered upward to a narrow tip, atop these were perched, precariously, a small ball of about twenty centimetres in diameter. Wendle turned to Westerman.

"I have brought you here to demonstrate why we Uniques have no need for crude mechanical weaponry," he said pointing to the pistol hung at Westerman's side. "Okay, I'm all ears," said the sceptical Englishman. Wendle turned and pointed to one of the balls.

"These objects are purely for target practice. Please use your gun and destroy one of them." With a shrug Westerman drew his pistol, aimed at the nearest ball and fired. The target exploded into several thousand pieces.

"Impressive!" said Wendle. "This is a new weapon to the Wardens, much more powerful than the standard thermal disruptors." Westerman holstered the gun and nodded, a new ball suddenly materialised atop the empty pedestal.

"Would you care to try again?" invited Wendle with a wry grin.

As Westerman drew his pistol one of the balls suddenly leapt into the air and then swooped towards him, he was too slow; it struck him in his stomach sending him tumbling onto the floor. Winded, he looked up to see the offending object flying towards him again; with a supreme effort he hurled himself to one side. The ball shot passed him, he brought his gun up and fired; the bolt narrowly missed its target and exploded against the courtyard wall. The object of his torment veered sharply into the air, performed a complex series of manoeuvres, and then abruptly dived towards Westerman; diving forwards the ball passed over him by a margin of a few centimetres, rolling onto his back, he aimed and fired. The bolt struck its target a glancing blow sending it spiralling into the sky, it had however slowed the object down; Westerman fired again and was rewarded with the aggressor exploding into small particles.

Breathing heavily from his exertions and the blow he had received, Westerman raised himself to his feet.

"You did well Steve. Well done!" said Wendle approaching him clapping.

"Okay. So what's the point of this?" breathed Westerman.

"Please go and stand over in that corner please. It is a protected area; the training targets will not bother you there," said Wendle walking to the centre of the square; doing as he was bid, settling into the corner and holstering his weapon, Westerman turned his attention to Wendle.

Nothing seemed to happen for long seconds and then at some unheard command, possibly telepathic, one of the balls shot across the square towards the Unique; at a distance of about a metre from its target the speeding object burst into cloud of dust, the only noise that Westerman heard was a brief, small, high pitched buzz. "What the?" he exclaimed.

Two further balls leapt from their positions towards Wendle, both exploded into nebulae of powder. A further three targets became airborne; one flew directly at the Unique, its companions veered away to more circuitous routes. The first target exploded and Wendle turned to face the second, which was approaching from his right, it too exploded into a haze of falling dust particles; the final aggressor of the ill fated trio was approaching rapidly from his rear, spinning around to face it, his eyes seemed to flash and the remaining ball joined its fellows in a cloud of powder.

Westerman stood transfixed by the spectacle he had just witnessed; Wendle walked towards him.

"How did you? What the?" he blustered. The Unique smiled and said.

"You have no idea how much power your body now carries, you no longer need to depend upon these primitive machines." Once again he gestured to Westerman's gun.

"How do you do that?" he asked, impressed and dumbfounded.

"We will show you; it only takes practice and obviously direction.

"When do we start?"

"As soon as you like, but I hope that you now understand why our people look upon your equipment with some apprehension." Westerman nodded slowly and undid the belt holding the weapon and lowered it to the ground.

"Okay I'll go along with that," he said.

"Please Steve, we know how this must make you feel very vulnerable, but it is an important gesture of trust towards us on your part."

"Come on then show me how to do this!" he replied eagerly walking to the centre of the square, smiling Wendle moved to join him.

"It is all about visualisation and will power. Choose one of the target balls." Nodding, Westerman took a step forward and pointed towards the central pedestal.

"Now look at the ball, concentrate on it! Imagine that the very structure of the object is visible to you; imagine the bonds between the very atoms laid bare before you." Westerman tried to conjure an image up in his mind of the connections, the invisible attraction between each atom to form the complex molecules. He suddenly became aware of a growing warm feeling throughout his body.

"Good, Good! I can feel the energy in your body; apply that energy in one moment, a moment of total disassociation!" pressed Wendle.

Westerman could feel the fire rising within him, at first he had felt that he was commencing a 'jump' but the sensation had modified into a more centralised burning, this burning now concentrated itself around the area of his eyes. A stab of white-hot pain shot through his temples, he heard a sound, not the faint buzz he had perceived before, this time it sounded like the scream of a thousand car tyres. An explosion followed, a loud deafening blast; the concussion threw the two men on to their backs on the floor.

Westerman was the first to regain some semblance of composure, as he struggled to his feet, he looked at the target ball; nothing remained of the object, also nothing remained of the pedestal and the nearest four of its companions, evidence of a massive blast showed its effects on the wall behind as deep cracks and scorched marks.

He turned to Wendle who had propped himself up on one arm and was surveying the devastation.

"I think that I need a bit more training and practice!" Wendle smiled thinly through the thick cloud of dust particles hanging in the atmosphere.

"You think?" he joked.

In the nearby underground observation area, Landon and Bolas, having just witnessed via hidden surveillance devices, the destruction caused by Westerman's effort, sat looking in silence, intently looking at the displays. Eventually Landon turned to Bolas.

"Look at the power levels generated by his blast. It's incredible!"

"Yes, it's really quite frightening. He will prove to be a very powerful ally to us," said Bolas in an admiring tone; Landon frowned at his read-outs.

"What if he does not want to be our ally?" Bolas looked sharply at Landon.

"How do you mean? Of course he will want to join us. He's Unique!"

"But what if he ever finds the truth behind his past?" Bolas breathed a heavy sigh and ran his fingers through his hair.

"That would be very unfortunate indeed." Landon nodded and the pair returned to their observations.

CHAPTER TWELVE

The Calaxian mother ship decelerated from supra-light speed as it neared the outer reaches of its target star system. The hyperspacial bubble surrounding the vessel dissipated and the massive, kilometres long, scarred and pockmarked cylinder winked into normal space with a silent concussion of light caused by the clash of titanic energies resulting form the intersection of the tear between two physically different universes.

The Calaxian commander hissed his displeasure at the momentary disjointed feeling and the nausea that it brought, he turned to see two of the younger members of the control room crew vomiting violently.

"Control yourselves!" he barked, whilst secretly harbouring a feeling of understanding nearly akin to sympathy. He turned his attention to the large display screen positioned on the forward facing bulkhead.

The star system ahead had been laid out graphically, indicating the relative distances and masses of the thirteen major astronomical bodies; as was the case with so many solar systems in the creature's experience, the outer planets were merely large collections of gaseous material surrounding unremarkable metallic cores. Whilst some of the components of the gigantic atmospheres could supply huge quantities of raw materials for various systems and processes, it was the inner worlds situated in the so called temperate belt that could furnish the organic materials required to feed the millions of Calaxians aboard the ship; that was their goal.

The commander studied the display, his experienced reptilian eyes weighing the pros and cons of a high-energy direct flight against using the gravity wells of the gas giants to slow the prodigious velocity still carried by the immense vessel. Ironically it was the presence of these very enormous planets and their vast gravity fields that stopped the Calaxian star ship from travelling nearer to the centre of the system with its star drive. The stable formation of the hyperspace bubble required for reaching faster than light velocities needed a very low ambient gravity presence.

One of the technicians, probably equivalent in ranking to a science officer, turned to face the commander and issued a stream of grunts, snarls and whistles.

"Sir, our preliminary scans show that the third and fourth planets are showing signs of inhabitation.

"Level?" snapped back the commander

"Level four sir, industrial, agrarian society class one!" Class one! Internally the leader groaned, class one! The smooth skinned bipedal race that seemed to be spread so widely across this galaxy, the same category of creature that had, on frequent occasions, caused so all sorts of problems, usually resulting in the loss of life and in some cases territory.

His attention returned to the display. Operating a control on a nearby panel, the orientation of the planets changed to show the 'overhead' view of the solar system, the orbits of the worlds graphically represented. "Course sir?" hissed the young helmsman

"Quiet!" he snarled, the ferocity of his reply bringing the room to a hush; he would have discipline on his command deck, turning to the station on his right he asked,

"What is our reserve status?" His question was directed towards a middle-aged female operative. It was an open secret amongst the bridge staff that the ageing commander held designs on her and it was obvious by the way she was using various cosmetics to display her mating scales to their alluring best that she would be receptive to his advances.

"Power is at sixty percent, water and food at fifty percent and current population levels are at ten cycles below saturation," She answered with the Calaxian equivalent of a sensual purr.

He opened his mouth to display his still impressive teeth to the female, she produced a suitably submissive gesture, and he could feel the lust stirring within his reproductive sack. Although he was advancing in years and this would probably be his last system assault he was still sure he would be able to show all these young pretenders a thing or two. He produced a guttural snarl of such viciousness that all the male Calaxians within the chamber jumped and cowered; the couple of female operatives present demurely pumped extra blood to their mating scales to indicate their total acceptance of the commanders claim over them.

With satisfaction, once again the display occupied his attention; presently he barked out the command,

"Low energy approach!" The control room became a blur of activity as the course corrections were computed, the odd operative or two shot a glance at their leader sat in his throne like chair at the centre of the bridge. He pretended to ignore their looks, he knew the meaning of them; the younger faction would prefer to blaze into orbit around one of the inhabited worlds and pound it into submission, he, on the other hand would creep up on the target worlds, making his command last as long as possible. It would take nearly two cycles to arrive at the first planet; during that time he would take full advantage of his position within the Calaxian hierarchy. He turned to look at the female on his right, she returned his leer with a suitable look of her own; he would definitely make the most of his command.

He stood up, made sure his enlarged reproductive sack was not too obvious, and with a last glance towards the object of his current desire he exited the control room for his personal quarters. Minutes later, after a respectful length of time had passed, the female excused herself and left the bridge to join her commander, she was followed out of the room by the lecherous leers of the young males.

CHAPTER THIRTEEN

Zalar had been on Bailon for almost two weeks, she was still in residence at the hotel, she had no idea at the time but the haul from her earlier robbery had been one of greater value than she had expected, with the effect of leaving her financially comfortable for at least a couple of months.

After some early social gaffs, she had started to fit into the Pizoka way of life. With some thought and a little bit of local knowledge, she had fabricated the plausible cover of being a wealthy landowner from the Southern continents taking the world tour to escape the painful memories of a particularly sordid affair. Once she had been in the hotel bar, talked to the barmaid and let a number of 'facts' slip in conversation; within a couple of days the story had spread, more or less, entirely throughout the town. She had assumed the name 'Tink-Bell', the origins of this being rooted in a childhood fable she had recalled.

At first boredom had been a serious factor in Zalar's day, however once the story of the wealthy young woman with a romantic past had been propagated, the steady stream of invitations to day and night social functions started.

Some of these invitations came from the local young men, which she summarily declined, citing the reason as being that she did not feel ready to become involved with anybody so soon after her last romantic encounter. This of course was not a lie; the open wound left through her heart and soul by the loss of Steve Westerman was still raw and edged with fire; she found herself missing him more and more, in the darkest moments, usually late at night when alone, the emotional floodgates opened and she was left a sobbing wreck, having to make real efforts to compose herself the following morning to face the everyday banality of Pizoka.

It was one of those particularly angst ridden occasions that Zalar drew back the curtains of her room, looked out at the busy main street and resolved to spend her time on this world in a more constructive manner. After all, this was her home world; she resolved to set about tracing her origin, her roots. For some strange reason she had always assumed that she was an orphan, rescued and brought up by the Wardens, but since the eradication of the control nanos a creeping doubt had brought the memories and facts surrounding her childhood into question.

Having dressed in a flattering pair of tight denims and a close fitting polo neck sweater she regarded herself in the full-length mirror, which hung on the wall of her room. She was aiming for an attractive and yet approachable look, the sweater was certainly showing off her assets perfectly; she wanted information and she was sure that approaching any man looking like this would surely not hinder her getting it.

After breakfast she approached the receptionist and enquired if the town had a central registration facility for births, deaths and marriages. Sure enough he was directed to a large white, stone built building at the end of the main street.

The sun was still quite warm in the Bailon autumn and the walk along the street was very pleasant; a large wheeled vehicle pulled up just ahead of her, the electromagnetic motor whined to a stop, a door at the front opened and a number of people disembarked. One of these, a young blond-haired woman saw Zalar and called out.

"Tink-Bell, Tink-Bell, It's me Diona!" Zalar recognised her and waved back, the woman came over to her.

"Hello Diona. How are you this morning?"

"Good! Good! We all missed you at the Zoozak bar last night."

"I'm sorry. I wasn't very good company last night; the old demons were out to play I'm afraid."

"Tink-Bell. You and your mystery man! You really should think about moving on," said Diona as she laid a comforting hand on Zalar's arm.

"I know, I Know. In fact I'm starting a new project to take my mind of things."

"What's all this about then?"

"I think that I have some relatives living in this area, so my parents once told me, I've decided to try and track them down," said Zalar, Diona frowned and vigorously shook her head.

"That doesn't sound like a plan likely to get you back on the 'man' trail to me," admonished the bubbly young woman.

"Sorry, but I'm still not ready for the dating game yet," answered Zalar truthfully.

"What a man he must have been," said Diona, raising her eyebrows skyward.

Zalar could feel her eyes beginning to water as the memory of her lost love surfaced again.

"He is!" she said, and with that she nodded to her acquaintance who smiled knowledgeably in return. They then separated and resumed their journeys to their respective destinations.

The records building proved to be coldly antiseptic in its décor, the reception lobby held a single desk, which was staffed by a very bored looking middle aged man, Zalar approached him and adopting an unashamedly attractive smile she said.

"I wonder if you can help me?"

The receptionist had noticed her approach and had made an unsuccessful attempt to tidy up the appearance of his badly fitting official uniform.

"Certainly, do you require any specific service?" he asked in a courteous and efficient manner.

"Yes, I'm wanting to try and trace some relatives and I was wondering if I could have a look at the register of births?" Zalar asked, maximising her most appealing smile.

"Do you have an appointment to use the terminals?" he replied.

This was a development that she had not anticipated, the whole culture of Pizoka was so laid back and relaxed that the concept of having to book something seemed a totally alien one.

"No. I'm afraid that I haven't," she replied.

"You should have an appointment, I'm sorry."

"Is there any way that you could fit me in please? I would really be so very grateful," she purred, noticing the way that the receptionist's gaze was repeatedly moving furtively to her chest.

"I'm only in town for today and I was really hoping to find out about my family," she continued, consciously standing upright to present her objects of fascination towards the man. At length he tore his gaze away from her tight polo neck and began to study an ancient looking appointments book on his desk.

"Well today is your lucky day," he said looking furtively from left to right.

"Cubicle four, through the door on the left is free for the next half hour." He nodded towards a glass door.

"Thank you very much…?" she said with an enquiring look.

"Mizoki," he offered enthusiastically.

"Mizoki? Thank you very much Mizoki," she beamed and started towards the door.

"What's your name?" he called after her and then quickly added, "I need to enter in the book the names of whoever uses the archives."

"Tink-Bell," she stopped and answered. The receptionist had suddenly gained confidence as he had watched the hypnotic sway of the young woman's hips receding from his desk; he plucked up all of his courage and asked. "Do you ever go in the Zoozak bar by any chance?"

Zalar started to walk towards the door again and smiling to herself she shouted over her shoulder.

"Sometimes, I'll see you in there perhaps?" The glass door closed behind her leaving Mizoki unconsciously adjusting the collar of his uniform, grinning inanely.

The cubicles were clearly marked with their identifying number and having located 'four' she entered the small room. Inside was a single desk and chair; a computer terminal was sited on the table, Zalar sat down and located the activation key; the display unit illuminated, presenting a menu of the options available.

Choosing births, a number of fields appeared on the screen; name, date of birth and place of birth. Looking furtively over her shoulder, she used the keyboard and entered 'Zalar' into the name field.

The search engine performed its crosschecking and referencing, eventually presenting one hundred and twenty three possible matches to the criteria. After a short pause for thought she typed 'Pizoka' into the place field and pressed the search key. After a few seconds, which seemed like a lifetime, the display changed and presented the result of the enquiry.

Four possible matches had been returned; Zalar looked closely at the information. Immediately she discounted the first two, they both had dates of death entries and their ages were well over a hundred years when they died.

She summarily dismissed the third entry as this also had a date of death, the final match looked more promising; eagerly she activated the detail option. Her heart dropped like a stone as she scanned through the information, a quick calculation revealed that this particular Zalar was still living in Pizoka and eighty years old.

She was crestfallen, about to leave, she returned the screen back to the search results display; it was at this point that the third person on the list suddenly captured her attention. It was the age of the person when she died, two years old; Zalar quickly activated the detail of the entry.

The date of death on this record led her to calculate that, if this person had still been alive, she would be thirty one years old, could this be her? Reading the detail, the parent's names were revealed as Boochka and Damena, could this be her father and mother? Further crosschecking showed that these people were still alive and living at an address in the Pizoka area.

Zalar realised that she was holding her breath, with a conscious effort she restored some calm to her raging emotions; was this her father and mother? If it was her own record she was viewing was she registered as dead? Whilst processing these questions she pressed the print function and a hard copy of the details emerged from a slot in the side of the terminal.

A scenario began to form within her mind; twenty-nine years ago did the Wardens abduct her? Perhaps this had been an initiative for some form of long-term recruitment, take children from some backwater planet and bring them up with the Warden doctrines, not to mention continued exposure to the effects of the control nanos. The more that she pursued this line of thinking, the more that it made sense to her; the jump terminus coordinates for this world were sited just outside Pizoka, this fact cut down the chances of coincidence dramatically; and of course after a prolonged period it is logical that she would have been declared dead. She shivered involuntarily, if this was all true, what had her parents been through in all the intervening years? How these poor people must have suffered; the rage directed against the Wardens began to well up inside her.

Restoring her self composure, she stood up and carefully took the sheet of paper, folded it and put it safely into the back pocket of her denims, turning off the data terminal she took a few seconds more to ensure the totally composure of herself and exited the cubicle.

In the reception area, Mizoki was in animated conversation with another uniformed individual; when Zalar entered the room he stopped talking abruptly leading her to think that she must be the topic under discussion.

Feeling more than a little flattered by this attention she exaggerated the swing of her hips.

"Did you find everything you wanted okay Tink-Bell?" enthused Mizoki.

"Yes thank you. Are you still on for that drink in Zoozak's?" she teased.

"Sure. Anytime," he replied, whilst giving a quick, proud glance to his colleague.

As she walked towards the exit she could easily visualise the two men nudging each other behind her just like a pair of schoolboys. She was just about to close the door when she caught the conversation that they had started.

"Oh. I forgot to tell you Mizoki. I was talking to Piron the other day and he babbling about seeing a ghost or something."

"That drunkard, what's he been saying now?"

"Apparently he was just outside town, staggering home after a nights partying I imagine, when he saw six men, all wearing robes, appear in the middle of the road in a flash of light!"

"No shit! What a complete loser that man is. You didn't believe him did you?"

"What do you take me for? Of course I didn't."

Zalar stopped dead in her tracks; a long cold shiver ran through her body.

Steve Westerman stood facing the pedestals, the balls atop four of them leapt towards him, almost simultaneously each one burst into a cloud of dust. Several more of the spherical objects materialised and shot from their resting places in ever more intricate trajectories and speeds, one by one they disintegrated. Another pair of the aggressive objects hurtled towards him from opposite directions, only a week ago they would have resulted in him waking up on the floor with a headache, not now however. He turned towards the nearest target, a barely audible high-pitched buzz, and a small flash from his eyes; it was gone. Holding out open palm in the direction of the second sphere, he stopped it dead in flight.

The internal drive mechanism of the device struggled to release itself from the invisible grip causing it to vibrate vigorously; Westerman destroyed another two balls and held a further one in mid-air by simple extending his other arm. The training cycle was now complete, no further spheres appeared on the pedestals, only the two captive mechanisms remained; smiling to himself he brought his hands together with a clap, the objects smashed into each other, exploding into a single mass of smoke, flame and debris.

"Bravo Steve! Bravo!" yelled Wendle as he emerged applauding from the 'safe' area.

"Very impressive!" said Bolas as he appeared from the alleyway. Still smiling, Westerman turned to Bolas and gave a small mock bow.

"I can really feel the objects in my mind. It's almost like second nature to me now," he said walking across the square to meet the two Uniques.

"Your powers are really coming under your control now, no longer being focused into single all powerful bursts of energy," commented Wendle.

"There's one particular area that we seem to be avoiding in my training," Westerman suddenly stated with a piercing look towards the two men.

"What's that Steve?" Bolas asked not particularly convincingly.

"You know very well what it is. I have repeatedly asked about being able to do some 'jump' training, every time my requests are fended off, politely I'll grant you, but still fended off." He stated, folding his arms across his chest in an openly unfriendly display of body language.

"We have to be sure that you can control the telekinetic energy within you before exploring how to channel it into an interstellar crossing," Wendle replied in what seemed like a slightly condescending manner.

"That's bullshit and you know it!" snapped Westerman. The Uniques began to look increasingly uncomfortable. "I know that there is a dampening field of some kind operating on me. Don't you think that I have tried to jump and nothing has happened?" He continued his verbal onslaught, the visible discomfort of the two men increased; they looked at each other.

"And that is another thing! I've been here God knows how long and there has not been a single telepathic thought I have picked up on. Does the jump inhibitor affect that part of my talents as well?" Westerman's barely contained anger threatened to erupt as his actions became more and more aggressive.

The Uniques looked back towards each other and eventually, with a shrug of his shoulders, Wendle turned to face Westerman.

"You are correct. We are stopping your teleportation abilities and it does effect other parts of your brain and so your gifts."

"Why?" growled Westerman

"We needed time to study the data we have been collecting on you," said Bolas glancing at Wendle for encouragement, "When we first became aware of you it was because the power that was being produced by your flight was of a magnitude unlike anything we have ever seen before. It was completely off the scale of anything we have experienced."

Westerman could sense that he was being told the truth; this was backed up by something Zalar had said about how different it was when they travelled together.

"Okay so I'll concede to being able to understand your curiosity about all this, but why have you waited until now to come clean about it?" he pressed even though he had calmed down a level or two.

"We felt that it was simple self-preservation. We did not know what you were or if you were a threat to us." Wendle said with a genuine twinge of regret in his voice, he continued. "We are not a race of people with a great population, when we breed we are not sure of our offspring being Unique. As you have seen the Wardens hunt us for our very essence to power their machines, our home world is in a very remote corner of the Galaxy and shielded against detection.

So you can appreciate our naturally defensive nature, we simply did not know what you were."

Westerman regarded the men before him, he actually believed that this was the truth; it did not however dissipate the feeling of being nothing better than a laboratory rat.

"Okay, so you are scared of something that you don't understand, but it does not alter the fact I am effectively a prisoner here."

"We apologise if you feel that way but security must be maintained for our people," offered Bolas. Westerman noticed that Landon had emerged from the alleyway and was crossing the square to join them.

"Come to join the party?" he asked sarcastically.

"Steve, please calm down. We have never meant you any harm, we merely wanted to study you, understand you. We wanted to know if we could trust you," said the new edition to the discussion.

"Don't talk to me about trust! You have separated me from my companion, incidentally the only person who has shown me any honesty since I left Earth, and you have imprisoned me on this world!" The anger began to steadily boil up inside of him.

"Please put yourself in our shoes for a moment. We did not know if you were a new Warden trick, or another threat from one of the many hostile factions in this Galaxy.

You have no idea what an unfriendly place this universe is; out there are literally hundreds of humanoid and non-humanoid races that prize our quantum DNA as highly as the Wardens. Ancient technology is spread throughout every star system and many of the indigenous people have understood the rudiments of its operation, they need our very lifeblood to run it. You could have been an agent for one of those factions!" Wendle stated animatedly, pointing expansively to the sky.

"Just one very major problem," replied Westerman after a few seconds thought, "how on Earth do I convince you that my intentions are not a threat to you?"

The three Uniques looked at each other and eventually turned back towards him.

"Time," stated Bolas, and with a small nod of his head, turned together with his companions and walked towards the alleyway.

Westerman had resolved to explore the small town that he had now become an unwilling resident of, and over the next three days he walked the narrow streets acquainting himself with the layout. The training had stopped following the confrontation, appearing to be left to his own devices, it was the on the third day that he made a truly startling discovery.

He had been walking along one of the larger roads of the town for about two hours and was a good eight kilometres from the small lodging house he had come to know as his home when the buildings abruptly ceased. The road continued ahead as straight as an arrow to the horizon, a tapering line of grey cobbles disappearing into the distance. The landscape had changed dramatically, small trees had petered out and the ground turned from rich earth into sand; he walked about one hundred metres further along the road and he was effectively stood in a desert.

Turning back towards the town he looked left and then right, all that he could see in either direction was the low Mediterranean style buildings; he resolved to walk slightly further along the road in order to get a better perspective on the size of the town, turning he had barely covered five paces when, smack!

An invisible force seemed to have struck him squarely across his face and chest, he had been propelled back by the impact a good three metres and had been dumped unceremoniously on his backside in the middle of the dusty road.

"Bastard!" he breathed as he dabbed at the trickle of blood that was now running down his top lip from his nose. Using the lap of his shirt he gently mopped his stinging nose; shortly the bleeding stopped and he climbed to his feet.

"What the hell did that?" he said quietly to himself and once again began advancing down the road, this time very slowly and with his arms extended in front of him. Three metres later he became aware of a tingling sensation in his fingertips and a definite resistance; one step further and it felt as if a giant mallet had struck his hands.

"Shit!" he yelped as he backed away, shaking his aching limbs.

The life returned to his digits and he stood and contemplated what could be blocking his way; he recognised that this must be some form of force field; naturally he then began to wonder at what was actually on the other side of the invisible barrier. What did the Uniques not want to be seen?

Looking about him to see if he could ascertain if anybody was watching his efforts, and then feeling foolish as he was probably under constant observation, smiling to himself he took a couple of steps back and then said to himself.

"Let's see how strong you are."

He reached out in the direction of the barrier with both hands, he concentrated using his telekinesis to probe the wall of energy. He could feel the force field deflecting his probes, he pushed harder, and the resistance grew and grew.

Mentally he focused the force he was applying against the obstruction into a conical configuration, the point of which he tried to burrow into the barrier; a small red dot appeared, floating in mid-air, a couple of metres from Westerman's out stretched hands. Closing his eyes he concentrated his strength into the 'wedge' he was driving into the force wall, modifying it's shape so that the tip was becoming thinner, sharper.

The solitary red spot was now the centre of an aerial display as narrow flashes of violet lightning radiated in all directions, the spot was now growing and changing from a flat disk to a cone shaped indentation; the colour also altered, moving from red through the spectrum to a bright orange, Westerman could feel the heat from the friction of the contact between the massive energies against the palms of his hands.

The lightning flashes grew in intensity and an entire twenty-metre diameter section of the barrier started to flash with iridescent colours. The point of conflict between the force field and Westerman's telekinesis had now grown to over half of a metre across and was a metre deep, its colour had moved to a brilliant blue-white, bordering on the ultra-violet.

Suddenly the larger section of the barrier stopped flashing and became transparent; Westerman recoiled from the vision as if he had been electrocuted.

A band of energy enclosed the now clear section of the invisible wall; this band had the appearance of the screen of a television set that had not been tuned in correctly. Away from the area that he had been trying to breach there was no change, giving the impression that a twenty-metre wide black hole had materialised in the scenery and at its heart a white disk, which was rapidly cooling and shrinking.

The lightning display had now stopped, allowing Westerman to move forward a couple of paces and stare out through the 'window' he had created. His senses reeled, gone was the desert; this was replaced by a night-time vista across a jagged rocky plain. The very same plain ended in the near distance against a sky filled with stars and gaseous clouds.

He gasped at the awesome spectacle ahead of him, an object slowly appeared above the foreshortened horizon, a small moon rose majestically into the starscape, and off into the distance the angry disk of a red sun moved across the heavens.

So entranced by this celestial display was Steve Westerman that he failed to register a brilliant flash of light behind him as Wendle and Landon materialised together with four other Uniques.

"Step away from the barrier Mister Westerman," said Wendle sternly. Behind Westerman as he turned to face him the area affected by his efforts had cooled to dull red and shrank to a coin sized spot, the transparent area had also began to contract, and with a noiseless explosion of light, disappeared leaving the desert horizon stretching into the false distance.

"This town is all there is, isn't it?" said Westerman

Landon slowly nodded.

"This is one gigantic artificial habitat on some god-forsaken asteroid isn't it?"

"We prefer to call it home," replied Wendle ironically. "Home, you've become such a paranoid society that you have shut yourself away in the back of beyond," he started to laugh, "what a farce! You are all prisoners here as much as I, you're imprisoned by your own fears, insecurities and phobias."

"We can leave when we want to, you are going absolutely nowhere!" snarled Landon.

Westerman looked at the six Uniques, they all gave the appearance of being tense, ready for action, he thought quickly. Should he fight them? Could he beat them? A sobering thought struck him, if he got into a fight with these people and won, what then? He could not escape from this place, he needed to locate the device that was stopping him from teleporting; he looked at his would be opponents and shrugged his shoulders, and walked towards them.

"Where are you going?" asked Landon, Smiling he pushed through, glancing over his shoulder as he walked away he said,

"Back to the Taverna, I'm starving." With that he continued back into the town gently whistling to himself. "What are we going to do about him?" said Landon

"I don't know. I don't think that he will ever trust us, also I doubt that he will ever join us," Bolas replied.

"Did you see the power at his command?" breathed Landon, gesturing over his right shoulder towards the invisible barrier behind them. Wendle thought for a while and then looked up into the azure blue sky.

"We may have to think about his destruction, we couldn't let that sort of power get into our enemies' hands." Landon nodded slowly and with that the six men disappeared in a flash of light.

Zalar walked down the street away from the records building, mentally composing herself. She was more than convinced that she had just heard an eye witness report of a team of Wardens arriving on Bailon, it was not a very large leap of imagination to realise the motive for their journey to this world.

She knew the standard procedure for planet fall, she had done it may times before; land and blend into the local population as much as possible, obtain intelligence about the area and then carry out the mission. They had come to find her and Steve; there could be no other possible explanation. The big problem was they could be anywhere in Pizoka; a man across the street looked at her, she froze in her tracks, was he a Warden? Should she run or grab the thermal disruptor from the clutch bag she was carrying and burn him in two?

The man smiled at her, she became more nervous, her hand reached inside her bag, the cold metal of the weapon reassuring to the touch.

A bundle of pure energy burst from a nearby door-way and resolved itself into a small child racing along the pavement; the man turned towards the little girl and grinned.

"Daddy!" yelled the youngster as she threw herself into his welcoming arms.

Zalar's eyes misted over as she released her grip from the disruptor, the man smiled at her once again, this time she returned the pleasure and set off back along the street to the hotel.

"You are going to have to get a grip of yourself girl," she said under her breath to herself.

The Calaxian multi-generational star ship had swung lazily through the gravity wells of the two giant gas plan-ets, the sheer strength of their attraction scrubbing off thousands of kilometres per hour from the vessels ve-locity. The leisurely fall towards the inner worlds of the system was now assured; only exertion of external, non-gravitational forces could stop the massive vehicle from swinging into the orbit of the fourth planet from the sun of this system in exactly nine days hence.

The Calaxian commander strode purposefully along the access corridor to the bridge, his heavily clawed feet clicking rhythmically on the metal deck. Ahead the two heavily armoured guards had seen his approach and snapped to attention. The commander allowed his mind to wander back to the days when guards were not needed on the star ships, the days before trans-galactic flight.

He was now nearing the end of his long life, he had seen the equivalent of five hundred Earth years pass by and despite his advanced age his memory was as sharp as ever. His birthplace had been this very vessel as it traversed the hyperspace of the intergalactic void; he had grown up looking at the gigantic viewing plates that showed the relative position of the enormous craft on its journey.

He had been at the very first landing on a world belonging to this galaxy; he clearly recalled his first meeting with one of the bipedal, warm blooded creatures that infested this region of space; he could also remember the screams as he fired his weapon and cut the animal in two. Soon he would start to lose his faculties and then a younger, ambitious Calaxian would challenge him for his coveted position; he would undoubtedly be killed, the circle of life completed.

The guards maintained their steadfast gaze as he walked past them. Guards on the bridge door! He recalled the mutiny of many years ago when a group of radical thinking Calaxian's had tried to take control of the vessel and return it to the mother galaxy. Many died that day and in consequence the ruling council had decreed that armed guards must always be present at the access points to critical areas.

One of the security detail moved slightly, his snout like mouth twitching and opening into a barely perceptible yawn; the commander brought his heavy, gloved fist around with lightning speed, striking the offending guard hard against the side of his face, the force of the blow sent the creature crashing into the corridor wall. Standing over him the elderly Calaxian issued a series of angry snarls.

"Don't you dare yawn in my presence, if I catch you falling asleep again on bridge watch you will either be dead or working in the defecation tanks. Do you understand?"

The target of his physical and verbal onslaught nodded subserviently and carefully avoided the piercing reptilian eyes of his superior. The commander suddenly swung around and gave the other guard a similar blow.

"The same goes for you too!" he spat at his second victim. Leaving the unfortunate subordinates he activated the code pad on the bridge door, entering as soon as the hatch had opened.

Upon his entry one of the crew hissed loudly and all his colleagues snapped to attention.

"Resume station!" he hissed as he approached his centrally placed chair, the bridge crew returned to their duties and carefully averted their gaze from the commander; in Calaxian etiquette, staring at a superior officer could and was interpreted as a direct challenge. The female who had been pleasuring him for the last few cycles did risk a momentary glance, he opened his mouth slightly to show his razor sharp teeth, a Calaxian show of domination; she bowed slightly and returned to her business.

"Any further intelligence on the target world?" he barked. "Post industrial society; nuclear fusion power generation with some light manufacturing, but mainly an agrarian basis for economy," answered a young male operating the science station.

"There is nothing unusual about them?"

"No Commander. They have no sophisticated warning devices and do not appear to have any planetary defences."

"Good, a nice easy one for a change," gloated the commander. The young science officer moved uncomfortably and said.

"Sir, we have picked up a couple of traces of an unusual energy signature."

"What type of energy?"

"Quantum Sir!"

Inwardly the elder Calaxian groaned, Quantum energy could only mean one thing, the Wardens.

"Maintain scans on the fourth planet, continuous scans! I want to know if there are any further 'unusual' traces." He snarled at the youngster who had looked back to his instruments and readied himself for the chastising blow that was bound to come his way.

It never came; the Commander stood up and walked towards the door, doing the Calaxian equivalent of muttering under his breath,

"Wardens. Fucking Wardens."

Westerman reclined on the bed in the room he had now come to call his own, it was early morning just before sunrise but the light had already risen to a level where he could make out the cracks in the plaster of the ceiling above.

His thoughts were full of Zalar this morning, and with these thoughts had returned the sick, empty feeling of loneliness. He was convinced that he needed to get to her and soon; a strange dread had clutched at his very soul that she either needed or would need his help. In the two days since the incident at the edge of the town, the Uniques no longer came to show him how to use his powers; he was left pretty much to his own devices. However, he suspected that they had got him under constant surveillance and all doors to potentially sensitive areas were proving very much out of bounds. Desperation had started to take hold in his search for the device that was inhibiting his jump capabilities. It was literally like looking for a needle in a haystack; it could be any shape or size, it could be anywhere, he had no idea where to start looking. Resolving to get up, as he was obviously not going to get back to sleep, he dressed, used the nearby bathroom, and then exited into the outside street.

The sky was adopting the familiar blue colour and the light level had nearly increased to full as the dawn broke. Of course he realised that the actual passage of the sun across the sky was a complete illusion, a holographic projection onto the energy barrier that enclosed this habitat; nevertheless, the rising sun still felt good against his skin.

Suddenly he became aware that there seemed to be a great number of people about for this hour of the day, he then noticed they all seemed to be heading in the same direction. Despite being able to 'jump' around the town easily the Uniques still walked over small to medium distances; he surmised that the energy expended would be too excessive for such distances, he could still remember how bad he felt doing too many teleportation's.

The density of people increased towards the other end of the street, Westerman decided to take a look at whatever was causing so much interest and set off in that direction. Presently he found himself in the middle of a throng heading for a small alleyway, he was swept along with the tide of people into the opening; the passage led, unsurprisingly, to a square. He realised that this was the same area he had materialised in on his arrival to this place.

The crowd had spread out around the edges of the plaza, leaving the central section clear, apart from the strange looking obelisk standing in the very middle. Everybody appeared to be looking towards the centre in anticipation, even though a deathly quiet hush had settled throughout the square, Westerman sensed that the telepathic chatter amongst these people would be deafening; looking at their faces every single person seemed to be genuinely excited.

An old man to his left abruptly pointed towards the obelisk, Westerman allowed his gaze to follow the man's direction; he could see nothing. Wait! Something was happening.

The obelisk was approximately two and a half metres tall and fashioned from a silver-bronze metal. It gave the appearance of two roughly pyramidal shapes placed on top of each other; the very apex of the uppermost point had now begun to glow.

At first Westerman had thought that it was a trick of the sunlight, but the glow was growing in intensity and now an audible whine could be distinguished. The excitement of the crowd was increasing with every passing second, proportional to the intensifying glow and the steadily rising pitch of the noise.

The tip of the obelisk was now incandescent and the sound threatened to deafen all the assembled mass in the square; suddenly the glow exploded into a blinding flash of pure white light, Westerman shielded his eyes as a purely reflex reaction. Slowly he lowered his hands and looked back across the square; the light had gone; the noise vanished. Beside the obelisk stood a blond-haired young woman, she looked about in abject terror. He noticed Wendle, Landon and Bolas step forward from the crowd to greet the woman, he suddenly comprehended that he had just witnessed the arrival of a new Unique.

Zalar emerged from the beauty salon, self-consciously patting her head; it felt strange to her to have shorter hair. She had had shoulder length locks for as long as she could remember. Turning and looking back into the shop window she examined her reflection, the person that looked back at her was totally alien in appearance to her. Not only had she got shorter hair but also now the familiar dark tresses had gone to be replaced by blond ones, she studied her new look; it was different, but necessity had imposed this drastic image change. The Wardens were here and she knew with unerring certainty that they would be looking for herself and Steve; this disguise, she hoped, would buy her some respite.

The thought of Steve Westerman brought a little smile to her face, would he approve of the new Zalar? A young man walked past and shot her a brief, crafty glance, he carried on walking but in the reflection of the window she clearly saw him turn to look at her again. Still smiling to herself she nodded to her reflection and left to make her way back to the hotel.

It was afternoon and the weather was quite good for the time of the Bailon year. The indigenous population were all dressed in lightweight casual wear, consisting of mostly shirts, slacks and skirts. She had been initially shocked at the variety of colours worn by everybody, this being such a marked contrast to the bland, dark and serviceable attire of the Wardens. At first shocked she now revelled in the wearing of the brightly coloured and patterned garments, they did seem to lift her spirits and the purchasing of a new addition to her wardrobe was a very pleasurable experience; when at her lowest ebb, missing

Steve and unsure about the future, a spot of retail therapy proved to be a very capable tonic.

As she neared the hotel her gaze drifted across the street to the ill fated store that had been victim to criminal fund raising activities, in the weeks that had passed the feeling of guilt she held inside of her had diminished very little.

Something caught her attention, she was about to enter the lobby of the hotel when, through the shop window, she saw the proprietor of the establishment talking to two men. You could call it instinct or a sixth-sense, but for whatever reason she froze in her tracks. There was something not right about the two individuals, something not right but strangely familiar; she slowly crossed the street in order to get a better look.

The afternoon volume of pedestrians allowed Zalar to get quite close to the shop front without increasing the opportunity to be seen, from a vantage point behind one to the trees that lined the road she was afforded a clear view of the activity within the premises. The reason for the familiarity of the two men was their clothing, they were both dressed in formal black fatigues, the identification of the style hit her like a thunderbolt; unmistakably Warden in origin.

She involuntarily ducked back behind the tree, her heart was pounding like a bass drum within her chest and she did not even dare to breath. Making a supreme effort to override her reflex panic response, she took a long deep breath; slowly exhaling she calmed her racing emotions and tentatively turned to look back into the store.

At that very moment the shop owner was leading the objects of her attention out of the door, she adjusted her position to maximise the cover that the broad trunk of the Bailon Oak provided, she could just overhear the conversation the group were having.

"Please come with me. I'll show you where they got into the building," said the proprietor, one of the men nodded and gestured for him to lead the way.

The trio disappeared down the alley beside the store, Zalar moved from her hiding place and carefully peered around the corner of the passage after them.

"This is where they got into the rear of the shop, this door leads to the backyard." The Wardens studied the door.

"Shit!" gasped Zalar to herself, as if in confirmation one of them pointed to the lock on the door and said.

"The mechanism has been totally burned out of its housing. Is this the method a thief would normally use to gain entry?"

"You tell me! I've been in business for nearly thirty years and this is the first time I've been robbed. But you're right, it would take a serious piece of thermal cutting equipment to do that, surely somebody must have seen something unusual like that."

One of the black-garbed men nodded and they were led into the backyard.

Zalar moved away and melted into the safety of the crowds on the street, she made her way across to the hotel. How stupid could she have been? She thought; the two Wardens would have easily identified the damage to the doors as being caused by a standard issue Warden thermal disruptor. She mentally ticked herself off again as she closed the lobby door behind her; they would know that she had been in this town, they would start to concentrate their search in the vicinity, and she needed to act fast.

The receptionist looked up from his station and the paperwork covering it, he did a double take as he recognised the attractive blond woman stood in front of him.

"Madam, I didn't realise it was you! Is this a new look for you?" he blustered trying to cover his embarrassment. "Yes, I fancied a change. Could I have my room key please?"

"Of course and if I may be so bold, this look is definitely you!" he said as he handed the key over. Controlling her flight reflex within her, she smiled appreciatively at the young man.

"Thank you very much, that's very kind," she purred and left to make her way to her room. She consoled herself that at least the disguise was working as she arrived outside her room.

Once inside, she closed and locked the door, resting her back against it, she let out a massive sigh of relief. Her mind was in abject turmoil; the sensible thing to do would be to get off this world as soon as possible, but she needed to stay in the area for when Westerman arrived, as she was sure he was going to. On the other hand the Wardens were here, and so soon. She had thought that it would have been a much longer period before they got here.

Abruptly she came to a decision. Although she was now effectively in disguise, she still feared that one of them would recognise her, almost certainly they would be carrying mini-computers and her image was sure to be available on them. She could not stay in the town; she took the printout from the records office out of her pocket and looked at the details on it; she studied the address. It was time to get reacquainted with her family she mused; so, with renewed resolve she began packing her clothes and equipment.

Westerman observed the greeting ceremony with a wry detachment, it brought back a good number of memories regarding his own arrival in this place; it also galvanised his determination to get away from the artificial habitat as soon as possible. He smiled to himself at the way that he could no longer think in terms of this place as a world anymore, the new arrival would be convinced that she was on a planet and not a piece of misshapen rock floating in space. He also smirked to himself that the term 'rock' would have conjured images in some people's minds back on Earth of the prison Alcatraz, he could not escape acknowledging the cosmic irony of the comparison. Yet again his thoughts turned to the absent Zalar, he was really missing her companionship tremendously, also he still harboured the dreaded fear that something dire may so be about to happen to her. Something caught his attention, interrupting his thoughts. Behind the newcomer the obelisk suddenly became decorated with a complex pattern of lights, this was totally unnoticed to the young woman. The patterns continued to become more and more intricate until a single faint beam of light, no wider than a pencil, lanced out from the top of the structure and touched the back of her head. The contact must have been without any sensation because the woman betrayed no signs of knowledge of the beam, it then as abruptly as it had started, switched off and the obelisk returned once more to its inert condition.

The smallest seed of an idea had been planted in Westerman's mind, what if this light was the actual mechanism by which the jump prevention was administered? It would make perfect sense to do this at the point of contact; perhaps he was on to something he thought to himself, he needed to investigate this development further.

The ceremony had finished and although he could barely hear the dialogue from his position, he realised that it was now time for the newcomer to be led away to the underground council chamber. Sure enough the greeting party led her away down the alleyway and subsequently the assembled crowd started to file out of the square after them; Westerman allowed himself to be swept along with the throng.

The small four seater ground car trundled capably along the narrow dirt road, clouds of light-brown dust billowed up behind it, the particles performing complicated manoeuvres in the air stream of the vehicle. The driver looked at the small rear view display on the dashboard and contemplated how long it was going to take him to get the machine clean again. Zalar registered the look on his face and enquired.

"Is it far from here?"

"Not far," came the curt reply.

The countryside through which they were moving had changed in appearance from the single storey dwellings of the suburbs to the neat, flat well groomed fields that were nearly all ploughed ready for the approaching Bailon winter. Zalar's attention was brought back to the road ahead as the driver let out a long bored sigh.

"Are the roads around here all like this?" she said hoping to engage the man in a tedium disturbing conversation. "Usually," he replied, "we should be grateful that the rains haven't started yet or we would be struggling."

"Does that make things a bit tricky?"

"Tricky doesn't even cover it! You need to have special tyres or a tracked vehicle, these roads become out and out swamp land."

"Do you often come out this way?" asked Zalar hoping to nurture the exchange further.

"Not often if I can help it. The folks around here are all farmers and usually my services are too expensive for them."

"Why are they all poor?" This question had been prompted by her desire to gain whatever background information she could, something to give her an insight into the people that could potentially be her long lost parents.

"Not all of them, but you know what farmers are like, always crying the poverty story," he chuckled gently.

The road ahead was as straight as an arrow, disappearing into the horizon, with the exception of a few shrubs and trees scattered around and about there was nothing but fields for as far as the eye could see.

The driver began to decelerate as a turning to the left began to resolve itself.

"Boochka's place is just along this lane," he said as he swung the vehicle into the turning, the wide tyres scrabbling for grip in the dust and gravel.

"Do you know these people?" she asked casually.

"Not very well, I've given Damena a ride from Pizoka market on a couple of occasions; she seems pleasant enough. Do you know them well?" he countered. She gave him a quick sideways glance and then replied,

"We used to be close a long time ago, but we sort of drifted apart."

The road wound around a complicated field boundary and then straightened out, heading towards a clump of trees in the middle distance,

"That's where we're heading," the driver said, pointing. Zalar felt a tightening in her chest start to manifest itself, she could feel her pulse quicken and her heart pounding.

Ten minutes later the collection of trees had revealed itself to be a copse of ancient Bailon Oaks, all towering at least fifty metres into the sky; nestled at its centre was a small collection of buildings. The ground car pulled up outside the largest structure in the group.

"Here we are," he said as he opened his door and stepped out, Zalar did the same. They both moved to the rear of the vehicle where the luggage storage compartment was located.

Having retrieved her cases and paid the driver the fee they had agreed, plus a sizeable gratuity, she started to walk towards the entrance to the building. Behind her the car turned round and raced off in an expanding cloud of dust back along the lane.

What would she say? She couldn't just walk up; knock on the door and say. "Hello I'm your long lost daughter." Somehow she did not think that the welcome would be what she had hoped for. These problems became irrelevant as around the corner of the building a mass of snarling teeth and skin appeared; it charged towards her and became identifiable as a small dog-like creature.

The animal was issuing a noise that was a strange cross between a bark and a hiss; it stopped approximately two metres away from Zalar, at this distance it was clear to see that a long time ago the origin of this species was undoubtedly reptilian. To compliment the warning bark it had also sprouted a ridge of pointed scales along its spine and extending to the tip of the whip-like tail; when extended the very tips of these scales changed colour to a vivid red, displaying a warning that was plain to see.

"Steady little fellow," she said soothingly. The creature responded by producing an even louder bark/hiss and braced itself as if ready to pounce.

Zalar reached inside her bag and took hold of her disruptor, she did not want to hurt this animal but, given its reptilian ancestry, its bite could well prove venomous. The snarling continued as it inched forward; she was about to pull her weapon from the inside the bag when she heard a voice, it shouted.

"Zoolot, bad Joolock!" The creature flattened its scales and changed their colour to a less threatening shade of red although it still maintained its unflinching stare upon her. Zalar removed her had from her bag and turned to the source of the voice.

The door had opened and from it had emerged an elderly, distinguished looking woman; her grey hair scraped back and held with a clasp to reveal a round, pleasant face that, although lined with age, was obviously once very attractive.

"Can I help you dear?" she said. Zalar had been stood just staring at the woman, she realised that a pregnant pause was being created; with an effort she forced herself to reply.

"Yes. I was wondering if you could help me, I'm looking for Boochka and Damena?" The woman smiled and said,

"I'm Damena, Boochka is working in the fields at the moment. What can I do for you?"

Zalar blinked as she found her eye watering slightly, she knew that for this to work she had to hold it together.

"My name is Tink-Bell." The elderly woman looked her up and down; comically, the circling animal she now knew as being a Joolock was unwittingly aping its mistress's actions.

"I'm pleased to meet you, but what can I do for you my dear?" She pressed.

"Well. This is kind of difficult to explain," offered Zalar as she collected her thoughts.

"That's okay my love, please take your time." The encouraging demeanour of the kindly old woman had made the task no easier for Zalar. She knew that initially she would have to lie to her, there was no way that the truth could be used, but still the thought of misleading the woman who could actually be her mother was proving to be an abhorrent one.

"I'm from the Southern Continent. I've been on a bit of a quest to discover my family's roots and some of my distant relatives have told me that I have kin in Pizoka.

My investigations have led me here I'm afraid." Damena looked carefully at the young woman's face; her eyes seemed sad but gave the impression of a very perceptive person.

"Your face is very familiar; you've certainly got Boochka's nose, perhaps it is on his side of the family." Zalar smiled and with more than a little relief replied,

"It could be, my relatives were very vague."

"Humm, where are you staying Tink-Bell?" The question took Zalar by surprise; taking a deep breath she played her bluff.

"Well I've actually just landed in the area and I was so wrapped up in my little project that I came straight here, could you recommend anywhere in the area?"

The elderly woman gave her a knowing smile.

"There's no where around here dear," she paused, looked Zalar up and down once more and continued, "you must stay with us of course."

"Oh! I couldn't possibly impose like that," blustered Zalar.

"Nonsense, after all you could be family."

"Well if you're quite sure? I'll pay towards my keep," she beamed; secretly this was a result that she could only have dreamed of.

"Of course I'm sure, and don't worry about paying I'm sure that we can find you the odd chore to do." Damena winked and chuckled; Zalar felt her heart melt.

"Come inside child," she said and with that she led the way into the building; the Joolock had sensed that there was no hostility between its mistress and the other person and had started to run around both of their legs, showing off, trying to ingratiate itself with the newcomer.

The inside of the building was typically rustic; a large living area that doubled as a kitchen and lounge; a large log fire crackled and blazed in a stone hearth, the flames casting their cosy warm light across the room. Zalar moved across to the inviting blaze and held the palms of her hands towards the heat; the ambience of the comfortable area warmed her through to her very soul. It felt right, it felt like home; as if in confirmation she could feel her eyes beginning to brim with tears, she swallowed the lump in her throat and turned, forcing a smile, to Damena.

"This is lovely. I could feel so relaxed here."

"Thank you very much dear. That's a great compliment, it may be humble but it's ours," said the elderly woman as she gestured, expansively around the room.

Zalar's attention was caught by a pair of small pictures on the top of a cupboard next to Damena, the light from the fire catching glass of the frame. She moved closer to look at the images and discovered that they were photographs of a young female child, very young and very pretty; her smiling face framed by a shock of thick dark hair.

"Who is that?" she asked, looking up at Damena. In the flickering firelight she could clearly see the older woman's eyes glistening; at length she answered.

"That's my daughter Zalar."

"She's beautiful. Where is she?" Zalar asked as earnestly as possible.

"I… I'm afraid that she's not with us anymore." Damena took the picture in her hands and looked at it for long seconds before she turned her attention back to Zalar and continued.

"She died many years ago."

A potentially devastating pang of heartache shot through the young woman, the agony inside of the other woman's voice was palpable; gently she reached out and took Damena's hand.

"I'm sorry to hear that, you must have loved her very much, I can tell." Looking down at Zalar's hand gently holding hers she said.

"Yes, I believe you can. It was a very long time ago but it still hurts." Nodding, Zalar squeezed her hand affectionately. Gathering herself, Damena wiped the tears from her eyes and said.

"Come. I'll show you where you can put your things and the way to your room."

"Will your husband be okay with me being here?"

"Don't worry about him, he'll be fine. It's not everyday that we get a beautiful young woman stopping with us; he'll think that it's his birthday!"

Sure enough Boochka returned to the house later that evening and Damena introduced Tink-Bell, (Zalar), to him. He was a broad shouldered man, possessing a body that had been honed by the countless seasons of working the land, his face having that weather beaten quality typical of people from an agricultural background. His eyes, however, were sharp and kindly, this being the first thing that had registered with Zalar as she shook the man's large rough hand.

Damena explained that she was a long lost, distant relative from the Southern Continent, Boochka studied the young woman's face for long tense seconds; Zalar began to think that he was not going to believe the cover story, but presently he said,

"It's always good to meet a long lost relation. Of course you should stay with us as long as you feel comfortable." He gently squeezed her hand and then turned to his wife.

"Now woman, where's my food!" he announced in a mock grandiose fashion. Damena smiled and responded.

"It will be on the table in two minutes, after you've washed those grubby hands."

Boochka went to the kitchen sink, as he passed Damena he playfully grabbed hold of her; playfully wrapping his arms around her, pulling her into an affectionate bear hug.

"Stop that or you will never get your supper! And, in case you hadn't noticed, we have a guest," she said, smiling whilst nestling into his strong embrace.

The watching Zalar could once again feel the unmistakable feeling of heartache spreading throughout her body, the pain emanating from all the lost years without knowing her parents, the loneliness of her childhood and the removal from the joy of seeing a couple so obviously in love with each other. Boochka unwillingly released his wife and made himself busy in the sink, Damena crossed the room to Zalar and gently laid her hand on her shoulder, saying softly.

"Are you alright Tink-Bell?"

"Yes. I'm fine. It's just that the whole room and the set up you have here has reminded me of something very dear to me," replied Zalar taking a deep breath and recomposing herself. Patting her arm before she left, Damena moved back to the stove and said,

"Please sit down over there," she indicated to a chair at the far end of the table, "his nib's likes to sit at this end next to the fire." Forcing a smile of acknowledgement, Zalar moved to her designated position and sat down. Boochka was drying his hands on a large towel as he said.

"Sorry I'm late tonight, but I was talking to old Jevan over by the north field; you know what he's like."

"Oh yes, he's just like an old woman sometimes. What's the illness he's be struck by?" said Damena as she began placing various receptacles of food on the table. "He's not ill this time believe it or not! Quite the opposite actually; he's really excited about something in the sky." "The sky?" asked the suddenly very focused Zalar.

"Yes. He was saying that he had found a new comet. He was pointing was it out to me, where it was in the sky," he explained as he settled into his favourite seat.

"Sorry, but did you say that you can actually see it," prompted Zalar.

"Don't take any notice Tink-Bell. I know old Jevan; he could possibly have seen this thing in the bottom of a tankard of ale," laughed Damena.

"No love! I've seen it too! I told you he showed me," insisted Boochka.

Perhaps it was the years of Warden training that was coming to the surface or some sixth sense but Zalar suddenly had a very bad feeling about the phenomena being discussed.

"Could you show me please?" she asked. Boochka looked up from the plate he was about to start filling with food and was all set to argue against moving from his chair when noticed the urgency that was apparent on the young woman's face, upon seeing this he stood up.

"Okay! Come on! I never could say no to a pretty face," he turned to Damena and smiled, "it won't take long dear; you come too."

The three of them walked out into the courtyard, the night sky had fully taken hold and through holes in the fleeting cloud cover the stars could be seen. Boochka looked around to get his bearings and then pointed up to a section of the sky.

"About there I reckon. We will have to wait for that cloud to go." Damena moved to her husband's side and nestled up to him for warmth against the night's chill.

Zalar wrapped her arms around herself after producing an involuntary shiver.

The clouds shifted endlessly across the black curtain of the sky, they appeared to be moving purposely, mischievously; refusing to unveil the portion of the starscape they wanted to see.

"Look! There!" cried Boochka, pointing.

Sure enough a dim star was trailing a tail of electric blue behind it.

"Oh that's pretty," said Damena, her husband looked at his wife's upturned face and held her tighter.

Zalar continued to observe the heavenly object, something was definitely not right, she couldn't figure out what it was; nevertheless it was causing her some anxiety.

"It must be very near. Look how it's moving against the stars," said Boochka. At that time a large section of the sky was clear, offering an unbroken opportunity to watch the object.

Suddenly Zalar realised what was wrong. The tail was varying in luminosity as they tracked its progress; a massive shiver ran down her spine, it was not the cold; she turned to the elderly couple and said in as calm a voice as she could manage.

"Thanks for showing me this, I've never seen one before, but I don't mean to be rude but I'm freezing!"

"You're right dear. Come on you big oaf, let's get some supper," said Damena as she broke from her husbands embrace and began leading him back into the house. Zalar followed and just prior to entering the welcoming doorway she glanced back up at the sky; there was no mistake in her mind. She had seen this spectacle before; it was not a comet, she knew that it was the final braking burn of a massive spaceship; her mind leapt ahead to a conclusion that seemed so obvious it made her shiver again. Calaxians!

CHAPTER FOURTEEN

Westerman walked around the 'reception' square carefully looking at the heavily patterned faces of the central obelisk; the mock sun was practically overhead in the azure sky casting only very small shadows. After weeks of searching around the small hamlet of the Uniques he was more convinced than ever that the strange structure before him was connected to the jump inhibiting field operating in this asteroid settlement. He had arrived at the conclusion after seeing the arrival of the 'new born' Unique and the simple fact there were no other structures like this in the entire town.

This was his fifth visit to the object and he still felt no nearer to gaining any insight into the operation, or more pertinently, the deactivation of the device. More frustrating was that he couldn't actually touch the machine; he had tried once only and discovered that a vicious little force field was in place. This energy barrier was only a scant couple of centimetres above the surface of the structure but it had the kick of a mule and had caused his hand to tingle for a good few hours after it had propelled him metres across the square.

He completed another circuit of the obelisk and stopped facing the enigmatic apparatus.

"I see that you are still wasting your time with the obelisk," said Wendle who had flashed into existence behind him.

"I suppose that it wouldn't do any good to tell you to fuck off!" replied Westerman without even glancing over his shoulder. The object of his scorn merely shrugged and walked over to stand by his side.

"I will be gracious enough to tell you that you are right about this piece of equipment; it is the teleportation restriction device." Still without looking at the Unique, Westerman replied.

"I had figured that much out all by myself."

"You cannot turn it off from here and the shielding is impregnable. So why waste your time?"

"Why won't you let me go?" asked Westerman.

"We can't risk you revealing the location of this world to our enemies either by design or by accident." Westerman finally turned to face his tormentor.

"Listen very carefully; I'll talk slowly so that the words will sink into your thick head. Unless I have some trait that allows me to remember the coordinates of places that I have visited, I wouldn't know how to find this shit hole! Oh, and by the way, you can cut the crap, this isn't a world or even a moon; it's a piece of rock you are hiding on."

Wendle smiled thinly.

"Be it ever so humble it is our home. You have seen what awaits us out in the universe; persecution and exploitation; we are all so very surprised that you will not join us."

"You know why I won't join you. You are stopping me going to the aid of a person that I hold so very dear. You are holding me prisoner!" spat Westerman.

"We have been through all this; Zalar is a Warden. You claim that she has broken her control programming; what if it's a ploy, a trap? What if as been engineered to ultimately reveal our location?"

"That's just paranoid delusional bullshit and you know it!" "Not to the Uniques. You have seen how their technology is based around our quantum DNA; if they captured this place they would have a massive source of materials from which to create even more devices of destructive potential. No! We are doing the galaxy a service by keeping our location secret."

Westerman threw back his head and issued a loud, brash laugh before turning his attention back to Wendle. "That is so very altruistic of you," he said sarcastically. "You are entitled to your opinion, just as we are."

"Okay given all this saving the galaxy crap, the hundred million dollar question; why am I still alive?"

Wendle produced a sickly grin and nodded.

"We are hoping that you will decide to join us, you have massive potential to be a truly powerful Unique; it would be a shame to waste such a valuable resource."

Westerman turned his attention back to the obelisk.

"I'm not an idiot! You are only going to stand me being a non-contributing burden for so long and then it's goodnight!" He drew his finger across his neck in a throat-slitting gesture and looked back towards Wendle. "You are a refreshingly perceptive individual Mister Westerman, it is a joy to converse with someone who has such an instantaneous grasp of situation."

"How long have I got?"

"Not long mister Westerman, not long!" answered Wendle who bowed slightly and then vanished in a flash of brilliant white light.

Westerman nodded his head ironically, although he had just been told that a death sentence hung over his head, it was not foremost in his mind; the fate of Zalar was the total occupation of his thoughts. He had experienced love before in the form of his dead wife Rachel but this affection for a dark haired woman from another world had consumed his soul; the longer they were apart the worse the heartache became and the more the feeling of dread grew. He did not know or understand how but he could sense that some dire event was about to overtake her, and he was convinced that he was the only one who could help. He was driven, he had to escape; it was imperative.

Once again he studied the obelisk, there had to be a way to get through the force field. A sound attracted his attention; turning he noticed that a number of people had started to congregate in the square, this could only me one thing; an arrival. The crowd continued to swell and position themselves around the perimeter of the area; Wendle reappeared accompanied by Landon, they made a beeline for Westerman, to where he stood beside the obelisk.

"Another lamb to the slaughter?" quipped Westerman. Wendle gave him a stern look and said,

"I do hope that you are not going to prove a nuisance Mister Westerman?"

"Me? Oh no, I'm just going to watch the show."

"Good. Because we would hate to have to resort to force at this time," said Landon menacingly.

"But not long eh?" sneered Westerman. Landon gave a thin smile and bowed slightly. At that very second the low, audible whine began and the two Uniques turned their attention to the incoming transit of one of their potential brethren, they moved towards the reception area leaving him stood a couple of metres away from the obelisk.

All eyes were concentrated upon the centre of the plaza; the expectation grew in tandem with the pitch of the noise being emitted from the machine. From where he was positioned Westerman could feel the power being generated by the device, he looked down at the hairs on the back of his hands and marvelled at the way they were quivering, he reasoned that there must have been a large static element to the energies being produced and manipulated.

A flash of light and a young man appeared in the reception area, his legs promptly gave way and he slumped forward unceremoniously on to his hands and knees, subsequently vomiting violently.

Something was different, Westerman could feel a tangible change in some stimuli in the surrounding atmosphere of the square; something was missing. Intuitively he swung his gaze away from the newcomer who was now being approached by Wendle and Landon, back to the obelisk. Acting on pure instinct he leapt forward and reached out his hand to touch the machine, bracing himself for the force field to violently repel his advances. Nothing happened!

His outstretched fingertips made contact with the face of the structure; he could feel the contours of the intricate symbolisation, it felt warm. Abruptly his hand was thrown away from the device as the shield resurrected itself, the tingling that he had experienced before flooded from the tips of his fingers to his shoulder and across his chest. Fortunately the assembled masses had mostly been too enthralled with the spectacle and ceremony of the arrival to notice Westerman's antics, the few that did witness his foolish action were smiling to themselves as he retreated a few steps, amused at the way he was shaking his stunned arm.

Returning the compliment he smiled back and further retreated to one of the corners of the square. He had touched the machine; the force field had been down, only for a few seconds granted, but it had been down. A plan formulated in his mind; he could not be sure but he thought that it was a pretty safe bet the shield was actually generated from inside the obelisk and the arrival of the newcomer demanded unfathomable amounts of energy for a successful execution, the power consumption must be that great that there was insufficient to maintain the screen.

Would the length of time offered by the temporary suspension be enough to successfully jump? What if they could intercept him again in mid-flight? These were obviously very pertinent questions to consider, but he now had hope, and to a desperate man that can prove to be a powerful inducement.

He could see Wendle and Landon beginning to lead the young man out of the square, he left his position of contemplation and pushed through the crowd towards Landon; eventually he was carried out of the square and down the narrow passage by the tide of people. Finally he caught up with the Unique in the outside street; he grabbed his arm, the man spun around to face him.

"What do you want Westerman?" he snapped, obviously surprised at being accosted in such a manner.

"Sorry. I was wondering how often you get new arrivals?"

"Why do you want to know?" Landon asked, his eyes narrowed as he looked at Westerman with suspicion.

"Oh nothing in particular, curiosity," he replied, still holding the other man's arm by the elbow, who was obviously impatient to go about his business.

"It varies from time to time. We sometimes have to wait for days or like today we have a couple within a few hours of each other, in fact we have another guest due in around two hours time. Now let me go!" he said firmly as he shook his arm free. With a final disdainful look he set off to catch up with Wendle and the newest arrival. "A couple of hours," Westerman said softly to himself. He rubbed his hands together in a gesture of excitement and set off towards his accommodation with a definite renewed spring in his step.

One and a half hours later Westerman sat at a table outside one of the town's many taverna, slowly sipping from an earthenware beaker. His attention was far removed from the brew inside the mug, which he assumed was a Unique approximation of a cross between tea and coffee, his focus was upon the alleyway that led to the reception square. From this position, some fifty metres away, he was carefully monitoring the movement of people around the passage entrance; he knew the traffic would increase when the newcomer was due.

It was mid afternoon and the street was busy; the taverna operator was giving him looks of disgust, probably because he was occupying a prime table and not eating very much. Westerman took a deliberately slow sip from his mug and then held it up in the manner of a toast towards the man; the recipient of this gesture huffed and turned his attention towards other tasks.

"And fuck you!" said Westerman under his breath and returned to his observations.

The quantity of people on the street seemed to have increased visibly; the flow of the pedestrians had definitely become focused towards the alleyway.

It was time. Taking a deep breath, he slipped from his table and plunged into the river of bodies and pushed his way forward.

In the square the masses spread out in their usual manner, around the outside of the reception area; Westerman made his way to roughly the same position he had occupied at his earlier visit. Wendle, Landon and Bolas emerged to take up their customary places; they noticed his attendance with a cursory glance and then turned their combined attention to the area where the newcomer would appear.

The now familiar whine started, Westerman looked up at the top of the obelisk, and the glow had also begun.

He gathered his thoughts up inside of himself; he knew he had to do this right; there would only ever be one chance as when he had played his hand there could never be another opportunity. The pitch and the volume of the noise increased, inside his mind, Westerman started to visualise a cylinder, which he then modified into a section of pipe about twenty centimetres in diameter by approximately half a metre long.

The sound and light reached its crescendo of intensity; in a blast of brilliant white light a middle aged woman materialised in the reception area, she swayed unsteadily; Westerman could feel the peculiar null sensation that told him that the shield was down.

From where he stood he extended his arms towards the obelisk, he took the mental image of the pipe and created an invisible, telekinetic energy version of it; he forced one of the open ends against the device.

Seconds later the force field reformed around the structure; light and bolts of charged energy erupted from around Westerman's 'force-pipe' where it interrupted the shield. Wendle and Landon spun around to see where the loud, crackling sound of an energy discharge was coming from as the force field tried to compensate for its incomplete condition by pumping more and more power into it. The noise increased along with the quantity and strength of the lightning bolts that were lancing out from the now visibly apparent hole in the obelisk's shield.

"What are you doing?" shouted Landon. Wendle set off across the courtyard to stop the attack; the crowd of people started to panic and back away form the potentially lethal display of raw energies competing against each other.

"Leave the device alone!" said Wendle as he went to grab Westerman; he never reached his goal as he was picked up and flung across the square by the invisible fist of Westerman's telekinetic power.

Landon braced himself and focused his own energies on the Earthman; his eyes flashed, sparks and flame exploded from a point in mid-air, a metre behind his targets head as his bolt struck Westerman's own hastily erected defensive shield.

The conflict occurring upon the surface of the obelisk was nearing a conclusion and Westerman was losing. The machine was bringing enormous quantities of energy to the battle, intent on completing the integrity of the force field; the hole had shrunk to half its original diameter, a major contributing factor to this being that the Uniques began sending bolt after bolt against him, which although splashing harmlessly against his shield, was diverting the energy away from the struggle against the machine.

In one last desperate act, he gathered as much power as he could from his reserves inside himself and focused it into a single blast. A pair of seemingly solid rods of white light, accompanied by a tortured screaming sound, exploded from his eyes and lanced through the hole in the force field.

A titanic explosion ripped across the square, the remaining people who had not fled were thrown like rag dolls against the enclosing walls, fragments of metal propelled at near supersonic speeds pierced unprotected bodies and an expanding ball of flame set clothing alight.

Westerman slowly picked himself up from the ground and looked at the surrounding carnage. People lay dead or dying, many moaned and wailed as the full extent of their injuries became apparent to them; nearby a woman screamed as she stared wide eyed down at her hand that was hanging by the an inconceivably slim piece of flesh from the bloody stump of her arm.

He turned his attention towards the obelisk, there was nothing left of the device with the exception of a very few smouldering pieces. Tentatively he investigated his own body for signs of injury, he had been lucky; the force screen he had erected to protect him from the Uniques attack had deflected almost all the effects of the blast. At that moment he became aware of a stinging sensation emanating from his cheek, he dabbed his hand to the source of the irritation; it felt wet and sore. He removed his hand revealing his fingers to be smeared with blood, he dabbed again; the flow did not seem to be great.

"What have you done?" was the hysterical shout from behind him, turning he saw Wendle scrambling to his feet and starting to limp towards him.

"What have you done?" he repeated.

"What I had to do!" exclaimed a stony faced Westerman. "It will take months to rebuild the machine! Countless Uniques could go unchecked on their first jump, they could die!" he entreated, Westerman stood his ground.

"I did what I had to do to survive! Your secret would have been safe with me!"

"You have no idea what's going on in the universe. No idea of the scale of the conflicts about to unfold," spat Wendle.

"No I haven't. You're right, I've met three alien species and they have all tried to do me harm! It is a hostile place so I need to be with people or a person I can trust and it is definitely not you lot!" said Westerman in measured tones.

"By person I suppose that you are referring to that Warden woman, Zalar. She will betray you, these are the ways of the Warden."

"I doubt it but time will tell."

Wendle suddenly straightened up and concentrated his gaze; his eyes flashed and his bolt bounced harmlessly of the force field that Westerman had flung up at the speed of thought. The Unique tried again; once more the blast of pure thought energy was deflected.

"You are a powerful Unique Steve Westerman, but we will find you, we will have our revenge against you."

"Oh shut the fuck up!" spat Westerman as he raised his arm, made a dismissive gesture and the Unique was lifted of his feet and thrown against one of the squares walls, coming to rest in an unconscious heap.

The surrounding crowd appeared to have shaken themselves back into action, they had started to close in around him; several bolts of telekinetic energy struck his shield and dissipated in a spectacular show of light and noise.

He said softly to himself, "Time to go." He closed his eyes and began to recreate the 'jump' feeling deep within, he could sense the energies building to a crescendo and then… Flash… A blinding, brilliant burst of the purest white light and Westerman disappeared.

Wendle had just recovered consciousness enough to see his tormentor vanish; he hurled insults and curses after the troublesome human in a fit of exasperation and feelings of futility.

The gargantuan mass of the Calaxian vessel slipped gently into its orbital position, millimetre perfect after its many light year journey. Along the crafts prodigious length a variety of protuberances began to sprout; inside the control room the commander surveyed the multitude of display screens that had now extruded themselves from the chambers ceiling, he turned to the science station.

"Any more evidence of quantum signatures?" he growled.

"Negative. Deep penetration scanners are about to come on line sir." Nodding the commander turned his attention back to the screens hovering within his peripheral vision.

He could not quantify his anxiety; he had performed many planetary raids but something about this particular operation was causing him a great deal of concern. He knew that he had come into contact with the Wardens before, they were not an especially ferocious body of warriors, they preferred to organise the native species into an opposing force rather than direct confrontation; at best a nuisance value he mused.

His second in command approached making the correct submissive gestures and adopting the accepted body language, however his eyes betrayed the fire of ambition, he coveted the commander's position.

"Sir, we are in position to launch. We have detected no planetary defences of any consequence, also there are no advanced detection systems operating, they don't even know we are here." gloated the reptilian creature. The commander continued his study of the screens, he knew he should give the order to commence the invasion cycle, but he wanted to make this young upstart wait, to show just exactly who was still in control. However in the back of his mind he still had the nagging dread regarding the blue-green planet that hung below his ship.

"Deep penetration scanners; anything new to report?" he snapped with a mock irritability designed to keep his subordinates on their toes.

"No new data commander," was the efficient answer from the science officer. Turning to his number two the ageing commander said.

"I think that you should start your invasion procedures. It looks like…" he was interrupted by a loud buzzer sounding from the science console; his gaze swung quickly around to a display on his left, an alert message announced its appearance by flashing menacingly.

"Sir, we have just detected a major quantum signature in the northern hemisphere," the junior officer yelled.

"I see it!" the commander growled impatiently.

"Should I continue with the invasion?" asked the second in command with an impatience that rivalled his superior. The older male rapidly turned to face his junior.

"No. I want to find more information about these readings before we launch our attack."

"But sir, we have superiority in numbers and weaponry; we could easily…." His words were silenced by the commander leaping from his chair with a burst of surprising agility and speed; knocking the upstart to the floor with a hefty backhanded slap.

"Don't ever question my orders!" he snarled, bending threateningly over the prone younger creature.

"As you command sir," replied the chastised inferior as he picked himself up and retired from the immediate vicinity of the command position.

"We will continue to observe this situation. There is no hurry," he turned his attention back to his number two, "patience is one of the principal virtues of a good officer." The younger Calaxian nodded his understanding as his superior returned to his chair. Discipline restored the older creature returned to his deliberations, he hoped that his display had adequately covered up any outward indications of the persisting feeling of dread that was clutching at the pit of his primary stomach.

A blinding flash of light proclaimed the arrival of Steve Westerman on Bailon; cautiously he looked at his new surroundings.

He had materialized in the middle of a thoroughfare of some description; the earthen road was lined on both sides by dry-stone walls, overhead the local vegetation's leaves attractively blocked out the midday sun. Whilst trying to decide which direction to take, he suddenly became aware of the fatigue creeping into his bones.

Moving to lean against one of the walls for support he started to take stock of his situation. Firstly he consoled himself that the tired feeling that had spread through his body must be a direct effect of the jump he had just made, not to mention his exertions back on the Unique's asteroid. Secondly, and most importantly, he was now desperate to locate Zalar; too long had he been away from her, many different scenarios of doom had played through his subconscious, but how would he find her?

He reasoned that the coordinates he had been given for Bailon would be the same as programmed into all the Warden jump devices, therefore this would be the place where she had also arrived on this world. He smiled to himself; perhaps he was stood in the very spot that she had occupied as she decided whether to walk left or right.

He knew that Zalar would have faced the same indecision, he tried to second-guess the way that her mind would have worked; he was fairly confident that local knowledge would not have been an advantage in her decision. She had been wounded in their struggle with the Wardens as they destroyed the Ring, he was also confident that she would have made her way towards a local centre of civilisation; a small town or village to seek medical assistance, but which way? The very nature of the terrain did not help in his decision making process, he could see no sign of any settlements in either direction. Abruptly, choosing to place his options in the hands of blind luck he turned to his right and set off at a brisk walk along the road.

After a few minutes he started to become aware that the climate on this world was markedly cooler that the artificial environment of the Uniques domicile; unfortunately the lightweight shirt and trousers he wore offered little protection against the cool breeze that was blowing steadily along the lane. He had no alternative but to pick up the pace and walk quicker to generate more internal warmth to stave off the chill; however his concern for the temperature of his surroundings suddenly became secondary as he became aware of a distant noise. This noise soon started to increase in volume very quickly.

He looked around for possible places of cover or tactical advantage, but the sound had something of a familiar quality about it, something reassuringly 'human'. With a flash of recognition he identified the noise; it was an engine, a single cylinder internal combustion engine. Seconds later his evaluation was confirmed as around a small bend in the road ahead appeared the Bailon equivalent of a motorcycle burst into view.

Westerman studied the rider as he quickly approached; he certainly did not look like a Warden or a Unique; deciding that bravery and trusting to luck was probably the best course of action, he stepped into the middle of the road and waved his arms, gesturing for the approaching vehicle to stop.

Fortunately the rider recognised Westerman's intentions and pulled steadily to a halt in front of him. The vehicle gave the appearance of a standard, Earth, 'off road' motorcycle with one major exception, the front forks divided into a two wheel arrangement, offering a bulkier profile when compared to what Westerman would have classed as being the norm. The rider killed the engine and still astride the machine, removed his heavy looking gauntlets.

"I wonder if you could help me?" asked Westerman. Reaching up, the pilot of the vehicle unclipped and swung upward the front section of the helmet revealing the wearer to be a young man, probably in his late teens or very early twenties. The man looked Westerman up and down and at length said,

"What do you want?" the suspicion in his voice was extremely evident.

"Thanks for stopping, I was wondering if you could tell me the direction to the nearest town?" the young man appeared to relax somewhat.

"Pizoka, it's straight ahead," he replied, gesturing towards the road in front of him; his gaze turned to the older man's face and focused on the cut across his cheek, "are you okay?"

Absentmindedly reaching up and touching the six centimetre gash, Westerman was rewarded with a sharp stab of pain.

"It's not as bad as it looks," he said covering his grimace against the pain with as pleasant a smile as he could muster, "I fell down a banking and cut myself on a rock or something."

The motorcyclist didn't give the impression of being too convinced by the explanation and at length he observed. "Whatever, it's your business," turning to look at the now darkening sky he continued, "look it's gonna rain. What the hell! Do you want a lift to Pizoka?"

"That would be great, thanks a bunch," Westerman blustered with true gratitude.

"Your not exactly dressed for the weather you know," observed the rider as he started the machines engine. "This must look pretty strange I guess?"

"Hey plenty of strange shit going on around here, comets appearing and disappearing; people materializing in flashes of light and weird robed men asking questions."

Westerman almost let his astonishment get the better of him; he knew that the young man could only be talking about the Wardens.

The motorcyclists gestured for him to climb on board the bike, saying,

"Just remember to hold on and don't try to lean on the corners, let me do that, just stay neutral."

Nodding, Westerman climbed aboard; seconds later they were speeding along the country lane, the dry-stone walls merging into a continuous blur on either side of them. The air seemed to have a multitude of small black flying insects in it; these were now impacting themselves against Westerman's face. Concentrating he produced a small, invisible force field around his head, the wind and organic debris now scattered harmlessly away.

Turning his attention to other, potentially pressing matters, he repeated the obvious fact in his head; the Wardens are here! That should have really come as no surprise to him, nevertheless, the affirmation of the fact did fill him with more than a hint of trepidation; he involuntarily shivered as the cool air drove into his bones as the vehicle sped onward.

Once again the pulse of concern had coursed through his soul, Zalar. He could not exorcise the thought from his mind that she was in grave danger, the desire to locate her as quickly as possible overwhelmed him once again.

The young man, who had proved to be an extremely capable handler of the machine, brought it to a halt at the intersection of two avenues, deep inside the town of Pizoka. Westerman climbed off the bike and thanked his benefactor; who, giving a small nod of acknowledgement raced away down the street in a flurry of noise and speed.

Standing on the pavement, he was suddenly struck by the enormity of the task he was confronted with in trying to locate his beloved. How could he hope to find a single person amongst all the, potentially, thousands living in this town? If indeed she was within the area of the settlement he was about to try and search in the first place.

Putting these negative thoughts to the very back of his mind he resolved to head into the centre of Pizoka and hopefully something there would assist him in his quest; another more pressing problem had begun to present itself however as the rain started to steadily fall. Luckily the street was only sparsely occupied so he formed a mental umbrella shaped shield above his head without attracting any attention as the rain was now diverted away from him a good ten centimetres above his head. Smiling to himself he mused how he ever managed to get through the day before he gained his Unique abilities.

Tens of kilometres away, Zalar had made her excuses and retired to her room; Boochka and Damena had so far made her stay on their farm one of the most pleasurable experiences she had ever had. Damena was always so pleased to see her; she and the elderly woman had talked long into the night on many occasions, Zalar had been very careful to keep her own stories of home and family very simple so as not to slip up at a later date when recounting things again.

One particular night, when Boochka had gone to bed, the two of them had sat together near the open fire, drinking a warmed home produced red wine, when quite out of the blue Damena had turned to Zalar and said,

"So my girl, who is this man?"

Zalar turned to face the woman, whose eyes were alight with insight and wisdom, redirecting her gaze to the glass in her hand she answered,

"His name is Steve Westerman."

"That is an unusual name," observed Damena.

"He's an unusual man."

"Not from these parts then?"

Zalar let out a little laugh and replied,

"You could say that."

Damena picked up on the wistful smile playing across the younger woman's features and continued to probe.

"What's he like?"

"Steve? Oh he's about my age, very strong willed and brave." Her voice trailed away as she became lost in her thoughts.

"You love him very much don't you," Damena gently stated.

"Is it that obvious?" countered Zalar as she returned her gaze back to the other woman's probing eyes.

"Tink-Bell, this may be none of my business, but what's he really like? Where is he?"

Zalar looked into the roaring fire, there seemed to be some comfort in the warmth and light of the flames.

"Two very good questions, as to where he is? I don't know; we have become separated during our travels. What's he really like? To be honest we haven't known each other very long, but he is very special; when I hear his voice it is like a light is switched on inside of me, when he touches me it is just like an electric shock."

Damena smiled knowledgeably and nodded encouragement for Zalar to continue.

"He can be very serious and then seconds later he can be equally as funny; in my eyes he is so heroic but his past has been rocked by tragedy, his partner and children were killed in a ground car accident, when he dwells upon this he can have his darker moments."

She looked across at the older woman, she was also lost in her own thoughts amongst the flames of the fire, and presently she said,

"Loss does that to you, me and Boochka still have our darker moments when we remember our daughter, Zalar."

Leaning over and placing her hand on the top of Damena's, Zalar said,

"I'm sure your daughter would have been very proud of you. "

A single tear rolled down the weather beaten cheek of the old woman, she squeezed Zalar's hand and looked into her eyes as she said simply,

"I know."

Zalar returned her thoughts to the present as she removed her rucksack from the bottom of the wardrobe in her room; from this she removed a rectangular device. Turning on the scanner she let her thoughts drift back to the couple going about their business downstairs whilst the machine booted up. She was one hundred and one percent convinced that these people were her parents, memories and resemblances had been giving her undeniable clues, and it felt so obviously right.

Her attention was dragged back to the scanner as it gave a small beep to announce its readiness; she activated the scanning function, setting it to orbital mode, the display changed its configuration to show a representation of the Bailon northern hemisphere. Sure enough directly above the pole an object was highlighted; the read out of mass and energy signatures scrolled up the right-hand side of the screen, confirming Zalar's worst fears, it was a Calaxian mother ship.

However, further examination of the engine heat readings showed that the vessel had been there a number of days, possibly not long after she had seen the 'comet'; but why had they not started their invasion? This was a strange development indeed, turning off the scanner and putting the equipment away in the wardrobe, she slumped heavily on to her bed, and she really wished that Steve had been here.

The rain had stopped and the dark grey clouds had begun to dissipate by the time Steve Westerman had emerged on the main street of Pizoka. At the present time the traffic was light allowing a fairly unimpeded view up and down the tree lined thoroughfare.

To Westerman it looked like an everyday, small town street in an everyday small town in rural England, he was actually finding the familiarity of the comparison quite comforting; he stopped and looked through the nearby shop window.

This was obviously a bakers; various loaves and cakes were displayed, the door opened and a young girl exited carrying her purchases, the smell of fresh baked bread surrounded him. This smell inevitably reminded him that he had not eaten for sometime and he was now starting to feel really quite hungry. He returned his attention to the window and caught sight of his own reflection; the gash across his cheek was clearly visible, it looked deep and angry, he should get it attended to, he thought, it would probably leave a scar.

It was during this examination of his wound that he glimpsed another reflection, this time across the road; two men stood in deep conversation, it was their clothing that was unmistakably familiar, Wardens!

Still using the window to carry out his surveillance, he carefully sidestepped to the shade of a nearby tree, the trunk of which was handily obscuring him from the two offending individuals. He changed his position in order to peer around the tree, it was obvious that he had not been noticed by them, they continued their discussion and surreptitiously showing each other information on small hand-held devices partially obscured by the wide sleeves of their robes.

At length they nodded to each other and set off in opposite directions along the street. Once they had disappeared from view, Westerman relaxed with his back against the cool, reassuringly sturdy bark of the tree, letting out a small sigh of relief; that had been close, he would have to be a whole lot more careful in future. His stomach let out a gargantuan rumble; this brought a smile to his face, he mused that he would probably starve to death a long time before the Wardens ever got their hands upon him at this rate, he needed food.

Looking along the street he noticed a sign, the translation nanos did their job, and the writing upon the sign resolved itself into 'Café', he took time to perform a quick glance up and down the road to make sure that the Wardens had not returned; they had not, he left the tree and made his way to the café door.

Upon entry he was once again struck by the near perfect similarity in décor and layout to almost any English café he may have been in before. He selected a table near to the window and took a seat, he wanted to be able to keep a weather eye onto the street, and if he was eating he did not want the Wardens spoiling the feast.

The tables were all covered with light blue tablecloths; in a holder in the centre he found a small, laminated menu; he picked it up and started to try and make sense of the bill of fare.

The big problem he immediately had was that the nanos could not translate the dishes names; normal, non-environmental specific words like 'and' or 'with' resolved themselves into perfect clarity, unfortunately the names of the meals did not have an English equivalent. He looked up feeling more than a little frustrated to see an attractive young woman approaching him; she was holding a small note pad in her hand. She was obviously the waitress.

"Can I help you?" she asked pleasantly. She looked up from her pad and noticed the gash along Westerman's face; he could clearly see her features harden and her body language change into a more defensive posture. "Does it look bad?" he asked deciding to tackle the issue head on.

"It does look very sore," she answered now feeling a little embarrassed; seeing her reaction Westerman suddenly felt that he should offer some form of explanation.

"I was on the back of a motorcycle and I caught a branch in the face," he said.

"You should get it looked at, it does look nasty," she replied with an attractive, sympathetic smile and then continued, "at least use our washroom and clean it up a bit."

He nodded and turned his attention back to the menu, no matter how long he looked at it nothing was making a great deal of sense; with a flash of inspiration he put the document down and looked up at the waitress.

"What's good today?"

"How hungry are you?" she swiftly countered with a glint in her eye.

"I could eat a horse!"

"A what?" was the puzzled reply, Westerman reddened slightly obviously this was an animal that did not have a Bailon equivalent.

"Sorry, it's a saying where I come from. I was trying to say that I am very hungry," he beamed at the young woman.

"One special coming up. What do you want to drink with that?"

"A beer,"

"A beer, no problem, do you want large or small?"

"Better make it a big one," he laughed as she nodded and noted the order on her pad.

"The washrooms through that door next to the counter," she said, pointing as she set off towards the kitchen entrance. Nodding, he got to his feet and started to make his way in the indicated direction, on his passage across the room he looked around at his fellow diners. He considered himself lucky, it must have been a quiet period of the day, and only three of the tables were occupied; two of these had couples sat at them, both of which seemed too engrossed in their conversations and food to bother about him. At a table near the washroom door was seated a solitary middle aged man; he was draining the last dregs of a hot drink from a white china mug when the waitress reappeared from behind the counter and crossed to the lone diner, she deposited a small slip of paper on the table and the man picked it up and after reading the slip, reached into his trouser pocket.

"Oh shit!" Westerman exclaimed inwardly to himself softly, "They use money."

This was one commodity that he did have at this moment, even if he did it would have been English currency; he somehow doubted that this would have been legal tender here. The waitress accepted the collection of coins from the customer and returned behind the counter, smiling sweetly to Westerman as she re-crossed his path, once behind the long wooden desk she deposited the money into an open, compartmentalised, flat box that was on a shelf. As he passed by the counter, Westerman could clearly see a substantial quantity of coins arranged by size in the various compartments; the germ of an idea formed inside of his mind.

After using the facilities to tend to the wound on his face, the girl and the motorcyclist both were right he should get it looked at, he practised the execution of his plan.

The washroom's vanity unit had two sinks inlaid into it and on the surrounding work surface a variety of items such as soaps and decorations had been arranged. One of the items was a glass tumbler, which had been filled with a collection of flat pebbles that had been lacquered to accentuate their natural colours; Westerman picked up the tumbler and emptied the pebbles into one of the sinks.

Stepping back as far as he could to simulate the distance he would be away from the money holder behind the counter, he reached out and held his hand open; a number of pebbles abruptly leapt from the sink and flew into his grasp. Smiling to himself he returned the pebbles back to the sink, arranging them into three separate piles.

Once again he repeated the exercise, this time focusing on just one of the small heap of stones, yet again they flew across the room into his hand.

"Yes!" he said to himself as a sense of triumph swept over him. He was not sure that his degree of control could be sensitive enough to do something like this; this feeling of elation soon turned into one of awe as he was hit by the stark realisation of how strong his powers actually were, of what he had become. He thought of the possibilities and was immediately stunned by how mind blowing they were; he had to shake himself out of this frame of mind.

He picked up the glass tumbler and replaced all of the pebbles to what approximated their original position, and then re-entered the café. The waitress stood behind the counter, there was no way he would be able to get to the money if she was there. He needed a diversion of some description.

The door opened and a couple of young men entered and shouted a welcome to the waitress, she smiled and waved affectionately back, one of the men went to a table, he pulled out a chair and was about to sit down. Just as his bottom was about to make contact with the seat, Westerman reached out with his mind and telekinetically yanked the chair away; the youth fell backwards on to the floor and in an attempt to regain his balance, he pulled the table over on top of himself.

The waitress rushed from behind the counter to the seen of the devastation saying.

"Janov, are you alright?"

All attention was now on the hapless youth, a woman from the couple in the nearest booth got to her feet to help him, barely concealing her amusement. This was the diversion that Westerman required, he reached out with his mind to the coin holder and from various compartments a collection of coins floated into the air and then shot into his welcoming grasp.

Approximately one hour later Westerman emerged from the café fully sated with the added bonus of now having some money in his pocket; of course he felt bad about the way he had dishonestly gained the cash, but he had made a small recompense by giving the young woman who had served him a good tip. He smiled to himself, which served to remind him of the tightness of the wound along the side of his face. He also was reminded of the inadequacy of his clothing as a cool breeze blew up the street; he needed more suitable attire, looking across the street he noticed a shop with a window display that was filled with men's clothing, smiling to himself once more he cross over the road and entered the retailer's.

The Calaxian commander shifted uneasily in his chair. There had been no further bursts of quantum energy detected on the planet to cause him any more secret consternation, the most powerful sensor arrays had only shown miniscule occurrences of the quantum effect and he knew that this was not unusual as a background phenomenon.

The second in command shifted restlessly behind him; he knew that his actions in delaying the invasion could be leading perilously close to giving the young Calaxian valid grounds to challenge for his position. He turned to the science station.

"Readings?" he growled. The science officer looked up.

"There is no change sir. No quantum energy bursts."

The old Calaxian nodded and took time to let his gaze wander across the collection of displays.

"Number two. How long before you can begin the invasion?"

The younger subordinate dragged himself away from leering at one of the female officers and replied.

"Two planetary cycles, commander. Loading of weapons is almost complete; troop embarkation can begin within one cycle."

The commander nodded again and made a show of flexing his four-fingered hand, extending his claws in a demonstration of strength.

"Science station, maintain all energy scans." He stood up and turned to face his second in command.

"Number two!" he hissed in a manner leaving the younger creature in no doubt who was still in charge.

"Begin the invasion cycle." He could immediately see the fires ignite in the reptilian eyes of his would be successor.

"Sir!" growled the second in command as he turned and raced from the control room, his body language displaying the release of the pent up frustration.

The commander watched him go and did the Calaxian equivalent of smiling to himself, he too felt the excitement of another invasion coursing through his veins, but still present in the back of his mind was the lingering dread.

Properly clothed and fed, Westerman actually felt in a much more positive frame of mind, a state of mind much more conducive to the search for Zalar, but where to start looking? He needed to try and put himself in her place, he needed to try and think like her; talk about getting in touch with my feminine side he mused to himself.

Her needs would be basically the same as his, food, drink, clothing and a place to stay. This line of thought brought him to the obvious revelation that he had nowhere to spend the night, of which there were unmistakable signs of its approach. The illuminated sign for a hotel swung invitingly in the breeze further along the street, he thought to himself that this was as good a place to start as any so he walked over to the establishment and entered the lobby; he approached the front desk.

"Good evening sir. Can I be of assistance?" asked the uniformed young man behind the desk.

"I hope so, have you got a room for the night?"

"Just the one night sir?"

"It could run into a couple of days I suppose, but just for tonight would be fine."

The clerk studied the bookings in a large diary and presently said,

"I have a single room available for the next three night's sir."

"Sounds great, I'll take it," said Westerman with a small internal sigh of relief. With the night closing in he did not want to be walking the streets trying to find a bed for the night.

The young clerk presented a bill for the accommodation, which he duly paid from the coins in his pockets, feeling more than a passing guilt that he had just performed a similar theft in the clothing shop as he had perpetrated in the café to swell his finances.

"Room 515, up the stairs, fifth floor," he said indicating the foot of the nearby staircase.

Just about to turn and leave, Westerman turned back to the clerk and said,

"I was wondering if by any chance you had had a friend of mine check in during the last few weeks." He offered the receptionist a coin of appropriate value for the divulgence of this information.

"What was his name?"

"It wasn't a he, it was a she. Her name is Zalar."

"That's funny; a couple of weird looking guys wearing robes were asking the same question a week or so ago." Westerman's heart skipped a beat. Wardens!

"I told them the same as I will tell you; I don't remember anybody of that name staying her recently."

Westerman nodded and put the money on the desk and turned to leave, he said,

"Thanks anyway." The young clerk picked up the coins and said,

"Excuse me sir." Westerman turned back to face him.

"The robed gentlemen described the lady in question to me, even showed me a picture of her on a small screen one of them was carrying; a very attractive woman if I may say so."

Westerman looked closely at the man's face, he was obviously not telling him the whole story; reaching into his pocket he produced another coin and offered it to the clerk who accepted it eagerly.

"Her name wasn't Zalar, it was Tink-Bell."

"You've seen her? Where is she now?" Westerman blustered.

"Easy now, it was a couple of weeks ago; she stayed for a while and then suddenly checked out one day."

The Englishman's heart sunk, such a near miss, so near and yet so far away.

"Why didn't you tell the other men this?" he asked, feeling deflated. The young man smiled.

"A few reasons sir, the main one is because she told me that if anybody wearing robes came asking about her; I knew nothing. Secondly; she paid me to keep my mouth shut," he said smugly.

"So why are you telling me?" he asked suspiciously.

"Well you did give me a good tip and more importantly she described you to me; didn't mention the cut though." Subconsciously reaching up to touch the wound he could feel the hope growing inside of him once more; he asked,

"Is there anything else?"

"Yes, but I'm afraid that I have to ask you a question or two." The receptionist was obviously enjoying the cloak and dagger aspect to this encounter a little too much. "Okay, go ahead, ask away," said Westerman, lowering his voice and leaning over the desk, nearer to the man. "What's your name? Not the one you've given for the room to be registered in, who the hell is John Smith anyway?"

"Steve, Steve Westerman," he replied smirking a little sheepishly.

"Okay that's the first one right. Where do you come from?"

Westerman was stopped in his tracks by the sheer gravity of this question. He suspected that give the right answer and he would be many steps further forward to being united with his lover; give the wrong one however and he would be back to square one. His inquisitor was starting to look a little bit nervous, taking a deep breath he said,

"I come from Earth."

The clerk smiled broadly and turned to reach inside a nearby cupboard and produced an envelope, which he then handed over to Steve Westerman with a flourish. "Thank you very much," Westerman said as with shaking hands he accepted the letter; he looked at the plain white envelope, across the front was clearly written, 'Steve'.

He reward the young receptionist with another coin and retired to his room, the last few metres to the door were covered in a barely disguised run; once inside he locked the door securely and drew the drapes. Turning on a small standard lamp that provided adequate illumination, he sat down heavily in an easy chair and gazed wistfully at the white rectangle in his hands.

He was physically shaking as he opened the envelope and removed the contents; he could feel his eyes begin to mist over as he unfolded the single sheet of paper and started to read the contents.

My Darling Steve,

If you are reading this you have found your way from wherever or whoever took you from me back to Bailon. I have been forced to go into hiding at a location in the nearby countryside; if you don't know it already my love I have bad news, the Wardens are here.

I think that I have found my natural birth parents and so I have decided to go to them, I'm not going to write down the location in case this letter gets into the wrong hands, I think I can trust Devin on the front desk, (I paid him enough!), not just to give this letter to anyone, but you know how 'persuasive' the Wardens can be.

I am well and looking forward to seeing you again someday soon, it seems like centuries since we last spoke or kissed, I am missing you oh so very much.

Please come and find me, I know that you are nothing if not resourceful and determined. I love you and I always will.

Your Zalar.

Westerman read the letter a further three times; by the time he had finished he could not decide whether he should be glad or sad. On one hand he knew that his beloved was alive, and at the time of writing the letter, well. However he still seemed a long way from being with her.

He mopped the tears from his eyes with the sleeve of his shirt; he had to think, where had she gone? Another line of potential enquiry struck him; how had she got to where she had gone?

With that he left the room and rushed down to the lobby.

Upon arrival the clerk was at his post, busy filling out various forms on the front desk.

"Devin?" said Westerman; the young man looked up smiling when he recognized him.

"What can I do for you Mister Smith?"

Westerman smiled, as he understood the misnomer.

"I need to ask you a couple more questions about Zalar." "I'm sorry sir but I don't know anybody of that name." Westerman looked at the young man; shocked. Was he holding out for more money? It was at that point in his deliberations that he caught a slight flicker in the receptionist's eye.

"As I said, I don't know anybody of that name." Once again his eyes flickered to the left, something was very wrong.

He could feel himself just about to lose his temper when Westerman looked to the clerks left; directly behind the young man there was a mirror hung on the wall, through this he could see one or two of the other doorways that opened into the lobby; in one of these stood two men, by their unmistakeable clothing he could tell immediately that they were Wardens. They appeared to be deep in conversation and had not noticed the conversation he was having at the front desk.

"If you would come into the office sir, we can discuss your missing luggage," said Devin, emerging from behind the counter and taking Westerman by the elbow, leading him towards a nearby doorway.

They entered the room, the receptionist made a point of looking at the Wardens before he closed the door.

"I don't think that they paid you any attention," he said. Westerman gave him a puzzled look and asked.

"Why are you doing this?"

"Let's just say that in my job I meet all kinds of people; some I like and some I don't. I like you and I liked your girlfriend," Westerman could not help himself blushing slightly at the reference to Zalar, Devin continued, "and I definitely do not like these guys! Since they showed up there have been stories going around about some really weird shit happening."

"What stories?" Westerman was suddenly very interested in this subject.

"All kinds of stuff, people appearing out of thin air, some of the townsfolk's personalities have changed overnight and don't forget the comet."

"Comet, what about a comet?"

"You're definitely not from these parts are you? We've had a comet appear out of nowhere one night, the next it was gone; I've got friends who are into astronomy and they tell me that we should have been able to see a comet for days, in fact one of them told me that he saw it and it's tail was pointing in the wrong direction. Weird shit eh?"

Westerman nodded, all this did not sound good. The appearances could easily be attributed to the Wardens 'jumping' on to this world and the personality changes sound suspiciously like the side effect of the application of their control nanos. The comet was unconnected, he thought, with his lover's former employees; if it wasn't a comet what could it be? He arrived at the conclusion that this phenomenon was actually a spacecraft of some kind; if so easily visible from the ground it had to be massive. Realisation hit him like a thunderbolt.

"Calaxians!" he said aloud.

"Who, what?" asked Devin.

"What?" replied Westerman trying to feign ignorance.

"Oh come on. I'm not stupid, you said Calaxians. Who or what are Calaxians?" pressed the clerk.

Westerman looked at the young mans eyes, they were full of excitement, wonder and anticipation of the unexplained; he could see the young mans soul was crying out for enlightenment.

"What the hell. It's not like I'm bound by a Star Trek style non-interference directive," he said softly to himself.

"What?" Devin queried.

"It's like this son, I'm about to tell you a couple of things that may just make your day or ruin it."

The clerk eagerly nodded encouragement to Westerman.

"Do you ever hear stories about outer space and people from other worlds? We call it science fiction."

"Oh you mean bug-eyed monsters and all that crap, oh yeah."

Unconsciously Westerman paused for effect, looking seriously at Devin.

"Well they haven't got bug-eyes, but what I can tell you is that you are actually talking to a man from a planet called Earth, which is many light years from here."

Devin looked at Westerman open mouthed for many long seconds and then promptly broke into a giggling fit. Eventually after what seemed like an age he regained his composure to say.

"Oh I see! Why all the quaint disguises? I mean an alien that looks just like a man? What a load of absolute rubbish!"

"I look like you because I am a man, just not from this world. There are many humanoid races spread out across the galaxy," replied Westerman, he was beginning to lose his patience.

"That's the biggest load of crap that I have…"

The door to the room in which they stood violently burst open; the two Wardens charged through it, their thermal disruptors already drawn and ready to fire.

As it transpired, fortune played its part in this encounter with the Wardens. The room that Devin had taken Westerman into had just one entrance door and this was situated in a corner; this opened inwards and the door itself provided a means of reducing the visibility of the targets for the attacking pair. With the speed of thought, Westerman pulled Devin towards him and erected an invisible force wall between the Wardens and themselves.

Twin ruby red beams of agitated particles lanced out from the disruptors and impacted into the screen and resulted in a brilliant display of pyrotechnics.

"What the fuck is going on?" shouted Devin as the Wardens fired yet again.

Westerman could not help but note to himself that the translation nanos seemed to have no problem with the more colourful words but could not cope with food names; once again the aggressors fired pulling him back from his private reverie.

His eyes flashed; one of the robed men's head exploded like an over ripe melon. His eyes flashed again; the second assailant's chest erupted open and with a muffled scream he fell backward on to the floor.

"What the fuck is going on?" reiterated the young man as Westerman released his grip upon him.

Dissolving his force wall, the Earthman walked over and examined the dead Wardens bodies, he said.

"What is going on is the type of shit that only happens in your very worst nightmares." The clerk stood, open mouthed, looking at Westerman, who continued talking. "All I told you earlier is absolutely true. I am from another world and these two pieces of shit are from yet another one; we are aliens!" He looked hard at Devin, the young man seemed to be gasping for air and panic was about to take over his entire body.

"Come on Devin; keep it together. I need your help, Zalar needs your help; this is going to sound crazy but the entire planet needs your help," said Westerman soothingly. The receptionist appeared to be responding to his words as, eventually, after taking in many gulps of air he dragged his wild gaze away from the shattered bodies of the Wardens and said.

"How can I help?"

"Good man!" said Westerman laying a reassuring hand on Devin's shoulder; the young man flinched slightly at his touch, but then relaxed.

"I really need to find Zalar,"

"Is she an alien too?"

"I'm afraid not. She's got specialist knowledge about these guys and also the ones responsible for the comet." He was careful not to say too much about the Calaxians, a reptilian race could well have been one culture shock too many.

"She checked out like I said; a few weeks ago," said Devin

"I don't suppose that she said where she was going?"
"No, I'm sorry."

"Shit!" spat Westerman, disappointed.

"She did ask me to call a private hire ground car for her though." The young man suddenly recalled.

"Please tell me that you always use the same one?" pleaded Westerman.

"I do until somebody gives me a bigger commission," Devin beamed.

"Alright, come on, you've got to call me a cab."

"Of course sir, right away."

Rubbing his hands in triumph and with a broad smile across his face he accompanied the receptionist back into the lobby.

"Devin," he said and once he had his attention he continued, "I want you to get as far away from town as you can; something's happening and I would like to think that you will be safe, so please, get out of town."

After looking into Westerman's eyes, Devin realised the severity with which he should treat this warning; he nodded saying,

"I will. But there's just one more thing sir."

"What?"

"She's blond now."

Westerman looked puzzled for a second or two and then with sudden realisation he laughed and followed the clerk towards the hotel door.

Devin had taken Westerman to a small house just off the main street; there he had been introduced to Marok, a driver who had proceeded to haggle over the cost of the fare to a location in the nearby countryside. Thirty minutes later and the very same ground car that had carried Zalar to her parent's farm, was repeating the task for Westerman.

The wheels threw up clouds of dust behind the vehicle, which was illuminated by the red taillights, giving the illusion of the ground car being rocket powered. The road ahead was being lit by a pair of double, high intensity spotlights, which picked out the twists and imperfections in the country lane.

Inside the machine, Westerman's heart was racing like a steam engine; the nearer he got to where Zalar could be, the more anxious he became. Any attempts at conversation with the surly Marok had long since been abandoned, as a form of distraction from the journey he focused upon the problem of the star ship, which he was sure would be Calaxian, orbiting Bailon.

This proved to be a cul-de-sac as a line of thought, he simply did not have the knowledge of these creatures to formulate a strategy; he needed Zalar. Yet again his thoughts had returned to his beloved.

Presently, the driver steered the car into a small lane that eventually led to a collection of modest buildings; the vehicles lights illuminated one of the structures with a doorway built into it. Westerman paid the driver, who promptly raced away into the night, and made his way to the entrance.

He could feel the perspiration on the palms of his hands as he reached up and rapped his knuckles on the wooden panelling of the door. From inside he heard voices.

"Who could this be at this time of night?" asked a woman's voice.

"We aren't going to find out unless we open it are we," answered another person, this time male.

A small light came on above the doorway, leaving Westerman standing in the middle of a puddle of illumination, making him feel very exposed. The door opened and an elderly man stood before him.

"Can I help you?" he said in a rich, commanding voice.

"I certainly hope so. I'm looking for someone, a very good friend of mine; a woman called Za…" he stopped himself and corrected, "Tink-Bell."

"And you are?" the man enquired suspiciously.

"My name is Steve, Steve Westerman. As I said I am an old friend of Tink-Bell, I heard that she was staying here?"

Boochka continued his suspicious observation; suddenly a woman appeared and heaved him out of the way.

"Did you say that your name was Steve Westerman?" she said excitedly.

"Yes madam I did," Westerman replied with the most disarming smile he could muster.

"Come in, come in! I'll just go and get her."

The elderly woman grabbed Westerman by the arm and dragged him through the door; Boochka looked on with bemusement.

"You wait right here, I'll get her."

Damena was obviously enjoying every second of this particular scenario and with an almost infant-like giggle she crossed to the bottom of a wooden staircase and shouted.

"Tink-bell, Tink-bell honey, could you come down for a minute?"

Westerman was sure that his heart was going to burst through his rib cage; it was pounding so strong as he fought the urge to run up the stairs.

"I'm on my way," was the muffled reply.

He could hear Zalar's footfalls on the bare wooden steps as she descended and got nearer and nearer; he was holding his breath, convinced he was about to pass out. "What is it?" Zalar said as she came into view; her eyes caught sight of Westerman.

"Steve!" she cried and raced across the room, throwing herself around her lover's neck.

They held each other in an intense embrace, neither one daring to let go in case the object of their hopes and desires would suddenly evaporate. Zalar nuzzled into his neck and breathed,

"Don't ever leave me again."

He squeezed his eyes tight shut in a vain attempt to stem the involuntary stream of tears running down his face, stinging as they ran through the cut on his cheek. He said softly,

"Not on your life."

The couple finally disentangled themselves from each other; she raised her hand and gently traced the line of the angry looking wound along the side of his face.

"Does that hurt?"

He smiled and replied.

"Only when I laugh!"

She smiled back in response and he looked deeply into her eyes, he could feel himself falling into those limpid pools; abruptly he pulled her towards him, their lips met in a frantic passionate kiss.

A nervous cough finally broke their embrace; they both turned to see Boochka and Damena watching them, a knowing smile spread across their faces.

"I'm forgetting my manners, Boochka and Damena, this is Steve Westerman," said Zalar, her voice full of pride. Westerman stepped forward and automatically offered his hand to shake; after a few awkward seconds the older man realised that he should take the hand, this was not a form greeting he was familiar with, he relaxed as the younger man shook the connected hands, vigorously.

"I see that you know each other very well," he said releasing his grip and returning to his wife's side. Reddening slightly Westerman replied.

"You could say that."

"That cut looks nasty Steve, do you want me to look at it for you?" offered Damena

Zalar smoothly interjected.

"I've got a medical kit in my bag up stairs; I can take care of that, I'll just go get it."

She turned to go up the steps.

"Tink-Bell, why don't you take Steve upstairs with you; I'm sure that the two of you must have plenty to catch up on and you don't want a pair of old fuddy duddies cramping your style," suggested Damena. Boochka made a small movement as if to protest but was very quickly silenced by a sly dig in the ribs from his wife.

"If you don't mind?" said Zalar.

"No go ahead, we'll catch up on all the gossip in the morning," encourage the older woman.

Zalar led Westerman up the staircase as Boochka turned to Damena; all set to give his opinion on their last exchange and voice his displeasure at seeing the couple disappear upstairs. Damena placed a silencing finger on his lips and said.

"Remember when we were young and in love?"

She removed her finger and he nodded; smiling she reached up and placed a tender kiss on her husbands cheek.

Twenty minutes later Zalar removed the medical device from Steve's cheek and the cut had gone; in its place there was a very faint red line.

"That should disappear in a few days. At least I won't have to call you scar face," she joked. Smiling thinly with mock disapproval he replied,

"Blondie!"

"What do you think of it?" She wound strands of her hair around her finger, teasingly.

"It suits you. It looks good," he answered as he moved over to where she had just sat down.

"I thought I'd lost you Steve."

Her head drooped, her manner becoming suddenly darker. Placing a comforting arm around her and drawing her close he breathed softly to her,

"I'm here now, that's all that matters."

Suddenly standing up, wriggling from his grasp, she moved to the other side of the room, agitated, annoyed. "Where were you? Where did you go? I was out of my mind with worry."

"Easy," he said, "I was kidnapped by the Uniques." He offered his explanation holding up his hands in a defensive gesture.

"The Uniques, what do you mean?" She shook her head in a vain attempt to understand what Westerman was telling her.

"The Uniques, people with powers just like me; they live together in secret, hiding from the Wardens and just about every other race in the galaxy."

"I've heard of such gatherings but I always thought they were a myth. Where do they live?" she said having calmed down somewhat.

"I don't know its location in terms of special coordinates, but I could jump there if I needed to; it's an asteroid, a cloaked colony, they are so afraid they are completely paranoid and xenophobic."

"Do they all have special abilities like you?" Zalar said as she sat in a chair opposite him.

"They have gifts, but you should see what I can do now." He smiled cheekily, the skin around his freshly healed wound feeling tight and new.

"What can you do?" she said immediately curious; in reply she received an even cheekier grin.

Sitting on the end of the bed Westerman looked at Zalar, she was the most beautiful creature he had ever laid his eyes upon.

"Come on tell me," she implored, joining in with his infectious smile.

Concentrating on the simple shirt that she was wearing, Westerman reached out mentally and using his telekinetic ability he slowly undid her buttons.

"What the?" Zalar said as she sat bolt upright in her chair.

"Relax. I won't hurt you," he said soothingly.

She sat back, placed her arms by her side and looked down at the fastenings on her shirt as they magically undid themselves.

"Just relax, you may enjoy this," he added. She looked at him sheepishly as the last button of the garment unfastened and was then flung open by unseen hands to reveal her bare chest; he gasped as he looked at her beautifully formed body and mentally reached out, caressing her heaving breasts.

"Oh!" she sighed. Her nipples becoming hard and erect almost instantly; standing up she crossed the room towards him, he stood up, concentrating as he mentally continued his stroking and caressing. Removing his sweater he moved to meet her, they came together in a powerful embrace; their lips locked, tongues darting eagerly into each other's mouths.

Westerman could feel her moving her breasts, hard and firm against his chest, her movements frantic and powerful. Breaking away from their kiss for the briefest of moments, she said.

"Steve I've got to have you!"

They tore each other's remaining clothes off in a passion-fuelled frenzy and then became entwined in an unsophisticated, short-lived joining. Desire, frustration and raw sexual energy combined to produce almost simultaneous orgasms of seemingly epic proportions; they lay together afterwards on the bed for long minutes, their bodies locked together, kissing and caressing in mutual worship.

"I do love you so very much," breathed Zalar, her body warm and still moving rhythmically against him.

"I love you too my princess," he replied, she smiled and her embraced tightened even further.

"I hope we haven't upset the natives, I think we got pretty loud," he said as he allowed his hand to trace the curve of her spine from the nape of her neck to the small of her back, causing her to shiver with pleasure.

"I think we're safe, they live over in the other wing of the building and the walls are fairly thick," she whispered. "That's good," he said, "because I'm still raring to go." She smiled and gently pushed him over on to his back; running her hand gently down his chest, across his stomach and further down until she tenderly made contact with his still erect member, he gasped aloud.

"So I see," purred Zalar, "we had better do something about that."

Slowly, she started to kiss her way down his body, following the same path as her hand. Softly kissing across his stomach and running the tip of her tongue along the line of his hip bones; her hair occasionally brushing, tantalizingly against his manhood, sending thrills throughout his body causing him to breathe heavily and emit small moans of pleasure.

She moved slightly further down his body and the moist warmth of her mouth closed around the tip of his organ; he groaned and squirmed as the delight that was coursing through his body became almost too much. Knowing that this exquisite treatment would only bring about the inevitable too quickly, he gently, but firmly grabbed her and pulled her up and on to the top of him; she sat astride his groin and only with a minimum of resistance, he was inside her.

Zalar let out a whimper of satisfaction as she moved to ensure that she had the full extent of his attention; gently he pulled her head towards his and they locked into a deep hungry kiss and slowly they began to move against each other.

Westerman could feel the shudders of pleasure running through his beloved's body, her kisses becoming more and more eager; abruptly she sat upright, head thrown back, breath short and moans of delight involuntarily escaping from her.

He knew her moment was near, just as he could feel his own climax building; reaching up he softly cupped her breasts and brushed her nipples with his finger tips,

Zalar's movements became even more frantic, her ecstasy becoming so strong that it was almost painful. "Oh God!" she yelled as the wave of her orgasm broke over her; she tossed her head from side to side and leaning forward, grabbed Westerman by the shoulders, sinking her nails into his flesh.

The stimulation had now proved to be too much for him, his thrusts became stronger and stronger; she hung on to his bucking body, feeling his climax near as he grew even harder inside her. With a grunt of bestial pleasure he exploded; his whole body a quiver with delight and magnificent sensations, the intensity of his orgasm overwhelmed Zalar and triggered another beautifully violent wave of erotic sensations through her own body as she climaxed again.

As the feelings of pleasure slowly diminished within them she collapsed into his arms, she lay on top of him in a warm, glowing embrace.

They awoke from their exertion-induced slumber a couple of hours later and lay, holding each other in the half-light of the darkened bedroom.

"I love you," he said softly. She snuggled further into his arms and replied.

"I love you too," she placed a kiss on his cheek and continued, "Why can't it be like this all the time"

"I know what you mean; I suppose we should really discuss our little problems."

"You mean the Wardens and the Calaxians?" she suggested, the distaste tangible in her voice.

"The very same, plus one other."

"What's that?" said a puzzled Zalar.

"Boochka and Damena, are they your parents?"

He felt her body tense against him, the pregnant pause eventually being broken as she eventually said.

"Yes."

"There's no doubt?" probed Westerman.

"No doubt, I manage to get hold of a sample of blood from a knife that Damena cut herself on; I ran the DNA scan on the medical unit, she's definitely my mother."

"Are you going to tell them?" Another pause filled the air between them.

"I don't know," she said hesitantly, "what do you think I should do Steve?"

"The same answer I'm afraid, I don't know." He kissed the top of her head as an act of encouragement.

Abruptly she got up off the bed and went to a cupboard, Westerman admired her figure in the dim light as she retrieved an object from a bag she had produced; God she was beautiful he thought as he could feel himself beginning to stir again, but more important matters needed his consideration.

She returned to the bed and resumed her position beside him, in her hand a small rectangular box; the screen on one of the sides of the device came to life, and its eerie glow throwing oddly shaped shadows about the room.

"What's that?" he asked

"A scanner, I wanted to show you how one of our mutual friends is doing."

She adjusted the settings and the display showed the star ship hanging above the northern hemisphere of Bailon.

"The Calaxians?" posed Westerman.

"Yes. I must say that I am impressed that you knew about them being here. Is that another of your special powers?" she queried with a wry smile.

"Huh? Oh no. I heard about the comet and put two and two together, luckily I got four," he answered smiling.

"I'm afraid I'm a bit confused."

"Why's that?"

"They normally don't wait this long before attacking, I don't understand it." She frowned at the display, her features illuminated by the light from the screen; Westerman also studied it and said,

"Perhaps something has got them spooked?"

"Perhaps something has," replied Zalar as she turned to look nervously at him.

"What's the matter?"

"Steve, I'll be honest, these powers you have are pretty frightening, and I think there's more that you haven't shown me," she said, carefully avoiding his gaze.

Reaching over he gently turned her to face him, looking deeply into her yes he said.

"Zalar, it's still me, still the same Earthman you fell in love with; okay so I've got some special abilities that other people may not have got, but it's no different from one person being able to juggle and another not."

"How many other Earthmen can teleport themselves across interstellar distances or move objects just by the power of their minds?"

Probably nobody, but I'm still flesh and blood. I still love you," he said as he gently pulled her towards him. As if giving a mental shrug of helplessness, she let the scanner drop from her hands and slid her arms around his broad shoulders; yet again they blended together into another passionate kiss, once again Westerman could feel his loins stirring into action.

"Do you think that our enemies could wait until the morning to have our undivided attention?" he mused, softly breaking contact with her lips. Zalar, with her body pressed firmly against his had felt the manifestation of his desire; she looked back into his eyes and whispered. "I think that they will have to."

With that there was nothing left to say; they continued their kiss and started to explore each others bodies, their subsequent love making lasting well into the early hours of the Bailon morning.

CHAPTER FIFTEEN

The Calaxian second in command entered the star ship's control room and came to attention beside his superior officer. This was simple Calaxian etiquette in action; he knew that he would have to stand there motionless until the commander acknowledged him.

Risking a miniscule, quick, sideways glance he could see the aging officer busying himself studying the various displays, pretending that he had not noticed the younger creatures arrival; how he hated the older Calaxian. One day all this would be his, he could afford to bide his time; besides, he had already had one run in with the commander, a second could possibly lead to his death.

Eventually the object of his loathing settled back into his throne-like chair and, without turning to look at junior, said,

"Report!"

"All invasion preparations are finalised sir," his voice thick with mock respect and efficiency.

"Science Station, Quantum activity?"

"Negative sir," was the reply. Upon hearing this, the commander stood up from his post and walked over to the large monitor that showed the Bailon northern hemisphere; abruptly he turned and glared at his second in command.

"Commence the invasion cycle. Start planetary bombardment immediately."

"Sir!" barked the young officer, his serpentine eyes shone with a great fire of delight; bowing he turned and briskly exited the control room, his clawed feet clicking rapidly upon the metallic deck.

Returning his gaze to the main display, the commander stared intently. The feeling of dread had not diminished, in fact it had increased; it was tangible as an overwhelming feeling of disaster, which he fought to control in case his body gave an involuntary shudder that would have given away his concerns to the assembled bridge crew.

Zalar and Westerman awoke late that morning, their previous night's exertions having worn the pair of them out; but now washed and dressed; they made their way down the stairs to the kitchen area.

"Morning, sleepy heads," said Damena as she beamed a knowing smile at the couple, turning from the food preparation to greet them.

"Help yourselves to breakfast. You must be hungry?" she probed playfully. Zalar blushed heavily and Westerman let out a nervously, embarrassed cough.

"Sit down, a hot drink is on its way," Damena said over two steaming mugs of a local breakfast beverage; Westerman accepted one and took a tentative sip.

"Tea!" he exclaimed.

"What?" said Zalar.

"Its tea, or a least it taste like tea," he replied and took a longer drink followed by a loud satisfied sigh as he savoured the flavour. "The best brew I've had in months," he commented as he settled contentedly into his seat.

"I'm glad that you approve. That cuts healed nicely I see," observed Damena.

"Yes, she's quite the magician don't you think?" Westerman answered as he reached over and affectionately rubbed Zalar's back; in return, she smiled sweetly at him.

"You always say the sweetest thi…"

She was interrupted by a loud beeping noise, appearing to emanate for inside the jacket she was wearing; she looked Westerman straight in the eyes, the dread and near panic was all too evident on her features.

Pulling the source of the noise, the scanner, from her pocket, she deftly pressed a combination of buttons; the noise stopped. She read the display; the briefest hint of open panic crossed her beautiful features, looking up from the miniature screen she yelled.

"Incoming!"

Westerman reacted first; jumping to his feet, he bounded over to the puzzled looking Damena.

"Zalar, under the table quick!" he said as he grabbed the confused older woman and propelled her onto her knees and forced her under the table; Zalar had already scrambled below the sturdy piece of furniture.

Joining them, Westerman forced himself between the two women and placing his arms around them; he concentrated and mentally formed a hemisphere of telekinetic energy above them.

A split second later the light streaming through the windows suddenly increased in brightness by several orders of magnitude, the air became filled with a cacophony of sound. The blast wave came next; the floor undulated, violently; the concussion from the detonation struck soon after.

Pieces of mortar, glass, crockery and other assorted household items flew randomly in all directions; Westerman's shield held as the table was ripped away from above them. Damena screamed as she opened her eyes to see a massive section of the wall of her kitchen shatter into fragments and hurl itself across the room. Westerman concentrated as hard as he could on maintaining the integrity of his screen.

The continuous rumbling slowly abated and the whirlwind of destruction eased until, finally, an eerie silence descended onto the devastated room. Damena's screams had also reduced to a breathless whimper, a visibly shaking Zalar clung to Westerman; the clouds of dust were now settling, making the true extent of the damage very apparent.

An entire wall had been blow off the side to the house, the debris had scattered inwards; beams and other assorted pieces of timber had come to rest at awkward angles throughout the room. One such item, a roofing support which had a twenty centimetre square section had collapsed and now was only supported by his protective force field and lay directly above the trio; faint lines of force flickered along the contact area. Still concentrating to hold the shield together, Westerman barked a command at Zalar.

"Quick Zalar, get Damena out of the house! I don't know how long I can keep the screen in one piece."

Zalar looked up and the potentially fatal mass of debris above them registered.

"Shit!" she said as she scrambled into action, dragging the older woman away from Westerman's side and unceremoniously bungling her out of the wrecked building via the newly created hole in the wall.

With the women out of danger, Westerman concentrated harder still and forced the timber further into the air, the sound of groaning wood and brick filled the room; piles of rubble shifted uneasily.

Once he had lifted the object as high as he dare, he scrambled to his feet and out into the courtyard, behind him he heard the splintering crash of the beam, followed by an even bigger impact as a large section of the roof fell down.

As he stood in the swirling clouds of dust, the women shambled over to join him.

"My house!" wailed Damena, Zalar gently holding and supporting her, trying to stem the tide of tears and anguish swamping the woman.

"Damena, please listen to me. Where is Boochka?" Westerman said laying his hand on her trembling shoulder.

"He... he was working on the drainage in the south field," she sobbed in reply; suddenly realisation of the motive behind the young mans question hit her.

"Oh my God, Boochka, what will have happened to him?" Hysteria mounted within the woman, Zalar took hold of her shoulders, gently shaking her to attention. "Damena, listen to me. Damena, where is the south field? Please show us."

Through all her pent up emotions the older woman recognised that her two companions were trying to help, she raised her arm and pointed across the courtyard, towards the fields.

"Out there, by the rock outcrop on the side of that hill." Westerman and Zalar looked towards the feature she had identified.

"Oh my god," breathed Westerman as he saw on the distant horizon an object that struck terror into the fabric of his soul; a large mushroom shaped cloud boiled into the sky. "Nuclear weapon?" he continued, half to himself and half a question directed to Zalar.

"No not nuclear, they use mass drivers to fire pieces of interstellar debris they collect during their entry into a targets solar system."

"Mass driver, what's that?"

"It's a device that uses magnetic forces to accelerate objects up to massive velocities and direct it towards a target. They usually fire things like large meteors or small asteroids," explained Zalar.

"So the sheer velocity of the object translates the mass of the lump of rock into destructive energy?"

"Yes that's right, in some respects we are lucky that they use this method, with an atomic weapon we could be dying now from the radioactive fall out."

"Lucky! You call this lucky?" abruptly yelled Damena, "my home destroyed, I don't how my husband is. You call this lucky!" Zalar gently embraced the woman to comfort her.

"Definitely the Calaxians then?" asked Westerman. Zalar looked over towards him and gave a small nod of confirmation.

"That was Pizoka?" he said pointing towards the expanding cloud. With her eyes filling with tears Zalar once again nodded.

Suddenly a flash in the sky caught their attention; a ball of fire raced across the sky at enormous speed, a roar filled the air marking its passage. Within seconds the object had disappeared over the horizon and a split second later that section of sky brightened visibly, as if a second sun was rising; a few seconds later the ground lurched beneath them as they watched the growth of another mushroom cloud commence.

"Mintako," said Damena thinly, the two women clinging on to each other for mutual solace.

"Steve, please can you go and find Boochka?" said Zalar, the worry tangible in her voice. He reached over and squeezed her arm, smiled and then walked a few paces in the direction of the south field where Boochka had been working.

"I'll be as quick as I can," he shouted over his shoulder and then vanished in a flash of brilliant white light.

Witnessing this Damena struggled her way free of Zalar's comforting grip, staring wide-eyed at the young woman.

"Who, what are you people?" she yelled, her voice thick with confusion and fear. Helplessly Zalar offered her open hand saying.

"We're friends."

Westerman materialised beside the rocky outcrop Damena had pointed towards, he nervously began to survey the surrounding countryside for any sign of the elderly man. The field near where he was standing was used to grow a crop of what looked very much like Earth barley, however the blast wave had flattened practically the entire field leaving a haphazardly interwoven mat of stalks. Tentatively he stepped into the remains of the crop, it crunched and broke beneath his feet; looking about he walked along the edge of the area.

Presently he thought that he could see a red object about fifty metres away, quickening his pace he crossed over to it and discovered a small four-wheeled vehicle, obviously agricultural in design, half submerged in a sea of branches, stalks and various vegetation that had been swept up against it. Reaching down he could feel that the engine was still warm; he reasoned that this must belong to Boochka.

Climbing on to the footplate of the machine to gain a better view, he carefully scanned the surrounding area for any further signs of the man; he saw nothing as a sudden darkness descend across the field. Looking skyward he could see that the mushroom cloud of debris had now begun to obscure the sunlight.

A faint sound snapped his attention back to the field, coming from the other side of the vehicle he could hear a faint moaning; he rushed to the source of the noise. Westerman almost fell on Boochka as he nearly blundered into the drainage ditch that the old man had been working upon when the blast struck. A cover of assorted foliage had blown over the top of the channel, almost fully camouflaging the prone individual.

"Easy fella, I've got you," said Westerman as he cleared away the debris. The older man looked in a bit of a battered state, blood smeared his face and his clothes were ripped in several places.

"Boochka, can you hear me? Are you alright?" he shouted as he knelt beside the ditch and reached down; the sound of his voice seemed to rouse the injured man. "Wha… What happened?" he stammered.

"Don't worry about that, let's get you out of here," said Westerman as comfortingly as he could, "can you get up?"

With a variety of gasps and sighs Boochka, and Westerman's help, climbed up the side of the ditch.

"Where does it hurt?"

"All over," Boochka stated and then suddenly, with a look of panic, shouted," Damena!"

"She's okay, a little concerned for you, but okay."

"We have to get back to the house, I need to see her," said Boochka as he stumbled forward unsteadily on his feet.

"You're in no fit state to walk, and that vehicle looks like it will take hours to dig out."

"But we have to get back, Damena needs me," pleaded the old man.

"You're right," said Westerman as he abruptly stepped forward and put his arms around Boochka; they vanished in a flash of light.

Zalar was gently cleaning Damena's face with a small damp cloth she had retrieved from the devastation of the farmhouse, the old woman had calmed down somewhat from her earlier agitated state but now the culture shock was starting to set in.

"Who are you people, what's happening here?" she asked in subdued manner.

"Who we are is a bit more difficult to explain; what's going on is just a tiny bit easier," answered Zalar, "the

333

blasts that are now occurring at all the major towns all over your world are being caused by an extra-terrestrial agency that is going to invade Bailon."

"Extra-terrestrials. Aliens?" Damena's eye's widened in disbelief.

"Yes, they are called Calaxians. They actually come from another galaxy."

"Can't we reason with them? Can't we put a stop to this senseless destruction?"

"Talking is pointless; it's been tried before. The Calaxians do not negotiate, they invade, conquer and strip the planet of all its resources before they move off and find another world."

"My god, some scientists believe that there is life on other planets but I never expected to find out that it was true in my lifetime," said a suddenly very calm Damena. Zalar stood up and looked towards the horizon and the ominous shapes of the mushroom clouds.

"I think that is pretty conclusive proof, don't you?" she said, managing to produce an ironic, thin smile. Damena stood up and moved to Zalar's side.

"Can I ask you something?" Zalar turned to face her.

"Sure. I'll do my best to answer as best I can."

"Why does Steve call you Zalar?"

This was a question that she had not been expecting; she looked at the ground, tears started to roll down her face as she began to sob uncontrollably. Gently Damena placed her fingers underneath Zalar's chin and lifted her head up until she was face to face with her; she looked at the young woman's face, her cheeks lined with the tracks made by the tears and the dust.

"It's my real name; I'm Zalar," she eventually said. The older woman continued to look into her eyes, her own suddenly widening with stark comprehension.

"You don't mean?" she gasped, Zalar nodded and softly said.

"I'm Zalar; I'm your daughter."

Damena took an unsteady step backward as if she had been actually struck by a massive object; looking at the ground she shook her head in disbelief.

"No! You're not my daughter, my Zalar is dead!"

"I am your daughter. I was abducted by another race called the Wardens; they raised me as one of their own, wiped my memories, put microscopic machines inside my body to control me. Steve rescued me and when my memories started to return I came back home to look for you," said Zalar as she advanced toward Damena, who promptly took another step backwards.

"This can't be true, this can't be happening." her voice started to fill with panic.

"I'm so sorry. I know that it's hard to understand, to take in, but it's true I've even compared our genetic make up; there's no mistake. I am your daughter."

Damena stood for long seconds staring hard at Zalar; eventually she said.

"I thought that there was some thing strangely familiar about you," she paused and then continued, "I don't understand why, but with everything else that is going on, I think that I believe you."

Zalar took another step towards Damena and simply held out her arms; tears poured down her face as she simply said.

"Mother"

She stepped forward and threw her arms around the younger woman; they embraced, hardly daring to breathe in case the moment vanished as if it was all a dream.

"Oh my darling," whispered Damena as she too began to uncontrollably weep tears of joy.

Such was the intensity of their embrace that they failed to notice a brilliant flash of light and the subsequent materialisation of Westerman and Boochka; the older man wide eyed and fighting to get out of the younger one's clutches.

"What the hell is going on?" he spluttered as he stumbled backwards, landing unceremoniously in a cloud of dust on his backside.

Now aware of their presence, Damena ran over and knelt beside her battered husband and threw her arms around him.

"Thank God you're okay," she said.

"Okay? What the bloody hell is going on here?" gasped Boochka, plainly struggling to comprehend the recent events.

"You are not going to believe it," said Damena.

"No shit!" he simply stated.

Over the next couple of hours, Damena tended to the, what turned out to be, superficial wounds on Boochka; Westerman and Zalar had purposely left the elderly couple alone to try and come to terms with all the new information that had been thrust upon them.

"You told Damena then?" said Westerman as they sat on a low wall watching the couple.

"Yes, I think that she took it well."

"A bad day to bury good news eh?" he joked with a smile. She smiled back and replied.

"Speaking of news; what are we going to do about the Calaxians?" Westerman frowned and looked at his hands.

"How long before they start to land?"

"It's normally about a couple of days, a day after the bombardment has been completed."

"I feel so helpless. I want to jump into that mother ship and blow the bastards to bits, but I don't know where it is, or how far away it is; I can't jump to it." He drove his fist into his palm in abject frustration.

"What do you mean?" asked Zalar trying to understand his angst.

"The Wardens gave me all their jump termini coordinates so I can use them to travel between worlds, I can also jump to places that I can physically see and as a final party piece I can also go to any place that I have physically stood at; I don't understand how but my brain logs the coordinates or something. But I can't jump to a new place that I can't see." he explained.

"I could supply you with the location of the Calaxian ship from my hand scanner."

"Sorry my love but all you could supply me with is a set of numbers and they would mean absolutely nothing to me at all, my subconscious would not register them; it would be meaningless gibberish."

"Oh," said Zalar suddenly deflated.

"Don't worry darling," he said laying his hand on her arm, "we'll think of something." He reached over a placed a small tender kiss on her cheek.

"Zalar?" said Boochka as he walked towards the couple, taking them by surprise; Zalar stood up and moved to meet him.

"Damena's been telling me one or two things," his strong voice trailing off in a wave of sudden helplessness.

"I know it's a massive amount to take in, but I'm afraid that it is all true," she said laying her hand gently upon his arm.

"It' all true?" he said looking into her eyes, his own full of tears.

"Yes it is daddy," she replied and flung her arms around the old mans broad shoulders, his own arms encircled her as he sobbed loudly with joy.

"Oh my little Zalar; I always knew that I would see you again. We went through all the motions, but deep down we both hoped and prayed that we would see you again."

Zalar had also begun to sob within the embrace; Damena now joined them to complete the family reunion, Westerman looked on with his eyes misting over as he was overwhelmed by the sight of unbridled joy amidst all the chaos and destruction; some joy could be found in the sadness.

After a respectful period he cleared his throat loudly to get their attention.

"I'm sorry to break up the party but we need to discuss what we are going to do about our friends," he said, pointing skywards.

"What can we do?" observed Boochka; Westerman nodded and replied,

"Not a great deal from down here, I need to get up to that ship."

"Can't you just vanish and reappear up there?" asked Damena.

"It doesn't work like that unfortunately mum," said Zalar, the two women exchanged a beaming smile between them as they both took pleasure from the use of the affectionate term.

"Yes, I'm afraid that it doesn't; I need to be able to see the ship with my own eyes and know the layout of the inside to get in there," he paused for thought and then continued, "Zalar do you have any schematics of the Calaxian ship or know where we can lay our hands on some?"

"I don't think that it is on this scanner," she said retrieving the device from her coat pocket and studying it for a few seconds. "There could be something on the general database machine in my kit bag. I'll go and get it." She moved off towards the partially destroyed house

"Be careful in there; it looks like it could collapse any minute," warned Westerman.

"I'll go with you," boomed Boochka, "It's been a good old house; she won't let us down now." The pair of them entered the ruin and very quickly disappeared from view. Damena approached Westerman.

"How are you son?" she asked with a voice full of warmth and tenderness.

"Okay I suppose. It's funny how quickly you can get used to things, the weird things I mean," he mused.

"Well we have a great debt of gratitude to you Steve; you brought our daughter home to us." The woman looked troubled to Westerman.

"What is it Damena?" he gently prompted.

"Are you an alien?" she asked in a barely audible whisper.

"I suppose that technically I am; I do come from another planet, Earth, a very long way from here. However, I understand physically I am no different from any other male inhabitant of Bailon."

"You've been travelling about space for a long time then?" she probed, awkwardly.

"Oh no, I'm a newcomer to this game; the wrong place at the wrong time I'm afraid."

"If Zalar believes in you, and that's good enough for me," she proclaimed and softly laid a calming hand on his arm.

"Thanks," he beamed and looked up to see Zalar and Boochka emerging from the ruined house, swinging by its straps in her hand was a rucksack.

"Got it, now we can see what is what," she said as she fished a small device from inside the bag. Her slim fingers danced over the machines controls and presently she handed it to Westerman, saying,

"That display shows all the main operational areas of the Calaxian star ships."

"What about all the big unlabelled areas?" he asked as he studied the miniature screen.

"Oh those are the living areas where the Calaxians sleep, play and so on. From what the Wardens know they are tailored to the individual crew's needs; a sort of home from home."

"I've identified the control room, how convenient for them to site it at the nose of the craft," he observed with more than a touch of irony in his voice.

Boochka, along with Damena, joined the younger couple, shaking his head.

"Does all this help us in any way?" he said. Westerman glanced at Zalar who returned the compliment nervously.

"Partly; If I could get near enough to actually see and identify a section of the hull, I could 'jump' on board," said Westerman.

"There's a really big but here though isn't there?" said Damena, Zalar slowly nodded her head.

"We have to be able to physically see the location of the ship to be able to travel to a position near enough to make the more accurate final jump," she explained.

"There's an even more basic problem, the first leg of the journey would be into outer space, so we would need space suits," interjected Westerman.

"Could you create a force field bubble, trapping the air until we got on board?" suggested Zalar.

"I don't really want to go down that route; you see I'm not sure if I can jump and maintain the screen, you've seen how much strength the teleportation takes out of me; remember on the ring when the ability left me? It was simple exhaustion."

"That's it the ring!" yelled a triumphant Zalar.

"What? The ring was destroyed," he replied.

"I know but there are other Warden ring stations out there, spread across the galaxy."

"And?" said a totally perplexed Westerman.

"Those rings all have storerooms on them, storerooms full of specialist equipment; space suits for example."

"Oh, I see!" he proclaimed with sudden comprehension, and continued, "so your plan is to travel to one of the stations, battle our way to a storeroom, collect the kit and then bring it back here?"

"Yes that's the idea, simple eh?" she grinned at her three companions.

"Oh yes, simple! Remember you got shot last time we tackled the Wardens, I don't want to lose you again; not for good especially."

Zalar smiled and moved closer to Westerman and planted a kiss on his lips.

"They won't be expecting anyone to do something as stupid as this, are they? Any how, I've got you to protect me now, haven't I?"

"Well seeing as you've got this all worked out, who am I to argue?" he shrugged helplessly.

"That's why I love you," she said and then suddenly became deep in thought.

"What's up now?" probed Westerman.

"I think I may just have come up with a brilliant idea for how we can get near to the Calaxian ship with the first jump," she said brightly.

"Now this is why I love you," stated Westerman closing upon her; soon they were in each other's warm embrace.

Boochka then turned to Damena and said. "If these two ever get around to leaving each other alone for a few minutes we could actually have a chance."

"You think? So you understood all that stuff about 'rings' and 'spacesuits' did you?" she asked. Boochka shrugged helplessly. "That's what I thought," she commented and turned her attention back to the cuddling couple.

Forty-five minutes later, Westerman and Zalar were saying their goodbyes in the dull light of the Bailon Sun as its rays battled their way through the dust that was now heavy in the atmosphere as a result of the Calaxian bombardment.

Damena was hugging Zalar, protectively; Boochka also had a defensive hand laid on the young woman's shoulder.

"Be careful my darling. Please come back to us," said the all too visibly distraught woman.

"Yeah, make sure that you come back, after all we don't want to lose you again," Boochka commented as Westerman walked over to the trio.

"I hate to be a kill joy but we really should be going; we've got to get on board that star ship before the landing craft are launched," he said, his voice laced with the regret he was feeling at having to take Zalar away from her parents.

"Please take care of our daughter Steve," entreated the tearful Damena.

"I will," replied Westerman as finally, with obvious regret, Zalar disengaged herself and stood by his side.

"And you look after yourself," added Boochka. Westerman smiled as he gave the old man the 'thumbs up' sign and turned to face Zalar.

"Well I'm ready. You're driving remember?"

Nodding, Zalar produced her jump engine and started to enter the destination coordinates.

"I've chosen ring station eight as our target, it's on the other side of the galaxy from the one we destroyed; I'm hoping that due to the distance involved they won't be expecting us there."

Westerman smiled encouragement and she closed her arms around his neck as she turned to look at her parents.

"If we don't get back before the invasion starts, grab what you can carry and head up into the hills; keep as far away as you can away from any town, village or any population centre." She could feel her eyes misting over again; she took a deep breath and said,

"I love you."

The couple smiled thinly back to her as they clung together for mutual comfort; tears streamed down Damena's face, Boochka's eyes were clearly watering as well.

With a final smile Zalar pressed the activation button and, together with Westerman, she disappeared in a flash of brilliant white light; the spectators to their departure continued to hold their embrace of mutual support for long minutes afterwards.

Tak-Foi-Cho hated the graveyard shift and to cap it all off he had also been lumbered with the routine maintenance of the 'jump' room; not that this was a particularly difficult task, there was actually very few moving parts in the teleportation related machinery. However on some occasions an incoming traveller would arrive a little 'hot', especially if a great distance had been covered and the heat generated is dissipated via massive heat exchangers, it was these devices that required regular attention.

He had only been a fully-fledged Warden for just over a solar year and yet he yearned to be out hopping across the galaxy, fighting the Calaxians or even better still tracking down the renegade Steve Westerman and the traitor Zalar. Like most humanoid civilisations bad news would spread quickly and the story of the destruction of the ring station had proved to be no exception to this universal constant. Every outpost knew of the evil Westerman and how he had used his powers to turn the head of the young Warden woman; it was even rumoured that various sexually based techniques had been employed in her coercion.

Tak-Foi-Cho had very easily been able to apply his own mental interpretation of this story; he had seen images of Zalar, she was beautiful; it had fired a secret fantasy that he would be the one to free her from Westerman's evil clutches, and in return for this service she would be eternally grateful to him; granting him anything in return. The potentially uncomfortable swelling now starting in his uniform brought him back to the real world from his fantasy, after all he thought to himself, he would never get very far in the ranks of the Wardens if he was discovered masturbating on duty. He smiled to himself and turned his wandering attention back to the machinery.

He heard the unmistakable 'click' of one of the reception relays operate; turning around he looked at a panel, which was set into the base of the 'landing' platform, he could immediately see from the sequence of displayed lights that there was a traveller inbound. Hastily closing the inspection cover he had been using, he stepped back from the platform.

Seconds later a blinding flash of light announced the arrival; his eyes adjusted to the changes in illumination within the room; a man and woman stood on the pad. The woman disentangled herself from the man's neck and turned to face Tak-Foi-Cho.

He looked at her, she was a tall, attractive blonde haired woman; her features looked familiar, he froze and shouted.

"My God, It's Zalar!"

Despite his inexperience the youth was quick and alert; he produced a thermal disruptor from beneath his robe and brought the weapon to bear, all erotic thoughts had disappeared from his mind to be replaced by murderous ones. He fired; Westerman stepped between the Warden and Zalar; he held out his hand, palm-facing Tak-Foi-Cho.

The ruby red beam of tortured particles stopped a metre short of its intended target; jagged bolts of energy erupted from the impact point on Westerman's telekinetic screen.

The young Warden ceased firing and was struck by a wave of abject panic and self-preservation, he turned and ran towards the doorway; Zalar drew her own weapon and prepared to fire.

"It's okay, I've got this!" Westerman said as he made a fist with his other hand and thrust it towards the fleeing man. Abruptly the Warden was plucked from his feet and flung against the unforgiving opposite corridor wall; the audible crunch of fracturing bones could clearly be heard from the impact, Tak-Foi-Cho slid into an unceremonious heap on the floor.

"Whoops. I think that I may have done that a little too hard," said Westerman. Zalar gave him a knowing look and moved to check the condition of the young

Warden; the corridor was clear as she proceeded to drag their victim back into the reception room.

"Is he dead?" asked Westerman.

Zalar nodded towards the smeared trail of blood that marked the path of the Wardens progress across the corridor.

"What do you think?" she replied as she rolled the body over to reveal the bloody, gory mess of his face; his eyes wide open staring lifelessly at the ceiling.

"Damn! I killed him and I only wanted to knock him out," he commented.

"Don't be too hard on yourself, I was going to blow the little bastards head off!" Zalar spat as she stood up and faced Westerman.

"You're really quite scary sometimes aren't you?" he mocked. Zalar smiled and said,

"Come on let's find the storeroom we need."

After stowing the Wardens body behind a removable wall panel inside the reception room, they cautiously made their way out into the corridor.

They walked for about thirty minutes before they arrived outside an innocuous looking doorway.

"I think that this is the environmental suit store," said Zalar as she moved towards the entrance. "Open!"

she stated in a loud clear voice. In almost immediate response the door opened and they entered.

"Lights!" was the next command to be issued. The room became illuminated revealing rows and rows of suits, each one having a helmet with a faceplate of reflective glass; the entire scene looked like a macabre butchers shop filled with racks of motionless pale beige bodies possessing a single shining eye.

"Which one is my size?" asked Westerman as he examined the nearest suit.

"It's a one size fits all situation, the only difference is that the ones on the left-hand side are male and the right-hand side's female," answered Zalar as she selected one of the garments.

"What's the difference?" posed Westerman, as he looked even closer.

"The plumbing, trust me you don't want to get the wrong one."

"Oh!" he said as he understood the reference and removed a male version from its hanger.

The unit was a great deal lighter than he had expected, the heaviest section appearing to be the large helmet assembly.

"Is this it?" No back pack?" he asked, carefully folding the suit to allow easier carriage.

"No back pack. These are environmental suits, designed for short exposure to space or any other harmful situation, they actually could be called or classified as escape suits," she replied.

"One very obvious question, how much air does this thing hold?" he looked nervously over at Zalar.

"More than you would think, if the conditions are right and the purifiers are working at optimum capacity it will supply you with breathable air for up to forty-eight hours."

Westerman gave an appreciative whistle as he returned his attention to the garment. It appeared to be made of a heavy, rubberised canvas, the thought of something so flimsy being able to protect him from the lethal environment of space was hard to swallow. Still he trusted Zalar completely, so he hoisted the bundle over his shoulder and having done the same with her burden, Zalar followed him out of the door into the corridor.

"What now?" he asked.

"We need to find the heavy weapon armoury," she answered looking up and down the slightly upward curving decks.

"Lost?" he said with a hint of sarcasm; she flashed a dismissive glare back at him and crossed to the opposite wall.

"Heavy armoury!" she commanded, loud and clear.

As on the previous ring, a path of lights appeared along the wall to guide them.

"Easy when you know how," Westerman quipped.

At that very moment a sirens wail pierced the silence of the corridor.

"Shit," breathed Zalar, "Intruder alert."

"Do you think they found the body?"

"No it's been too quick, shit, shit!" she exclaimed.

"What's wrong?"

"How could I have been so stupid? They must have tied voice recognition into the guide programs; it must have identified my voice on the direction request as an unrecognised pattern," she explained.

"No not unrecognised; you were a Warden, it won't have been erased, they've flagged your voice to raise the alarm," he commented with an air of absolute conviction. "We need to get going; they will pin-point our position within seconds!" she yelled over her shoulder as she started a steady trot along the corridor in the direction indicated by the moving wall lights.

"Here we go again," said Westerman under his breath as he set off in pursuit of her.

It was nearly fifteen minutes later that they encountered their first resistance; two Wardens erupted from a doorway and discharged their weapon. Westerman had been prepared for such an eventuality and whilst they had been running along the corridor he had maintained a three-metre square force screen, both in front of and behind them, as they ran.

The twin beams of highly energetic particles impacted upon the force field, throwing lurid violet sparks in every direction, their points of contact just a few centimetres short of his chest and Zalar's face.

She raised her own disruptor and prepared to return fire, she was too late; Westerman's eyes flashed twice. One of the Wardens fell to his knees clutching helplessly at the gaping hole that had appeared in his chest; the other unfortunate fell over backwards, his head completely disintegrated.

"What the?" said Zalar glancing sharply towards Westerman.

"Another gift I'm afraid," he offered sheepishly.

"How many more have you got?" she said with a nervous smile.

"You're okay, that's the lot. I think?" he replied, embarrassment heavy in his voice.

"I fell in love with a simple human who then goes and turns into a superman before my eyes," she remarked to herself, shaking her head.

"You still love me then?" he mocked. Smiling back she brushed her hair away from her face and said.

"Oh, it may take more than a few gifts to put me off."

He smiled as he moved nearer and laid a comforting hand on her back.

"Come on, I think that we should pick up the pace a little," he said as they started to run along the corridor again.

They met no further resistance until they had almost reached the armoury; once again a pair of Wardens leapt from a doorway and fired at them. On this occasion however, one of their attackers was carrying one of the newer, more powerful weapons, the type that Westerman had favoured.

The bolt of charged plasma struck the defensive shield creating an effect that was totally different from the standard thermal disruptor. Faced with so much energy the blast could not be dissipated into the surrounding atmosphere; the entire force screen flexed like a massive sheet of invisible rubber, Westerman was lifted off his feet and hurled backwards, coming to rest a good three metres away. The concussion had knocked the very breath out of his lungs; he laid helplessly on his back gasping for air.

The unforeseen effect of the two titanic energies colliding had taken the Wardens by surprise also, Zalar seized upon this opportunity and fired her weapon twice; both shots struck their respective targets and both of the robed figures fell to the floor, both dead with large smouldering holes in their chests.

"Are you okay Steve?" yelled Zalar as she rushed to his side.

"I… I think so," he gasped.

"Well it looked pretty spectacular," she smiled as she bent over him.

"Unexpected, I'll give you that one," he observed as, with her help, he clambered to his feet.

"Your screen still saved you though," she offered as she held his upper arm to steady him.

"Yeah, but I wouldn't like to do that one very often."

"Are you sure you're okay?" she pressed.

"I'll be fine," he said as reassuringly as he could, retrieving his dropped space suit, "where's the armoury," he continued in an attempt to deflect some of Zalar's concerns.

"Just ahead, I can see it highlighted by the guide program."

"Good, all this running is wearing me out," he said with a smile.

At that moment another Warden burst from a doorway just in front of them, his disruptor raised.

"Oh do fuck off!" shouted Westerman; the air filled with a high-pitched scream and a pair of incandescent beams erupted from his eyes. The attacker exploded into small gory fragments, spraying a film of red slime over the nearby corridor wall.

"Steve!" said Zalar in disbelief.

"Sorry, I didn't have time to control the power of the blast," he said with the demeanour of a naughty schoolboy. She shook her head and walked towards the armoury door; Westerman shrugged and trotted over to her side.

"One problem," she said, deep in thought.

"Isn't there always?"

"This door will now have a defence screen," she nodded towards the entrance and bent down to pick up the dead Warden's discarded weapon. She threw the disruptor under-hand at the door; the device seemed to stop in mid-air and then crumple into a ball of sparks, flame and debris.

Westerman whistled, Zalar looked at him and nodded.

"How do we get around this one?" he asked.

"I'm not sure. I don't think that you can do the 'jumping in' trick; this room will be full of narrow aisles and racking," she replied thoughtfully.

"I don't want to appear in the middle of something," he agreed.

"We've got to do something pretty quick, I would imagine that there will be dozens of Wardens on their way as we speak."

Westerman thought for a short while and then with a sudden decisive flash of inspiration, he said.

"I've got an idea. Keep a look out for trouble; what I am going to do will take all of my concentration."

Nodding, Zalar checked the settings on her disruptor and moved to stand vigil in the middle of the corridor.

Facing the door, Westerman extended his arms and started to mentally create a cone of force as he had done previously on the Unique settlement; he drove the point hard into the entrance's force field, sparks and sheets of electric blue flame radiated from the point of contact.

He applied more pressure and his telekinetic energy bit deeper into the shield, an audible hum began to resonate up and down the corridor; the same hum increased in volume at an exponential rate and soon rivalled the wailing of the intruder alarm, still echoing around the inside of the ring.

The circuits and controlling programs for the doors security systems detected the power drain in the shield being caused by Westerman's assault and compensated by ploughing even more energy into the screen generators. Sweat visible on his brow, his eyes closed tight in total concentration, Westerman leaned further into the field;

a new, greater intensity of pyrotechnics burst from the contact point.

On the surface of the shield a halo of bright red light approximately twenty centimetres in diameter was clearly visible with flashes of ultraviolet light emanating from its outer edge; the central null area was growing, very slowly, but growing. The loud humming had now become a deafening shriek, Zalar briefly interrupted her sentry duties to look at Westerman; his back was towards her but she saw that his outstretched arms and shoulders shook with the sustained effort, his silhouette framed by flashing, pulsating light generated by his struggle against the shield. Something attracted her attention off to her right.

A flash of light heralded the materialisation of a group of six Wardens; she spun around to bring her weapon to bear. Unfortunately, the would-be attackers had not given any consideration of their orientation with regard to their targets in their haste to 'jump' into the fray; they had appeared with their backs towards Zalar and now had to turn around to fire. This presented the woman with valuable split seconds of opportunity, giving her the time needed to send several beams of death into the groups midst.

Four of the Wardens were dispatched immediately, their inert bodies nearly burnt in two falling heavily to the floor. One of the survivors threw himself clear and fired his weapon in Zalar's general direction; the ruby red beam splashed harmlessly against the corridor wall a full metre wide of its intended mark. Once again Zalar fired; one more Warden fell to his knees with a smoking hole through his chest; the sole surviving attacker produced a jump device from under his robe and promptly vanished from the conflict to an unknown location.

The tortured sound of the overloading generators was now at a deafening pitch and volume; the hole in the shield had grown to half of a metre in diameter, the remainder of the screen awash with an angry looking bright red glow. Westerman gathered what remaining strength he had and with a supreme effort he pushed the cone of telekinetic force as hard as he could.

Flames and debris flew from various sections of the wall surrounding the armoury door; the sound abruptly ceased as the security field evaporated; Westerman sagged forward, his arms burning with fatigue.

"Jesus! That took some effort," he cried as he shifted his weight back to steady himself.

"You did it!" shouted Zalar as she moved to his side, he smiled thinly back at her, nodding.

"Open!" she commanded. The door stayed resolutely closed.

"The mechanism is probably fried," she offered looking around, "What we need is another key."

Crossing to the smouldering heap of bodies she retrieved one of the newer style plasma disruptors from a dead Warden; returning she smiled and said to Westerman.

"This should do the trick."

The door exploded in tiny fragments as the weapons bolt of energy struck it; when the dust and smoke had cleared their way was very clearly no longer barred.

"You get scarier," said Westerman playfully.

"I've got a good teacher," she retorted as she winked and led the way into the Armoury.

Westerman stood guard by the door as Zalar moved up and down the racks of equipment; to the casual observer this room could have been in any storeroom of any factory on Earth, rectangular boxes of varying dimensions were stack innocuously on the shelves. Eventually finding what she was after she shouted,

"Steve, this is what I came for. Can you give me a hand?"

He joined her and she pointed to a crate constructed from a plastic material, it was roughly two metres long and half a metre square.

"What is it?" Westerman asked. Zalar simply smiled and tapped her forefinger on the side of her nose.

"Wait and see. It's a surprise," she purred. Looking around at the boxes of machinery, he said.

"This may be a daft question, but this is supposed to be a heavy weapons store, do we have any bombs in here?"

"How big and what type?" she replied making an expansive gesture.

"Very big and very dirty," he leered menacingly.

Zalar looked around for a few moments and then went over to a metre square plastic crate.

"Ten megatons and nuclear?" she breathed seductively to him.

"I take it we are singing from the same hymn sheet on this one," he remarked casually, however this was greeted with a puzzled look.

"Sorry, I don't understand you Steve," she said.

"Sorry my darling, it was an Earth saying. I meant to say we have got the same idea," he corrected as he mockingly raised his eyebrows skyward.

"Oh, I see," she realised enthusiastically.

"Can we set it off okay?"

"Should be able to; the activation circuits are pretty straight forward and self contained."

With that she unfastened the lid of the crate and proceeded to press a sequence of buttons on the device inside.

Westerman looked on in awe and admiration; her slim, shapely figure bent provocatively over the bomb to allow her maximum access to the controls.

"If this is a dream, I hope I never wake up from it," he said softly to himself. He allowed his gaze to linger on her backside for a while and then snapped his attention back to the job in hand, after all this was not the time or place and he could feel he was becoming aroused by the sight of his beloved's beautiful body.

A beam of tortured particles lanced past his head and struck the nearby racking; Westerman spun around to see a lone Warden standing in the doorway, his weapon ready to fire again. With a reflex defensive action he formed a force field in front of his weapon; it fired and the disruptors discharge reflected back off the telekinetic energy screen. The Warden screamed as his tunic burst into flames; Westerman's eyes flashed twice and the attackers chest exploded, the corpse then falling into a heap of burning flesh and clothing.

"Don't ever talk to me about being scary," quipped Zalar, he smiled back to her sourly.

"Are we all up and running?" he asked.

"Two minute countdown awaiting activation sir!" she barked whilst performing a mock salute.

"Can they deactivate the bomb after the countdown has started?"

"Not a chance," she beamed in answer.

"Okay let's get this crate of yours and scram." He walked over and grasped one of the carrying handles attached to the box; whatever was inside was not as heavy as he had anticipated, and with minimal effort he dragged it into the aisle.

"I think that we should stand it on its end so that we can put our arms around it for the jump," said Zalar, and with a nod from Westerman they lifted the crate into a vertical position.

"Are you going to do the honours Zalar?" he said gesturing regally towards the bomb.

"It would be my pleasure," she replied and reached into the open case. Combinations of switches were operated and a low, powerful sounding hum started emanating from the device.

"Right, take us back home please Steve," she said, wrapping her arms around the erect packing case; her space suit draped over her shoulder. After giving a brief nod of acknowledgement, Westerman copied Zalar's stance and pressed himself against the opposite side of the box; he reached around and interlocked his arms with hers.

He realised at that moment why the responsibility for the trip back to Bailon was his, Zalar had only the coordinates for the regular landing site programmed into her jump engine; Westerman had physically stood in the courtyard of Boochka and Damena's farmstead. He closed his eyes and concentrated on the target location, he felt the power of the jump building up inside him; the hum from the nuclear device continued to build towards its catastrophic crescendo, he gently squeezed Zalar's arm to offer reassurance as they vanished in a brilliant flash of white light.

The illumination of their departure had barely faded as a trio of Wardens burst through the destroyed doorway; they fired wildly, their beams carving the air of the unoccupied armoury.

"They've gone," said one of them.

"I wonder what they wanted in here?" posed another.

The third Warden held up his hand to silence his comrades; they all stood in silence and listened.

"What's that humming sound?" he asked.

In horror they all simultaneously identified the source of the noise, in vain they reached for their jump engines;

it was too late, critical mass was achieved and the nuclear warhead detonated instantly vaporising them.

The ball of boiling plasma continued to expand, even the exotic material of the ring station's construction, which had endured countless years in space, yielded under the assault of such concentrated titanic forces; its integrity failed. A section of the station blew into fragments, the rest of the structure contorted into unfeasibly complex shapes and started to break apart; finally with the magnetic containment fields gone, the mini-sun being held at the centre of the rapidly disintegrating ring, flared into a miniature supernova; anything within a five million cubic kilometre area was destroyed by either impact with the debris or exposure to high energy particles.

CHAPTER SIXTEEN

Westerman and Zalar materialised in the customary flash of light in the dead centre of the area immediately outside of her parents homestead. The light from their 'jump' receded and the darkness of the Bailon night closed in upon the travellers, their precious cargo stood like a dark grey monolith in their grasp.

The arrival had brought Boochka and Damena out from their place of shelter, inside one of the nearby farm buildings; they approached holding crude oil burning lamps in their hands.

"Zalar, are you all right?" asked Westerman as he extricated his hands and arms from her grasp.

"Yes, yes," she replied as she remembered to start breathing again.

"Zalar, Steve. Are you both okay?" said Damena, who continued, "We didn't know how long you were going to be."

"We're fine," said Zalar who then ran to meet the couple and hugged them warmly in turn.

"What's with the oil lamps?" queried Westerman nodding towards the poor source of illumination.

"Power grids gone. So have the communications and imager system," said Boochka gravely.

"Standard Calaxian assault tactics. Knock out the power and communications; it makes things easier for them when they land," Zalar stated.

"Talking of all things related to invasions, how long before they start thinking about planet fall?" asked Westerman as he looked up into the clear night sky.

Zalar produced her hand scanner and began to configure the device to the correct mode.

"Uh oh!" she said.

"That doesn't sound very promising my dear," observed Damena.

"The mother ship is nearly back into geo-stationary polar position; they will launch the landing craft within hours of achieving that orbit," Zalar stated in a very serious way. "We have to stop them before they launch, once down here on the surface they will be too spread out; we won't be able to stop them," Westerman stated with a stony face.

"What's in the box?" asked Boochka in an effort to lighten the mood.

"Ah! The answer to our prayers," smiled Zalar, her eyes sparkling in the lamplight.

"What?" said Boochka looking at Westerman.

"Don't ask me, this is all your daughters' idea," he answered nodding in her general direction and adding a shrug.

"Give me a hand Steve," Zalar said, suddenly very animated.

Under her guidance they manhandled the crate into the furthest corner of the yard, laying it down with the clearly marked lid pointing upwards; Damena and her husband had moved closer to watch in silent bemusement. Zalar reached down and pressed a sequence of buttons upon a panel on the box.

"Stand back!" she yelled as she shepherded her companions to a safe distance from the device.

For long seconds nothing happened; suddenly the lid rose up at one end and folded back upon itself, the sides them flopped to the ground raising small clouds of dust. The machinery inside the case had been revealed and whilst most of the mechanism was clearly alien to Westerman, he immediately recognised a lethal looking one and a half metre long dart-like missile nestling in the middle of the package.

"Now that looks interesting," he mused.

The equipment continued to hypnotically unpack itself; control panels unfurled, support struts extended and various lights started to wink on and off. After a matter of a few short minutes the package had resolved into a launching station for the enclosed projectile; a barely audible hum had begun, hinting at the potential power of the weapon.

"I'm impressed darling," Westerman commented.

"Well what do you get the man who has everything?" chirped Zalar.

"What good is that little thing going to do against the massive ship in orbit?" asked Boochka. Westerman cocked an eyebrow towards Zalar and added,

"He has a point. My first concern is that it is not big enough to reach the altitude needed, let alone the payload necessary to destroy a Calaxian star ship."

The knowledgeable grin on Zalar's face widened even further as she motioned her audience to move nearer to the device. It sat, a mixture of dull silver metal and shiny hydraulic struts, in its own pool of illumination; the young woman laid her hand upon the cool metal of the nose cone of the missile proudly and said.

"Mum, Dad, Steve; I'd like to introduce you to the Zoltar class surface to orbit missile. It has a range of just over ten thousand kilometres and the destructive power of ten kilotons." Westerman brightened appreciably.

"So this could reach the ship?" he said, almost incredulously.

"It could and if it hit in the correct place it would destroy it," she replied with great relish. Her astonished onlookers exchanged hopeful smiles.

"So it's the answer to our prayers dear," said Damena. Zalar's mood darkened slightly.

"I said it could destroy it," she paused to let her words sink in and then continued, "but it won't."

"Shit!" said Westerman as he stubbed the toe of his boot into the ground in frustration.

"The Calaxian's have energy and kinetic weapon deflector screens around their vessels."

"Damn it" sighed Boochka. Zalar continued.

"The actual screen has a dual purpose, one is defensive in case of attack; the other is to deflect any debris that they may run into whilst travelling through space. At the velocities they operate at even a particle of dust would impact with phenomenal energy."

"I see, but if that is the case how will this help us?" said Westerman gesturing towards the missile.

"I'm surprised that you have not picked up on this by now Steve; as with anything I do, it concerns you."

"What? I don't follow you," he replied, confused. Damena and Boochka looked at Zalar and then Westerman. Zalar laughed out loud and then marched over and placed a hand on Westerman's shoulder and reached forward to plant a light kiss on his lips.

"My darling, it's your jump abilities," Westerman shook his head. She continued, "when the Wardens jump the coordinates of the termini are hard coded into their devices; they downloaded all those into your brain, but once you have physically been to a location you can jump there also."

"Yeah, I know all this but how does this help us?" he commented, still unclear of her motives.

"You have one final trick up your sleeve; you can also jump to a point that is actually visible to you." She paused and waited for her point to become obvious.

"And?" he said, beginning to become frustrated.

"And, we don't have to physically hit the ship and destroy it; all we have to do is make sure that the explosion against the shields is visible to you."

The simplicity and transparency of Zalar's plan hit him like a thunderbolt; he moved over to the young woman and wrapped his arms around her, kissed her and then lifted her off of her feet.

"Oh I do love you," he said.

"Can somebody please explain this to us?" stated a still confused Damena.

Westerman put Zalar down and after another quick peck on her cheek he turned to the elderly couple.

"Your daughter's a genius! She's right; all I have got to do is see the missiles explosion and then I will have a reference point to make the jump to. We put on the suits," he gestured to the environmental suits piled on the nearby ground. "When I see the blast, I jump to that point; we will be in space beside the Calaxian ship. Once I've got a reference point I can use the diagram Zalar's supplied and jump directly on board. Simple!" Boochka whistled long and low; Damena shook her head.

"Sounds awfully dangerous Steve," she said.

"It's the only way if we are going to save Bailon," Zalar responded with deadly seriousness. Westerman broke his embrace and crossed to the pile of spacesuits.

"We had better get a move on. How long before the ship's in position?" he asked.

"I reckon it's just about there. My scan shows that its speed is down to a few metres per second," Zalar replied studying her scanning device, its illuminated screen giving her face an eerie pale blue glow. Westerman retrieved the suits and crossed to her side. "Sorry love," he said sheepishly, "but you will have to show me what to do with this." Nodding to the garments hung like a pair of deflated tailors dummies in his hands. She smiled and took hers from him.

"Come on, let's go into the barn over there," she prompted and took him by the arm into the nearby building.

Ten minutes later Westerman and Zalar rejoined her parents, the younger couple clad in the environmental suits they had liberated from the Wardens. The material the garments were constructed from had been activated and was now reconfigured to their individual requirements.

"Suits you," said Westerman as he looked appreciatively at the way the protective cloth was now cupping Zalar's firm backside. Looking around in response she realised the focus of his attention.

"Steve! My parents are here," she said as she felt her cheeks flush with embarrassment; he shrugged in silent reply.

"Well you both look the part," observed Boochka in an attempt to break the growing atmosphere of departure tension. Damena looked silently on, her eyes misty from the floods of tears she was holding back.

"Can you program the attack coordinates for the missile from the scanner?" asked Westerman in a business-like tone designed to snap Zalar from the reverie that had descended upon her as she looked at her parents.

"Uh? Yes," she replied and redirected her attention to the scanning device.

"They've stopped," she announced.

"Where are they?" queried Westerman.

"The coordinates are; seven – five – two ..."

"No. Where are they?" interrupted Westerman. She looked up from her computations in puzzlement; he stood gesturing upwards, towards the night sky.

"Oh! Sorry," she said feeling a bit foolish.

"I need to know where to look," he offered smiling. Studying her display she turned and pointed to a section of the sky to the north.

"You see the four really bright stars that form the rectangle?"

Westerman located the area of sky she was indicating to him; they were extremely lucky, any cloud did not obscure the Bailon starscape on this night.

"Got it!" he said enthusiastically.

"The right-hand bottom corner star, the Calaxians are very near there," she further explained.

Westerman looked away from the target towards the horizon, even in the night he could clearly see a bank of clouds gathering; the deed would have to be done soon. "Okay, let's do this," he said with a renewed determination in his voice, Zalar nodded and walked over to the missile and started to press a sequence of buttons on one of the panels. Westerman approached Boochka and Damena.

"I'm sorry it's now or never I'm afraid, the weather could close in soon or even worse they could begin their landings," he said to the couple. Damena reached out her hand and laid it upon his arm.

"Look after our daughter Steve," she said softly, her face glistening in the lamplight, revealing the tracks of the tears rolling down her cheeks. He placed his gloved hand on top of hers and said,

"I will, you have my word on it."

"That's good enough for us son," said Boochka placing his hand on Westerman's shoulder.

"We have a heartbeat!" exclaimed Zalar as a powerful throbbing noise suddenly interrupted the quiet of the night air; with almost reverential respect she backed away from the assembly and joined her companions.

Damena threw her arms around her daughter's shoulders and drew her into a powerful embrace.

"Oh please look after yourself my darling," she entreated. Zalar returned her hug and said.

"Don't worry I'll be fine, I've got a superman to protect me."

Westerman looked to the ground in embarrassment as Boochka joined his wife and daughter in a three-way hug. However his feeling of inadequacy and discomfort was abruptly cut short as the launcher emitted a long loud beep; he spun around to face the device.

The throbbing pulses of power quickened noticeably and the tail section of the sleek dart had begun to glow; reluctantly Zalar broke away from her parents grasp.

"Here we go!" she shouted above the building volume of noise.

Suddenly the glow exploded into a blast of cold white light and the projectile leapt into the night sky. There was no flaming tail to see ascending into the heavens, only a dazzlingly bright ball of light climbing ever upwards, its velocity increasing with every split second. The throbbing noise subsided only to be replaced by the roar of tortured air as the missile pushed faster and faster through its molecules.

A loud bang, just like a very loud thunderclap, suddenly assaulted their hearing; Westerman glanced at Zalar and shouted.

"Was that a sonic boom?"

She nodded her reply as the point of brilliant light faded into the blackness of the night, Westerman moved to Zalar's side.

"How long?" he asked.

"About five minutes, that's all," she replied softly as the background noise had now receded.

"What's powering that thing?"

"A forced photon pulse," she replied as she watched the sky, her elegant upturned chin catching the light from the launcher.

"It's powered by light?" asked Boochka shaking his head in bewilderment.

"That's right Dad; a highly compressed and focused beam of photon particles," she said proudly. Westerman gently laid his hand on her shoulder.

"We have to get ready my love," he said with his voice purposefully tinged with regret; she nodded and went over and planted a kiss on the cheek of her mother and father and then returned to Westerman.

"Put the hood of the suit over your head and press the green button on your wrist pad," she instructed.

First locating the control he did as he had been instructed. When the hood was in position and the front piece of the material made contact with the appropriate section of the neck of the suit, it suddenly hardened and morphed into a rigid shell, with similar appearance to a motorcycle crash helmet; a number of lights switched on inside the unit and the reassuring hiss of the circulating air could clearly be heard in the background.

Zalar caught his attention as she gesticulated for him to press another button on the control pad; he complied with her request.

"Can you hear me?" Her voice filled his helmet with perfect clarity.

"Yes," he said, "crystal clear."

"It's nearly impact time Steve," she said as she moved nearer to him.

"Have I told you lately that I love you?" he said, seeing her smiling eyes through the faceplate of her helmet.

"Not enough," she replied. His arm encircled her waist as she placed one arm around his shoulder; in her other hand she held a thermal disruptor in deadly readiness. Together they nodded to Boochka and Damena and then turned their attention back to the night sky.

The Calaxian commander sat with his attention firmly focused on the screen that was showing the data being relayed from the science station console.

Three clear quantum signatures had been detected on the surface of Bailon in the last few hours; one could be clearly identified as belonging to a Warden Jump engine, but the other two readings were the ones giving cause for concern.

"You are sure that these readings are correct?" hissed the commander.

"Sir!" was the tacit reply from the science officer.

Of course they were correct he mused to himself, the power levels recorded for the second set of readings were astonishing; five times the magnitude of a normal Warden jump signature, what could this mean, a new weapon? Still the feeling of uneasiness persisted.

"Commander, incoming missile!" shouted one of the tactical bridge team. The commander pressed a nearby control stud and the main display changed to show the scanner read out.

A single line arced its way from the representation of the planets surface, a single dot on the screen showed the position of the attacking object; a dotted line projected the expected flight path, there could be no doubt of its intended target.

"Tactical analysis?"

"Standard Warden photonic drive surface to orbit missile; yield well below our shields capacities," answered the tactical officer with almost robot-like efficiency.

The senior officer did the Calaxian equivalent of a smug smile; he knew that this puny weapon offered no threat to his vessel.

"Shall I destroy it sir?" asked one of the weapons officers.

"No! I will not give such a puny, ineffectual assault against us the credence of expending our weapons energy upon it. Let it impact upon our shields," replied the commander making a dismissive gesture with his clawed hand.

The projectile continued along its flight path and when within two kilometres of the gargantuan bulk of the star ship it collided with the energy screen, blooming into a vivid violet-white silent explosion of light.

Watching the puddle of blinding light grow and then dissipate, the commander allowed a razor toothed grin to spread across his reptilian features.

Westerman and Zalar saw the explosion and watched as a small point of light grew in size and intensity until it was clearly visible as a roughly round area of brilliant violet-white.

"Got it!" shouted Westerman.

"Are you ready?" asked Zalar; he placed his faceplate against hers and replied,

"As I will ever be."

She watched as he closed his eyes and they were suddenly engulfed in a blinding white light, which cleared as abruptly as it had appeared to reveal that they were floating in the blackness of space; surrounded by countless stars.

Westerman looked down and below him hung the planet Bailon. The feeling of weightlessness made the scene unreal; it was as if he was standing in the middle of some bizarre dream, only the mass of Zalar still in his grasp brought any tangible trace of reality to the scenario.

"Are you okay?" he asked gently; her voice came through his helmet's speakers bringing another facet of reality to him.

"I think so…oh!"

"What's wrong?" he said as he tried to turn her around to face him.

"I don't feel so good, I feel sick," she replied.

He manoeuvred her into a position where her faceplate was pressing hard up against his and said.

"Zalar, look into my eyes; try to relax, breath deeply."

She gingerly opened her eyes and looked deeply into his.

"That's it. Concentrate; tell your brain that you are the right way up. There's nothing wrong." He could clearly hear her breathing becoming steadier, more relaxed.

"How come you are such an expert on free-fall sickness?" she asked between breaths, her eyes smiling at him through the two panes of Plexiglas.

"Too many science fiction movies I think." He gave her a small squeeze of encouragement.

"I think that I'll be okay," she said.

"Good, because I need you now; where is the Calaxian ship?"

Tentatively they separated from each other and allowed themselves to drift a few centimetres apart; Westerman slowly turned and looked upwards.

"Oh my god!" he exclaimed.

Directly above them was the titanic mass of the star ship; it was so big that it entirely blotted out any stars overhead.

"Fucking hell!" said Zalar.

"I know what you mean," he answered. It was impossible to gauge their distance from the vessel; its bulk seemed to disappear in all directions. Zalar was the first to recover from this feeling of insignificance, lifting her hand scanner from its belt clip she began to manipulate the display.

"We are two and a half kilometres away from the hull," she said as she focused on the readings to further help combat the feelings of sickness.

"Where is the control room?" he asked.

"Back up that way," she said, clumsily gesturing to her left, the action inducing a slow spinning motion to begin.

"Steady. Don't try to stop yourself, let me join you," he instructed her in response to the increased rate of her breathing.

"We are just outside the defence screens Steve and I think that we are falling towards them," she said with an urgency that did not require any further clarification to Westerman.

"I need to see the diagram of the ships internal layout so that I can make the jump inside."

Zalar put the scanner back onto her belt and retrieved the database device; anticipating his request she had placed the graphics he required into the quick retrieval memory, with the operation of a couple of controls the small screen showed everything Westerman needed.

Taking the machine from Zalar's grasp he looked at the slowly rotating mass of the Calaxian craft; the little display in his hand showed the internal layout of the vessel and also some external features. He desperately searched for any point of reference; in his helmet he could hear Zalar's breathing becoming more and more laboured, knew that she would not be able to hold on for much longer.

Just at the very limit of his field of vision he saw something, a large needle like protrusion had come into view; he glanced back at the display, the exact same object was clearly visible on the screen.

"Zalar, hang on! I think that I've got it," he said excitedly. She did not answer him back; all he could hear was gasping and the occasional thick belch followed by a gulp coming from the stricken woman.

On the display he could see that directly below the base of the structure he had identified ran a large access corridor; looking at the needle and comparing the distances he pulled Zalar tight against him, he took a deep breath and concentrated. The slowly tumbling pair vanished in a flash of light.

They materialised midair in the target corridor; the gravity field of the Calaxian vessel took hold and they fell one and a half metres onto the hard metallic decking in an unceremonious heap.

"Offff!" exclaimed Westerman as he landed on his back with the majority of the bulk of Zalar landing across his midriff.

"Ow!" she yelled as she rolled from the top of him.

"You've some need to complain," he gasped as he struggled to replace the air that had just been knocked out of his lungs.

"Press the red button on the wrist pad," she said as she carried out this operation. Her helmet detached itself from the front of her suit and collapsed into its hood configuration; Westerman did the same and was immediately struck by a strong pungent aroma.

"What the hell is that smell?" he gagged; Zalar wrinkled her nose up in distaste.

"That my love is roughly three million Calaxians," she replied slowly.

"The smelly bastards, have they all shit themselves?"

"It's a closed ecology. After long voyages and or when the population reaches a certain critical point I would imagine that the recycling technology is, shall we say, stretched."

"Smelly bastards," he stated again, she grinned at him and took the portable database from his gloved hand.

"The control room is back that way," she advised, pointing along the corridor.

"We really need to destroy this piece of shit and get out of here," he spat as he looked down the corridor.

"We need to stop the invasion first. I'm thinking that if we stop the order being given that would be the best way of doing it."

Westerman nodded and started to walk towards the control room.

"How far?" he asked as Zalar joined him.

"About two kilometres."

"Jesus! This thing is massive." She merely nodded in reply as she adjusted the output level of her thermal disruptor to a lethal setting.

The corridor was as straight as an arrow and roughly five metres square with supporting braces positioned at fifty metres intervals; this layout gave the slightly unsettling effect of walking down an infinite tunnel with no end in sight.

"It messes with your head," commented Westerman.

"It sure does," she replied as she looked at the screen of her handheld device, "there's another corridor joining this one in about one hundred metres."

Westerman nodded and mentally snapped an invisible telekinetic force wall into existence roughly five metres in front of them.

"Keep a sharp lookout," he said.

Presently the entrance to the other corridor became obvious; signalling with his hand he moved to the opposite wall, Zalar did the same with her weapon ready; her finger hovering over the firing stud.

They were ten metres from the aperture when a rhythmic clicking became barely audible; they snapped a quick glance at each other to confirm that they had both heard the noise as two Calaxians emerged. The creatures reacted with lightning reflexes; they drew their weapons from the belts that encircled their small, scaly waists and fired.

Twin beams of agitated particles lanced out towards Westerman and Zalar, only to impact in a maelstrom of pyrotechnics against the force wall.

Zalar fired once and one of the reptilian beings was practically cut in two; Westerman's eyes flashed and the remaining attackers head exploded into gory fragments accompanied by a dull wet, splattering sound.

"I don't think that I'll ever get used to that," said Zalar with a mock grimace of repulsion on her face.

"Nag, nag, nag," mocked Westerman as they strode over the bodies.

"Is your screen still up?" she asked; he turned and nodded in confirmation.

"Good," she continued and moved closer by his side.

The rest of their progress along the access corridor was uneventful and eventually the illusion of the never-ending tunnel started to evaporate as the actual end became more and more visible.

"There should be an opening to our left at the end," said Zalar consulting her database. Westerman moved over to the corridor wall and craned his neck forward around one of the supports.

"I see it, no guards," he observed and smiled.

"The control room must be guarded, it's got to be," she offered.

They arrived at the doorway, it lead to another smaller corridor; this one curved around to the right and was sharply elevated. Westerman entered slowly.

"Be careful Steve," Zalar whispered. He turned and gave her a wink and then slowly began to edge up the passageway.

The curve eventually straightened out but the uphill nature continued; he could now see that their way was barred fifty metres ahead by a solid metal door and two very bored looking Calaxians. At Westerman's gesturing the two humans retreated back down the corridor around the bend until out of sight.

"Is that the control room?" he whispered.

"Yes."

"We need to get rid of those guards, the door could be locked but I think we can deal with that," he mused.

"I think that the guards are your department," she said with a smile.

"You're right, come on." He smiled back and started to edge slowly back up the passage.

The two sentries were not actually looking down the corridor, making Westerman's task so much easier. Once he had a clear view of them his eyes flashed twice in quick succession; equally rapidly the guards heads exploded, both bodies now rested in a bloody heap in front of the door.

"Come on. We need to get in before anybody arrives and finds this mess," he observed as he advanced upon the entrance.

"Mess is the word, you need a shovel," she commented as she gingerly picked her way through the carnage.

The control room door was totally featureless, but the frame contained a single, square panel about two centimetres square.

"Ready?" asked Westerman as he prepared to place his finger upon the control.

"No!" cried Zalar as she knocked his hand away.

"What's wrong?" he said, slightly annoyed.

"I think that this is a bio-metric sensor lock, when you touch the pad it senses the composition of the digit operating it," she explained.

"And it would have sensed a non-Calaxian using it," he said in sudden realisation.

"Yes, it would have activated an alarm or even a security screen on the door."

"We can't jump in because I don't know the layout inside," he commented.

"Don't worry I've got an idea," she said brightly and started to make adjustments to the settings on her disruptor.

With the precision of a surgeon, Zalar moved over to one of the dead guards and using the beam from her weapon, configured to its narrowest setting, she neatly sliced off one of the alien's hands.

"This should do the trick," she said passing the gruesome trophy to Westerman.

"Charming," he observed as he gingerly accepted the offering.

Moving back to the door he placed the forefinger of the hand onto the panel.

The commander looked viciously at his science officer.

"What do you mean you detected a quantum signature outside the ship?" he growled, showing his fearsome array of teeth.

"Sir, I was reviewing the previous external sensor logs and I found the reading," answered the cowering object of the superior's wrath.

"How long ago?"

"Not long sir, almost immediately after the Warden missile impacted on our defence screens."

The commander suddenly became very concerned.

"Show me the readings quickly!" he barked.

The display on the status screen showed the facts and figures of the quantum trace in question; the elderly Calaxian suddenly had his concern elevated by several orders of magnitude. The trace matched exactly the previously unidentified, powerful recordings; he reached for a control to order a ship wide alert, the bridge door slid open almost silently behind him.

He never managed to see who had entered his command without his permission, a ruby red beam of accelerated particles drilled a hole through his skull killing him instantly. One of the tactical officers had barely enough time to shout, "Wardens!" before his chest exploded.

Ten officers occupied the control room at this particular time and due to the Calaxian paranoia surrounding their promotion system the only individual carrying a weapon was the commander, this circumstance ensured that resistance to the invasion of the bridge was practically zero.

Within thirty seconds all the reptilian aliens were dead; Westerman surveyed the room.

"I think that we are secure," he said with satisfaction as he used the severed Calaxian hand to operate the control and seal the hatch behind them.

"I should be able to interpret their status panels using my hand scanner," said Zalar, taking the device from her belt and crossing to the dead commander's station.

"I'll make doubly sure that we are all alone," offered Westerman, walking around the control room; using his boot to turn over the bodies.

"Oh shit!" cried Zalar.

"What's wrong?"

"The invasion cycle can't be stopped from here. The order has been given and now it is in the hands of the sub-commanders; it is a procedure created for the very eventuality that we have enacted. They launch when loading is complete.

"Shit!" spat Westerman

"Exactly," replied Zalar.

"Have they begun to launch yet?" he asked. The young woman pressed a sequence of buttons on her hand held device and then operated a number of controls on one of the bridge panels.

"No!" she said with a mixture of relief and triumph.

"Good, that means that we are not too late. We have got to think of something," he said as he pushed the dead body of the science officer from its chair and sat down; his brow furrowed with deep concentration.

"Can we blow the ship up from here?"

"No, I'm sorry but once again the Calaxians feudal based society would not allow them to trust a small group of individuals with enough centralised power for such a momentous decision," she offered.

"What can we do from here?"

"Well, we have weapons, science station and navigation," she said with a shrug. Westerman sprang to his feet.

"Zalar! Do we control propulsion as well as navigation?" "Yes but? Oh I see," she beamed a massive smile across the room at him.

"We need to move the ship away from Bailon," he said with a renewed urgency, Zalar was already busy studying the control panels and the various screens.

"If we can get this thing moving there is a failsafe that will not allow the landing bay doors to open," she announced victoriously. Westerman crossed over to her, put his arms around her waist and gave her a heavy kiss on the lips.

"Come on then, let's get going," he said.

"Can you sit at that station over there Steve?"

"This one?" he replied as he reached the large control desk.

"Yes, sit down and do what I tell you," she ordered as she depressed a large array of buttons.

"Yes sir!" he answered mockingly; she allowed herself a brief look towards him to flash an affectionate smile.

"The bank of switches, the red ones in the top right-hand corner, throw them all into the downwards position."

Westerman did as he was instructed and a variety of lights winked into life in response.

"Steve. On the bottom left-hand side; the three sliders, see them?" Westerman nodded confirmation, Zalar continued, "Good, knock them all into the furthest upward position."

Hardly the briefest of a pause after he had carried out his instructions a barely perceptible shudder ran thorough the length of the ship.

"We're moving!" she yelled.

"Good girl," he called back with a broad grin upon his face.

The three fusion drive exhaust nozzles at the stern of the Calaxian vessel started blasting out the hundreds of kilometres long tongues of plasma; their brilliance far greater than the Bailon sun.

Damena and Boochka looked up in fear and amazement at the strange, eerie false dawn that had broken about them, their eyes soon adapting to focus on the brilliant smudge of light in the night sky.

"Zalar?" breathed Damena. Boochka said nothing, he just held his wife even tighter to him.

Deep in the bowels of the Star ship, the Calaxian second in command stood on an overhead gantry menacingly observing the loading of the invasion force onto the sixteen landing vehicles below him. The sheer weight of the numbers of foot soldiers to embark always caused a bottleneck in the conquest procedure mused the restless officer; still, he comforted himself, if the old fool on the bridge had given the order as soon as they had entered orbit the process would have been advanced much further.

"How long?" he growled down at a subordinate stood at a console on the next level down.

"We're above ninety percent loaded on transports one to eight, the other six are at around eighty percent," responded the junior officer efficiently as he looked up. Always the same, the last six craft were the furthest away from the designated military area, once he was commander he would arrange to billet some of the troops in the general habitat area; sure, some of the council would kick up a fuss but deployment would be so much quicker.

He started to walk along the gantry that ran the length of the embarkation bay suspended from the roof by unfeasibly thin looking struts, his progress made the walkway bounce slightly. Below, the landing craft looked like fat, triangular darts, each capable of carrying up to thirty thousand troops, albeit in appallingly cramped conditions. This capacity was of course compromised by the transportation of equipment and heavy armaments, but soon there would be close to five hundred thousand, vicious Calaxians falling towards the world below.

An exceptionally strong vibration passed along the walkway, stopping the second in command in his reptilian tracks; this was unusual, the gantry never felt this unstable, this was a totally unfamiliar sensation. The years of living on the multi-generational vessel had honed his sensitivity to the various nuances of the crafts behaviour, he immediately recognised the cause of the phenomenon; the main fusion drives had been activated. What was that old fool doing in the control room?

He looked down; the entire invasion force had stopped in its collective mid-stride and stood looking in bewilderment at each other. Uttering an oath of interstellar origin, the second in command turned and sprinted along the gantry in the direction of the bridge. Below several of the sub-officers saw their superior's actions and began to make their own way forwards.

The Calaxian star ship was truly massive in its proportions; therefore the acceleration produced by the mighty fusion torches could hardly be described as breath taking. Zalar studied the various readouts decorating the navigation panels; they had been operating under full thrust for nearly thirty minutes and their speed had only just topped two hundred kilometres per hour. She knew that this vehicle was certainly no sprinter; the motors were designed to operate for many years at a time, providing a constant thrust, to climb relentlessly out of a star's gravity well and attain a critical velocity for the star drive to be activated. Westerman looked over at her.

"How are we doing?" he asked.

"Slowly," she said, but brightening continued, "but we've just reached the velocity for the hanger doors to be automatically dead-locked."

"That's good news. Speaking of locking the door, is there anything that we can do about our own entrance?" He gestured towards the control room hatch.

Zalar looked down at a nearby control panel and after a few seconds she smiled and pressed a few buttons.

"We're locked in," she announced.

"Good because I think that somebody or something must have realised by now that we are on the move," he offered.

"You are probably right. Can I ask you a question Steve?"

"Sure, fire away," he responded.

"Now that we've got this thing moving, what are we going to do with it? I've been all through the data and there is no way that we can blow this thing up from here, but on the plus side of things this is the only place that it can be controlled from."

"Believe it or not I have actually been giving this some thought, and the only course of action I think would be viable is to crash this bloody thing into something," he said as he looked her straight in the eyes.

"I think that you are probably right, but what or where?"

"The Sun," he replied, matter of factly.

"Wow! You really think on a grand scale don't you," she observed.

"How long would it take us to reach it?"

Zalar looked down at the instrument panels and then back at her hand-held; after a couple of minute's computations she said,

"We are starting to build a bit of pace up now, and of course we would be using the sun's gravity well to add acceleration so the trip should take about ten days."

"Shit! That's a long time," Westerman gasped as he agitatedly ran his fingers through his hair.

"We will have a hell of a job holding them off for that length of time; we won't be able to abandon ship until it's nearly all over in case they break in and take avoiding action," he mused biting his bottom lip in concentration.

Zalar continued to study the various panels and her equipment.

"We could have an opportunity to pick up more speed in about twelve hours time, that's when we will achieve ram-scoop activation velocity," she offered with a seductively wicked glint in her eye.

"Sorry, you've lost me in techno-babble."

"At the moment we are burning Hydrogen from the internal storage tanks to fuel the fusion reaction; at ram-scoop speeds the velocity is sufficient for the stray particles or atoms of hydrogen that we are flying through to become concentrated enough to be funnelled into the reactors and used," she explained.

"I remember reading once that outer space was not a perfect vacuum, is that what you mean?"

"Yes, that's right. But the nearer we get to the sun the concentration increases further still; material blown out of the star in the solar wind will act like a supercharger, the reaction will become stronger, our speed could increase exponentially." Zalar actually appeared to becoming excited by this turn of events.

"Do we need to make any course corrections or anything?" asked Westerman.

"Already done and laid in."

"Good, so all we have to do is wait," he said and sat back in his chair.

"Do you want something to eat?"

"Could be hungry, where are we going to get something? We can't exactly order take away or get drive-through."

"Come over here with me," she said, extending her hand towards him. He accepted her offer and she led him over to the far side of the room and pointed to a section of the wall.

"Oh yes," he said with a smile. Zalar was pointing to what was immediately recognisable as one of the food dispensing alcoves he had previously seen; obviously this unit had been looted by the Calaxians from some Ancient artefact and integrated into the bridge layout.

"Does it work?" he asked.

"Let's see. Coffee, white medium blend," she said aloud, clearly.

The mechanism activated and a mug of steaming beverage appeared on the alcoves internal platform.

"Yes!" he said, taking this as a sign that good fortune could be finally coming their way.

Thirty minutes later they sat together on one of the more unimportant consoles; having sated their hungers, Westerman looked around sheepishly.

"What's wrong Steve?" she asked.

"This is a bit embarrassing, where are the toilet facilities?"

She smiled and pointed to a small closet door situated near the control room entrance.

"Over there. Don't expect anything fancy, it could just be a hole in the deck," she said and began laughing.

"Cute!" he said with a grimace as he walked over and opened the door.

Thankfully the room he entered held no unpleasant surprises; in fact he actually found it amusing that a race of reptiles from another galaxy had come up with more or less the same solutions to a common problem. The tiny bathroom even came with a small hand basin together with a recognisable tap arrangement; he splashed the cool water from it over his face to refresh himself.

"Okay?" Zalar asked with a smile as he re-entered the control room.

"Never better," he stated as he sat down beside her.

"How fast are we going now?" he asked, Zalar consulted the instruments and replied.

"About two thousand kilometres per hour."

"What are we going to do about the rest of the crew when they try to break in here?" the concern all too apparent on her face.

"I'm not going to tell you that I've got some master plan I'm afraid," he answered honestly.

"We really need to have some contingency," she pressed.

"You're right. Let's get these bodies into the access corridor for a start, I think that it may start to get a bit ripe in here," he said as he stood up.

"And?" she pressed.

"I'm thinking," he said with a smile as he grabbed the nearest body to him and began dragging it towards the door.

The second in command had already found the two dead bodies in the main corridor, he quickly realised that the vessel being in motion was possibly not the actions of the commander; could it be possible that there was somebody else aboard the ship, the Wardens?

He quickly dismissed them as the likely culprits on the grounds of this being a too overt action for that particular cowardly race of humanoids. A group of eight sub-officers joined him in his deliberations.

"Wardens?" asked one of them.

"Those spineless, smooth skinned animals?" spat the senior officer, "not a chance."

"But sir," said another of the group.

"What is it?" snapped his superior.

"I was in the control room a while ago; we were attacked by a Warden surface to orbit missile. I saw it explode harmlessly against our shields on my monitor before I left for the embarkation area."

Some new weapon perhaps, thought the leader; could it be that the old fool had been right to be concerned by all the quantum readings? He dismissed this train of thought as being of no consequence as he would have to act.

"I'm convinced that the bridge has been compromised, we must assume that the commander is dead; therefore I take charge."

The assembled creatures hissed their obedience.

"Quickly, go to the armoury and bring weapons; light side arms and a large portable laser cannon. Quickly!" he snapped and the group split up as four of their number ran off down the corridor to fetch the armaments.

The newly installed commander gestured the remaining Calaxians to follow him as he moved towards the entrance to the bridge access passageway.

"Quietly," he hissed through his needle sharp teeth.

Luckily, when Westerman and Zalar had opened the control room door the only Calaxians waiting outside were the dead guards; they dragged the deceased bridge crew into the passageway and stacked them on one side so as to not block a potential escape route.

"You stay here and keep the door open for me. I'm going to have a little look around," Westerman said as he unceremoniously dumped the last body on top of the pile. Zalar nodded, she did not have to say the words because the expression on her face shouted, 'be careful', louder than any voice could possible utter; slowly Westerman started to inch his way down the curving tunnel towards the main corridor. Eventually he could see the opening at the end, the difference in illumination between the inside and the outside of the passageway producing easily discernable shadows.

Meanwhile, out in the main corridor the weaponry had arrived and with a wave of his clawed fist the commander waved his troops forward; they moved towards the entrance to the access tunnel in near total silence.

Westerman stood at the corridor entrance, he was convinced that he could hear nothing apart from the background throbbing of the massive engines in the distance; he counted to three and then stepped through the gateway onto the main corridor.

The Calaxian and Westerman nearly collided, face-to-face, both parties jumped back in a startled, reflex, reaction. Reptilian instincts of the aliens enabled them to recover from the surprise quickest; the commander brought the weapon in his hand on the human.

Having no time to concentrate on the erection of a force shield, Westerman's own survival instincts took over and he blindly threw himself back into the control room access tunnel; the Calaxian fired and a beam of deadly energy struck the bulkhead where is target had been stood; the metal bubbled and spat, sparks showered in all directions. Several more beams were fired into the passage entrance as Westerman scrambled away, half crawling and half running; he could feel the heat radiating from the impact points around him.

The Calaxians had thought better of entering the doorway however, this gave him the opportunity he needed and concentrating, he threw up an invisible telekinetic force wall, totally sealing off the access way. The lethal rays struck the shield, jagged bolts of static and a large quantity of exotic energies filled the tunnel; but the screen held, Westerman began to feel back in control of the situation.

The attacking aliens could now clearly see their target but were starting to become increasingly perplexed as to why their efforts were not reaching the human; even more annoyingly the source of their problem was now standing up and walking away towards the control room smiling.

Westerman allowed himself to get around the curve of the tunnel and nearly to the bridge entrance before he let the shield drop, he could still hear the scream and crackles from the weapons impacts; Zalar stood waiting in the doorway, a concerned look upon her face.

"Get ready to shut the door, we've got company!" he yelled as he broke into a run towards her. He mentally let the screen drop and several beams of energy lanced into the passage behind him.

"No shit! Come on," she shouted. Within an instant he was through the door and Zalar used the severed hand to close it behind him.

"Better lock that darling," he called. She was already at the console and operating the necessary controls.

"Already there," she said with a thin smile.

"Wow! That was close; I nearly walked straight into them," he laughed as she nervously walked over and stood beside him, he slipped his arm around her waist; she was shaking.

"Hey, it's okay. You're safe," he said reassuringly.

"I know, I know," she commented softly.

"Can they get through that door?" he asked with a nod in the entrances direction.

"Not with small arms but I imagine some of their heavy stuff can."

"I thought as much, we need a plan. How long before the ship is so near the sun that it will be beyond the point of no return?"

Zalar unwillingly left his comforting embrace and consulted the instruments on the navigation panel, and after a couple of minute's deliberation she took a deep breath and said.

"About eight days, give or take."

"That's two days lower than the original estimate," he observed, puzzled.

"That's because I didn't factor in the increase in speed with the ram-scoop. I missed it out because it looks like the system hasn't been used for years," she mused, still looking at the displays.

"Not used? It will work won't it?" he pressed, more than a little concerned.

"Oh it will work, I think." Westerman gave her a sideways glance.

"It looks like that drive format is a hangover from their pre-faster than light days," she continued. "When the Calaxians first decided to go walkabout and expand into the cosmos, they did not have faster than light capability; they simply used fusion reaction rockets. Eventually, as things developed, more technology from conquered worlds became available enabling the engines of their fleet to evolve; one of the subjugated races had the ram-scoop and it was incorporated.

However this was, as far as the Wardens could tell, a relatively short lived era, very soon after they stumbled onto the FTL drive and the ram-scoop became obsolete; the system simply has not been removed."

"How old is this ship?" he asked laying his hand upon the cold metal of the internal superstructure.

"No idea, we, or should I say the Wardens, believe that the Calaxian vessels could be thousands of years old," she observed.

"Back to the problem in hand, eight days?" he said, lost in thought.

"The good thing is that they cannot control things from anywhere but here, so all we have to do is hold out," she offered.

"Only!" he replied.

For the next few hours they debated the next best course of action; however the issue rapidly came to a head.

Zalar had sat on the floor next to the door, fatigued by all the mental exertion as another brilliant idea had just been torpedoed by impracticality; she let her back lay against the metal of the hatch.

"Ow!" she yelled as she jumped to her feet.

"What's wrong?" asked Westerman as he rushed over to her.

"The hatch. It's so hot to the touch," Zalar observed as she eased her garment away from her shoulder to check her skin for any damage.

"Are you okay?" asked a concerned Westerman.

"Yeah, I'm fine. It just took me by surprise, that's all," she reassured him.

Westerman approached the section of the door in question and held out his hand towards it; from a few centimetres away he could clearly feel the heat.

"I think our friends are trying to get in," he said.

"Makes sense, they must be using some heavy duty form of heat ray. If you can't open the doors burn the entire wall away."

"We had better think of something fast, I think that it is starting to glow."

He pointed at an area in the centre of the hatch, it had begun to visibly change colour; a wisp of smoke curled upwards from the affected area.

"Quick Zalar, we need to see the schematics of the ship in this area."

Within seconds one of the main displays showed a cut away diagram of the star ship; Zalar manipulated the controls and the section they occupied expanded to fill the screen.

"That's the control room," indicated Zalar as she pointed at the screen.

"What's all the empty area with no detail around us?" he asked, gesturing to the large blank areas on three sides of the bridge.

"I'm not sure. That's the control room, there is the access tunnel, I've no idea what's in there," she answered, obviously puzzled.

Westerman turned back to the door, an area thirty centimetres in diameter was now glowing dull scarlet and this area was visibly growing by the second.

"Water tanks!" cried Zalar triumphantly; Westerman snapped his attention back to the screen and said with an air of puzzlement,

"Water?"

"Water, they use it for fuel for the fusion engines; heavy water to be precise, a couple of a million litres of the stuff."

"Does the access tunnel go through the middle of it?" he asked with the germ of an idea growing rapidly in his mind. Zalar studied the schematic, altering the orientation of the display to allow a three hundred and sixty degree view around the passage. Finally she said, "Yes it does, it's completely enclosed."

"Good. Here quick, give me a hand with my spacesuit. I've got an idea," he said with a renewed enthusiasm as he picked the garment up and started to climb into it.

A few short minutes later, environmental suit in place with the exception of the helmet, he directed Zalar's attention back to the diagram on the monitor.

"Tell me if I am wrong, but the other end of the control room access tunnel; that's a door isn't it?" he asked pointing to the screen. She studied the plans and at length nodded, saying.

"It's an emergency pressure door. I suppose you want to know how to activate it?"

He leaned over and planted a large kiss on her cheek.

"That's why I love you," he stated cheerfully.

A spitting sound made them both turn towards the control room door; it had now started to glow bright orange as the Calaxians poured megawatts of focused energy into it.

"It won't hold much longer," Zalar said.

"The pressure door?" prompted Westerman, pulling her attention back to the diagram.

"The control is on the main corridor wall next to the entrance. You had better take our friend with you," she replied holding up the severed Calaxian hand.

"Will it work?" he asked as he gingerly accepted the gruesome item.

"Should do, it's the same security clearance as the bridge door."

He took a step back from Zalar and closed his eyes in concentration, a split second later he vanished in a flash of light.

He materialised just outside the entrance to the access tunnel in the main corridor, his sudden appearance took the two Calaxians by total surprise; he dealt with them easily, one being decapitated by a telekinetic burst and the other by having his head twisted around by Westerman's psychic manipulations.

Quickly he located the door controls and, stepping just inside the passage, he reached outside and activated the mechanism; the door slid closed behind him with a barely audible hiss.

Holding one hand outstretched in front of him, he constructed a mental force wall and began to edge upwards and around the curve in the tunnel towards the control room.

Soon he could see the group of three aliens, they all were busy watching their efforts against the bridge door; in front of them there was a device mounted on a tripod, obviously the weapon they were using to burn through the metal of the door.

With all attention being focused upon their handiwork, Westerman had no trouble disposing of the aliens; his eyes flashed three times in quick succession, equally quickly there were three dull, wet concussions, the decapitated bodies fell in an untidy heap.

The weapon continued to fire its unwavering beam of destruction at the door, the point of contact now white hot. Westerman approached the device; on its body was mounted a small control panel which was covered by a seemingly unfeasible number of buttons. Cursing he looked around at the rest of the weapon, he had assumed that there would be a trigger mechanism of some description; he was obviously mistaken.

On the point of desperation, because he feared the integrity of the control room door was fading fast, he grabbed the machine and physically turned the beam away from its target. The particle stream wavered as sparks and sheets of flame flickered across the passageway; the heat from the tortured entrance hatch could be clearly felt on his face.

Eventually he had turned the ray through ninety degrees and it was now blasting away at the wall of the passage; barely in the nick of time he wrapped his protective shield around himself as a wall of flame erupted from the new point of impact. Backing away slightly, he could see through the distortion created by his own mental force field that the door was now cooling rapidly; he could not discern any signs that it had been penetrated; his plan just may have a chance.

Moving back down the inclined and curving tunnel, leaving the device to do its work, he positioned himself on the curve so as to be just able to see the doorway; he knew he needed to ensure that any uninvited guests did not spoil the party he was planning. Seconds stretched into long minutes; time appeared to be moving at a glacial pace, he could still hear the high pitched whine of the weapon, what was taking so long? He had just resolved to move back up the tunnel to check on progress when he heard a dull explosion, closely followed by the unmistakable sound of gushing water; a split second later a wall of liquid was speeding towards him.

Barely in time he closed the hood of his suit, the flexible nature of the material transformed into the hard shell of a helmet just as the mini tidal wave knocked him clean off his feet; the force of the torrent drove him back along the passage, tumbling end over end until he slammed against the pressure door.

The access tunnel flooded rapidly and once completely awash the current subsided abruptly. Westerman swam and clawed his way back along the passageway to check on the control room door; his prayers were answered, it had held. Relieved he looked at the gaping hole through which the thousands of litres of fluid had raced in. He felt a bump against his helmet that made him try to turn around in panic; the headless body of one of the dead Calaxians floated by. It was time to leave he decided and with that he vanished in a flash.

Zalar jumped backwards with a squeal as Westerman flashed into existence in the control room, his appearance accompanied by a large splash as the water that had surrounded him also arrived. Deactivating the helmet from his suit, he beamed a broad grin across the room at her.

"I take it that you have been successful?" she said having regained her composure.

"Sure have. There must be a quarter of a million litres of water between us and the main corridor," he said with smug satisfaction

"And if they try to break through the pressure door on the access passage they'll flood the main corridor," she observed.

"Exactly," Westerman added triumphantly as he began removing his suit equipment.

"I'm afraid that I have lost our door key in the water," he said gesturing towards the hatch.

"We shouldn't need it, should we?" she asked, a tinge of consternation colouring her tone.

He moved over to where she stood and placed a comforting arm around her.

"You're all wet," she said with mock disgust and playfully pushed him away. Adopting a more business-like manner, Westerman looked at the display screens.

"What are you looking for?" she asked.

"We could do with some external views of the ship, they could try and do something reckless," he mused.

"No problem," she replied and operating a sequence of controls, the monitors changed their displays to show various sections of the star ship's exterior; a quick check revealed no activity.

"Looks all clear at the moment," he commented.

"Come on, let's get you out of those wet things," Zalar purred seductively. In response he smiled broadly as he allowed her to start undoing the suits various fastenings.

Hours later they lay together naked on a large sheet of material they had found in a storage locker to cover the deck. They had made slow and deliberate love; exploring each other's bodies, revelling in the feeling of the victory, the removed threat and security. Zalar's head rested upon his chest, her arm draped lightly across his stomach.

"What do we do after all this is over?" she asked as he gently stroked her hair reassuringly, the very touch of her acting as a soothing balm for his soul.

"That's what I've been wondering. Will it ever be over?" he replied distantly. She lifted her head and looked into his eyes.

"We can't think like that can we," she offered.

"You're right of course, but the scale of our struggle will be enormous. Look at the facts, just the two of us against three enemies, the Uniques, the Wardens and the Calaxians. They all have their own agendas and we are on the outside of all those plans."

"There must be somebody we can find to ally themselves with us. I would think the people of Bailon are going to be pretty grateful for one."

"Don't think that I haven't considered them, but with respect, compared to our enemies your people are primitive," he observed.

"So I'm primitive am I?" Zalar retorted with mock indignation. He leaned forwards and kissed her saying,

"You know what I mean."

"Of course I do my love," she said cuddling into his chest, "just don't be so quick to discount us."

"Point taken," he conceded.

Suddenly the entire spacecraft shuddered, both Westerman and Zalar jumped to their feet.

"What the?" he breathed as he looked at the display screens hoping to see something that would explain the phenomenon. Zalar had immediately gone to the main navigation console; after checking various instruments she turned to face him and with a broad smile on her face she announced,

"The ram-scoop has been activated."

"Can we see it? Is there anything to see?" He had unconsciously adopted the look of an inquisitive schoolboy, Zalar found the never ending awe of the unknown in his eyes so attractive.

"I think we can do something," she teased and began operating the display controls.

Whilst she bent over the panel, Westerman could not help himself allowing his eyes to wander over her beautiful naked body silhouetted in the glow of the main viewing screen, which held the growing image of the Bailon sun. He realised that he should stop his ogling as his body was beginning to respond in all too obvious ways.

"Over here on this screen," she said. He went and stood beside her.

On the display was a view of the nose of the star ship; barely visible was a translucent blue area that extended outwards into space. Occasionally bright flashes of a ghostly light erupted along the outer edge of the blue area.

"What am I looking at?" Westerman asked.

"The blue is an area of charged particles being trapped by a magnetic field; the same magnetic field is funnelling the hydrogen and other exotic elements from the solar wind into the ram-scoops, there," she explained and pointed to the large funnel shape protuberances that had extended from the ships outer hull.

"Steve, can I ask you a question?" she purred.

"What is it my love?" he said, still engrossed in the spectacle on the monitor.

"Is that for me?" she asked. He looked at her and she nodded downward towards his groin, he coloured slightly and said softly.

"All yours darling, it is all yours."

Good," she cooed as they fell together in a passionate embrace and returned to their makeshift bed.

CHAPTER SEVENTEEN

The next few days passed by more or less uneventfully as the mighty vessel accelerated remorselessly towards the Bailon sun; no actual physical assault had been attempted upon the control room, however a brief piece of excitement did break the monotony for Westerman and Zalar.

It was the third day of their one-way trip to oblivion and Zalar noticed a row of red warning lights had illuminated on one of the status panels; she immediately investigated, her trusty handheld database in her hand at the ready.

"What's up?" said Westerman, pushing a plate full of fruit he was consuming to one side.

"They're up to something in the landing craft bays," she replied.

"Can we see what's happening?"

"Way ahead of you, I'm just bringing the internal monitors on line," she said efficiently.

After about five minutes the display screens had still not resolved into anything but snow and static.

"Have they sabotaged them?" he offered.

"Shit! I never thought of that," she cursed to herself, "I'll bring up the external views of the landing bay doors."

The screen flickered and the static was replaced by the crystal clear image of the massive doors, they were opening.

"They can't seriously be trying that!" she exclaimed.

"Trying what?" he asked, confused.

"They've overridden the door releases; they are trying to launch some of the landing craft. They must be trying to escape in them; it's suicide!" Zalar cried in horror.

"I'm sorry. You've lost me on this one," he replied totally bemused.

"No it's me who should be sorry; I keep forgetting that you don't come from an advanced race."

He felt himself bristle and responded.

"What do you mean not advanced?"

Zalar immediately realised the error of her assertion.

"Sorry. That came out all wrong; I was trying to say that there is no way that you could know the mechanics involved in operating a craft at what is now approaching relativistic speeds," she explained in a conciliatory tone. Westerman smiled back at her and said,

"Okay enlighten me."

Taking a deep breath, Zalar scratched her head looking for inspiration as to where to start his education;

she used the pause as an opportunity to check the view screen, the doors were still opening slowly.

"You remember I told you about the Calaxian star ships having a protective shield around them for two reasons; to defend against attacks and protect against space debris whilst underway?" she asked.

"Yeah sure," he answered nodding encouragement for her to continue.

"Well as the speed increases the potential damage from one of these impacts increases exponentially. It's all about the build up of kinetic energy you see; we are now moving at many thousands of kilometres per hour, one speck of dust could have the energy of a not too inconsiderable bomb."

"That's why we have the corona of fiery energy running before us," he said.

"Yes, that's right. It's where the space dust is being vaporised into its component atoms by our forward shields; the energy released is producing the heat and light," Zalar enthused, visibly taking pride in his ability to grasp the situation.

"Okay I'm with all this stuff, but how does their escape attempt have to be suicide?"

"Now we are really moving fast, the energy from the front shield is so great that it does not have time to dissipate before we arrive at the impact point; it spreads around the ship's other shields."

"I think I know what you mean, a slipstream effect," he said triumphantly.

"Exactly," she agreed and the continued, "so basically you have a constant stream of energy and interstellar particles flowing from nose to stern all around the vessel, just metres away from the hull."

"So when the landing craft emerges into space it will be torn apart?"

Zalar nodded grimly, Westerman turned his attention back to the screen saying.

"This could be worth seeing. I wish that I had some popcorn." He glanced back at her, his face bearing a broad grin.

"The doors are fully open," she announced after consulting the various readouts.

Nothing happened for long minutes as they sat watching the display screen and then suddenly the landing craft slowly began to emerge.

The vessel inched outwards into space in a lateral orientation; occasionally small sparks of flame were seen as miniature rocket motors, attitude jets, fired nudging the craft into its adjusted attitude.

Westerman realised that he was holding his breath, feeling foolish he turned to Zalar; she too was engrossed in the unfolding drama.

"How far away from the ship is the slipstream?" he asked.

"I'm not sure, let me check," she replied as she checked a nearby console. Presently she turned back to observe the progress of the landing craft and said,

"At this section of the hull it's about fifty to sixty metres."

In silence Zalar reached out and took hold of his hand, together they watched, spellbound, as the Calaxian vessel crept into space; the long vehicle's stubby wing flashed.

Pieces of metal sprayed away from the point of impact into the stream of high-energy particles; the entire vessel shuddered and its orientation changed rapidly. Such was the force of the collision between the leading edge of the machines aerodynamic surface and the slipstream that the entire ship was now being dragged into the stream of energy.

As they watched from the safety of the control room, Westerman and Zalar saw the Calaxian landing craft pulled deeper and deeper into the deadly tide. Metal panels boiled away instantaneously; within a scant few seconds the spaceship disappeared in a flash of destruction.

The Calaxians never attempted to launch another craft.

Four days later, Westerman and Zalar stood on the bridge, their environmental suits in place, side by side looking at the main viewing screen. It was time for them to leave, the control room had already become too hot to bear; inside the cool protection of their suits they watched the final act of this drama unfold.

The sun was now completely filling the screen, despite the instrument being set at its lowest magnification; the brightness had also been corrected to its lowest level but still proved intolerable to the naked eye.

Westerman turned to look at Zalar; he could not see her face through the faceplate of her helmet as it had automatically adopted a golden reflective finish to protect her from the intensity of the light.

"I think that it is time to go," he said, she turned towards him.

"I think that you are right, nothing can save the ship now; the shields are starting to overload."

They had heard nothing from the millions of Calaxians on board the vessel, they had seen them via the internal closed circuit viewing facility, but there had been no attempt to storm the bridge.

The entire crew now seemed resigned to their fate and had retired to their individual quarters to spend the last few hours indulging personal activities. A day or two before Westerman and Zalar had witnessed various fights, several of the creatures indulging in a mass sexual practice and a large number of them drinking a variety of liquids from assorted containers. Steve made the connection between the fighting and the lack of beverages, perhaps these creatures were in nature not all that dissimilar to humans after all.

The corridors were deserted now, the aliens preferring a private death; Zalar speculated that a good number of them would have chosen to take their own lives rather than the fiery ending awaiting them.

"Do they have a God?" asked Westerman.

"Do you know I'm not actually sure," Zalar replied.

"How much longer is it?"

"The forward shield will fail within a few minutes, we must go," she said urgently as she moved into his embrace.

"Your wish is my command my love." He closed his arms around her tightly.

"I can't wait to get out of here," she observed with a shudder.

"I know what you mean; it already feels like a ghost ship."

Abruptly a shudder ran through the decking, nearly shaking them off their feet.

"Next stop Bailon!" shouted Westerman as he closed his eyes and began to concentrate; an instant later the couple vanished from the control room, the brilliance of their exit still visible against the light from the main viewer.

Ten million kilometres away from the Bailon sun the defensive shields of the Calaxian star ship finally lost their struggle against the relentless pounding of the solar radiation. Despite its many hundreds of thousands of metric tonnes bulk, once the energy screen was gone it took a matter of a few seconds for the destruction of the vessel.

Metal boiled away, composite materials failed, evaporated and flesh dissolved; in a final cataclysmic event the fusion reactors lost collective integrity and their energies released in a rapid series of explosions. The vessel and all its occupants were gone, destroyed without a trace as the force of the explosions and the might of the sun stripped all the materials back to their atomic format.

One hundred and fifty million kilometres away on Bailon practically nobody witnessed the death of the Calaxian vessel, the intensity of the destruction masked by light from the life-giving star.

A small group of individuals did register the passing of the aliens however, huddled in an abandoned farmhouse, about twenty kilometres south of Pizoka; six robed men sat studying their handheld database devices. One of the group rose to his feet and addressed his colleagues.

"The Calaxian vessel has been destroyed, do you all confirm?" he asked, they all nodded their agreement.

"No malfunction would have caused this event, and the Calaxians are not prone to acts of suicide; we can only assume that some external agency must have orchestrated this."

Once again all heads nodded in silent agreement with the synopsis.

"I think that only one thing could have done this, a Unique," he further stated.

"But the Uniques never take direct action like this, they hide away somewhere and just exist," said one of the men, the standing Warden smiled thinly down at his colleague.

"You are right of course, but I can think of one Unique who has demonstrated that he would get involved," he said evenly.

"Westerman, Steve Westerman!" said one of the Wardens jumping to his feet.

"Exactly, it's logical, this is his chosen mate's home world everything fits into place."

One of the groups number stood up and walked over to the doorway and looked out across the Bailon countryside.

"He will be coming back here, Zalar originates from this area. We have him!" he said triumphantly.

The others stood up as he turned back around to face them.

"Concentrate your search on trying to find Zalar's parents, if they are still alive."

"We have got them on this downloaded local census database," said on of the group looking up from his handheld.

"We've got him," breathed another of the group, menacingly.

CHAPTER EIGHTEEN

Westerman and Zalar flashed into existence more or less dead centre of the courtyard outside the complex of farm buildings that was Boochka and Damena's homestead.

It was daytime and, judging by the position of the sun, around noon. The orientation of their materialisation had deposited them facing the damaged area of the farmhouse. It was immediately obvious that the reconstruction work had begun in earnest as a tubular steel scaffolding arrangement now enclosed the building; also several piles of debris gave testimony to the clear up operation.

They undid the latches on their helmet assemblies and rolled back the now flexible material. The air smelt clean and fresh, Zalar took a deep lungful and then slowly breathed out.

"That's better," she exclaimed as she started to loosen some of the environmental suits fastenings.

"You're not kidding. Things were starting to get a bit hot and smelly inside these things," responded Westerman, with a grimace of distaste. He also breathed deeply from the clean air and felt a little light headed from the increased oxygen content of the Bailon atmosphere; it was then that he noticed the increase in volume and variety of the background noise. He had over the past few days got used to the distant rumble of the engines and the clicks and whirrs of the relays; now, however, he could hear the breeze rustling the leaves of the trees and birdsong was all around him.

The sky was a beautiful azure, with only the occasional cloud drifting about threatening to obscure the suns warming rays. Looking up at the ball of nuclear fire in the sky, Westerman shook his head in wonder.

"A minute or two ago, we were up there," he mused; Zalar turned her attention skywards and said,

"It all sometimes seems like a dream."

"Not a nightmare then?" he offered turning to face her. She smiled and turned to face him.

"With you there, how could it be?"

He placed his arm around her shoulder and gently pulled her into his embrace, their lips met and the kissed.

"And what do you think you are doing with my daughter?" exclaimed a woman's voice from behind them. Turning they saw Damena rushing across the courtyard towards them, Boochka emerged from inside another building.

"Are you both okay?" she cried as tears of joy and relief filled her eyes.

"We're fine Mum," Zalar replied as she was engulfed in, firstly Damena's and then Boochka's embrace.

"Did you succeed?" pressed Boochka as he released his daughter and grasped Westerman's hand.

"We did, the Calaxian vessel is destroyed," Westerman answered, not without a hint of pride in his voice.

"We were so worried, it's been so many days," said the older woman as she moved over to embrace Westerman.

"We kept looking at the sky; we didn't see any explosion or anything like that. What have you done with them?" asked Boochka, taking a quick nervous glance up at the sky.

"You wouldn't believe it dad, we flew them into the sun," Zalar replied in a matter of fact manner.

"Are you alright?" Damena asked her husband. Westerman looked over at the older man; tears ran down his ruddy cheeks. Zalar went over to her father and threw her arms around him.

"What's wrong daddy?" she breathed in his ear.

"I thought that I would never hear anybody call me that ever again," he softly sobbed; Zalar held him tighter as her own tears steadily flowed from her eyes.

Damena looked on with pride and happiness; at length she turned to Westerman and said,

"Thank you for giving us our daughter back Steve." Embarrassed, he looked to the ground and replied,

"There's no need to thank me, Zalar has given me my life back. I would do anything for her."

She laid her arm around his shoulder and kissed him gently on the cheek.

"I know you would," she said softly.

"Damena, can I ask you a question?"

"Sure Steve, anything of course."

"I was just curious about something, please don't take this the wrong way but you accepted that Zalar was your daughter very easily."

Damena took a step away from him and looked him steadily in the eyes.

"Please, I don't want to offend you but whilst we have been up there we have had a lot of spare time on our hands and it is just something that I was thinking and have become curious about," he offered, desperate not to either spoil the moment or hurt the woman's feelings. At length a smile crept across Damena's face and she replaced her arm around his shoulder.

"You are a pretty sharp person aren't you Steve?" she said quietly and continued. "There were many reasons that I accepted Zalar so quickly; I suppose that the main one was mother's intuition, I connected with her as soon as I met her and lets not forget, I think that there is a major family resemblance."

Westerman looked her square in the eyes and raised his eyebrows in a gesture that said he clearly thought that there was something she was not telling him. Damena picked up on his suspicion and quickly said,

"Okay, Okay. I did have the feelings that I was talking about and after Zalar had been with us for a while I started to wonder if this woman called Tink-Bell really could be Zalar; I mean she looked the correct age and everything so I did a little checking."

"How do you mean checking?" he asked, glancing over to confirm that the subject of their conversation was not listening.

"At the time Zalar was born there had been a good few cases of children going missing, so in an attempt to make it difficult for anybody to kidnap an infant and then pass them off as your own, because that is what the authorities thought was happening, every new born was issued with a genetic id tag."

Westerman nodded encouragement to the woman; he could tell that this secret was one that she really needed to get off her chest.

"The tags are very small and easy to use; all you have to do is hold them against a person's skin and if it is a match a small indicator on it changes to green," she explained.

"How big are they?" asked Westerman.

Damena held her thumb and forefinger approximately three centimetres apart.

"That small," he commented, and then continued, "I think that I can see where this is going; you had the tag in your hand and you held it against Zalar and bingo!"

Damena nodded sheepishly in confirmation of his hypothesis, and quickly added.

"It was late one night when we were having girl talk over a drink or two; talking about you as I recall."

"Oh great, It's my fault is it?" he joked.

"You won't tell her will you?" Damena urged the concern tangible in her voice.

Westerman leaned closer and whispered softly in her ear.

"What do you think?"

Damena hugged him firmly and said,

"Thank you."

About an hour later the four of them sat inside one of the rooms of the farmhouse that had not been too badly affected by the Calaxian bombardment; Damena had cleaned out any debris and to the casual observer it looked as if nothing untoward had happened.

Boochka and Westerman were engaged in deep discussion about the state of the Bailon essential services whilst, Damena and Zalar exchanged comments on their respective partners.

"So how long before the electricity was back on?" asked Westerman.

"It was only a matter of a couple of days. Our generation plants are mostly renewable based; tidal, wind and so on, all that needed repairing was the distribution grid," answered Boochka as he regarded the large glass of locally brewed ale in his hand.

"What about communications?"

"That's going to take longer. We have local messaging via short range transmitters but the long range stuff was all situated in the towns; so when those bloody lizards destroyed the towns the global net went with it," he growled and then took a large gulp from the glass.

"Do you have communication satellites?" enquired Westerman.

"Communication, what?"

"Satellites, they are small devices in orbit around Bailon, used for communication linkage around the world."

"Never heard of anything like that before, how do they work?" Boochka pressed, Westerman smiled and replied,

"To tell the truth, I only understand the basic principles, we have them back on my home world, Earth."

"What's Earth like Steve?" asked the older man, leaning forward in his chair.

"Just like Bailon; grass, trees, people. It's all very much the same."

"That's incredible; a planet on the other side of the galaxy, just like ours." Boochka's eyes drifted off into the distance, his thoughts billions and billions of kilometres away.

"Boochka, I've got of a delicate subject that I need to discuss," said Westerman, they both turned and looked at their respective partners; the women seemed engrossed in their own discussion.

"What is it Steve?"

"You know that we've told you about the various factions fighting for supremacy out there in the galaxy?"

"The Calaxians, the Wardens and the Uniques?" commented Boochka.

"Yes that's right, well just prior to the Calaxians the Wardens arrived here."

"Why have they come here? Was it because of the Calaxians?"

"No, I'm afraid that they are here for us," answered Westerman darkly.

"Oh, so you are on the run from these people."

"Yes we are, they knew that Zalar had come from Bailon so they reasoned that she would return here," explained Westerman.

"Well they were right weren't they," observed the older man.

Westerman nodded gravely, took a deep breath and said,

"And that is why we cannot stay here for long."

Like a thunderbolt the realisation hit Zalar's father; he could be saying goodbye to his daughter when he had only just been reunited with her.

"Perhaps the Wardens have been killed in the Calaxian first strike?" he said as he clutched at any hope of losing Zalar, Westerman held his gaze and slowly shook his head.

"Sorry Boochka, the Wardens would have been equipped with the same detectors as Zalar. They knew the invading craft was here, they knew of the bombardment tactics. In any case they would only have sent others to take their place."

Slowly nodding, the gentle giant of a man started to see the logic of Westerman's argument; he looked across the room at Zalar and then returned his attention to the young man.

"Of course you're right, when do you have to leave?" he reluctantly conceded.

"A couple of days I think," Westerman replied and then nodding towards the two women continued, "could you tell Damena?"

"Thanks for that!" Boochka snorted and then nodded slowly.

"Thank you," said a very grateful Westerman.

Zalar and Damena suddenly seemed to have reached a decision of some kind; they stood up and approached the conversing men.

"We're having a party," said Zalar.

"No buts!" scolded Damena and continued, "We are going to celebrate the return of our daughter properly." Realising through many years of experience that it was pointless to argue, Boochka simply said,

"When is this happening?"

"Tomorrow night," stated Zalar with finality, her eyes ablaze with joy and excitement; Westerman and Boochka exchanged fleeting glances, the more discerning observer would have picked up on the uneasy nature of their interaction.

"I want a word with you Steve Westerman," said Zalar as she dragged him out off his chair and out of the house into the courtyard.

"What have I done now?" he asked with a mock resignation.

"We really must get you out of that suit," she purred as she gave him a knowing wink.

"Oh, I see," he said as their pace across the courtyard increased.

The Wardens rendezvoused back at the old farmhouse they had used for their previous meetings. The light was fading quickly as the Bailon dusk drew in about them; the sunset a mass of bright red, orange and browns, accentuated by the dust still remaining in the atmosphere from the Calaxian attack.

"Report!" barked the senior figure of the group.

"I think that I have discovered the location of the parents of Zalar," responded one of the assembled men.

"Share the information."

With that command the Wardens produced their handheld devices and, following the activation of a control sequence, the mini-computers linked over an ultra secure, short range, wireless network.

"Transmitting data," said one of them.

On all of the machines the location and layout of Zalar's parents homestead appeared.

"Good! We will coordinate our assault for tomorrow night," stated the leader in a triumphant manner.

"You are leading the attack, Toll-Khan?" enquired one of the Wardens.

"No, I will be in charge on this one!" answered a loud unidentified voice from the shadows. A robed figure emerged from his concealment in the gloom. Toll-Khan gestured towards the stranger and said,

"The attack will be led by Tang-Zal-Far. He has experience with the renegade Zalar and Steve Westerman."

The new addition to the deadly group grinned back at his assembled colleagues, his eyes wild with rage and vengeance.

The following day Westerman awoke and automatically stretched out his arm to encircle Zalar, but she was not there; still half asleep he patted the bed in a vain attempt to find her. Finally realising that he was alone, he propped himself up on his elbows and looked around the room.

Westerman had slept like a baby, which could of course have been assisted by the extended lovemaking session they had indulged in. Swinging his legs around onto the floor, he got up and after getting dressed, made his way to the bathroom; the cold water he found there more than adequate to fully wake himself.

No longer drowsy, he could feel hunger growing in the pit of his stomach; how long had he been asleep? What time was it?

After not finding anybody in the makeshift kitchen, he made his way into the courtyard, which had been totally transformed. Long tables were covered with crisp, clean white cloths; he spied Damena busily draping brightly coloured lengths of ribbon over of the courtyard's decorative bushes.

"Wow!" he said as he approached her.

"Good morning Steve, or should I say afternoon?" she replied cheerfully.

Suddenly feeling guilty about the fact he was going to take her daughter away again, Westerman found he was unable to look the older woman in the eye.

"Steve," she said as she gently rested her hand on his shoulder, "I know. Boochka has told me everything."

"I'm sorry," he said as he raised his eyes to meet hers.

"I know you are son and I know why you are doing it; Zalar's safety is the most important thing to us. We understand."

She placed her arms around his neck and gave him an encouraging squeeze, he could actually feel his anxiety easing through her actions; at length she released him and adopting a more business like manner she said,

"I'll bet you're hungry?"

"Absolutely famished," he confirmed.

"We saved some breakfast for you, come on," said Damena as she led him to a small table in the corner.

There he found a selection of bread and cheeses; sitting down, he began to munch his way through the rustic fare.

"How many people are coming to the get together?" he asked between mouthfuls.

"About fifty we think," was the reply.

"How many?" Westerman spluttered.

"About fifty, When the story got out that my long lost daughter is back and brought with her a man who has saved the planet, it is amazing how fast news travels and how many people want to meet you."

Westerman could feel himself colouring up with embarrassment; Damena spotted this and quickly added,

"Please you have not got to worry about it; they are all friends and if you are pestered either Boochka or I will step in and save you."

Swallowing hard, he continued his meal; Zalar emerged from a nearby doorway carrying a large box.

"Where do you want this mum?" she said happily; she noticed Westerman, practically threw the box onto the nearest table and ran over to him.

"Missed me?" he said, smiling broadly up at her.

"You bet!" she answered, throwing her arms around his neck and smothering him in kisses.

"I'll get on with the jobs then?" commented Damena, busying herself and moving away from the couple.

"Zalar sit down a minute or two please, there's something that I really need to talk to you about," he said pushing a chair out from the table; she accepted the invitation asking,

"What is it Steve?"

"You know that we have got to leave here soon, don't you?" he said sadly.

She looked him squarely in the eyes, he could see the tears beginning to instantly well up inside of her; gently taking her hand he continued softly.

"I'm sorry my love, but we have to."

She nodded slowly, choking back the tears and sobbed. "I figured as much, the Wardens?"

"Yes and possibly the Uniques too," he replied gravely. "This is not fair, I've only just found my parents again after all this time!" the anger at the injustice of it all plain in her voice.

"I know, I know; but it is for their protection as well. What if they got caught up in the middle of something and got hurt? How would you feel then?"

After a long pause she looked away from him towards her mother and said,

"I know that you are right; it's just so hard."

Westerman leaned over and pulled her towards him, drawing her into his arms for comfort.

"How soon?" she asked, her voice breaking and laden with grief.

"Soon, but we are still going to have this party before we go," he whispered positively. She broke from his arms and looked at him, saying.

"You bet we are!"

The rest of the afternoon was spent preparing the courtyard for the evening's entertainment.

Damena had almost magically produced a multitude of cakes, deserts and cooked meat products to satisfy the guests, Boochka had conjured up three barrels of his locally produced ale; it had taken a great deal of lifting to raise these final items onto one of the tables.

Eventually everything was set and the old man celebrated by pulling two large tankards of the foaming beverage, he offered one to Westerman.

"Your health!" growled Boochka as he lifted the vessel and proceeded to drain the contents.

"Your health!" echoed Westerman as he began to imbibe the brown liquid.

"Not bad," he commented, the taste very reminiscent of a beer he had once had back on Earth.

"Huh, not bad he says. It's the finest," Boochka blustered.

"Of course it is," quickly retorted Westerman.

"You two aren't about to get drunk before the party are you?" shouted Zalar.

"No, we're just checking that it is okay," answered Westerman with a sly wink to his male companion.

"Like mother, like daughter," whispered Boochka.

"Everything's ready," announced Damena, "let's go and get changed everyone. No family of mine is going to greet our guests looking like a set of tramps."

"Come on let's get ready," said a suddenly sad looking Zalar. Westerman grabbed her hand and gave it an affectionate squeeze.

"I'll be okay," she said in response.

"Of course you will," he agreed as he slipped his arm around her slim waist and walked with her back to the house.

The older couple watched them depart; they looked at each other and then both gave a silent nod of resignation as they also held hands and walked across the courtyard.

The sun had just begun to set as the first guests arrived; they arrived in an assortment of ground cars and agricultural vehicles, every visitor bore a bottle of some description containing his or her own particular brand of beverage. Westerman watched with silent amusement, this was destined to be one hell of a drinking session, his thoughts drifted back to some of the family barbeques he had attended back home; the similarity in format was striking given the vast intervening number of light years.

"You okay?" asked Zalar. He had not seen her approaching, she carried two glasses; one was offered to him, which he took and tasted the contents.

"Now that's good," he said, Zalar nodded with smug approval.

"I thought that it would be to your liking," she cooed.

"A toast to us,"

"May we be together forever," she said.

"Cheers!" called Westerman as the glasses clinked together.

"Do you still love me then?" Zalar moved closer to him, he could feel the heat of her body through their clothes. "Oh darling, I have never loved anybody so much in my life," he breathed.

"You know all the right things to say don't you?"

"Only when it's the truth," he insisted.

"I know." And with that their lips met in a passionate kiss.

Music played from a small box in the middle of one of the tables, its style not dissimilar to Earth country,

Westerman had observed. The guests stood around in many groups, Damena and Boochka moved amongst them offering drink or food; everybody seemed to be enjoying themselves.

Totally unknown to all attendees of the party, a group of seven robed figures was moving, silently through the night; their progress across a nearby field towards the homestead unimpeded.

As they reached the outskirts of the farm buildings, Tang-Zal-Far held his hand aloft to halt his fellow Wardens; he observed the party ahead, his teeth shone in the glow from the gathering. This was perfect, a natural distraction, he actually imagined he could taste the revenge in his mouth. He gathered his colleagues about him.

"Listen very carefully," he whispered," we will wait until later, they are all consuming alcoholic products so after a short time their affectivity will be severely diminished." One of two of the Wardens quickly glanced over their shoulders at the revellers and nodded their tacit agreement. Tang-Zal-Far continued to outline his tactics. "In the meantime we will spread out around the perimeter of the area and in one hours time I want you all to converge to within twenty metres of the central area. Do you all understand?"

The assembled group nodded their agreement once again.

"I will give the signal to attack over our short range communicators; there must be no attack before that time. Do I make myself clear?" he emphasised.

"What if we run into one of them before your signal?" asked one of the junior Wardens.

"In such a case you must not allow the alarm to be raised; use force if necessary to maintain our secrecy." Glancing over his shoulder towards the merrymakers he continued, "Nobody must survive this; there must be no witnesses, lethal force."

A number of them grinned, showing their approval; Tang-Zal-Far gave a gesture to disperse the group, saying.

"One final thing, Westerman and the traitor Zalar are to be mine to kill; nobody else must fire upon them, clear?" His voice had adopted a threatening demonic quality. The others stopped and looked back towards him; in the illumination offered by the nearby party they could see his features set in steely determination. Silently they all indicated their acceptance of his directive and then melted away into the night to take their respective positions.

The party had really begun to come alive, Boochka and Damena had proudly introduced their daughter to the majority of the neighbours and everybody had started to kick back and relax. Several of the guests were dancing, whilst most of the rest seemed to be either talking or drinking, everybody seemed happy.

In a lull between another round of 'meet and greet', Zalar located Westerman and after skilfully weaving her way through the throng to him, he greeted her with a broad warm smile; excusing himself from a middle aged woman he was talking to they moved to a slightly quieter place.

"Hello you," he said warmly to Zalar.

"Hello to you too, do you come here often?" she joked in reply.

"How's it all going? It seems ages since I last spoke to you." His arm encircled her waist as she nestled into him.

"I know what you mean; everybody seems to want to talk to me. I'm constantly being introduced to people that I am supposed to know from when I was a child," she agreed.

"I'm glad that we decided not to make our involvement in stopping the attack common knowledge."

"You're right," she said as she rolled her eyes skywards, "that would have been a step too far for these people to take."

"Too bloody right, mind you, I have nearly tripped up a couple of times by people asking me where I come from."

"The southern continent is a much easier option than a planet several thousand light years away," she observed.

"I know, but when the conversation gets around to specific cities in the southern continent, I'm screwed," he said. She looked into his eyes and purred,

"If I had my way, you would be."

"Easy now tiger," he whispered back with a mock shocked expression.

Zalar became suddenly serious and lowered her gaze to his chest.

"I wish we could just settle here and raise children," she breathed wistfully. Gently stroking her hair, Westerman allowed himself to join her in a moment of reverie.

"Yes that would be nice," he conceded, "this does seem like a friendly place to live. Obviously apart from the occasional war-like reptilian race and other assorted aliens."

She looked up at him, smiled and playfully slapped his arm.

"You always have to spoil the moment, don't you?" she joked.

"Sorry I thought that you were on a downer."

"No, I'm okay. I was just dreaming."

"One day my love, one day," he said and gently laid a kiss upon her hair.

"This looks serious!" commented a loud voice from behind the cuddling couple.

Westerman and Zalar turned; it was Boochka and Damena.

"No, we're fine dad," said Zalar.

"Don't try and kid a kidder," stated her grinning parent.

"Just dreaming, we were just dreaming," offered Westerman.

Damena had two glasses in her hands; she offered them to the younger couple.

"Thanks Damena," said Westerman, accepting his drink as Zalar took the other.

"It's a good party," observed Damena.

"Sure is," agreed Boochka

Westerman had just taken a mouthful of the cool fluid from his glass when all hell broke loose.

Tang-Zal-Far raised his short-range communicator to his lips and after a brief pause, he said coldly and clearly, "Now!"

He moved from his position in the shadows of a small outbuilding and raised his thermal disruptor; he pressed the firing stud and a ruby red beam of death lanced out towards the crowd of partygoers.

From their positions around the perimeter of the celebration area the other six Wardens all followed suit; screams of agony and panic erupted into the night air. The advancing robed figures fired again and again, the Bailonians fell to the ground in increasing lifeless numbers.

The glass fell from Westerman's hand as he heard the first scream, turning he clearly saw a beam of lethal particles cut through the darkness and strike a middle-aged male squarely in the chest. Damena screamed as another pencil thin shaft of destruction narrowly missed her and struck a nearby fence, blowing it into splinters.

Westerman reacted, with almost an instantaneous effort he spun around to face Zalar and her parents, an invisible bubble of telekinetic force popped into existence around them as several more disruptor beams lanced towards their position.

The fireworks display produced by the impact of the tortured particle streams and the force field set off intense flashes of brilliance illuminating the surrounding courtyard.

"What the hell is going on?" yelled Boochka, raising his voice to make himself heard above the crackle of the discharge from Westerman's shield.

"We're under attack! Wardens!" shouted Zalar as she instinctively pulled her parents closer to Westerman.

Although deep in concentrated effort holding the shields integrity, Westerman was able to direct a nod towards Zalar to show his appreciation of her actions; he shrank the bubble to the smaller area, with his charges nearer, he required. The smaller the area, the stronger his shield could be. Huddled at the centre of a now glowing ball of protective energy, the four of them could now turn their attention to the surrounding carnage.

The ruby red beams of energy continued to flicker and the victims continued to fall, their tortured screams loudly filling the night sky.

"Oh god no, please no," whimpered a distraught Damena.

"Steve! Look over there!" yelled Zalar, he turned his head and looked in the same direction as her.

He could clearly see a figure silhouetted against the light from a window in the main house; whilst he watched a deadly shaft of light from the end of the individuals' out-stretched arm, it was a Warden.

"You Bastard!" spat Westerman, his eyes flashed and the shadowy figure convulsed as if hit by a mighty fist and fell to the ground dead.

"What's going on?" screamed Boochka, Damena was now in his arms; her face buried deeply in his chest to block out the nightmarish scenes.

"Keep close to Steve dad, he's put a shield around us to protect us but you've got to stay close," pleaded Zalar as she grabbed her father's arm. He looked at his daughter for a brief moment and then gave a terse nod of understanding.

Westerman continued to look around to try and locate the sources of the disruptor fire in the surrounding darkness; he saw the faint outline of another attacker, once his eyes flashed and was this time gruesomely rewarded with the sound of a damp explosion confirming that his telekinetic bolt had found its target.

"We've got to get away from the centre of the courtyard," Westerman shouted as two more impacts upon his screen produced a radial display of dissipating energy, Zalar nodded and pointed towards a nearby large table away to her left.

"If we could get these two over there, the fire is coming predominantly from the other direction," she explained. Immediately Westerman understood; the two Wardens he had killed were now a missing segment from their circle of death, Zalar's potential cover was in the fire free segment. He nodded and between them they forcefully herded Boochka and Damena towards the table.

The screams were starting to diminish in both quantity and audible volume as the remaining Wardens relentlessly cut the defenceless people down; the small group cowering inside the sphere of lifesaving force finally reached their goal. Westerman concentrated his power and inserted an invisible force wedge under the legs of the table and drove it home; in slow motion the item of furniture rose up and fell onto its side. Between them, Westerman and Zalar shepherded the older couple behind the makeshift barrier, away from the Wardens line of fire.

All the guests now lay dead or dying in the courtyard; the target for the attacker's weapons was now definitely the shielded group, repeatedly the ruby red beams struck the force wall, lines of force radiated outward from the impact areas accompanied by static discharges and a deafening crackling sound.

"How long can you stand this?" Zalar shouted to Westerman; she could see the beads of perspiration on his forehead, testimony to the constant mental effort.

"I… I don't know. Every blast takes a little more out of my strength," he cried.

"I need a weapon, if I could fight back I could take the some of the pressure off you," she said as she began scouring the surrounding area for anything she could use.

"Zalar, look over there, on the floor," Westerman shouted pointing to his right.

In the dark she could just make out a tubular object laid on the ground, it lay beside what appeared to be a heap of clothes; one of the Wardens blasts struck the shield and the resulting energy discharged illuminated the area she was looking at. In the burst of light she realised that the pile of rags was actually the body of one of the Wardens, more importantly beside this bloody heap the tubular object resolved itself as a thermal disruptor.

"Steve! Look, a disruptor. I'm going to make a run for it," she cried.

"No! Stay there!" shouted Westerman, "leave this to me," he added.

"But?" she gasped in reply, feeling helpless in her current situation.

"Trust me," he smiled at her as he extended his open hand towards the weapon.

For long seconds nothing happened, but then abruptly the device leapt into the air and shot into Westerman's grasp.

"What the?" breathed Boochka as he witnessed the seemingly impossible.

Gently, with mock reverence, Westerman presented the retrieved weapon to Zalar; with a broad grin she accepted it.

"What are you?" asked Boochka incredulously.

"He's unique dad, and I love him," answered Zalar with evident pride in her voice as she swung her disruptor around to bear on the source of the incoming beams of death.

"I've contracted my shield to just the size of the tabletop," said Westerman, his eyes closed in concentration.

"Got you," Zalar said as she peered around the edge of the upturned piece of furniture.

A ruby beam lanced out from the darkness and struck the defensive screen; Zalar fired back at its source and was rewarded with an agonising scream, which pierced the night.

"Another down," acknowledged Westerman.

"There's still another three out there I think," Zalar replied as she ducked back behind the shield to avoid the incoming torrent of fire.

"We need another plan, if I could see them; I could end this very quickly."

"We need some illumination!" she stated with a flash of inspiration.

"What?"

"You know how you picked up the disruptor from the ground, could you hold something in mid air in the same way?"

"I suppose I could, what have you got in mind?"

Another volley of beams struck the shield causing Westerman to almost physically stagger backward from the impacts.

"We had better do whatever you're planning pretty soon, I'm beginning to sag a bit here," he said, the concern obvious in his face and voice.

Zalar nodded and slid open a small panel on the base of her weapon; expertly she pulled out a small circuit jumper from its position in a grid of sockets and then replaced it into a different pair of holes. Closing the access panel she turned the weapon over and adjusted its output to the maximum setting.

"Are you ready?" she asked him.

"To do what?" he replied, confused.

"When I tell you take this from my hand and hold it in the air, about fifty metres above the centre of the courtyard."

He nodded and Zalar pressed the firing stud on the device; immediately the weapon began to visibly vibrate in her open hand and a high pitched whine filled the air. For Long seconds she observed the weapon as the noise became louder and higher in pitch; the beam emitter at business end of the disruptor had begun to glow.

"Ready?" she said, briefly glancing over at Westerman.

"Okay," he breathed back at her as he prepared his concentration.

"Now!" she cried.

Westerman extended his open hand towards the increasingly animated device; it rose slowly from Zalar's palm and into the night sky. In a smooth arc he brought his arm around to point towards the area of sky he wanted his charge to reside in, after a small pause the now fiercely glowing object tracked the motion of his arm.

The incoming blasts had now ceased as the Wardens attentions had also turned towards the cylinder that now hung above the centre of the courtyard.

"Don't look at it," instructed Zalar.

Westerman had barely time to shield his eyes when the disruptor exploded into a ball of expanding, dazzling white light; Zalar had reprogrammed the device to overload by causing a forced chamber firing, with the emitter crystal deactivated the generated energy had no way to be released, the explosion had been inevitable.

As the glare of the explosion started to recede, Westerman uncovered his eyes; across the courtyard he could clearly see three Wardens in the remaining illumination, they all stood with their arms across their faces trying to blot out the blinding light.

His eyes flashed twice and two of the robed figures fell backwards as a large area of their chests exploded outwards. The third realised he was in danger and instinctively produced his jump engine, ready to make his hasty getaway.

"Oh no you don't," growled Westerman as he extended his hand towards the Warden; the small box was torn from his grasp, the sound of snapping digits clearly audible.

"Eat shit and die!" yelled Westerman as his eyes flashed brightly, the man's head exploded dramatically and his lifeless body fell to the ground.

Standing up, Westerman allowed his mental wall of force to dissolve. He surveyed the courtyard, it was littered with the bodies of the party guests; Boochka released Damena into Zalar's care and went to stand beside him.

"I can't believe this has just happened," Boochka said, shaking his head, stunned by the scale of the carnage.

"I'm sorry that this had to happen here. If we had gone away yesterday all these people would still be alive," Westerman stated shaking his own head in disbelief.

"You can't hold yourself responsible for this son."

"Thank you, you're being kind but we all know that this all down to me."

"Now listen to me!" growled Boochka, the force of his voice shocking Westerman to attention, "these creatures, the Wardens, the Calaxians, you didn't create them. You don't direct their actions; you stood up to them, you've saved our entire planet."

Slowly Westerman recognised the logic of the older mans words; it did help but he couldn't shed the mantle of responsibility easily.

"Thank you," he said, Boochka nodded and they both turned and moved over to the women.

Damena seemed to have calmed down under Zalar's close attention, Boochka put his strong arm around his wife's shoulders and drew her into the protection of his warm embrace, Westerman followed suit and did the same to Zalar, she responded by wrapping her arms around his waist as they stood together in mutual comfort; suddenly as she looked over Westerman's shoulder a movement caught her eye.

Tang-Zal-Far had purposefully hung back during the Wardens assault on the party. He had carefully worked his way around the perimeter of the courtyard, using the cover of darkness, to arrive at a position less than fifty metres away from Westerman, Zalar and the two remaining Bailonians. He had been all set to discharge his weapon at the group when he had seen the glowing disruptor climb into the sky; instantly recognising the threat posed by the overloading device, he had scrambled away from the courtyard and thrown himself behind a low wall as protection against the blast he knew was imminent.

He had continued to cower in his place of refuge for long minutes after the battle had concluded, his face still shielded by his robe, as he strained to listen for clues as to the situation back in the yard.

Voices, he could clearly make out voices. He slowly uncovered his head and tentatively opened his eyes; no blinding light, the darkness had once again cloaked the area, remaining behind the stonework he sat up and listened intently to the conversation; Westerman blaming himself for all the deaths, and so he should thought the Warden.

With deliberate care he inched his way from his place of hiding and began to move towards the quartet, moving from one area of shadow to another. They had not seen him, the element of surprise would be squarely on his side and he crept closer still.

Tang-Zal-Far could clearly make out the individuals in the subdued illumination; they were stood in pairs, Westerman and Zalar nearest to him; perfect! The troublesome Earthman had his back towards him; slowly and deliberately he raised his disruptor.

Taking careful aim he readied the weapon for firing; revenge, satisfaction and an all host of other emotions raced through his body, he wanted to savour this moment as he experienced an almost sexual joy. His finger fell upon the firing stud.

The circuit was almost closed when, over Westerman's shoulder, Zalar opened her eyes from the bliss of her embrace and saw the Warden.

The young woman realised in a split second that their attacker was about to fire; reacting instinctively and with a strength born of desperation, she pushed Westerman aside as the weapon discharged; a pencil thin beam of death sliced through the blackness of the night.

Whilst falling to the ground as a result of Zalar's action, Westerman saw the ray narrowly pass him by; he hit the ground and rolled over into a kneeling position and swiftly turned to face his attacker. The Warden was running towards him, his disruptor firing again, Westerman thrust his open palm forward and deflected the incoming blasts with a hastily erected force screen; his eyes flashed and Tang-Zal-Far's right knee shattered sending him tumbling to the ground.

The crippled Warden tried to get upright to fire again and Westerman prepared to finish him off; he was too late, Boochka had used the opportunity to retrieve a stout piece of timber and with a mighty effort he ran over to the robed man and struck him squarely with it at the side of the head.

Tang-Zal-Far's skull shattered instantly, he was dead before his body had collapsed to the ground.

"Bastard!" spat Westerman, getting to his feet and approaching the lifeless heap to make sure he was finished. Suddenly a woman's anguished scream pierced the night, echoing across the now still courtyard.

Westerman spun around to the source of the sound; Damena stood with her hands in front of her mouth, eyes wide open with terror looking at her daughter.

Zalar was kneeling with her hands clasped firmly to her chest; she looked up unsteadily at Westerman, a smile half formed on her lips as she took her hands away and looked down at them; they were smeared with blood.

Westerman looked at her questioning eyes and then allowed his gaze to move down to her chest, he could feel his heart shattering into a million pieces as he saw the neat hole from which a steady trickle of blood ran; the hole marking the passage of the beam from the Wardens weapon as it had passed through her.

"Zalar!" he wailed.

She looked deep into his eyes and smiled lovingly back at him.

"I'm sorry Steve," she said, a single tear rolled down her face, as she simply fell forwards onto the cold brick-work of the courtyard, dead.

CHAPTER NINETEEN

The cold light of the dawn had chased away the darkness of the night and illuminated the solemn gathering around the unlit funeral pyre, atop of which, wrapped in a simple white shroud lay Zalar's body.

Westerman stood apart from the grieving parents, he preferred the known quantity of his own distress against the additional burden of the elderly couples extreme sadness that proximity to them would bring. Away to his left a man dressed in a ceremonial gown was speaking words of comfort and hope; although clearly audible he did not hear them, they were lost in the nebula of the emotional fog that surrounded him.

It was three days since Zalar's death, Westerman had gone through the motions of the daily routine but he was not mentally there; every time he closed his eyes he could see his beloved knelt before him, looking up at him with her eyes full of incredulity, this was too much for him to bear. Boochka and Damena had made the effort to console him but they too were swept up in their own tide of remorse and loss to be able to offer any objective comfort; also he thought that he could see burning deep within their eyes a smouldering fire of animosity towards him, they had not said anything but he was sure that they blamed him for their daughters death.

The speaker stopped and walked towards a nearby-lit brazier, pulling two flaming torches from the crucible, he approached the couple; they accepted the burning items and began to solemnly walk towards the pyre.

Damena stopped and turned to look at Westerman, she could see his cheeks glistening in the early morning light. Gently placing her hand on her husbands arm she guided him over to the grief stricken Earthman.

"Steve? Please," she said, her voice trembling as she offered her torch to Westerman.

He looked up at her and then to the stern features of Boochka, who after a pause, nodded.

"It's what she would have wanted," whispered Damena as he accepted her charge.

At an unspoken signal the two men stepped forward to the pyre; in unison they both presented their torches to the base of the wooden structure and the kindling ignited.

Some form of accelerant had been applied to the fuel because flames quickly engulfed the base of the pyre and as the intensity of the blaze grew Westerman and Boochka withdrew to stand either side of Damena. Rapidly the flames increased until they were leaping high into the sky, Westerman closed his eyes again; once again he could see

Zalar knelt before him, she mouthed the words 'Steve', he reopened his eyes to see the blaze now totally engulfing her body.

"Zalar," he groaned, tears steadily streaming down his face. He felt Damena's hand slip inside his own; a woefully inadequate squeeze was exchanged, but he could not bear to turn and look at the woman beside him.

The three of them stood watching the flames rage, consuming their loved ones remains; such was the intensity of the blaze that nothing of the body could be seen, but with each glowing ember or fragment of ash that climbed into the air, borne on the thermal currents, he could imagine that another part of the beautiful creature he had loved was ascending to some higher plain.

Quite suddenly the two metre high burning construction collapsed in upon itself, as it was designed to do, a shower of sparks and flame erupted upwards; it seemed as though Zalar's very essence had made its final escape. This was the long established and traditional signal that the funeral ceremony was completed, Damena and Boochka turned and started to walk away, feeling numb and helpless, Westerman allowed himself to be led away. Briefly he looked over his shoulder at the fiery heap.

"Goodbye my love," he said softly and then turned away to accompany the elderly couple back to the farmstead.

For the following three days, Westerman tried to immerse himself in the everyday banality of the daily grind; he awoke, rose, bathed and joined Boochka and Damena for breakfast. He thought that he had actually detected a thawing of the icy atmosphere between the three of them, the majority of which seemed to emanate from the older man; Damena however had begun to cling to Westerman, it was as if he represented her last physical link with Zalar. He tolerated this but in all honesty he was finding the attention and the motive behind it very wearing.

This particular morning Westerman sat down in the makeshift kitchen and after they had exchanged the usual pleasantries he announced.

"I've decided that I should be moving on."

Damena reacted first, dropping the utensil in her hand.

"No! You can't go, tell him Boochka," she wailed, her eyes wild with emotion.

Boochka turned and looked long and hard into the younger man's eyes and after a while said gently.

"I'm sorry my love, but you are going to have to let him go."

"No! Zalar would have wanted him to stay, it's his home now," she yelled, slumping forward, her arms supporting her grief racked body.

"I have to go. I'm sorry," Westerman said softly.

Damena sat down heavily in her chair, her head in her hands, her soft sobbing echoing throughout the room; Westerman could feel his own tears welling up from deep inside of him, abruptly he stated,

"I'm sorry but I have to." With that he stood up and walked briskly through the door into the courtyard; Boochka stood up and moved to his wife's side and gently laying his hand on her heaving shoulder said,

"He's right my love. We have to let him go, we can't cling on to him to satisfy our own selfish needs."

"You resent him for Zalar's death don't you?" Damena replied.

"What?"

"I said you resent him for our daughter's death," she pressed, her face raised to look with red-rimmed eyes at her husband.

Faced with this direct onslaught from his wife, the gentle giant of a man collapsed into a chair beside her; tears streamed down his face. Damena quickly recognised his torment and placed her arm around his shoulder.

"I... I don't blame him," he whispered and continued, "I feel resentment towards him because he knew our daughter in later life more than we did. I'm jealous of him."

The couple looked into each other's eyes and fell into an embrace of mutual comfort.

"I know, I know," breathed Damena as they clung to each other. After long minutes had passed, Boochka extricated himself from her welcomed clutches.

"He must go you know," he said.

"I know," she eventually, reluctantly answered.

"He will be hunted by the Wardens and if he stays here it would be an obvious place for them to look."

"Don't you think that I know that!" she yelled with an anger that gave Boochka a start.

"He's my only link with our daughter, the daughter that we thought was dead and we would never see again; and now we never will," her tirade continued.

Reaching across the table, his hands closed firmly around hers; he gripped her tightly and said,

"She's dead now, but Steve's alive. We can't be selfish in this, he has to leave but I think that he would prefer to do it with our blessing; he feels that he has let us down, he didn't protect Zalar; he feels responsible."

Slowly the wisdom of her husband's words started to crystallise within Damena's mind; she knew that he was right; it was a selfish conceit on her part. Forcing a tearful smile she said.

"You're a wise man Boochka."

He returned her smile thinly and added,

"You have your moments too."

The couple hugged each other again and in silent agreement, they separated, stood up and walked hand in hand towards the door that led to the courtyard.

Westerman was leaning against a wooden picket fence at the far end of the yard, he looked out with unseeing eyes across the surrounding countryside; clouds scurried overhead in the morning breeze producing intricate patterns of light and shade over the fields as they obscured the suns rays.

His thoughts were consumed with the yawning chasm of loss and loneliness he felt in his soul, Zalar had meant absolutely everything to him; in fact he was feeling more than just a passing pang of guilt at never fully showing her how much he really had loved her. So wrapped up in his reverie, he did not notice the elderly couple approaching.

"Steve?" said Damena gently, Westerman gave a start and turned to face them.

"Oh? Hi, I didn't hear you. I was miles away," he said somewhat awkwardly.

"It's okay son," said Boochka, laying a calming hand on his shoulder.

"We've been talking, and you are right, you can't stay here. The Wardens will find you again," stated Damena, her eyes heavy with tears.

"She's right, you must go," her husband added in a show of united resolve.

Westerman nodded and looked at the ground.

"I'm sorry that I couldn't protect her," he said, his voice cracking. Boochka gently rubbed his shoulder saying.

"We know that you are, but it wasn't your fault."

Looking up form the ground into the old man's eyes he could see the truth within them; he nodded and walked away from the couple, it was time to pack.

Two hours later the three of them stood in the centre of the courtyard. Westerman had packed a few clothes into a backpack together with some assorted toiletries and his environmental suit, he also had Zalar's backpack full of the Warden devices; he was ready to go.

He had dressed in a pair of denims, shirt and lightweight coat; he had reasoned that his attire would be suitable for where he had decided to go.

"Have you got everything?" asked Damena as she fussed over his coat.

"He knows what he is doing mother," said Boochka humorously.

"I'm good to go," said Westerman. Damena flung her arms around him and kissed him warmly on the cheek. Westerman offered his hand to Boochka, who took it and shook it gratefully as Damena dragged them all into group hug, which lasted for many minutes. Eventually extricating themselves they all looked at each other with tears streaming down their faces.

"Will we see you again?" asked Damena, her voice strained.

"I hope so," replied Westerman, he hoped his positive tone would comfort her.

"Take good care Steve," said Boochka as another tear escaped from his left eye and raced down his rugged cheek.

"Right; stand back!" Westerman said with an air of finality, picking up his bags. He began to concentrate and immediately felt the jump energies building inside.

"Where will you go?" shouted Damena.

Westerman smiled sweetly and said simply,

"I'm going home."

With that he vanished into the welcoming brilliance of the flash of dazzling, pure white light.

Damena turned and buried herself in Boochka's warm chest, the old man wrapping his arms around her whilst he looked wistfully up into the sky and allowed his mind to drift away to far away places at the very edge of his imagination. He couldn't help observing to himself that the universe had suddenly become a very much smaller place.

THE END

Steve Westerman's adventures
will continue in 'The Unique Problem'.

AUTHOR BIOGRAPHY

Heath A. Hague was born in the County of South Yorkshire, Northern England on the 8th October 1958.

After leaving education he has had a fair selection of jobs, from Salesman to Lumberjack. However in later years he has made the field of Computers his profession.

Always being interested in the genre of Sci-fi, as a hobby he has written a few short stories over the years. The Unique series is the crowning glory of his work so far.

Printed in the United Kingdom
by Lightning Source UK Ltd.
135535UK00001B/1-30/P